the Adventurists

the Adventurists

stories
by

Richard
Butner

Small Beer Press
Easthampton, MA

Small Beer Press
150 Pleasant Street #306
Easthampton, MA 01027
smallbeerpress.com
weightlessbooks.com
bookmoonbooks.com
info@smallbeerpress.com

Distributed to the trade by Consortium.

Library of Congress Cataloging-in-Publication Data

Names: Butner, Richard, author.
Title: The adventurists : stories / Richard Butner.
Description: First edition. | Easthampton, MA : Small Beer Press, [2022] |
    Summary: "The rules are always clear but never fully known in the first
    collection of Richard Butner's allusive and elusive, nostalgic and
    modernist stories"-- Provided by publisher.
Identifiers: LCCN 2021017254 (print) | LCCN 2021017255 (ebook) | ISBN
    9781618731944 (paperback) | ISBN 9781618731951 (ebook)
Subjects: LCGFT: Short stories.
Classification: LCC PS3552.U8296 A66 2022 (print) | LCC PS3552.U8296
    (ebook) | DDC 813/.54--dc23
LC record available at https://lccn.loc.gov/2021017254
LC ebook record available at https://lccn.loc.gov/2021017255

First edition 1 2 3 4 5 6 7 8 9

Set in Centaur MT. Titles in Futura.
Printed on 30% PCR recycled paper by the Versa Press in East Peoria, IL.
Author photo © 2021 by Areon Mobasher. All rights reserved.
Cover illustration © 2021 by Wesley Allsbrook (wesleyallsbrook.com). All rights reserved.

This book is dedicated to John Kessel.

Contents

Adventure   I

Holderhaven   23

Scenes from the Renaissance   50

Ash City Stomp   72

Horses Blow Up Dog City   87

The Master Key   104

Circa   121

At the Fair   141

Pete and Earl   151

The Ornithopter   164

Stronghold   185

Delta Function   205

Give Up   224

Chemistry Set   241

Under Green   261

Sunnyside   283

Adventure

On the ferry to the island, I saw a man dressed as a jester. His image flashed into view in my side mirror as I sat there half-dozing behind the steering wheel. It was midday as we chugged along across the sound, and the sun glared off the smattering of pickups and SUVs and vans on the deck. For a second I thought I had dreamed him.

I turned in the seat and looked out the back window and there he still was, just his head and what looked like the end of a fishing rod visible. He was standing out on the back of the boat. He was looking up at the sky, not squinting. Farther behind him a flock of gulls followed the boat. His head slowly lowered until he was staring straight at me.

I spun and sank back into my seat, slumping so that I wasn't visible in the side mirror. I wasn't in the mood to talk to some kind of street performer who fished, or some fisherman who was heavily into cosplay. I was tired and hungry. I was looking forward to seeing my old friend Virginia, getting the tour of this odd little island that wasn't close to much of anything, drinking a beer or two, getting away from the world if only for one night. She would probably know the story of the jester. She knew all the stories.

The ferry docked and I was one of the first off, and Virginia met me in the parking lot next to the abandoned Coast

Guard barracks. Virginia was wheeling around an oxygen tank fitted with tiny clear tubes that swooped up to her nose.

"You hadn't mentioned this," I said.

"There are some things I'm not going to talk about," she said. She tapped the silver canister. "This is one of them. The first rule of oxygen tank club is, you do not talk about oxygen tank club."

She pulled a plastic bottle from her back pocket and handed it to me. Bug spray.

"You're going to need this," she said. "The mosquitoes are no joke here."

The jester trudged off the ramp of the ferry, carrying only his fishing pole. I asked Virginia if she knew who it was, and she just shook her head.

"You get a lot of people in costume out here?"

"In the summer, there are occasional infestations of pirates. Lately there've been mermaids, too. Never seen a jester before."

I had been hoping for at least a sliver of adventure. Maybe seeing Virginia for one night after so many years wasn't going to fix my life, but if it did, all the better. On the phone she'd said something like, "I've got something important I want to give you, you have to come pick it up." This was suddenly a very different sort of trip, one that included an oxygen tank.

Or maybe it wasn't. Maybe it was one of Virginia's pranks. When we were younger, she stole this gimmick off of *WKRP in Cincinnati,* and always had a bandage on some visible part of her. She wore one across the bridge of her nose for a year solid. Every time someone asked her what had happened, she said that she couldn't really talk about the details. An oxygen tank. I wouldn't put it past her.

"What do you think he wants?" I asked.

"Let's say . . ." Virginia said, and then she paused. That was the introduction to all her great improvisations.

"Let's say he wants me. Call him Death's Fool. See his staff?"

I squinted and saw that the fishing rod wasn't a fishing rod or a normal walking stick. At the tip there was a little doll-sized figure of a jester, also holding a staff.

"Okay," I said.

"I've never been much afraid of anything—you know that—or even if I was, I would just run toward the fear, not away from it. But that right there is Death's Fool, and maybe he doesn't notice me yet but he will. Stay out of his way when he makes his move."

Virginia bent over at the waist and started coughing and laughing at the same time, holding her hand up to fend off any possible assistance.

I laughed too.

"I think I could take him," I said. The skinny jester with the funny stick had left the parking lot. "I've been working out. Krav Maga. Needed to drop some pounds."

I opened the passenger door so she could get in. "Your Krav Maga workout is no match for Death's Fool. Besides, he came here on the boat with you. How do I know you're not working together? Here, let me drive."

Twenty-five years earlier, I'd watched as Virginia head-butted a would-be thief, a guy who walked into the bar where she was working and leaned over the counter trying to grab money from the cash register. She knocked him flat out. She called the cops with one hand while fishing some ice out of the cooler and holding it to her forehead with the other.

"Well, maybe he's gone now. I don't see him anymore."

"He's still there. Where's he gonna go? Striding off into the Atlantic? He's probably waiting in the lobby of the inn right now."

3

Virginia had been the caretaker of Blackbeard's Hideout for a few years. She knew I wasn't particularly happy sitting in a cubicle designing catalogs for a medical equipment supply house. Now there was an oxygen tank. We talked on the phone maybe two or three times a year, and she always asked me to come visit, and finally there I was visiting. Hadn't actually seen her live and in person in twenty years. She was going gray. I was too.

Virginia was my oldest friend.

"I guess we won't be going for a run on the beach," I said.

She went to get in the driver's side of the car, pulling the oxygen tank behind her.

"No run on the beach, no swimming, no diving, no horseplay."

"Whatever you say." I looked back toward the sound, where the ferry that had dropped me off was already chugging back into the distance.

Virginia started the car and we pulled onto the main street, what seemed like the only street. Surprisingly, she obeyed the 25 mph speed limit. Speed limits had never really been her forte.

To our right was the harbor, mostly empty docks. To the left there were houses and the occasional restaurant or bar or kayak rental hut. Nubbin's Grill. The Rusty Cutlass. All of them still boarded up for the off-season, even though it was a warm March. Then a low brick wall around a small cemetery, iron gates with an anchor motif. Death's Fool sat on top of the wall, staff in hand, staring off into the distance. I pointed him out to Virginia.

"Want to see if he needs a ride anywhere?"

"Hell no," said Virginia.

Just as we rolled past he looked over at our car and smiled. I couldn't tell if he was looking at me or at Virginia. He had no teeth.

4

We lurched to a halt, clouds of gray dust billowing up from the gravel lot at the side of Blackbeard's Hideout. I moved slowly, deliberately, trying to match Virginia's pace as I retrieved my bag and walked past the 19th-century pointing finger sign up to the screened porch that was seeded with rocking chairs. The building was a dark two-story hulk, more barn than hotel, down a side street from the main road. A fan inside the engine compartment of the car spun to a stop, clanking. Beyond the hotel, the side road curved off to the left. There were vacation houses with white picket fences, and everywhere the gnarled scrub pines.

Virginia went in first through the screen and front doors, not locked. Inside the lobby was a big open space, concrete floor with doors all around, a balcony with the same, all of it dimly lit. There was an old Cheerwine machine that whirred away. There was a pool table and there were bicycles stacked against the wall. I spotted Virginia's unicycle, the one with the zebra print seat. There was also a small boat built into the floor that said *Adventure* on the side. Virginia walked around and stepped through an opening into the boat, which evidently was the reservations desk. She slid a brass key on a diamond-shaped fob over to me. "How about Room 102? It's right next to the caretaker's apartment." She gestured to a door, cracked open, near the boat.

A scraggly white cat with bent whiskers and chewed-off ears shambled out from the opening into the lobby. "You remember Lightning," she said. The cat made its way toward us, in no hurry. I did remember Lightning. Lightning had been her cat when we were kids, decades ago. I remembered Lightning zooming around her parents' split-level house. Lightning stalking my shoelaces. Lightning shambling into the room to deliver a huge cockroach corpse to me. Maybe Virginia always got white cats and always named them Lightning and this was Lightning Mark Two, or Mark Three. No way it could be the same old Lightning, unless she'd had him cloned. I tried to think if she'd ever mentioned pets in her calls or letters, but couldn't recall.

"Meow," said Lightning, walking into the boat and then jumping onto the desk chair and then the desk. Virginia proffered her hand and Lightning bonked into it. He batted at the oxygen tubes as if rearranging them, then settled down on top of a big leather-bound book.

"Give him a scritch," she said, so I leaned over and tickled him under his chin. He'd always liked that. All cats like that. This couldn't be the same Lightning. His fur was so thin, I could see the pink skin underneath. His purr was a loud thrum, just like the old Lightning's.

"He's happy to see you," she said.

Lightning stood up and bonked against my shirt, leaving a patch of white hairs. Then back to my hand. I picked up my bag and took it to room 102. On the door, a spray of dried flowers hung from a nail. The stems were dusty gray but the dried blossoms were red with yellow tips.

"What's the flower?"

"Blanket flowers," she said. "We call 'em Joe Bells. Joe Bell: jilted lover from further up the coast, wandering the island. Folks left him baskets of food and he returned them filled with blanket flowers. Then one day he was found in his boat, dead, surrounded by the flowers. That's the story, anyway. I've got them planted around the swimming pool. They grow anywhere—might as well be weeds."

"What does Lightning think of Joe Bells?"

"Lightning is more interested in the vole, shrew, and mouse population. As far as flora goes, he's a purist. I grow catnip for him in the herb garden."

Lightning had come over and was patiently waiting for me to open the door to room 102.

"Is this place built on a Native American burial ground? Do you often get the urge to type the same sentence over and over during the winter months?"

She laughed but then immediately started wheezing in spasms. I rushed over but she waved me off.

"That doesn't sound good."

"Sounds fine to me," she said. "Don't worry, we don't have a room 237."

The room was more rustic than piratical, with a double bed, a red Naugahyde recliner, and a wooden dresser. The carpeting was worn through in spots and lumpy in other spots. No television. The window was half-covered by a bright red curtain, tied back with rope. I threw my bag on the bed, then pulled out my toiletries bag and put it on the sink in the tiny bathroom. Lightning had followed me into the room and made his way from the recliner to the top of the dresser in two tentative hops. He slumped down and lay there with his head over the edge. It looked like it would be very uncomfortable, even for a cat. It also looked exactly like how Lightning, the Lightning of my youth, had lain on the coffee table in the living room of the split-level house where Virginia lived.

I was startled by a sound outside. At first I thought it was a dog snarling. Lightning didn't move from his spot. I went to the window, standing far enough back so that I wouldn't be seen. In the side lot of the hotel there was a spindly young boy, no more than twelve. He had a plastic cutlass in one hand, and wore a long black coat belted with a red sash. On his head, a black pirate hat, which bore a skull and crossbones logo in case there was any doubt.

"Arrr!" said the boy. Over and over, while shaking his cutlass at the air, at the building, at all the points of the compass. He would stylishly pose for a second, hands on hips, then start up again with the yelling and the swordplay.

I let the curtain fall all the way across the window, not wanting to incur the wrath of the tiny buccaneer.

The one piece of art on the walls was a print of a coat of arms, very English, a busy array of lions and unicorns and crowns and roses. At the bottom a banner read "Semper Eadem." Instinctively I pulled my phone out, but there was no signal. I walked over to Lightning.

"Lightning," I said, "can you translate, hmmm?"

Lightning stood up when I said his name. I reached over to give him a pat and he leaned back on his back legs and clutched my hand gently between his front paws. He held on for a few seconds and then let go, back onto all fours. It was, of course, something that the old Lightning had done many times.

"Where should we go eat, Lightning?" I asked. "Let's go talk to Virginia."

She was sitting in the reception desk boat, absently spinning a little ship's wheel that was bolted to the desk.

"The *Adventure?*"

"Yeah. One of Blackbeard's ships was the *Adventure.* The other was the *Queen Anne's Revenge.* They found that one. Never found the *Adventure,* though."

"And here it's been sitting in this hotel all along. You should notify the historic preservation office. Hey, what's with ye olde coat of arms in my room?"

"That is, perhaps not surprisingly, Queen Anne's."

"The Latin bit? The slogan?"

"Semper eadem: always the same."

"Good luck with that, Queen Anne. Hey, they got any restaurants on this here island?"

"Oh yeah, we've got tacos and pan-Asian and a wine bar and a bakery and a pizza place. And seafood, of course. And none of them are open for the season yet. The pub is open, where you can get all the fried brown food you'd ever need. But let's just eat here. I can make sandwiches, and I've got beer. You still drink beer, right?"

"I still drink beer."

"Besides, Death's Fool might spot me if we went out somewhere."

"I'll protect you."

"I don't think you'd be much up against Death's Fool. We should stay here with Lightning. Death's Fool hates cats. It's like an allergy. Confuses him. It. Them. I don't know what gender Death's Fool is."

"Let's go with 'him,'" I said.

Lightning entered on cue and went into the boat. Virginia pulled him up into her lap. He hung his head down over the ledge of her knee.

"When do I get this artifact of great importance? Is it some of Blackbeard's treasure?"

"You in a rush? Ferry doesn't leave until tomorrow morning."

I shrugged a shrug that Virginia had seen a thousand times before.

"All right," she said.

She turned up the regulator knob on her oxygen tank, dumped Lightning out of her lap, and got up.

"I can get it, just tell me where—"

"I'll get it, hang on."

She went into the caretaker's apartment and then came back with a dark blob in her hands. When she got back in the boat she tossed it over to me.

It was my old Norfolk jacket. I'd bought it at a thrift store sophomore year. I'd been in an extremely brief tweedy British explorer phase. Then Virginia had taken it from me, saying it looked better on her than it did on me. Which was true. She would roll the sleeves up and wear it as a top in cool weather, stashing beers in the voluminous pockets.

"Still fits you," she said.

"Only because of this ridiculous diet I'm on."

"Looks like it's working."

"Well, this is awkward. I show up here empty-handed, and you've given me this jacket."

"That's not a jacket, that's a historic artifact. Also, it's your jacket, remember?"

"Yeah. You know what else you could give me, Virginia? Wisdom."

She laughed.

"Could I say anything more eloquent than 'hang in there, baby,' the line from the old cat poster? You want platitudes? I've got books full of them—my ex started sending them to me. I guess he feels sorry or that's his ass-backwards way of apologizing or something. Live, keep going, all that."

"I've tried living and keeping going."

"Me too, and look where it's got me." She thought for a moment. "Seriously? OK, Virginia's rules. Follow your obsessions. Honor complexity. And, I dunno, maybe take up unicycling. Although it's probably too late for you to take up unicycling. But you knew all of that already."

"Yeah."

"Excuse me again, will ya?"

She went back into the caretaker's apartment, moving slowly. I thought about obsessions and complexity as I rummaged through the pockets of the jacket. I tried to think of the last thing I'd been truly obsessed with, but nothing came to mind. In the jacket there was half a tube of old butter rum

Lifesavers, a butane lighter, and a packet of sugar. One of Virginia's party tricks was opening a packet of sugar and drizzling the grains through the flame of a lighter, which when done correctly produced a big stream of crackling fire. Always a hit on the back patios of rental houses and dive bars, and only one time did a fire extinguisher have to be deployed. I wondered when the last time was that she'd done that trick. I wondered if she still had the knack.

She was gone for a while, long enough for Lightning to go investigate, and then finally they returned together.

I brandished the lighter and the sugar. "Can you still do this one?"

She rattled the plastic tubes that led to the ever-present tank. "I don't really go in for tricks anymore, especially ones that involve open flames."

She came over and sat next to me on the couch.

"There's an island story, one that I actually believe. A ship wrecked off the coast here, one carrying a circus and menagerie. Circus costumes washed up on the shore. Carcasses of hippopotamuses, giraffes, camels, lions, and tigers washed up on the shore. But two horses survived and roamed the island for years, performing circus tricks for anyone they came across in hope of getting a treat. Eventually they just faded into the herd of wild ponies that already lived here. I think about those two horses a lot."

Lightning smashed into my leg. I leaned down to pet him. I could feel bumps, growths, under his patchy fur.

"You know, Blackbeard tried to go straight," she said. "After blockading Charleston for weeks, he surrendered to the governor. Promised he'd stop with all the pirating. He moved inland, married a local woman. His fourteenth wife, by some accounts. Didn't last, though. You should go see the Point. That's point with a capital P. Most historic part of the island. Blackbeard died there. In the *Adventure.*"

"The boat that's never been found."

"Yeah. Walk out of here, turn right and then head down the road to the lighthouse, then keep going past it. Look for a green gate and an informative plaque; that's where the trail to the point starts. Stay on the trail. Keep an eye out for Death's Fool. And for mosquitoes. You might want to spray yourself again."

"Aren't you going to come with?"

She coughed again, wheezing wetly into her hand. "I'm tired. Maybe I'll work on a trick for you, that one with a playing card and a shot of whiskey and a shot of water. Go on. If you leave now you can watch the sunset from there. Take a flashlight."

I took a flashlight, doused myself with more bug spray, put on my sunglasses, and set out.

I walked out to the road, where there was a Canada goose milling around by the roadside. Just as I turned right it fanned out its wings and started honking at me. I kept going—it was only a bird—but then it attacked, flying up and pecking at me. I batted at it, which I'm sure looked hilarious to any islanders watching. It was a lot better at dodging me than I was at dodging it. I fell backward onto some crushed gravel. The bird did not let up, flying over and continuing to jab at me. I heard a window slam open from the hotel.

"Stand up and take your sunglasses off!" she said.

Still under attack from the goose, I complied as quickly as I could.

"Now spread your arms out."

I did that, and suddenly the goose backed down and backed away.

"You OK?" she said. I shook the dust off of myself.

"I don't think it broke the skin. I thought they only attacked when defending their young?"

"You thought wrong. That one, he's lonely. Been hanging around here, not paired up. Single male goose. The seasons are so weird now, I'm not sure when he'll migrate. If he'll migrate."

"So you have a special power of kinship with animals now, too?"

"No, I'm just not a dingbat who goes wandering around not paying attention. Now get going."

I found the green gate past the lighthouse. There was a slot at the bottom of the informative plaque that contained one lonely sunbleached informative brochure. I stuffed it in my back pocket. I wished that there was a brochure on all the various diseases and conditions that required use of an oxygen tank. My phone was still useless. No bars.

The trail ran by a white picket fence next to an old house. After the house the fence changed into stacks of driftwood, some of it hung with shells and horseshoe crab carapaces. After some sandy hills the fences stopped and I entered the maritime forest. The gnarled live oaks had already sprouted new leaves so I was surrounded by a canopy of green. The trail ran up and down hummocks, past salt marshes and yaupon thickets, with no sign of habitation of any kind.

I felt alone on the island, as if I might as well have been back in the time of the pirates. The only noises were the noises of birds, birds that I could not identify, chirping and peeping and squawking. I tried to imagine walking over the next rise and finding Blackbeard and a convocation of fellow pirates there. I skimmed the brochure as I walked and learned that indeed this exact area had been where he and his men holed up in between plundering runs. And that the largest convention of pirates ever had been held there, right there. There was no trace, just sandy soil and trees. Then I got to the cistern and the grave.

I consulted the brochure again. The round brick cistern was covered now. The twentieth-century owner of the property was buried there next to his horse. He must've loved that horse. I wondered which one of them died first.

I kept going on the path. The trees thinned out and now it was mostly high grass and then over a final dune there was the sound, placid in the fading rays of the sun. Directly ahead of me in the water was where Blackbeard had been anchored in the *Adventure* when he was ambushed and killed by the Royal Navy, his body swimming around Lieutenant Maynard's ship three times after it had been beheaded. There were no boats nearby that I could see. Far to the south was another island at the other side of the inlet.

I tried to imagine it in the early morning hours, in 1718, multiple ships occupying the channel. Cannon fire, guns and grenades, ships ablaze, the clank of cutlass and dagger. The groans of men killing and being killed. The sun was sinking low now, setting the water on fire.

And as I stood there, balancing on a cinder block against which the corpses of two jellyfish beat in the rhythm of the waves, someone ran into my legs from behind, knocking me down on onto all fours in the shallows. It was the pirate boy.

"Arrr," the pirate boy said, brandishing his plastic cutlass.

I still hurt from where the goose had pecked at me, and that gave me the idea to fend the boy off in the same way. I stood, pushed my sunglasses back on my head, and spread my arms wide to make myself as big as possible.

The boy ran at me and whacked me in the crotch with his toy sword. I collapsed.

"Arrr!" he said again, emphatically. Then he ran up the beach, toward some lights in the distance. I rolled over to a sitting position and waited for this new pain to subside.

It was starting to get seriously dark, so I retraced my steps down the path and back to the hotel.

Virginia had left the porch light on at the hotel. Moths big and small bashed themselves senseless against it. The door to the lobby was open and I trudged in. My shoes were full of sand and even though I'd doused myself in spray, I still had a couple insect bites. Plus the aches and pains inflicted by the goose and the pirate boy. I needed a drink.

"Get any good photos?" she said.

"Nah," I offered. I didn't mention the pirate boy. If she had secrets, well, I could have secrets too. "What are my beer options?"

"Just random cheap stuff, I'm afraid. I don't drink much beer anymore. Switched to vodka and grapefruit a while back. Get some vitamin C with my vitamin A. The fridge is in my apartment, check it out. And fix me a drink."

I went and got a randomly cheap beer and made her a vodka and grapefruit.

We sat on the screened porch, me and Virginia with Lightning playing the part of the elephant in the room. Virginia turned the light off so the only illumination was the occasional sweep of the lighthouse.

Lightning took an interest in something on the other side of the screen, standing on his hind legs and pawing away without extending his claws. When my eyes adjusted, I realized that it was the goose.

"Your familiar is good at making friends," I said.

"Oh yeah, they're pals, at least as long as they stay on either side of the screen. And the goose visits Lightning pretty often. If you take my hint."

I took the hint. That's why I said: "Tell me a story." It was one of our oldest routines. One would say "tell me a story" and the other had to make up something right then. Virginia had always been a lot better at it than I was.

"Tell me a story about Death's Fool."

And so she did.

Once there was a citadel in the mountains ruled by a Queen. The citadel sat on a plateau at the top of a pass. There were seven gates, and the gate to the east was called the Gate of Cats, and the gatekeeper there was a man with a son and a daughter. The Gate of Cats sat at the top of a long, steep climb up from the valley below, and the doors of that gate rarely opened.

But one day, there was a rapping at the gate, and the gate-keeper was not there to hear it, for he was at the temple lighting incense and praying to the gods. The son and the daughter—their mother had died years ago—were there, and sat listening to the sharp knocks, four at a time and then a long pause and then another four, and so on.

Finally the daughter went to the gate and slid the spy door open. The son crept up slowly behind and watched.

"Let me in," said the thing beyond the gate. Its voice sounded like the stone wheel that the miller used to grind grain. The thing at the gate rode a goat sidesaddle. The goat was bigger than any goat that the daughter had ever seen. Behind the rider, a rooster perched on the goat's rump.

"Who calls at the Gate of Cats?" said the daughter. She had heard her father say this before.

"Death's Fool," replied the thing on the goat.

That doesn't make sense. You said that Death's Fool was allergic to cats.

OK, it's the Gate of Owls. Happy?

Carry on.

It carried a staff, at the top of which there was a figure that looked like a miniature of Death's Fool, which in turn held a tiny staff, at the top of which there was an even tinier figure, and so on. Death's Fool gently touched the ground with the tip, and the rooster crowed, and the goat bleated, and when these things happened the locks and latches to the gate clanked open. The boy and girl ran off to find their father. Death's Fool nudged the gate and it slowly swung wide open. The goat shuffled through the gate, past the rocky ground of the pass and onto the flat packed earth of the citadel.

When the boy and girl got to the temple, they found their father the gatekeeper lying supine beneath the altar. A rivulet of blood dripped from his open mouth. The children screamed and cried. But they were not alone in the temple. The gilded doors of the royal chamber opened and the Queen emerged.

"O Queen," the daughter said, "Death's Fool is here!"

But the Queen paid them no mind. She rushed straight to the body that lay beneath the altar, and the children gave way, because she was the Queen. She knelt and felt the chest of the gatekeeper, which no longer held a warm beating heart. She turned her face away from the children.

"Go home," she said. "Go back to the Gate of Owls."

The children did as the Queen said, because everyone did as the Queen said. They rubbed their tears away with their sleeves and walked down the aisle between the benches and out into the sunlight. But they did not go to the Gate of Owls, because outside was something even more wondrous. Lying on top of the grave where she'd been buried, dressed in gauzy white that could not possibly have been the same shroud she'd been buried in, was their mother, pale and whole again. Her bright hair shone in the sun. They ran to her and embraced her.

"I have been dreaming of you," she said. "And now you're here."

The children were so amazed that all they could say was "Mother! Mother!" and hug her more and cry more.

"Where is your father?" she asked, and that shocked them back into what they'd witnessed only moments before.

"Father is dead!" they cried.

"Well then, there's nothing we can do about that. Come with me, children."

And with that their mother stood, as nimble as a fox, and took them hand in hand back in the direction of the Gate of Owls.

As they walked, their mother began to sing a song, and it was a song the children had never heard before, and the song went like this:

> At break of day
> We sit and weigh
> The rights from wrongs
> The words from songs
> We pull and push
> We taste and touch
> The games we'll play
> At break of day

As they walked along the Queen and her Guardian Prime, her constant companion, rode past them. The Queen's horse wore a bell and everyone knew its tone and knew to kneel and avert their gaze when the Queen rode by. The children heard the bell and fell to their knees and stared at the ground, but their mother did not. Their mother remained standing, and turned toward the sound, and there was the Queen, swaying as she rode along, with her fiery hair and upturned nose.

Their mother snorted at the Queen, as if she were a pig. But before the Queen could respond—and surely this would mean some kind of punishment—from the opposite direction there was the cry of a rooster, and there came Death's Fool aboard his great goat. The Queen tugged the reins and stopped her horse, and waited as Death's Fool arrived. The goat shambled up the street until it stood in the shadow of the Queen's horse.

"Who are you?" said the Queen.

"I am Death's Fool."

"We have known Death here."

"I am not Death. I am Death's Fool. Today is my day, and this place is my place now."

Death's Fool wore motley in stark white and black, off-kilter stripes and patches that were hard to focus on. Death's Fool shimmered in the sunlight. The rooster had black and white feathers and the goat was white with a black mask and mantle.

The Queen commanded the Guardian Prime to banish Death's Fool. The Guardian Prime rode up past the Queen but then the rooster crowed and the goat bleated and at this his horse stopped and would go no further. The Guardian Prime dismounted and moved toward Death's Fool but then before he could touch the nose of the goat, the rooster crowed again and the goat bleated and the Guardian Prime could go no further.

"I am going to sit on your throne," said Death's Fool to the Queen. "And if I want to dance a jig I shall stand up and dance a jig. And if I want to play a tune I will rip out your shinbone and make a flute of it. And if I want to beat a drum I will tear out your skull and tap it like a tabor."

The great goat stirred and shifted in the direction of the palace.

"Stop," the Queen said. "Take all the treasure that you can, but leave this place, and come here again no more."

"Very well; it is done," Death's Fool said, and touched his staff to the ground, and though no one could see it at the time, the treasures in the royal storehouses vanished. All the gold, all the silver, all the rubies, everything. Death's Fool continued, unimpeded, on to one of the gates in the west, and left the city and was never seen again.

The mother took her children by the hand and led them along the path to the Gate of Owls.

When they got to the gatehouse, the children broke down in tears, for even though they had regained a mother, they had still lost a father.

Their mother packed as much as she could into satchels for the three of them, and worked the locks and latches of the Gate of Owls open, and led the son and daughter out and down the steep path.

The little monarchy in the mountains eventually faded away. And no one knows what happened to the mother and her children.

So, there's your story.

That was not the end of the night. We stayed up and talked.

We talked about old times, people and events from years ago, some of it rehashed to death and some of it things I hadn't heard in decades. We talked about Butts on Parade, each of us blaming the idea on the other. We talked about that one summer I spent watching *Monty Python* reruns in the basement of her parents' house after getting off my shitty job polishing tabletops at the furniture factory. We talked about the circle of fifths, which she once again tried to explain to me and which I once again could not fathom at all, given that my musical career ended with the recorder in the sixth grade, whereas her musical career had extended all the way to the island, where she would sit in with the cover bands that played the pub at the height of the season. We talked about the time that she entered the father/son swim meet with her dad and they cruised to victory, pissing off the other families, him wearing a Speedo and doing the backstroke with a cig in his mouth and her in an American flag one-piece. I talked about how she was my diving board hero when we were kids.

"You always had that ability to land on your feet."

"You don't land on your feet in the water."

"You know what I mean."

"Until, until, until."

She raised her drink and said, "Here's to the *Adventure*."

"To the *Adventure*," I replied, and clicked my beer against her glass.

We talked and talked and then she said, "I want you to have something else besides the jacket." So we talked about that for a while.

And then she was tired, and went in to bed. I stayed up a while, finishing off a third beer, wondering who else I'd have to battle to get off of the island.

In the morning I drove to the ferry, Virginia in the passenger seat and Lightning in her lap, the Norfolk jacket and Lightning's dish in the floorboard. I stopped in the parking lot. We both got out. She spread the Norfolk jacket on the seat and Lightning curled up on top of it. She closed the door.

"Come back when you can't stay so long," she said.

"Well, I know how to get here now. So when I can find the free time, I'll come down," I lied.

We hugged, for the first time that trip, and I felt just how little there was left of her, and she pushed me away and smiled.

"OK, that's it," she said.

"Yes."

I got in my car and got in line to roll on to the ferry. And then we were pulling away, and I got out and left Lightning asleep in the car and stood near the fantail as the boat chugged out of the harbor, looking at Virginia, who waved every so often just to make me wave back. In the distance behind her, I spotted the jester, slowly walking toward her.

Holderhaven

In 1911, Nerissa and Jorn Holder move into Holderhaven.

In 1966, Nerissa Holder dies, having outlived her husband, both sons, and a son-in-law.

In 1983, Holderhaven opens as a country house museum.

In 2003, Rudy needs a summer job. His friend at college, Bill Mills, says he can pull some strings. Bill does not need a summer job. Bill's family is not quite as wealthy as the Holders had been, but they are rich enough. Bill's father is Ol' Dick Mills. Dick Mills's house does not have a name. It is much smaller than Holderhaven, but it still has a tennis court, a swimming pool, and a separate climate-controlled warehouse for his collection of vintage Jaguar convertibles. Ol' Dick Mills knows everyone in the county. Everyone who matters, at least. He places a call to Harriet Diamond, supervisor of operations at the Holderhaven House Museum.

Holderhaven has four floors, including a basement. Sixty-four rooms. The first and second floors are open to the public, as long as the public stays behind the velvet ropes and doesn't try to touch the leather-topped parquetry desk in Mrs. Holder's den, or the tapestries hanging on the balcony walls of the central hall. The board plans to open the basement to the public soon. The top floor, originally for storage, is occupied by the museum staff. Harriet Diamond has an office. Mary Holder Hodgson has an office on the top floor too, with access to the roof walk, but she is rarely around. Rudy gets to stay in a bedroom on the top floor for the summer. The bedroom had been the major-domo's originally. In the 1960s it had been renovated as a teen-ager's hideout. As far as amenities are concerned, it is not much different from Rudy's dorm room.

Rudy is not particularly qualified to work in the house. He is studying math, not architectural preservation. The museum employs specialists to conserve the artwork, to clean the tapestries, to preserve the library books, to ensure that the flowers outside match the photographs of the gardens from the 1920s. That has been the great project of the museum: to send the house back in time. To erase the renovations and redecorations done by the family over the course of the 20th century. To make the house suitable for population by flappers, bootleggers, and gentlemen in straw boater hats. Mary Holder Hodgson has decided that the 1920s would be good for business. Competition in the house museum market is stiff. Everyone is second place to the Biltmore House. Everyone is trying harder. For a time, Mary Holder Hodgson pushes to come out with Holderhaven branded wine. But grapes had never been grown on the estate, and the board nixes this plan. Plans to re-create the 1920s continue.

Rudy is given keys and alarm codes. For the first weeks of the summer, he and Bill Mills spend their off hours together. Bill Mills is an avid moviegoer. Bill is looking forward to the next Matrix movie.

In 1974, Harriet Diamond is a Black Panther. She wears a black beret, a shiny black leather jacket, dark sunglasses, and a stern expression as she delivers breakfasts to hungry schoolchildren. In addition to holding a Black Panther ID card, she also holds a membership card to the Women's Auxiliary to the White Knights of the Ku Klux Klan. She and all her fellow Panthers sent in fake photos to a PO box address they saw on a flier stapled to a telephone pole. They all received Klan cards. There was no membership fee.

"Know your enemy," Harriet said. Sending off for the Klan cards was her idea.

In 2003, a black-and-white photograph of herself and the other Panthers sits on Harriet Diamond's desk. Rudy steals glances between the photo and Ms. Diamond, trying to interpolate the path between the two endpoints. He wonders if Ms. Diamond feels conflicted as an African-American about working in a place like Holderhaven. He never asks her about this, though. In Harriet Diamond's wallet, she still carries her Panther and her Klan membership cards. They are creased and torn now. Realistically old, unlike Holderhaven, which is constantly policed for any sign of decay.

Harriet Diamond is not surprised that Rudy's knowledge of upkeep and repair is not quite as expansive as Ol' Dick Mills implied it would be when he got Rudy the job. Rudy painted houses the previous summer.

"Rudy, what do you know about carpentry?"

"Not much, Ms. Diamond."

"What do you know about plastering?"

"Not much, Ms. Diamond."
"What do you know about, oh, swimming pool filtration?"
"Not much, Ms. Diamond, but I'm a quick study."
"What do you know about secret passages?"

In 1910, Nerissa Holder works with architect Irving Gill on the house plans. She supervises every aspect of planning and construction. Mr. Gill wants an asymmetrical design, with only one wing. Mrs. Holder asks for two wings off the grand central hall. The primary building material will be rough granite stones, with a clay tile roof. She asks Mr. Gill to design matching structures in miniature for the separate servants' quarters and for a playhouse for the children she plans to begin producing. And she asks for a secret passage. No one but Mr. Holder is to know about the secret passage. She works closely with Mr. Gill to ensure this. After the house is built, she burns the blueprints in the fireplace in the great hall. She adds them to the fire one page at a time, ensuring that each is completely consumed, leaving no trace.

In 1911, the secret passage exists. It begins in Mrs. Holder's closet in the master bedroom. Clothes hang to either side. Pressing on the back wall panel at doorknob height pops a magnetic catch so that the entire panel swings open. There is no landing; the spiral staircase begins immediately, down a shaft barely wider than a chimney. The interior is black and featureless, and there is no source of light inside. Any traveler in the secret passage would navigate by feel. The staircase leads all the way to the basement, bypassing the first floor. The basement is a floor of amusements: a party room with large granite fireplace, a billiards room, a one-lane bowling alley, an indoor swimming pool, an elaborate bar with mirrored walls. The secret passage exit is disguised as one of the mirrored panels behind the bar.

In 2003, there are no plans to put the secret passage on the public tour. Instead, it is to be fixed up for the wealthiest donors. A bonus for them. They are also going to get to use the bowling alley and swimming pool in the basement on special occasions. Harriet Diamond gives Rudy the task, for most of June, of fixing up the secret passage.

The secret passage is not the only unusual feature of the house. There is a safe in the master bedroom, behind a painting of a fox hunt. The painting is now hinged to the wall to make it easier for the docents to swing it away dramatically as they tell schoolchildren the tale of Mr. Holder's money. There is an impressive collection of taxidermied animals in the library. Because of the harsh chemicals used—arsenic and mercury—they have been encased in plastic. Mr. Holder had been a keen naturalist, and his love of nature is another paragraph in the script that the docents memorize.

When asked, Mary Holder Hodgson says she is not sure why there is a secret passage. Because the passage is not going to be placed on the public tour, there is no need to "interpret" it. When Harriet reveals the existence of the passage to Rudy, he asks her why it exists.

"Rich people," she says, lowering her head to gaze at him over the top of her reading glasses. This is the only answer she gives.

Tours continue through the summer, so Rudy cannot leave the upper entrance open as he works. He places a fan at the lower entrance, trying to pull out the hot still air. He wears a mask, which makes breathing more difficult. First he sands the rust off the metal stairs, beneath a worklight tethered to a long orange extension cord. He starts at the top, wielding sandpaper and steel wool, dripping sweat, trying not to make too much noise. The docents are used to seeing workers painting a hallway or trimming the hedges, but Rudy wants to keep the secret passage a secret.

He has been sanding for a week when he makes the discovery. Swinging the light around, he notices scratches in the wall. About halfway up the climb, someone had carved a word. The letters are blockish and clumsy, all capitals. Perhaps this word was carved in the dark. The word is LIZZA. Following that name are tally marks, two sets of five plus four more.

Rudy tells Harriet Diamond many things, but he does not yet tell her about his discovery in the secret passage.

The history of Holderhaven is available in a coffee table book. It is also spelled out on a series of kiosks in the tour entrance area, which Harriet refers to as the emergency room. It's the converted garage. Behind velvet ropes sits a 1930 Rolls, not actually one that belonged to the Holders. The original car was totaled in the wreck that killed Crosby Holder, the eldest son, in 1932. The garage is where you buy your ticket and where, if you want more than the docents will tell you, you can learn about the history of the Holder estate. Rudy cursorily read the kiosks when he first started working at Holderhaven. Harriet asked him to check them for typos. She seemed pleased rather than annoyed when he found and fixed two: Pennslvania and capitol instead of capital. Now he returns to the kiosks, looking for mention of anyone named Lizza. He finds none, not even an Elizabeth. Not one on the family tree chart. Not one in the endless paragraphs on Mrs. Holder's various projects: her unsuccessful attempt to cultivate tulips, her more successful dairy operation, the school she founded to instruct the servants. No

mention of a Lizza in the descriptions of the famous personages who stopped by Holderhaven to play croquet or to dance
the Charleston. These personages included Charles Lindbergh
and Calvin Coolidge.

Bill Mills calls up Rudy, wanting to go to a movie and then
out to Jay's, his favorite bar. Rudy begs off, says he is feeling ill.
He stays up late working on Harriet's computer, looking up
more genealogy, looking up the names of Lindbergh's wife. Her
name was Anne, not Lizza. Coolidge's wife's name was Grace.

Finally he gives up and goes back to the secret passage
with a flashlight. He pores over the walls looking for any other
marks. For anything at all, but finds nothing. No hidden chamber. Just the inscription.

It is against the rules, but that night Rudy steps past the
velvet rope and sleeps on the Holders' bed, with the door to the
secret passage left open. There is no pillow on the bed. There
is no pillow on any bed in the restored rooms of Holderhaven.
Mrs. Holder believed that it was healthier to sleep without a
pillow, to preserve the youthful straightness of the spine. Rudy
does not have any revelatory dreams.

In 1899, Holderhaven does not exist. Mr. William Bagge, sheep
farmer, owns a small tract that will form the heart of the 1,066-
acre Holder estate. Mr. Bagge's daughter is born. After Mr. Bagge's
death, his wife and daughter will go to work for the Holders.
His daughter's name is Elizabeth, but she is called Lizza.

In 2003, Rudy and Harriet are having a conversation.

"What do you think the secret passage was for?" Rudy
asks.

"Jorn Holder was a strange man. Maybe to make it easier to run down and get a nightcap from the bar? We know he liked to take over from the bartender and mix drinks. Maybe he liked to appear suddenly behind the bar at parties."

"Seems like a pretty useless trick to go to so much trouble."

Harriet is moving numbers around in a spreadsheet as she talks.

"He couldn't swim, either, but that didn't stop him from building a pool. And I hear he was lousy at bowling, too. How's the bowling alley coming?"

Rudy shrugs and winces. In addition to the secret passage, he is tasked with repainting the bowling alley. The restoration consultant, a big man named James, has chosen a color called Peach Surprise that is the closest match to the original paint. The bowling alley, though small, is airy and temperate compared to the secret passage. Rudy has inspected all of its nooks and crevices for markings or bits of papers and found nothing. He has not actually started painting it yet.

"Speaking of tricks, pick a card," Harriet says. She proffers a deck to Rudy.

"Do I get to inspect the deck first?" he asks.

"No, you don't get to inspect the deck. What, don't you trust me?"

"All right, Harriet, I trust you."

He pulls a card from the set fanned out before him. He tries to pull it from a non-obvious place in the deck. Not the middle. Not either end. Not halfway between the middle and the end. The card is the jack of diamonds.

"Don't show me the card," Harriet says.

"Is this a comment on me?" Rudy asks. "Because if it is, I don't get it."

"I don't know what you're talking about. Put the card back in the deck."

He slides the card in, again to a place that he thinks is the least likely.

Harriet raps the top of the deck sharply, then carefully flips over the top card.

"Is this your card?"

The card is the nine of clubs. Rudy really wants the trick to work, but he doesn't want to lie. So instead he just waits. She repeats the question.

"No, Harriet. It's close, though!"

Harriet scrunches her brow.

"Not your card, huh? Damn. All right, sort through the deck and find it for me."

She hands him the pack, which he flips over and begins sifting through. To Rudy it looks like a standard deck of cards. He can't find the jack of diamonds, though, even though he'd just put it back in there.

"Hang on, hang on, I'm feeling something," Harriet says. "Stand up."

He stands up.

"Put your hand in your left trouser pocket."

He puts his hand in. There is the usual junk: assorted change, a little pocket pen, his lucky paper clip. There is also a playing card. Rudy pulls the card out slowly, and as he does he unconsciously takes a step back from Harriet. The card is the jack of diamonds.

"Pretty good, huh?"

"Damn good, Harriet."

In 1912, Crosby is born, the first of Jorn and Nerissa's three children. Immediately after the birth, Jorn Holder commissions a painting and a statue. The painting is a portrait of a prepubescent girl, clad only in a diaphanous white dress. She clutches a spray of white flowers and has a pixie grin on her face. She has sharp cheekbones and a snub nose. The painting hangs over the mantel in his office. The statue is bronze, placed in the terraced garden, in the center of a circular slate walkway surrounded by rhododendron and azalea. The terraced garden is on the north side of the east wing, visible from the master suite and from Mr. Holder's office. The statue is of the same young girl. She is nude, facing toward the house, her arms spread to display the bounty of the garden and grounds. Mr. Holder calls her "Lady Liberty."

In 2003, Rudy continues his investigations. He is surrounded by objects, rooms full of them. He is surrounded by texts. Books in the library. Paperwork in Harriet's office. Mary Holder Hodgson's office is always locked, but he imagines she has some records too. It turns out that most of the surviving records from Holderhaven are now kept in a vault at the university. Not available to the public. Someone is doing a dissertation, but she is out of town for the summer. Rudy sends the doctoral student an email, but gets no response.

Rudy imagines all these objects, all this text, laid out in a giant matrix. He is slowly picking his way through each cell in the matrix. He looks in the big maintenance building that's hidden at the end of a paved pathway in the woods. It's a modern structure, built after Holderhaven's transformation into a museum. The gardeners' tools and machinery are kept there. There is also furniture from the now deprecated mid-century era of Holderhaven. Rudy carefully inspects the jumble of bent plywood chairs and steel and fiberglass tables, but he finds no graffiti, no spoor of the mysterious Lizza. He looks in the playhouse and the servants' quarters too, but finds nothing of interest.

Rudy takes the keys to these buildings back to Harriet's office, to replace them on their labeled hooks. He plops down in Harriet's chair, spins to face the shelf on the far wall. There is a series of boxes, labeled with years starting with 1923. He starts to pull the earliest one off the shelf.

"You don't want to touch that one," Harriet says, from the doorway. "That's what they call a valuable collector's item. Those have nothing to do with the house. It's my complete set of back issues of *The Linking Ring*. I'm reading through them on my lunch breaks."

Rudy raises his eyebrows, not comprehending.

"The magazine of IBM, the International Brotherhood of Magicians. They don't have an International Sisterhood, so I make do."

"I'm sorry, I wasn't trying to snoop through your stuff."

Rudy gets up and moves to the chair on the other side of the desk. Harriet takes up her position behind the desk.

"How's the bowling alley coming?" Harriet asks.

"Uh, it's taking longer than expected."

"Has to be done by the party, which is next Friday. What are you looking for in the maintenance shed, anyway?"

Rudy hesitates.

"And don't lie."

So he doesn't. He tells her about the inscription in the secret passage.

He offers to take her to see it, but she declines.

"I believe you. I don't need to see it."

Harriet tells him that the name Lizza does not ring a bell with her. Not the name of any family members. Not the name of any of the servants that she can recall. Harriet pulls her copy of the coffee table book from the shelf. She points out the photograph on page 27: "Crosby, the governess Mags, Alvis,

unidentified women and Jorn at Holderhaven, circa 1915."
Three-year-old Crosby is wearing a suit that matches his father's.
They stand at either end of the group of women. One of the
women is holding Crosby's younger brother, Alvis, in her arms.
On top of the hill in the distance sits Holderhaven. The women
all wear white dresses. Six women are unidentified; any of them
could be Lizza. Mags wears her hair in a bun perched on the top
of her head. Her hand rests on young Crosby's shoulder.

"There are a lot of unidentified people who passed through
these hallowed halls," she says. So many names, especially servants' names, are practically lost to history. Possibly recorded
on census rolls, probably never engraved on a tombstone, just a
dimly remembered story to their descendents. At any given time,
especially in the early days of Holderhaven, there would have
been cooks, laundresses, gardeners, maids, nurses. Someone to
set the pins in the bowling alley. A chauffeur, whose name does
survive, as does the name of the majordomo: Arthur Doyle.

"No relation to Sherlock Holmes," Harriet says. "Trust
me."

"We could just ask Ms. Hodgson," Rudy says. "Maybe
she knows some lore that didn't get set down in the book."

"Mary Holder Hodgson can tell you a whole other book's
worth of family history. If you want to talk about the ill-fated
attempt to bottle and sell salad dressing made on the estate
during the Depression, she can tell you all about it. If you want
to know all about her uncle Alvis's pet monkey that he kept in a
cage next to the swimming pool, she can reel off a list of all the
furniture and objets d'art that it broke or ruined every time it
escaped during its two-year tenure in the house. If you want to
talk about Nerissa Holder's fondness for tomato pudding and
lamb sandwiches at her whist club luncheons, she will recite the
entire menu and then teach you to play whist. Which is a boring

damn game, by the way. But she didn't even know about the secret passage's existence—it had been sealed shut for decades when the restoration architects discovered it while they were drawing up plans. I doubt she wants to know that some girl's name is scratched on the wall in there next to some tally marks.

"Also, she always keeps her office locked. And she's the only one with the key."

In 1965, two magicians visit Hattie Diamond's fourth grade class. She and nine of her classmates pose for a photograph with them. The magicians, both of them white men, wear bow ties and plaid tuxedos. This photograph is published in the September issue of *The Linking Ring*.

In 1916, Jorn Holder dies. The cause of death printed in the *Daily Lookout* is a combination of gastritis and exhaustion. Nerissa has the painting of the young girl removed from Jorn's office and the nude statue removed from the terraced garden. Alone one night soon after, she burns the painting in the fireplace in the great hall. Later she will donate the statue to be melted down for the war effort. She has a large marble obelisk constructed and put in the place of the statue, a cenotaph for Jorn, whose remains were sent back to the old Holder family cemetery in Pennsylvania. Almost nine months after Jorn's death, on Christmas Day, Nerissa bears their final child, a girl, Noelle.

The secret passage is not the only way to traverse the floors of Holderhaven. There is an elevator, but it is locked shut, deemed unsafe and too expensive to repair. There is a dumbwaiter, too, merely broken. And of course there are stairs; narrow ones to get up to the top floor where Harriet works and Rudy lives, grand ones on either side of the central fireplace to ascend from the first floor to the second, less grand ones to descend to the basement. Rudy wonders if the elevator holds any secrets, or the dumbwaiter. The dumbwaiter compartment itself is stuck between floors. He manages to pry open the doors and finds nothing but a black chimney, a secret passage in miniature. No scratches, no hidden messages. He crawls up as far as he can, which is not far, searching with a flashlight and finding nothing.

Holderhaven has its own ghost story. Everyone who works there, including Harriet, knows the story. The ghost in the story is Mrs. Holder. A portrait of her hangs over the fireplace in the great hall. In the portrait, Nerissa Holder is thirty-one years old. A little brass lamp illuminates the portrait, night and day. The story is, if the lamp is shut off at night, Mrs. Holder's ghost will emerge from the portrait.

Rudy hears this story from Harriet, but assumes it is merely to keep him in his room at night, instead of wandering about in the dark house pretending to be an early 20th century aristocrat. Going beyond the velvet ropes, sitting in the chairs that are never to be sat in again.

Rudy decides to ask Mrs. Holder herself about Lizza. He waits until midnight, goes downstairs and positions one of the dining room chairs in front of the portrait. He flicks off the light switch next to the mantel and takes a seat. And waits. In the portrait, Mrs. Holder is kindly and radiant. She looks like Rudy's high school world history teacher, Ms. Raney. The same knowing smile, the same piercing green eyes. Rudy has seen actual photographs of Mrs. Holder, and the portrait is a vast improvement. His eyes adjust to the darkness. It's a full moon outside but it remains extremely dim in the grand hall. On the third floor, the windows are normal glass, but on the public floors, the windows have been coated to keep out the damaging rays of the sun. Mrs. Holder does not emerge from the painting. Her mouth does not even move. Rudy conjures up a mental image of Mrs. Holder talking to him, but in reality the thin painted smile does not vibrate in the least. Mrs. Holder says nothing. Rudy keeps waiting. It takes time to prove a hypothesis, he thinks, wondering if hypothesis is the right word. Rudy is also falling asleep.

He thinks about leaving his mark in Holderhaven, just as Lizza did. Not scratched into the wall of the secret passage, though. Something even sneakier. Maybe written in permanent marker on the bottom of one of the circular stair treads. Who would ever look there? Rudy and his signature doodle, a hyperbolic spiral. Permanent, or as permanent as anything in the house, living on unseen until the house collapsed or burned or until someone decided to repaint the bottom of the treads on the circular stairway. When would that ever happen?

He is jarred awake by a noise, or possibly just a dream of a noise. He focuses on Mrs. Holder but she is as flat and lifeless as ever. The noise had not come from the painting. The noise had come from inside the secret passage.

Rudy flips the light switch back on, replaces the dining room chair, and slips upstairs to the master bedroom. He pushes the panel in the back of the closet and it pops open. He leans into the passage.

"Mrs. Holder? Nerissa Holder?"

And then, after a moment: "Lizza?"

He is met with silence. He goes and gets a flashlight from his room, walks down the stairs and back up, but he finds nothing amiss. On his way back up the steps, he stops at the marks. Checks them with the flashlight—no change. He reaches out

and touches the wall, brushing his palm over the scratchings.
The marks are warm.

"Lizza?"

He turns and sits on the steps, flicking the flashlight off.
He hears no more noises, though, and after a time he goes up to
his room and to bed.

Downtown one Saturday at the end of June, the annual Sum-
mersplosion is happening, and Harriet is one of the entertain-
ers. Rudy catches the bus to see her perform. She does sets on
the side stage at noon, three, and six. In between she roams
the crowd, doing close-up magic. She wears a gold robe with
embroidered stars, and a turban with a large ruby brooch. Rudy
gets there in time to see the finale of her three o'clock set. It's a
card trick. The audience volunteer, a middle-aged white man in
khaki shorts, discovers that the card he chose from the deck and
signed with a permanent marker has vanished from a locked
box and reappeared underneath his baseball cap. The crowd
goes wild.

Rudy buys a hot dog and a plastic cup of beer from a tent
set up by the local microbrewery. Across the square, a reggae
band on the main stage has started up a song about a shantytown.
Rudy walks along looking at the craft booths as he polishes off
the hot dog and the beer. Pottery, beads, beads made from pottery, pottery featuring beads. He turns the corner and sees Harriet working the crowd. She has a brass urn in one hand. With
the other hand she is discovering gold coins on the person of a
young girl holding a helium balloon. The girl is extremely tick-
lish; she cackles as Harriet plucks coins from her armpits, from
behind her ears, from out of her shoes. Endlessly they appear,
and endlessly Harriet tosses them into her urn, which makes a

loud clinking sound each time. Finally Harriet goes to work on the father of the girl with the balloon. Harriet is a lot bolder here than she is at Holderhaven. She displays an empty hand, then reaches around behind the man to pull a gold coin from his butt. The girl with the balloon spasms with laughter. Harriet tosses the coin into her bucket, clink, bows, and moves on.

Rudy walks up to her before she can find another victim.

"Great show, Harriet," he says. She is squinting at him, not responding to the compliment.

"What is that?" she asks. Her arm shoots out near his head, to pluck something from behind his ear. She holds it up between them. It's a key.

"Look what you had behind your ear. Didn't your mother tell you to wash back there? Looks like the key to Mary Holder Hodgson's office to me. Maybe you better hang on to it."

She presses the key into his hand.

"No, Harriet, I—"

"You take the key, do what you need to do. If I got caught snooping in there, it'd cost me my job. Magic pays well by the hour but it's not enough to pay the bills."

"Thanks, Harriet."

"For what?" she says loudly, then she pulls a gold coin out of his nose and drops it in her bucket.

Rudy pockets the key and takes the next bus back to Holderhaven.

The sun is still out when Rudy unlocks Mary Holder Hodgson's office and slips inside. He is immediately confounded. The office is much emptier than he'd expected. The desk is bare except for a computer monitor and an inbox. Unlike Harriet's computer, Mary's is password-protected. He tries a few passwords, but none of them work: Holderhaven, Hodgson, Nerissa, passage. He types in Lizza, feeling sure that it's the one, but when he hits the Enter key the same "access denied" message appears. He flips through the papers in the inbox, but nothing looks promising. They are mostly current magazines and newspapers, or clippings related to the Holderhaven House Museum. Nothing that looks old or archival. The desk is unlocked but contains mostly cosmetics. One drawer contains only skin creams.

The walls are covered in framed photographs: Mary Holder Hodgson shaking Ol' Dick Mills's hand as he offers her a check and mugs for the camera, Mary Holder Hodgson showing Nancy Reagan around the great hall, pointing at the fake medieval tapestries. There is a locked cabinet next to the desk. For all Rudy knows, there might be another safe hidden behind one of the framed photos. So he checks behind each one, finding only bare walls.

An unabridged dictionary and a large, leather-bound Bible sit on top of the locked cabinet. Rudy flips open the Bible. It opens to a section in the center for a family tree, but this has not been filled in. Pressed between the pages is a small stack of old, fading photographs. He sorts through them. None look promising. Color snapshots from the 1950s and 1960s, children sledding, children hunting for Easter eggs on the grounds. An old black-and-white photo of the portico, with curvy edges. He checks the backs of the photographs for writing, finds none.

The photograph of the house feels thicker than the rest, because it's actually two photographs stuck together. Rudy carefully pries the photographs apart with his thumbnail.

In the photograph, Jorn Holder stands next to a statue of a girl in the terraced garden. Her nude torso touches his clothed torso. She has her arms outstretched, and his arm is draped over her shoulders. Jorn is smiling.

For a moment, Rudy can't breathe. He commits the photograph to memory, and replaces it and the other pictures in the Bible.

The door to the roof walk is not locked. Rudy walks out and up the steps to the flat tile spine of the roof. Most of the 1,066 acres of the Holder estate have been sold off long ago, but he squints and tries to imagine the surrounding countryside covered in green woods and pastures instead of parking lots and strip malls, lined with dirt paths instead of asphalt roads. The sun goes down and he says goodbye to the day.

The next weekend is the annual reception for the patrons of the house. This year they celebrate the imminent opening, thanks to their donations, of the bowling alley, the swimming pool, the bar, and the party room, the same rooms that Rudy and the conservators have been trying to put in order. The patrons love doing things that ordinary visitors are not allowed to do. The frisson of going beyond the velvet rope is their reward for donating the hundreds of thousands of dollars that it takes to keep the place running.

Harriet asks Rudy if he is going to attend.

"I'm invited? I don't have to work the reception?"

"No. Mary Holder Hodgson suggested that you might be able to assist the caterers, but I talked her out of that."

"Thanks, Harriet," Rudy says.

"You might even get to meet some folks who really were in the Klan," she adds, as if that is a bonus.

The party invitations suggest that attendees dress up in the style of the 1920s. Bill Mills loans Rudy an ivory linen suit. Bill goes in a top hat and tails, as if he'd walked out of a Monopoly set. Rudy scrounges up some spectator shoes at a thrift store, but he cannot find a straw boater hat. Bill's suit is a little too big for him.

Ol' Dick Mills is a platinum patron of Holderhaven. Platinum is $10,000 a year and up. Platinum members are listed in the brochure, on a plaque in the entry hall, and in the back of the coffee table book. As it turns out, the platinum members, most of the patrons in fact, are not interested in dressing up in the style of the 1920s. There are a few people who make an attempt. The men are all would-be gangsters, in black shirts and white ties. The women are all would-be molls, in short dresses and shiny headbands.

Harriet wears her mentalist outfit, an embroidered wrap dress and turban with a large fake ruby affixed to the front. Harriet's husband, Harvey Roseboro, does not attend. Harvey never attends functions at Holderhaven.

The croquet lawn is lit up, and there are tents and tables set up on the south lawn. Most patrons circulate through the party room to take a cursory glance at the restoration before retiring to the tables outdoors to smoke and talk. Waiters circulate with trays of champagne, trays of foie gras on toast. Rudy politely turns down the champagne. Instead he orders a Maiden's Prayer, an authentic Prohibition-era cocktail, at the bar. He looked up the recipe earlier in the day, from the *Savoy Hotel Cocktail Book* in the house library. Gin, Cointreau, lemon juice, orange juice. The bartender is happy to make something that's not yet another bourbon and ginger ale. Twelve-year-old bourbon, bottle after bottle, drowning in a sea of ginger ale, sucked down by the platinum members who don't like champagne because it gives them gas. Ol' Dick Mills, he prefers single-malt scotch doused with Coke.

Bill Mills is drinking both champagne and beer. He and Harriet and Rudy stand together, making small talk. Ol' Dick

Mills has long since retreated to a table outside where he can smoke with his cronies.

"Hey, do a trick," Bill says to Harriet.

"I am doing a trick. I'm reading your mind," she says, then she asks Rudy to get her another glass of that Austrian rosé.

Rudy goes, and Bill decides it's time to go to the bathroom.

"The seal is broken!" he announces, for the benefit of anyone who cannot read his mind.

The bathroom in the basement is still not renovated. There are portable toilets set up outside, twice as big as the type used by construction workers. They are hooked up to running water. An attendant sits next to them in a folding chair, supervising a stack of cotton towels.

Rudy returns with Harriet's wine, and Bill re-enters the party room from the hall. They both notice the young woman at the same time. Ella is standing by the hearth, next to the restored mural. Ella is extremely short. Ella has had the most success dressing in the style of the 1920s. She wears a loose slim dress, gray with a white collar, and a single long strand of pearls. Most importantly, she wears a cloche hat. Like Rudy and Bill, she is significantly younger than any of the other attendees at the reception, except for the waiters and bartender, and the waiters and bartender are all male.

After a few more minutes of conversation, Harriet says to Rudy: "Why don't you stop staring, and just go talk to her."

Rudy walks over to Ella. She's still scrutinizing the mural.

"It was just restored," he says. "We can't identify every-one, though." The mural is of a party scene, caricatures of the Holder family and their close friends. Painted in the 1920s, when Mrs. Holder was courted by many men but deigned to marry none of them, it was covered with geometric wallpaper in the 1950s, when Mrs. Holder declared that looking at a mural with so many dead people in it was exhausting.

"Well, that's clearly Jean Lilly, the polo player," she says, pointing to a tall man with a big nose and mustache carrying a polo mallet over his shoulder. "My grandfather told me about him."

"Your grandfather knew the Holders?"

"Yes. His father was their attorney."

Ella has a pronounced gap between her top two front teeth. Rudy finds it fascinating, but tries not to stare.

They continue to talk about the people in the mural before moving on to talking about themselves. Ella is leaving the next day for Geneva, to get an early start on her JYA: junior year abroad.

Bill Mills walks up with two glasses of champagne and tries to hand one to Ella.

"I never touch the stuff," she says. "I'm more of a scotch woman."

"Go get the lady some scotch," Bill says to Rudy. "The good kind." Rudy does not budge. Ella suggests that they all walk to the bar to peruse the scotch selection.

"Rudy's the houseboy here, he should get your scotch," Bill notes.

They go to the bar and Ella chooses her scotch.

"Neat," she says to the bartender.

"Neato!" the bartender replies.

Bill offers to give her a ride in his convertible after she finishes her drink. As he says this, he slugs back a half glass of champagne in one gulp. Ella says that she does not ride with strange men in convertibles.

"I'm not a strange man, I'm Bill Mills. Son of Ol' Dick Mills."

Ella laughs.

Rudy and Ella attempt to continue their conversation. Bill continues to talk about his car and about what a nice night it is and how great the stars look and the wind feels when you're driving in your convertible at night.

"You're in no condition to drive," Ella says.

"She's right," Rudy adds, although he remembers more than one occasion when he rode in a car driven by a drunken and insistent Bill.

Bill is unaccustomed to so much disapproval, so he goes off to find more alcohol. Ella and Rudy step outside. They pass the tent and the croquet lawn, wandering through the gardens around the house. They walk slowly and look up to confirm at least part of Bill's assertion: the stars do look beautiful.

Rudy learns that Ella attends Smith College. She will return directly to Smith after her European jaunt. She likes Smith, but complains about the lack of boys. In addition to Geneva, she plans to spend time in Prague and Berlin. She's majoring in environmental science and policy, but is considering law school.

Rudy reciprocates, talking about university, and about his summer with Holderhaven and Harriet Diamond. They pass through the pergola and into the terraced garden. Bill Mills is there. In the interim he has had four more glasses of champagne, and he has misplaced his top hat. He is urinating on the marble obelisk.

"Ella Minnow Pee!" he observes loudly, when he realizes who it is that has happened upon him. He zips up and wipes his hands on his pants.

Ella seems tolerant of Bill Mills, so Rudy follows her lead. The three of them sit together on a bench in the terraced garden. Inside Rudy is imagining fighting with Bill. Fencing with him. Throwing down his glove to defend the lady's honor. He took fencing to fulfill his physical education requirement, but he wasn't very good at it. Bill keeps staring at Ella's chest, even though the flapper dress is neither revealing nor form-fitting.

"Are you a shy boy, Bill Mills?" Ella asks. "Because it doesn't seem you like to make eye contact."

"Are those things real?" Bill asks. "I thought flatters had flap chests.

"I mean—"

"Are you saying I have a flappy chest?"

Ella twists from side to side, sending the strand of pearls swinging. She and Rudy both laugh, but Rudy is worried that this will only antagonize Bill. Bill is already nodding off, though, and he does not respond.

Rudy leans in and whispers to Ella.

"I know where we can go," he says. "I want to show you something."

They go inside, slip behind the now-empty bar. Rudy clicks the mirrored panel open and then stands aside and says, "Watch your step."

She climbs up and he follows. Halfway up he tells her to stop.

"Give me your hand," he says.

"Don't try anything stupid," she says. "Or you will be filled with regret as you go tumbling down these stairs. Also pain."

"Not stupid," he says.

She gives him her hand and he traces the outline of the inscription in the secret passage.

They ascend to the master bedroom and plunk down on the floor, on the safe side of the velvet rope. Rudy removes the linen jacket, and she kicks off her heels.

"I found a photograph last week. I think it has something to do with those marks. That marker that Bill was peeing on? Didn't used to be there. It used to be a statue of an extremely young, extremely naked girl."

"Yes, that was her," Ella says, staring at the bricked-up fireplace. "And now I guess we know that her name was Lizza. I'd always heard her referred to as 'that poor girl,' never a name."

"Wait, back up," Rudy says, his mind on fire. "You know who left those marks in the passage?"

"I've got a pretty good idea. Hello? My great-grandfather? Attorney to the family?"

"I have a lot of questions to ask you," Rudy says. So he does. He offers to swear himself to secrecy, if she'll just tell him everything she knows about Lizza. Ella laughs.

"I don't care about secrecy," she says. "Tell Harriet Diamond. Tell Bill Mills. Don't bother telling Mary Holder Hodgson, because I'm sure she knows some version of the story, unless she's in complete denial.

"Jorn Holder had always liked little girls, ever since he'd been a little boy. Nerissa Holder had mistaken his lack of ardor for gentlemanliness when they were courting, but clearly this became a problem after they were married. So instead of trying to dampen Jorn's passion, she merely redirected it for her own ends. Allowed him to molest his favorite servant girl, as long as he—I hope this doesn't offend your delicate sensibilities—made the deposit with Nerissa. Of course as time went on he got bolder. Thus, the statue of the nude girl in the garden. When the secret passage was discovered when they were restoring the house as a museum, well, anyone who knew the story could figure out what it had been used for.

"So this went on, Lizza acting as the catalyst for Nerissa to generate children. Then Jorn dies, under mysterious circumstances."

"Lizza killed him!" Rudy says.

"I have no idea. I suppose it's possible. The story I heard was that Nerissa killed him, because he'd gone insane and actually thought he could marry the girl. Maybe he really died of gastritis and exhaustion? My great-grandfather never saw the body. That was his story, as my dad told it to me one night when he'd had too many martinis: that Nerissa killed Jorn, and then had the servant girl and her mother paid off and sent far away. Clearly when Jorn dies, it's right around the time of conception of the last child, Noelle. Nerissa then has the secret passage sealed off and begins the task of raising her brood. Anyway, that's quite a discovery you've made there. The fourteen marks . . . do you think she was fourteen when her semi-conjugal visits ended? Do you think there were only fourteen of them? That can't be."

"No. I wonder if any of the platinum level patrons will notice them."

"Hope not. You can bet that Mary Holder Hodgson will have them covered up if she notices them."

"Can I ask you another question?" Rudy says. "It has nothing to do with Jorn Holder, Capitalist Pedophile."

"The answer is no," Ella says. "Because I'm leaving for Europe tomorrow."

"That's not the question. The question is, why didn't you get braces?"

"Oh. I did have braces, when I was a kid. My teeth started moving again."

"Is the answer to that other question still no?" Rudy asks.

"Come here," Ella says.

Later she gives Rudy a printed card with her email address, and he scrawls his on the back of one of her cards. Ella leaves at midnight, as workers are packing up the chairs and tables and tents.

Bill Mills wakes up on the concrete bench, alone. He makes his way to his car only to find that the car keys are no longer in his pocket. He is briefly furious before he passes out again in the back seat.

In 1916, Lizza Bagge prepares for another night. She leaves the house where the other servants live, telling her mother that Mrs. Holder has once again asked her to clean the mirrors behind the bar. Mrs. Holder feels that this is a job best done at night. Lizza takes the wooden cleaning box and carries it up the hill, entering the house through the door to the swimming pool. The lights remain on in the pool area; the still water glows green. She walks down the hall, past the bowling alley and billiards room, into the party room and then back behind the bar. She sets the wooden box down on the floor. She removes her belt and her white dress and stands, wearing only her slip, examining herself in the mirrored panel. She will turn seventeen soon, but she still has the same face and the same slim build she has had all of her teenage years. Sharp cheekbones, bobbed nose. You'll fill out, just you wait, her mother often says to her.

She opens the cabinet next to the icebox, moves items aside as she looks for one particular implement. There, behind the punch bowl and a stack of Bakelite ashtrays, she finds it. She looks back to see if anyone can see her, then she pops open the door in the mirror. She steps in and up, pulling the panel closed behind her. Then she's climbing the stairs, ice pick in hand.

Later, she will go swimming.

Scenes from the Renaissance

Bob paid his twelve dollars and went to find the Queen. The gatekeeper had given him a courtesy map. The gatekeeper had been asking many of the patrons in line if they were carrying weapons, but he did not ask Bob this question.

Bob inspected his map, comparing it against what he could see of the landscape. It had rained the night before, and the trees and tents were still wet. The grounds were muddy. The village was shaped like a broken circle where the ends didn't quite meet; he had entered at the six o'clock position. The fields were lined with shops and food stands, tents and stages; at the far end of the circle, if he proceeded around counter-clockwise, there was an arena. On the map, the center of the circle was empty. The map showed tents and stages and other buildings, but none of the text made sense to Bob. It wasn't written in an alphabet he understood.

A nearby Fool walked over, jingling as he approached. He planted himself in front of Bob and then began to convulse, as if he were about to vomit up something. He produced a gold button from his mouth. He held it up so that Bob could see the figure on it. The design was of a snake eating its tail. The Fool snapped his fingers and the button disappeared.

"You were supposed to meet me at the privies half an hour ago," said the Fool, whose real name was Chuck.

"I got held up in traffic, and—"

The Fool held his finger to his lips and nodded at another nearby patron, a bearded man in a black velvet tunic, who was mumbling to himself and staring at the ground as if he'd dropped something. The wave of the Fool's head sent a blast of perfume up Bob's nose. He reeked of lemons and sandalwood.

"Presto!" the Fool said. He waved his hand again and the button reappeared. This time it was threaded on a purple string.

"This is a magic button," the Fool announced, winking at Bob. "And this is magic string. It will bring you peace and contentment."

"How much?" Bob asked.

"Five dollars."

"No, not how much does it cost. How much peace and contentment will it bring me?"

"It *is* magic." The Fool looked around—the mumbling man had moved along. "Let's do this quickly. I have to stay in character. Give me the money."

"I'm doing you the big favor, and it costs me five bucks?"

"I'll pay you back later," the Fool said.

"In what, gold doubloons? You don't have the right kind of currency to pay me back. You couldn't even get me a complimentary ticket to get in, and the only reason I'm here is to help you with your plan."

"You're doing the noble thing, Bob. And besides, I think you *will* achieve peace and contentment."

Bob didn't care about the peace or contentment. He cared about seeing her face again. It had been ten years.

He gave a bill to the Fool, who tucked it into a pouch on his belt and then handed over the button and string.

"Place it on your left wrist," the Fool said. "Closest to your heart, and to the future."

Bob slid the string over his left hand. "I thought you were some kind of nobility, not a jester."

"I have a few different personas. They needed me in this garb today; half the cast came down with the flux, including the regular Fool."

"I was wondering, could you help me with this map?"

The Fool plucked the map out of Bob's hand and examined it.

"You were given the wrong one. This is the rune map," he said. "It's for Vikings only."

"There are Vikings here?"

"You really haven't been to one of these before, have you? Look around, there are many peoples here. Of course, most of them don't belong here. Vikings, too early. Pirates, too late, except for the sad ones that insist on calling themselves the Queen's privateers."

The Fool put his hand up to his brow and did a quick pirouette, surveying the crowds.

"*Most* people here do not exist. None of the musicians, except for that tall fellow with the lute and his friend with the sackbut. None of the belly dancers, certainly. Nor the kilted folk, as stylish as they may be. Nor any of the young fellows at the jousting arena. Not with all that plastic armor."

As he spoke, the Fool mimed all of the people he described: a stout strum for the lutanist, a shake of the hips for the belly dancers, a thrust with a sword for the fighters.

"But she exists?"

"She's as close as it gets, yes. Very accurate. Which is the problem. So, have you thought up a story to tell?"

"Yes," Bob said. "Remember spring of senior year, when she was playing Ophelia in the Little Theater's production of *Hamlet?*"

Back then she jumped at any chance to do Shakespeare or Marlowe, but at school it was always abridged versions of Broadway musical faves of the 1950s. She did those shows too, she and Chuck always the romantic leads, Bob behind the light board or sound board or up on the fly rail.

"I'd pick her up every night after rehearsal and we'd hang out. So at dress rehearsal one night she wanders out of the theater still in costume—this corset and wispy gown. Not just in costume but in character too. We went to Spring Garden Pizza, that place where they used to crank Mudhoney and Screaming Trees, remember? It's still open, but the music they play nowadays sucks. She goes floating in and she's still talking in that 'hath' and 'dost' talk."

"Yes, I'm familiar with that talk," the Fool said, spreading his hands wide to indicate their surroundings. "I speak it all weekend, every weekend."

"Well, the guys behind the counter went nuts, started mocking her. When they brought our pizza out, two guys carried it, and they both curtsied before they put it on the table. They said something really dumb like, 'Here's your pie, princess.'

"That was the first time I felt comfortable enough to play along with her. I went to the door and picked up an umbrella and started swinging it like a sword. I was shouting at the counter guys, calling them varlets and knaves and stuff, challenging them to duels, pretending to fend them off with the umbrella. At the same time, with my other hand, I boxed up our pizza. We made our escape, I threw down the umbrella, and we ended up laughing about it and eating it in the park."

"Yeah, that should work," the Fool said.

"Doesn't anyone else notice that she's really the Queen?" Bob asked.

"I don't think so. Up close, it's fairly smelly and nasty. So most people don't get that close. The ones who do, they tend not to remember once they are away from her. And if anyone does remember, what are they going to think? They're going to think, damn, that was an authentic Elizabethan experience I had today."

Far down the slope from Bob and the Fool, from inside the unmapped center of the village, a parade emerged. There were trumpets and bagpipes. People marched out and away, a riot of reds and blacks and purples.

"What's that?" Bob asked.

"Let me see," the Fool said. He made a cylinder with both hands and looked through as if it were a telescope. "Ah, I see the Royal Feces Examiner. And the Royal Butterfly Shoveler . . . there's the Keeper of Tigers and Horses."

He looked up from his imaginary telescope, glancing over at Bob.

"It's a joke, Bob," the Fool said. "We don't have feces examiners and tiger keepers."

"Is she in there?"

"Of course she is, it's the Royal Parade."

Bob took a few steps towards the Queen's Parade, but he was so transfixed trying to pick her out of the crowd, he didn't see the large rock in his way.

"Look out!" the Fool said, but it was too late: Bob tripped over the rock and fell down onto the muddy slope. He skidded, painting himself with a stripe of muck from ankle to shoulder.

The Fool walked over and helped him up, then dabbed at him with the rune map, scraping off the filth.

"Well, now you're quite a bit more accurate. What is this?"

The Fool tapped a ring on the pinky of Bob's right hand.

"It's her class ring. We traded them, and then never made the swap back after she went off to college."

"And you're still wearing it? And you still have long hair. Please, tell me that number I dialed wasn't a second line in your parents' basement."

"No, Chuck, I'm not living in my parents' basement. What's wrong with my hair?"

"Nothing's wrong, sorry. Look, I really appreciate this," the Fool said. "I appreciate that you believe me about what's happened to her. But please, stick to the plan. Catch up with her when there's no crowd around. Beyond that, just have fun. Walk around. Play along."

"Is that you?" Bob asked, sniffing.

"Is what me?"

"That smell, it's like you doused yourself in three different flavors of Aqua Velva."

"Occupational hazard. I'd rather smell that than some of the people around here. You'll see. Or smell. Listen, I have to go; if the program director sees me out of character, I'll get fired, and then I'll be the Queen's ex-boyfriend too."

The Fool, bells jingling, walked off toward a door in the fence that bore a sign: "Participants Only." Bob tried to get a glimpse beyond, but it swung shut too quickly.

"Screw you, Chuck," Bob said.

Bob brushed at the remaining mud on his clothes, but only succeeded in getting his hands dirty. The parade in the distance was gone now, and he couldn't even hear the music anymore. He ambled in that general direction, though, past the crowds of people who, according to Chuck, did not exist. It had been ten years, what was an hour or two more? He wasn't in a rush, and besides, this was her world now. He wanted to explore it. He came upon a wooden sign in the shape of a hand with pointing finger. It said "Joust to the Death at the hour of five." He walked past this, down to where a stage was set up underneath a large sycamore tree. He took tiny steps down the slippery slope. The mud sucked at his shoes.

On stage a juggler put down his batons and picked up three small swords. The patrons, seated on low wooden benches, clapped perfunctorily. After juggling the swords behind his back, through his legs, and high into the air, he dropped two of them. From his apron he produced an apple.

"You, sir!" he said, pointing straight at Bob. "Here!"

He tossed the apple to Bob, who slipped a bit while catching it, but managed not to fall into the mud.

"Hurl that apple at me and I shall cleave it."

Bob stood still. He looked down at the apple, which now bore his muddy handprint.

"Cleave it?" he asked.

The crowd murmured. "Cleave it, cleave it in twain like the devil's hoof," the juggler replied.

"Throw it," someone called out from the crowd.

Bob tossed it underhand toward the juggler, who brought the sword down like an executioner, blade flashing in the noonday sun. The apple split in half and fell to the stage. The crowd applauded.

"Funny word, cleave," said the Nun, who'd walked up beside Bob. She'd managed to find a spot of grass to stand in. "The Bible says: 'Cleave to one another, and two shall become one.'"

"That's beautiful," Bob said.

"But it also means its opposite. Cleave as in cling," she said, placing her hands together as if in prayer. "Cleave as in split." She separated her hands, stretching her arms wide before dropping them to her sides.

She wore a brown robe and cloak. If she'd fallen in the mud, it did not show.

"There is a jest here, concerning Anne of Cleves . . . but I am no jester."

"Is Anne here today?" Bob asked.

"She shouldn't be. It's too late for her."

"I hope it's not too late for me. Do you have a map I can borrow? I got the wrong one."

"I have no map," the Nun said. "But, I took a pledge of poverty, chastity, and obedience. So what else would you have this poor virgin do for you?"

"Well, first I wanted to find out more about this village. I'm new here," Bob said. "Eventually I'll need to find the Queen."

"She's easy to find," the Nun said. "But difficult to see."

"It's pretty important. I, ah, traveled through time to get here."

Bob gestured at his clothing. He wore jeans, high-top canvas sneakers, and a long-sleeved T-shirt. The Nun looked him over from head to toe.

"Of course you did. Are you sure you're not a witch?"

"If I was a witch I'd cast a spell to get my map back. And then I'd cast a spell to be able to read the damn thing. Also I'd magically clean my clothes."

"That doesn't sound like any witchcraft I've ever heard of."

"If you really want to know, your Queen dabbled in witchcraft. This was in high school, before she was Queen. She used to read tarot cards."

"God's Teeth! Don't speak such things! In her youth the Queen studied with the noted scholar Roger Ascham. Under his guidance, she read the classics, history, and theology, and learned six languages."

"Actually she just took Latin, like me, with Mr. Saylor. SPQR. Senatus Populusque Romanae."

"I strongly doubt this, but no matter. I can show you around the village, if that's what you wish."

Bob extended his arm to the Nun and raised his eyebrows.

"That's an anachronism," the Nun said.

Bob kept his arm out.

"That's me, Mr. Anachronism," he said. "But you can call me Bob."

After a moment, she hooked her hand around his elbow, and then they began to walk.

They passed a row of shops and tents where sellers hawked wares of all types. There was a brisk business in jewelry, candles, knives, nachos and cheese.

At a table selling figurines, a gangly boy in green tights was scrutinizing the statue of a nude, winged woman.

"Fairies are way cooler than dragons," the boy said, speaking to the young woman behind the table.

The Nun sniffed at this, and tugged Bob farther away from the boy and the merchant girl.

"You might have a better chance of meeting the Queen, of making a good impression, if you were properly attired," she said.

"I am properly attired, considering I'm a time traveler from four hundred years in the future."

"Yes, but there is the witch problem . . . and the filth problem."

Bob nodded. The Nun was right. Chuck's plan didn't require him to be clean or to be much of anything other than good old Bob, a psychic blast from the Queen's past. But he wasn't here for Chuck, not really. He was here for himself. Surely being attired as a gentleman from her era would impress the Queen.

They had stopped in front of a booth selling clothing: baggy white shirts, brocaded velvet gowns, floppy caps and jaunty feathered hats, thigh-high leather boots.

The Nun showed him what was accurate garb for a high-ranking lord, a spy or diplomat. It turned out to be very expensive; even just to rent an outfit for the day took most of the money he'd brought. He stuck his wallet into the leather belt pouch and left his muddy clothes and shoes in a stack at the back of the booth.

Three women walked by in matching outfits: brown bodices and skirts, white shirts beneath. Unlike many of the women of the village, these three wore shirts that actually covered their chests. Their sleeves, though, were furrowed with red and gold pleats. One carried a cage containing a white dove and a black dove. One carried a bundle of roses. The other carried nothing.

"We perform for a nickel," the one with nothing said.

Bob pulled a handful of change from his pouch and picked through it. He had one of those gold dollar coins, the one with the native American on it. Or was she a suffragette? And what was her name? Bob was sure he knew her name, but couldn't think of it in that instant. He felt a little wobbly. Authentic clothing was hot. The tights he now wore itched.

He picked the dollar coin and tossed it to the woman who carried nothing. She snatched it out of the air and then handed it to the woman with the birds. Bird woman slid it into the cage.

The women started barking like dogs. The one with the birds had a deep, throaty bark, like a mastiff. The one with roses yipped like a terrier. The one with nothing but good catching ability howled. Their eyes rolled back in their heads. Their sunshine sleeves flapped and billowed as they waved their arms in ecstatic agony.

Bob looked over at the Nun.

"Laira," she said. "An epidemic of hysterical barking in women. It broke out in France in the early seventeenth century."

"I thought this was the late sixteenth century," Bob said. "This epidemic is in your future."

"Not my future, Mr. Anachronism. My future is a life of service to my husband, the Lord God."

The three women continued their barking and snarling.

"If they charge a nickel, and I gave them a dollar, is it going to last twenty times longer than usual?" Bob asked.

"No," said the woman with the roses. All three were normal again. Quiet, with the red receding from their cheeks so that they were once again pale as moons. "Instead, please accept this."

She handed him a rose, a pink rose, and kissed him on the cheek.

The three women walked off to look for their next victim.

"The war is over," the Nun said, pointing at the rose. Bob just shrugged. "It's time to move on."

"Funny, she told me that once," Bob said.

They continued walking past a wooden platform where a quartet of musicians played recorders to a small crowd gathered there.

"Are you sure we're headed in the right direction?" Bob asked.

"It's just a big broken circle, with the gates at one end and the joust arena at the other, and a hundred ways to spend your money in between."

"What's in the middle of the circle?" Bob asked.

"That's where we live.

"See, this leads to the Queen's court," the Nun continued, pointing to a banner hanging from a wooden post. There was an elaborate design drawn in black, swirls of interlocking strokes making up the overall shape. In the center were two letters, E and R.

"Emergency Room?" Bob asked. "Eternal Relationship?"

"Elizabeth Regina," the Nun said.

"That's not her name. Her name is . . . crap! I can't remember her name. But Elizabeth, that's not it."

"Why don't you tell me your history with the Queen?" the Nun said. "Maybe that will jog your memory."

"We were friends in high school, she and I and Chuck, too. You know him, the Fool?"

"One of many," the Nun said.

"Drama Club all four years . . . those two were always on stage, I was setting up lights or running the sound board. It surprised me as much as anybody one night at a cast party when she started making out with me.

"But then we graduated, and she went off to New York to live and to study acting seriously. It helped that her family had money. She moved on, and at first I tried to move on too. It's not like I've been celibate for ten years, especially when I was going to college. But she's my one true love. The first year she was away, she sent me a letter at Christmas. I still send her a birthday card every year, and those are never returned, but that was the last I heard of her until quite recently."

The Nun looked on calmly, gravely.

"I've got that last letter from her in my wallet, but I've got it up here too." He tapped the side of his head.

"It was all about how tiny her apartment was, and how beautiful the city was just after a big snowfall. She signed it 'Love Always.' Why would she sign that if she didn't mean it?

"The night before she left town, we got a bottle of cheap white wine at this one convenience store that didn't check ID, and went out to the park near school. We sat on top of a picnic table and drank and talked about the past. A lot of stories that began with 'do you remember?' It didn't occur to me until after she left that we didn't talk about the future at all."

The Vikings, the belly dancers, the pirates, they weren't in this part of the village. Everyone here, the peasants and the upper classes, the burghers and beggars, were all Elizabethan.

"Where did everyone go?" he asked.

The Nun shrugged, then said: "Maybe, like you, they all went off to buy an accurate appearance. Soon the streets will be full of spies, and diplomats."

Bob was having second thoughts about ditching his real clothes. Now he was just another Elizabethan gentleman, one of many. Nothing special.

"Have you noticed anything strange about the Queen?" he asked.

"Strange?"

"Like, during the week, don't all you folks just hang out in regular clothes?"

"Yes."

"But she doesn't, right?"

"No, she and Chuck stay in her pavilion."

"Doesn't that make you wonder?"

"There are a lot of harmless eccentrics in this business, Bob. Some take their eccentricities a little more seriously than others. Although, now that you mention it, no one really goes near their pavilion. It always smells like a privy there."

Bob held his left hand up and showed the button to the Nun.

"The fool gave me this," he said.

"That's not his usual favor," the Nun said. "Usually he gives out these cheap rocks. 'Fairy stones.' That snake is striking himself."

"Yeah, weird. This is supposed to bring me peace and contentment. It's all part of Chuck's plan."

The trail they were on wound past a hut where a blacksmith hammered a bar of red-hot iron on an anvil. Just past the blacksmith a hawker at a small clearing called out to them, inquiring as to whether Bob would care to test his prowess with a fencing foil.

Bob grasped at his belt but there was no sword nor scabbard there. He needed a weapon.

He handed the fencing master one of the last of the gold coins from his purse and he handed the pink rose to the Nun. The fencing master fitted him with a wire mesh helmet and long leather gauntlets, then handed him a sword. It was long and the pointed tip was blunted with a cork.

"Are you sure this is a wise course of action?" the Nun called out.

"Yes," said Bob from inside the wire mask. "I studied the foil and saber with Lord Howard. I mean, Coach Howard. Two semesters."

The fencing master donned his own protection, saying: "Touches to the torso above the waist—only those count."

"Straight to the heart," Bob said.

They raised their swords to their faces, then squared off. Bob eased down into a crouch. In a flash the fencing master was on him, shuffling quickly past after scoring a touch on Bob's right shoulder.

Bob immediately dropped his sword, clutching at his limp right arm with his left. He yelped in pain. The fencing master dropped his helmet and ran over.

"What's wrong?"

"I'm hit," Bob said.

"Impossible," the fencing master said, bringing up his foil. The harmless cork still sat on the tip.

"Look," Bob said, dipping his hand under his shirt and bringing it back out, stained red.

"My god!" the fencing master said. "Wait here, I'll get first aid."

The fencing master dashed off.

"How bad is it?" the Nun asked. "It shouldn't take long for the first aid crew to get here, they can patch you up. How did it happen?"

"I don't know. I'm fine. I need one of these."

Bob took up his foil in his left hand, removed the cork tip, and slid it into his belt.

"What are you doing?"

"I'm going to find the Queen. I'll find a surgeon later."

"You're taking this much too seriously," the Nun said. "Just sit and wait for the medical crew, OK?"

This was no Nun at all, not speaking as she did.

There was a thick hedge that enclosed part of the fencing arena. He couldn't remember any hedges on the map. He walked to the hedge.

"Where are you going?" the Nun asked, but he ignored her.

He bent the branches back as best he could and fought his way through the barrier. Beyond the hedge was the back of a tent, a wall of rough gray canvas. He moved around it until he found a seam, then slipped inside.

It took him a moment to adjust to the shadows, but as his vision cleared he thought of the Fool saying, "Very accurate." Scattered through the tent were tables, chairs, and benches. He wandered through the maze they formed, trying to look as if he belonged. The tent was populated with gentlemen playing games: draughts, and a game that looked very much like backgammon. Others played card games, but they were not any card games he knew. Not at first. Then the name came to him: Forced Victory. Played with a . . . tarot deck. He watched a hand between four gentlemen who were dressed similarly to himself, although their hats had wider brims and longer plumes.

At the other end of the tent sat a table where a barmaid was pouring out tankards of ale from a large barrel. Bob approached.

"One please," he said to the barmaid.

"That'll be sixpence," the barmaid said.

Bob looked in his pouch and found a small silver coin, which he plunked on the table. She handed an ale to Bob which he took to a corner of the tent, where a backgammon set and a gilded box for cards lay unattended on the table.

He twiddled the button, still lassoed to his left wrist.

"You haven't brought me peace and contentment yet."

He sipped his ale and tried to clear his head. Something was going on here, something more than what Chuck had told him about on the phone. He felt disconnected from the Bob who loved pizza and Mudhoney records.

He nudged aside the backgammon set to get at the cards. His parents had had a backgammon set. He and the Queen would steal beers and stay up all night playing backgammon down in the basement.

He picked up the box and slid the cards out. He shuffled them and pulled three off the top: the Ace of Cups, the Five of Cups, the Wheel of Fortune.

He had no idea what they meant. The ace looked bountiful, but the five cups were all overturned and empty. The Wheel of Fortune, that was easy enough to figure out. That was how he'd lived his life, spinning the wheel to see what came up.

He replaced those cards and sifted through the pack, pulling out three cards: a knight, a queen, and the Fool.

Bob's guts roiled. A breeze flapped the front door of the tent, but it was not a refreshing breeze. It smelled like a stable.

Bob picked up the Fool card and tore it to pieces, letting them cascade onto the ground.

"That's your fortune," he said.

The gentlemen at the other tables turned to glance at Bob, but then went right back to their game. Bob stood up and took another sip of his ale. It tasted spoiled. He walked out of the tent.

The street smelled worse than a stable, even though Bob could see no horses. It smelled worse than the dumpster that sat in his apartment parking lot. Mud-covered peasants pulled their own carts by hand. On a nearby cart Bob saw whole fish for sale, their eyes cloudy, flies buzzing around their gills. There were wooden buildings here that Bob did not recall being on the map he'd seen. Shops, a tavern, what looked like houses. One establishment had a sign advertising a pit for fighting cocks.

He made his way to a less filthy part of the street.

The Nun was already there. She still held the pink rose.

"Hurry," she said, waving him over. "It's almost time for the joust!"

She extended her arm, but he merely looked down and furrowed his brow.

"This way," she said.

They proceeded down an alley that opened onto a glen. This led to a larger open space surrounded by wooden bleachers, the joust arena. At the far end sat a two-story structure, bedecked with colorful flags. Lions covered the flags, on two legs and four: gold on red, black on blue, red on gold. The people wearing similar colors were all here too. It was a feast for the eyes but not for the nose.

The ceremony was already underway.

Bob said: "I'm supposed to catch her while no crowd is around."

"It's too late for that."

The royal stand was populated with the Queen and all her court. Chuck, now clad as a gentleman, stood by her side. In the arena, the master at arms trotted around on his horse, explaining the rules and backstory of the joust to the people gathered there.

In the center of it all, like the prow of a ship, the Queen stood, almost blinding in a white dress studded with decorative gold buttons. She wore no crown; instead her red hair was festooned with pearls, an inversion of the gold and white of the dress. Less a dress than a piece of stage scenery inhabited by the Queen: a cape arching into angel's wings behind, the skirt supported from beneath to form a circular table around her. No ruff collar, but rather two lacy epaulets on her shoulders and then a low straight bodice that revealed an expanse of white skin.

He scanned the rest of the crowd. Everyone wore Elizabethan clothing. The master at arms was introducing the two knights who would fight to the death.

"What's your plan?" the Nun asked.

"My plan is to see her again, to get as close as possible. All I have to offer her, to show my devotion, are this rose, and words." Bob held out his hand to take the rose from the Nun.

"Devotion? That is not devotion, that is—"

The Nun did not finish her sentence. Her eyes widened and she lurched forward suddenly and bit the head off of the rose before Bob could take it from her, shaking her head as if she were a dog tearing into a rabbit.

After savaging the rose, sending petals flying, she fell down on all fours and started barking. She had a deep bark. She snarled, too, but didn't appear ready to bite. Instead she turned and crawled back off away from the arena.

Bob worried that this would attract attention, but the eyes of the crowd, the eyes of the lords and ladies in the royal stand, all were trained on the arena, where both knights had now been introduced. Bob drifted back behind the wooden bleachers, working his way around to get close to the royal stand. He peered up to see Chuck whispering in the Queen's ear. Near the royal stand, the stench was almost unbearable, but no one seemed to notice. Or if they did notice, they nonchalantly held scented rags up to their faces as they whispered to each other. Up close Bob could see that the hands holding these rags were filthy.

The master at arms had finished introducing the two knights who were to battle. One wore black and green, the other blue and silver. Their first test would be with the lance, but before they could take up these weapons from the squires, Bob rushed out through the fence and into the arena itself, kneeling down in the mud just below the Queen.

He looked up and saw that she was still beautiful, her skin was still pale without even a freckle. But as he studied her face he noticed that she was starting to wrinkle around the eyes. She was pale, literally paper white, thanks to makeup. He could see that this pigment covered a large boil next to her lip. She looked tired, and stiff, as if her dress was holding her up instead of vice versa.

The stench of the arena seemed to be the most concentrated around her. Nausea swept over him again, and he could barely speak without gagging.

"Your Majesty, I am here from a faraway land," Bob said. "I must speak quickly."

He said this quietly, so that only she and the others on the royal stand could hear. The crowd gathered on the wooden stands murmured at this breach of protocol, and the two knights trotted up on their horses, flanking Bob. The Queen half-smiled. Everyone was looking to her for their cue. The lords and ladies at the far ends of the stand whispered behind their fans.

"A faraway land?" the Queen said. "Yet you look familiar to me." He could smell her breath from where he knelt. It smelled like rotting garbage.

"It's me, Bob."

"What a foolish name, Bob. Why hast thou come here?"

Bob fished in his pouch, pulling out the letter and a photograph. Faded and bent, the picture showed her sitting on his lap, taken in an old-fashioned photo booth they'd discovered at an amusement park. In the photograph he had long hair, and her T-shirt read: "Touch Me, I'm Sick." Bob held the letter and photo up so the Queen could see. The smell coming from her was almost unbearable.

"That's us. Remember?"

The Queen took the photograph and held it behind her fan. She looked slightly puzzled.

Bob thought about the speech he'd tried to memorize, the stories. This was his cue.

"You can bring her back," Chuck had said on the phone.

But he didn't know if he wanted to bring her back. He just knew he wanted to start again with her. Maybe he could start again in the sixteenth century. Maybe they were already stuck there. She was his one true love, that was what mattered.

It didn't matter that the sixteenth century was pretty disgusting, not balanced against his love.

Before he could begin a speech, a speech for himself and not for Chuck, Chuck leapt down from the royal stand.

Chuck snatched Bob's left wrist, holding it up so the Queen could see the button and purple string. Bob did not resist.

"Surely this is the sign of a thief, or a witch, stealing from the Queen."

Looking up at her, Bob realized that one of the buttons on her dress *was* missing. The one closest to her heart. The buttons were gold, with the design of a snake eating its tail. He twisted his arm out of Chuck's grasp.

"What is the punishment for stealing from the Queen, for witchcraft and thievery?" Chuck asked.

"Beheading," the Queen said.

"Guards, seize this man," Chuck said.

"Remember that time," Bob said quickly, "when I taught you to drive?"

The Queen held up her hand, and the guards stayed put.

"Remember how the hot metal of the car felt against your back? A car, not a chariot, not a carriage, not a horse. A rusted-out 1979 Volvo sedan. I showed you how the transmission worked, and then you tried it, and we went back and forth a few times, heaving and stalling across that parking lot, until one time when we were switching seats you stopped me, pulled me against you on the passenger door?"

He thought of the letter he held in his hand, and in his mind. It had been his totem and touchstone for so long. The words were still the same . . . but now that he saw her, something about them had changed. It wasn't her appearance, nor the stench that seemed to emanate directly from her. It was the acting. She'd always been acting. That letter he'd treasured was just a two-page string of cliches that ended in "Love Always" but meant nothing.

The Queen's expression changed a bit as she glanced at the photo again. She furrowed her brow, as if examining the closest detail. Then she looked back down at Bob.

"Your Majesty," Chuck said, but she waved him off.

"My name is Amanda; you know that, Chuck," the Queen said.

The stench was gone, evaporated into the late afternoon.

"I remember the car, and the kiss, Bob. But now I'm the Queen, and the audience is waiting for their joust to the death.

"You were always noble, Bob. Yes. But life is too short to be noble," the Queen said.

Bob reached around his wrist and removed the button, yanking it from the purple string. He was tired of games, and delusions, and ready to give up his part.

"This is not stolen, merely borrowed. And now, returned," Bob said, averting his gaze as he held the button up to the Queen.

"Thank you," she said, accepting his gift.

He stood and looked the Queen straight in the eye. From behind him, the court murmured at this breach of protocol.

"Goodbye," Bob said, bowing his head to her.

"Fare thee well, Bob," she said, but she did not return the bow. It wasn't what Queens did.

He didn't ask for the photograph back. He turned and walked slowly out of the courtyard. A breeze blew, flapping the colorful flags and sending in sweet-smelling air: honeysuckle and lavender. The Vikings and the pirates had reappeared, standing in behind the throngs of the Elizabethans. There were the belly dancers, too, and men in kilts. His own muddy clothes were waiting for him at the back of a tent.

If he looked back, would she still be there? He didn't turn around.

He felt peaceful, and contented.

Ash City Stomp

She had dated Secrest for six weeks before she asked for the Big Favor. The Big Favor sounded like, "I need to get to Asheville to check out the art therapy program in their psychology grad school," but in reality she had hard drugs that needed to be transported to an old boyfriend of hers in the mountains, and the engine in her 1982 Ford Escort had caught fire on the expressway earlier that spring.

Secrest was stable, a high school geometry teacher who still went to see bands at the Mad Monk and Axis most nights of the week. They had met at the birthday party of a mutual friend who lived in Southport. She had signified her attraction to him by hurling pieces of wet cardboard at him at two a.m. as he walked (in his wingtip Doc Martens) to his fully operative and freshly waxed blue 1990 Honda Civic wagon.

The Big Favor started in Wilmington, North Carolina, where they both lived. He had packed the night before—a single duffel bag. She had a pink Samsonite train case (busted lock, $1.98 from the American Way thrift store) and two large paper grocery bags full of various items, as well as some suggestions for motels in Asheville and sights to see along the way. These suggestions were scrawled on the back of a flyer for a show they'd attended the week before. The band had been a jazz quartet from New York, led by a guy playing saxophone. She hated saxophones. Secrest had loved the show, but she'd been forced to drink to excess to make it through to the end of all the screeching and tootling, even though she'd been trying to cut back on the drinking and smoking and related activities ever since they'd started dating.

That was one of the reasons she liked Secrest—it had been a lot easier to quit her bad habits around him. He had a calming influence. She'd actually met him several months before, when he still had those unfashionably pointy sideburns. She pegged him as a sap the minute he mentioned that he was a high school teacher. But at the Southport birthday party they had ended up conversing, and he surprised her with his interests, with the bands and books and movies he liked and disliked. Since they'd started dating she had stopped taking half-pints of Wild Turkey in her purse when she worked lunch shifts at the Second Story Restaurant. His friends were used to hunching on the stoop outside his apartment to smoke, but she simply did without and stayed inside in the air-conditioning.

Hauling a load of drugs up to ex-boyfriend Rusty, though, was an old bad habit that paid too well to give up, at least not right away.

She compared her travel suggestions with his; he had scoured guidebooks at the local public library for information on budget motels, and he'd downloaded an online version of *North Carolina Scenic Byways*. His suggestions included several Civil War and Revolutionary War sites. Her suggestions included Rock City, which he vetoed because it turned out Rock City was in Tennessee, and the Devil's Stomping Ground, which he agreed to and did more research on at the library the next day.

"The Devil's Stomping Ground," he read from his notes, "is a perfect circle in the midst of the woods.

"According to natives, the Devil paces the circle every night, concocting his evil snares for mankind and trampling over anything growing in the circle or anything left in the circle."

"That's what the dude at the club said," she said without looking up from her sketchbook. She was sketching what looked like ornate wrought-iron railings such as you'd find in New Orleans. She really did want to get into grad school in art therapy.

"Of course, it's not really a historical site, but I guess it's doable," Secrest said. "It's only an hour out of our way, according to Triple A."

"So, there you go."

"This could be the beginning of something big, too—there are a lot of these Devil spots in the United States. We should probably try to hit them all at some point. After you get out of grad school, I mean."

"OK." It wasn't the first time he had alluded to their relationship as a long-term one, even though the question of love, let alone something as specific as marriage, had yet to come up directly in their conversations. She didn't know how to react when he did this, but he didn't seem deflated by her ambivalence.

That was how the trip came together. She had tried to get an interview with someone in the art therapy program, but they never called back. Still, she finished putting together a portfolio.

The morning of the Big Favor, she awoke to a curiously spacious bed. He was up already. Not in the apartment. She peeked out through the blinds over the air conditioner and saw him inside the car, carefully cleaning the windshield with paper towels and glass cleaner. She put her clothes on and went down to the street. It was already a hazy, muggy day. He had cleaned the entire interior of the car, which she'd always thought of as spotless in the first place. The windshield glistened. All of the books and papers she had strewn around on the passenger floor-board, all of the empty coffee cups and wadded-up napkins that had accumulated there since she'd started dating him, all of the stains on the dashboard, all were gone.

"What are you doing?" she asked, truly bewildered.

"Can't go on a road trip in a dirty car," he said, smiling. He adjusted a new travel-size box of tissues between the two front seats and stashed a few packets of antiseptic wipes in the glove compartment before crawling out of the car with the cleaning supplies. As they walked up the steps to his apartment she gazed back at the car in wonder, noting that he'd even scoured the tires. She remembered the story he'd told of trying to get a vanity plate for the car, a single zero. North Carolina DMV wouldn't allow it, for reasons as vague as any Supreme Court ruling. Neither would they allow two zeroes. He made it all the way up to five zeroes and they still wouldn't allow it. So he gave up and got the fairly random HDS-1800.

After several cups of coffee, she repacked her train case and grocery bags four times while he sat on the stoop reading the newspaper. They left a little after nine a.m., and she could tell that he was rankled that they didn't leave before nine sharp. It always took her a long time to get ready, whether or not she was carefully taping baggies of drugs inside the underwear she had on.

Once they made it north out of Wilmington, the drive was uneventful. He kept the needle exactly on 65, even though the Honda didn't have cruise control. He stayed in the rightmost lane except when passing the occasional driver who wasn't doing the speed limit. After he had recounted some current events he'd gleaned from the paper, they dug into the plastic case of mix tapes he had stashed under his seat. She nixed the jazz, and he vetoed the country tapes she'd brought along as too depressing, so they compromised and listened to some forties bluegrass he'd taped especially for the trip.

"You're going to be hearing a lot of this when you're in grad school in the mountains," he said.

She was bored before they even hit Burgaw, and her sketch pad was in the hatchback. She pawed the dash for the Sharpie that she'd left there, then switched to the glovebox where she found it living in parallel with a tire gauge and a McDonald's coffee stirrer. She carefully lettered WWSD on the knuckles of her left hand.

What Would Satan Do? Satan would not screw around, that's for sure. Satan would have no trouble hauling some drugs to the mountains. She flipped her hand over and stared at it, fingers down. Upside down, because the D was malformed, it looked like OSMM. Oh Such Magnificent Miracles. Ontological Secrets Mystify Millions. Other Saviors Make Mistakes.

In Newton Grove, she demanded a pee break, and she recovered her sketch pad from the hatch. Just past Raleigh, they left the interstate and found the Devil's Stomping Ground with few problems, even though there was only a single sign. She had imagined there'd be more to it, a visitor's center or something, at least a parking lot. Instead there was a metal sign that had been blasted with a shotgun more than once, and a dirt trail. He slowed the Honda and pulled off onto the grassy shoulder. Traffic was light on the state road, just the occasional overloaded pickup swooshing by on the way to Bear Creek and Bennett and farther west to Whynot. He pulled his camera from the duffel bag, checked that all the car doors were locked, and led the way down the trail into the woods. It was just after noon on a cloudy day, and the air smelled thickly of pine resin. Squirrels chased each other from tree to tree, chattering and shrieking.

It was only two hundred yards to the clearing. The trees opened up onto a circle about forty feet across. The circle was covered in short, wiry grass, but as the guidebook had said, none grew along the outer edge. The clearing was ringed by a dirt path. Nothing grew there, but the path was not empty. It was strewn with litter: smashed beer bottles, cigarette butts, shredded pages from hunting and porno magazines were all ground into the dust. These were not the strangest things on the path, though.

The strangest thing on the path was the Devil. He was marching around the path, counter clockwise; just then he was directly across the clearing from them. They stood and waited for him to walk around to their side.

The Devil was rail thin, wearing a too-large red union suit that had long since faded to pink. It draped over his caved-in chest in front and bagged down almost to his knees in the seat. A tattered red bath towel was tied around his neck, serving as a cape. He wore muddy red suede shoes that looked like they'd been part of a Christmas elf costume. His black hair was tousled from the wind, swooping back on the sides but sticking straight up on the top of his head. His cheeks bore the pockmarks of acne scars; above them, he wore gold Elvis Presley-style sunglasses. His downcast eyes seemed to be focusing on the black hairs sprouting from his chin and upper lip, too sparse to merit being called a goatee.

"This must be the place," she said.

The Devil approached, neither quickening nor slowing his pace. She could tell that this was unnerving Secrest a bit. Whenever he was nervous, he sniffed, and that was what he was doing. Sniffing.

"You smell something?" asked the Devil, pushing his sunglasses to the top of his head. "Fire and/or brimstone, perhaps?" The Devil held up both hands and waggled them. His fingers were covered in black grime.

Secrest just stood still, but she leaned over and smelled the Devil's hand.

"Motor oil!" she pronounced. The Devil reeked of motor oil and rancid sweat masked by cheap aftershave. "Did your car break down?"

"I don't know nothing about any car," the Devil said. "All I know about is various plots involving souls, and about trying to keep anything fresh or green or good out of this path. But speaking of cars, if you're heading west on I-40, can I catch a ride with y'all?"

"Uh, no," Secrest said, then he turned to her. "Come on, let's go. There's nothing to see here." He sniffed again.

"Nothing to see?" cried the Devil. "Look at this circle! You see how clean it is? You know how long it took me to fix this place up?"

"Actually, it's filthy," Secrest said, poking his toe at the shattered remains of a whiskey bottle, grinding the clear glass into a candy bar wrapper beneath.

The Devil paused and glanced down to either side.

"Well, you should've seen it a while back."

Secrest turned to leave, tugging gently at her sleeve. She followed but said, "C'mon, I've picked up tons of hitchhikers in my time, and I've never been messed with. Besides, there's two of us, and he's a scrawny little dude."

"A scrawny little schizophrenic."

"He's funny. Live a little, give the guy a ride. You've read *On the Road*, right?"

"Yes. *The Subterraneans* was better." Secrest hesitated, as if reconsidering, which gave the Devil time to creep up right behind them.

"Stay on the path!" the Devil said, smiling. "Forward, march!"

Secrest sighed and turned back toward the path to the car. They marched along for a few more steps, and then he suddenly reached down, picked up a handful of dirt, then spun and hurled it at the Devil.

The Devil sputtered and threw his hands up far too late to keep from getting pelted with dirt and gravel.

"Go away!" Secrest said. He looked like he was trying to shoo a particularly ferocious dog.

"What did you do that for? You've ruined my outfit."

She walked over and helped brush the dirt off. "C'mon, now you've *got* to give him a ride." The Devil looked down at her hand and saw the letters there.

"Ah, yep, what would Satan do? Satan would catch a ride with you fine folks, that's what he'd do. Much obliged."

From there back to the interstate the Devil acted as a chatty tour guide, pointing out abandoned gold mines and Indian mounds along the way. Secrest had the windows down, so the Devil had to shout over the wind blowing through the cabin of the Honda. Secrest wouldn't turn on the AC until he hit the interstate. "It's not efficient to operate the air conditioning until you're cruising at highway speeds," he had told her. That was fine with her; the wind helped to blow some of the stink off of the Devil.

A highway sign showed that they were twenty-five miles out of Winston-Salem. "Camel City coming up," the Devil said, keeping up his patter.

"Yeah, today we've rolled through Oak City, the Bull City, the Gate City, all the fabulous trucker cities of North Carolina," Secrest replied. "What's the nickname for Asheville?"

"Ash City," said the Devil.

"Fair enough," Secrest said.

They got back on the interstate near Greensboro, and Secrest rolled up all the power windows. When he punched the AC button on the dash, though, nothing happened. The little blue LED failed to light. Secrest punched the button over and over, but no cool air came out. He sniffed and rolled down all of the windows again.

He took the next exit and pulled into the parking lot of a large truck stop, stopping far from the swarms of eighteen wheelers. He got out and popped the hood.

"You guys should check out the truck stop," he said. "Buy a magazine or something." In the few weeks she'd known Secrest, she'd seen him like this several times. Silent, focused, just like solving a problem in math class. She hated it when he acted this way, and stalked off to find the restroom.

When she returned, he was sitting in the driver's seat, rubbing his hands with an antiseptic wipe.

"What's the verdict?"

"Unknown. I checked the fuses, the drive belt to the compressor, the wires to the compressor . . . nothing looks broken. I'll have to take it to the shop when we get back to Wilmington. You don't have a nail brush in your purse, do you?"

"A what?"

"A nail brush, for cleaning under your fingernails. Never mind."

"Don't forget me," the Devil said, throwing open the back door. He had a large plastic bag in his hand. Secrest pulled back onto the road and turned down the entrance ramp. The Devil pulled out a packaged apple pie, a can of lemonade, and a copy of *Barely Legal* magazine and set them on the seat next to him. Secrest glanced back at the Devil in the rearview as he sped up to enter the stream of traffic.

"What have you got back there?"

"Pie and a drink. Want some?"

"No, I want you to put them away. You're going to get the back seat all dirty."

The Devil folded down one of the rear seats to get into the hatch compartment.

"What are you *doing?*" asked Secrest, staring up into the rearview. The car drifted lazily into the path of a Cadillac in the center lane until Secrest looked down from the mirror and swerved back.

She turned to look at what was going on and got a faceful of baggy pink Devil butt.

The Devil didn't respond; he just continued rummaging. Finally he turned and gave a satisfied sigh. He had a roll of duct tape from Secrest's emergency kit, and he zipped off a long piece. Starting at the front of the floorboards in the back seat, he fixed the tape to the carpet, rolled it up over the transmission hump and over to the other side, carefully bisecting the cabin. A gleaming silver snake guarding the back seat of the car.

"I get to be dirty on this side," he said. "You can do whatever you want up there." Then he picked up his copy of *Barely Legal* and started thumbing through it, holding the magazine up so it covered his face.

Secrest didn't argue.

She looked over at him and noticed he was preoccupied with other matters. Secrest's hands, still dirty from poking around in the engine compartment, had stained the pristine blue plastic of the steering wheel, and he rubbed at these stains as he drove along.

She could see the speedometer from her seat, and he was over the speed limit, inching up past 70 steadily. He'd also started hanging out in the middle lane, not returning immediately to the safety of the right lane after he passed someone. Traffic thinned out as the land changed from flat plains to rolling hills, but he still stayed in the middle lane. Plenty of folks drove ten miles over the speed limit. That was standard. Secrest probably attracted more attention the way he normally drove—folks were always zooming up behind him in the right lane, cursing at him because he had the gall to do the speed limit. Now he was acting more like a normal driver—breaking the speed limit, changing lanes.

The Devil sat silently on the hump in the middle of the back seat, concentrating on the road ahead. The pie wrapper and empty can rolled around on the seat next to him. She watched the speedometer inch its way up. At 75 Secrest suddenly started to pull over through the empty right lane into the emergency lane.

"What are you doing?" she asked. Then she craned her head around just in time to catch the first blips of the siren from the trooper's car. Blue lights flashed from the dash of the unmarked black sedan.

The Devil leaned forward and whispered in her ear. "Be cool, I'll handle this," he said.

"Goddamn!" she said, and this curse invoked a daydream. In her daydream, she keeps saying "Goddamn!" over and over. Secrest is busy with slowing down, putting his hazard lights on, and stopping in the emergency lane. The Devil is not in her daydream. She pops the door handle and jumps out while he's still rolling to a stop, losing her footing and scraping her knees and elbows against the pavement as she rolls to the grassy shoulder. She stands up, starts running into the trees along the side of the road. As she goes, she reaches up under her skirt and peels the Ziploc from her panties, but it's already broken open. Little white packets fly through the air in all directions. They break open, too, and it's snowing as she charges off into the woods.

The trooper chases her, and just as the last packet flies from her fingertips, he tackles her. She starts to cry.

Outside of her daydream, the state trooper asked Secrest for his license and registration. He retrieved these from the glove compartment, where they were stacked on top of a pile of oil change receipts and maps. The trooper carefully watched Secrest's hand, inches away from her drug-laden crotch, as he did this. She was sitting on her own hands.

"Ma'am, could you please move your hands to where I can see them?"

She slid her hands out and placed them flat on top of her thighs.

The trooper took the registration certificate and Secrest's license, but he kept glancing back and forth from them to her hands.

"Nice tattoo, isn't it, officer?" the Devil said, pointing to the smeared letters on her knuckles. The trooper slid his mirrored sunglasses a fraction and peered into the back seat of the car, staring the Devil in the eye.

"Not really. You should see the tattoos my Amy got the minute she went off to the college. I won't even get into the piercings."

"Kids these days . . . ," said the Devil.

"Yep. What are you gonna do?" The trooper pushed his sunglasses back up on his nose and straightened up. "Well, anyway, here's your paperwork. Try to watch your speed out there, now." He smiled and handed the cards back to Secrest.

They stopped for gas near Morganton. There was a Phillips 66 there.

"The mother road," Secrest said.

"Last section decommissioned in 1984, and now all we have are these lousy gas stations," said the Devil.

"Ooh, *1984*. Doubleplusungood," Secrest said.

"I'll pump," the Devil said. "Premium or regular?"

"Doubleplusregular."

Inside, Secrest got a large bottle of spring water, another packet of travel-size tissues, and breath mints. She stared at the array of snacks and the jeweled colors of the bottles of soda, trying to decide. Behind the counter, a teenage boy tuned a banjo, twanging away on the strings while fiddling with the tuning pegs.

It took her a long time to decide to forgo snacks altogether, and it took the teenager a long time to tune the banjo. She tried to think of a joke about *Deliverance*, but couldn't. Secrest went up to pay, and she headed for the door.

She went around to the side of the building to the ladies' room. The lock was busted. She sat to pee, carefully maintaining the position of the payload in her underwear. The door swung open and the Devil walked in.

"You know, I've been wanting to get into your panties ever since we met."

"Get the *hell* out of here, or I'll start screaming," she said.

"Oh, that's a funny one," the Devil said. "But I'm staying right here. You owe me."

"I don't owe you anything." She was trying to remember if she had anything sharp in her purse.

"Of course you do. Why do you think that cop didn't haul your ass out of the car? You have me to thank for that, for the fact that all that shit in your panties is intact, and for the fact that you're not rotting in one of their cages right about now."

"OK, for one thing, I don't know what you're talking about. For another, get out of here or the screaming really starts."

"What I'm talking about is all that smack you've got taped inside your underwear. The dope. *Las drogas*. I want you to give it to me, all of it, right now. That stuff is bad for you, in case you hadn't heard, and it can get you in a world of trouble."

"Screw you. You're not getting any of it. I was serious about the screaming part."

But then it didn't matter, because Secrest came in right behind the Devil. He spun the Devil around by the shoulder and kneed him in the crotch. It was the first time she'd ever seen him do anything remotely resembling violence. The Devil crumpled to the concrete floor.

"Screw you both," the Devil gasped. "I'll take the Greyhound bus anywhere I want to ride."

They checked in at the Economy Lodge in Asheville. Secrest checked the film in his camera and folded up an AAA map of downtown into his pocket and set out to see the sights.

"The historic district is almost a perfect square," he declared, as if he'd made a scientific discovery. "So I'd like to walk every street in the grid. I figure I'll get started today with the up and down and finish up tomorrow on the back and forth while you're at the university. Want to come with?"

She told him she was tired and crashed out on top of the musty comforter with all of her clothes on while the overworked air conditioner chugged away.

She met Rusty at a bar called Hot Spot. It had been less than two years since she'd seen him, but he had to have lost close to fifty pounds, and his hair, once a luxurious mass, was now thinning and stringy. He still got that same giddy smile when he caught sight of her, though, and he rocked back and forth with inaudible laughter. They walked back to his place on McDowell Street, where he gave her the $900 he owed her plus $600 for the drugs in her underwear. They celebrated the deal by getting high in his second floor bedroom, sitting on the end of the bed and staring out the gable window over the rooftops of old downtown as the fan whirred rhythmically overhead. After a few minutes, he collapsed onto his back, let out a long sigh, and then was silent.

She was daydreaming again. In her daydream, Secrest is out walking the maze, crisscrossing through the streets until he sees the Devil walking toward him from the opposite direction. The Devil's shoes look even filthier, and his goatee has vanished into the rest of the stubble on his face. His shirt is stained with sweat under the arms and around the collar, turning the pink to black.

"Not you again," Secrest says, kicking the nearest lamppost with the toe of his wingtip. "I was almost finished with walking every street in the historic district." He looks away, back toward the green hills of the Pisgah Forest to the south, then turns back, as if the Devil will have vanished in the interim.

"Yes, you're very good at staying on the path," the Devil says. "But now it's time for a little detour. Your girlfriend is sitting in an apartment on McDowell Street."

"Oh, really?" says Secrest.

"Yes, and the police are closing in, because an old friend of hers has ratted her out to the cops. They're probably climbing the stairs right now."

Or maybe he says, "An old friend of hers is dying on the bed next to her right now."

Anyway, the Devil reaches out and grabs Secrest's hand, shaking it energetically.

"Thanks for the ride, buddy," he says.

Then Secrest comes running up the street to save her.

Horses Blow Up Dog City

Hanes was repainting the front window of the store, filling the thick black outlines of the letters in sparkling candy-apple red, when Carlos came back from lunch with the news. It had been a quiet day: no sales all morning, just dirty looks and double-takes from passersby. The new logo looked good, but red and black stains spotted the sidewalk beneath his feet. Metalflake paint was hard to get, but Hanes got it from the same sources as all the other junk that populated his shop, Changes: Antique Technology and Silver Salts. Retro chic, and therefore the painted front window. It was there not just to attract the collectors he lived off of. Mainly he just liked the way it made the store look. Stable.

Carlos was running and his new hair flapped against his skull with every clunky step. So the news, which Carlos brought back every day from the decidedly unstable front window of the Flower Ball burger stand, must've been pretty important.

"Grover's dead. They found his body in the desert. He just walked out into it and died."

Carlos was breathing hard and after those three sentences the urgency drained out of him. He slumped his shoulders, looked away, across the street in the direction of the crystal-blue waters of the Hudson. Then he grabbed Hanes tight around the biceps for a second before walking into the store.

California Joe was just making his way down to the end of Washington Street, waving his laminated permits and chanting his usual midday rant. It was something Hanes heard every day. "Fire it up! Hey, killer, spare some change? Fire it up . . ." It was directed at no one in particular.

Hanes carefully closed up the paint tin, pushed his way into the store, and announced, "We're closed" to the three Malaysians who were scrutinizing the Gunfight game machine in the corner. They didn't complain. They'd been in town for a week, staying with family, wheedling Hanes daily for a deal on the thing.

Carlos had wisely retreated upstairs, leaving the downstairs photography vault empty for Hanes, who entered and sealed that door behind him and thought about how dumb he was for crying about a death that, in sudden retrospect, he should have seen coming a long time ago.

The photo vault, a gray room usually filled with the non-smell of polypropylene and stainless steel, now smelled like paint, even through the tears. His sinuses, relined over a year before, were still sensitive. It wasn't enough contamination to worry about; the purifier could handle it. He sat for a moment on the ledge next to the tinted Acrylite window, waiting for the tears to subside, checking his hands for wet paint flecks. Then he opened his personal drawer in the big Neumade cabinet, pulled out the box labeled "2004–2005." He picked up the stack of positives he'd taken with the old Mamiyaflex, tossed them onto the light table. The colors still bugged him, skewed toward cyan because he had to process them himself. Everyone looked slightly ghoulish.

He took the photos up and one by one they showed just how small his world had been in the past two years: Grover surrounded by his puppet menagerie, the first publicity photo, one Hanes had done for free. Grover in the store, pretending to dance with the Omnibot 2000. A blurry shot Carlos took, of Hanes with his arm around Lexene, which should've been filed in an earlier box. Grover and Lexene returning from the first tour, goofing with movie-star sunglasses and scarves.

The boxes, the vault, the whole store, were about preserving things. The photo-positives and their surreal colors would be around for another hundred years, easy, and they were the originals, silver and dyes, not some high-res scans.

It surprised Hanes that Grover's image hadn't vanished from all the slivers of celluloid in the store.

She wouldn't have heard the news. Hanes spent a lot of time in the past because that was his job; Lexene was just plain disconnected. Grover's management wouldn't try to contact her; Hanes knew that, too. They'd been on the outs since the last tour fell apart. They'd lost her Synaptic Six, her lighting and video rig, in transit from Mexico City. To them it was a worthless piece of junk, dead-end neural technology. They had offered to buy her a current model, but she turned them down. The Synaptic was what made Lexene's lights unique—too old to be of much use to anyone else, too young to be an antique.

Hanes stacked the plastic-clad slides together, locked them in his drawer, and then he locked Carlos in the store.

He'd have to walk to her place—Lexene didn't wear a phone, she wouldn't pay for most tangle channels, just had a little one-way box of Grover's, one possession out of the small pile he'd left at her place when he moved to LA. Mainly she sat in her tiny walk-up, drafting designs that would never get produced, reading books. Even though she tried hard to be chronically unemployable, "difficult," she still had to say no more often than anyone else Hanes knew. No to the managers, directors, and A&R goons who blundered out through the tunnel to track her down on her home turf. Yes to a select few, yes to people or shows or bands or ideas she loved, and that was her living. She could've had a nice life in an apartment in a restricted part of Manhattan, wall-to-wall design work, never have to touch a lighting panel or a video camera again. Instead she lived in Jersey and burned up a lot of time hanging out with Carlos and Hanes, going out on the road a few months out of the year to operate the Synaptic by hand.

Her place was a short walk. Hanes got there, did the mudras to get in the front door, and then, later, her door. A book about *fin de siècle* fads and fashion trends that he'd downloaded for her the week before was lying flat open on the enormous kidney-bean drafting table, almost finished. Hanes had skimmed it. The book was a shuck, written by one of those scammer profs at University Online, but it was full of raw data and good photos, and was therefore interesting. The text, though—it had taken the author six years to digest and analyze what Hanes and Lexene had lived through and worn like skin.

Lexene was on her bed, staring coolly at the tangle box between her boots, twisting her straight red hair in knots with her left hand.

Neither one talked. The box wasn't on a news channel. It was a live feed from a public-access show in San Diego. The emcee, a droll fourteen-year-old with crenellated ears, notches big enough to see even on the tiny screen, was talking about how learning the true names of Jesus had saved him from a life of crime. Behind him, another shape, less definite. A face just over the left shoulder of the Christian boy. Someone was mimicking his earnest sermon on the wonders of religion and linguistics. That someone was Grover.

Hanes hadn't planned any big speech for Lexene in the first place. He'd planned to tell her, "He's dead," and so he did.

"Really?" Lexene said, clicking her boots together over the screen. "He's right there. He's been making fun of this kid for the past fifteen minutes."

Back out in the street, Hanes and Lexene remained silent as footage of the recovery of Grover's body flashed across the front windows of bakeries, bars, markets. His adopted hometown was awash in the event, looping it over and over from every possible angle, cutting in shots of distraught fans all over the world. One Russian boy was dressed as the Sad Little Jester, the puppet that came out and explained the moral at the end of "Horses Blow Up Dog City."

"God, I met that guy when we played St. Petersburg," Lexene said. "He came to the show in that same get-up. Grover made him come up on stage."

Then Grover plodded in front of the crowd of Russian kids gathered to mourn his death. They didn't seem to notice.

"This sucks," Lexene announced. "This is really going to suck if they start tagging Grover all over the place."

The prank wasn't anywhere near the first of its kind. The Enquirer channel said it was space aliens, but their transmissions never seemed to get tagged.

Common knowledge was that this anonymous group of Belgian grad students was behind it, sampling images from the tangle into this big diamond block of storage, cobbling together moving images that had never occurred in reality, spitting them back out to invade channels at random. The year before they'd sent out snippets of world leaders engaged in various marginally legal sex acts, and the TSA had to go public on their inability to shut all of the transmissions down. No one could detect the source of the rogue packets; they just showed up and super-imposed themselves, unannounced and unwelcome. Mainly it was just showing off: the images attacked other packets that were encrypted with a supposedly uncrackable algorithm. There was nothing political about it. No demands, no manifestos, no public claims of responsibility.

"Stupid kids," Hanes said, assuming his role as the gruff middle-aged man. "They'll get tired of it soon, especially with Grover saturating the legitimate channels."

As it turned out, the Belgians were bigger fans of Grover than Hanes had predicted.

Hanes had met Grover a couple of months after returning from a long shopping trip to Australia. He was one of Lexene's dis-coveries. She always needed folks to eat out with, because she never cooked, and with Hanes out of town that meant she had to find another dining partner. Grover simply appeared to fill the void. After Hanes got back, the dining party numbered three.

Grover met them at the door of the storage space he was living in, and Hanes thought he looked all of seventeen or eigh-teen. A frail, curly-haired kid, hunched over. Lexene told him later that he was twenty-six.

Inside, there wasn't a square inch of bare cement. Every-thing had been decorated—the walls, the floor, the ceiling, the bed, even the tangle box and the chemical toilet—covered over in sky-blue and white. It was like being suspended in a bubble in the air. Clouds all around. And on top of this substrate sat the marionettes. They came in all sizes, some with two legs, some with four. The biggest was an eagle with a human head, lifelessly crumpled on top of the work table. They were all people or anthropomorphized animals: rabbits, a mouse dressed up like a chef, two horses, some beasts that Hanes couldn't identify. All done in those same shades of bone gray and blue. Some actually were just skeletons; all were fragile looking.

"Hi," Grover had said, in that nervous, quiet voice. "Do you like the puppets?"

Lexene and Hanes walked aimlessly for a while, and finally she said, "Can I make some calls at the store?" Hanes nodded, and they turned back down Washington. That was when the surface tension in Lexene finally burst.

"It was so obvious. It was such a dumb cliché, no one ever figured it would come true. Remind me never to work with disturbed geniuses who can't handle fame, OK? How fucking cornball . . ." Lexene was getting as emotional as she ever got in front of other humans, which meant she was walking even faster than normal, fidgeting obsessively with her hair.

In the window of the bagel place, Grover was pogoing like a bunny through the middle of a show on the Catastrophe channel . . . a fleet of plankton harvesters churning through water the color of rust. Opposing view text scrolled up the bottom half of the display, carefully timed to deflate all the statements the main announcer was making. From the outside it was just nonsense, mirror writing. Grover's image hopped all around the window. Boing, boing, boing. To Hanes, the wide, toothy smile on his face, a smile that had never existed outside of the tangle, was utterly unconvincing.

The day after their first dinner together, all three went on a local shopping trip. They drove down to Englishtown, to an open-air market that Hanes knew about. "Most collectible stuff for the best prices, the shortest distance from New York." Grover seemed fascinated by the rolling countryside so close to the urban sprawl of New Jersey/New York. He said it reminded him of growing up in Georgia, but he didn't say anything else about Georgia. Still, he opened up fast, faster than Hanes was accustomed to. He ended up crouching between the front bucket seats, so his squeaky voice could be heard over the roar of the van.

He seemed to have an encyclopedic knowledge of the most trivial subjects: breakfast cereals and which had the optimal flavor, kung fu fighting styles (from the old flicks where you couldn't pick whether the good guys won or not), and cartoons—why the endless Looney Tunes remakes of the Singing Frog episode weren't half as good as the original. He'd watched a *lot* of tangle, but it didn't affect his mind the way the Surgeon General said it would. All the useless facts, the endless permutations of the same old sitcom plot elements, Grover cobbled all that detritus and scree together and it became fascinating to hear him talk about it.

That day in Englishtown they found the Omnibot 2000, the robot that you programmed with old magnetic tapes.

"Cassettes," the Greek said.

"Little boxes," Grover said.

The Greek had a stack of the tapes in the back of his station wagon, most of which, surprisingly, hadn't melted or lost their fragile oxide coating. That was the hardest part, getting software for the old machines. It was a gold mine if you found tapes and disks that still worked. The robot was in perfect condition too, and the Greek only wanted sixty for it. Hanes talked him down to forty just for the hell of it, and convinced him to throw in an old Atari, too.

"Don't they understand what this stuff is worth?" Grover asked, walking back to the van with Hanes, who cradled the Omnibot like a newborn child.

"Collectors never drive to Englishtown," Hanes said. "They'd rather give me the money."

"My dad had an Atari like this one. I wasn't supposed to touch it." His face got dull. "'Sixty-four bits!' That's what he'd yell at me when he caught me playing with it. 'Get your hands off of them sixty-four bits!' He could play it for hours, until his wrists got sore."

That was the only time Grover mentioned the existence of his father.

Hanes tried to stay busy the next few days, working through a backlog of mail-order business, checking and rechecking inventory. Carlos worked the register and stayed out of his way. Lexene was staying in a Manhattan hotel, running up an enormous room service bill, so she could avoid the press and have a phone. The press was choking hard on the question, "Why does a childlike millionaire, famous puppeteer, walk out into the desert and die of exposure?" and filling up airtime with footage from the last show at Madison Square Garden, the one that started with "Mr. Sloth's Underwater Birthday Party." There was talk of starting a Grover channel but his management sat on the rights to the rest of the footage they owned.

Lexene walked into the store a week later, a week in which the press had related that Grover's mother died of cancer five years before, his father was in a private penal institution in Colorado, and his management was "deeply saddened by the recent events."

"I'm hungry," Lexene announced.

═══

The first tour was originally just Grover and Lexene, road cases for the puppets and her lighting board, a van. They stopped in at the store before getting on the train to the rental place in Paterson. Because it had a phone, the store had become their base of operations; they had to stop in to get the final tour schedule. After a barrage down the east coast, there were a lot of days off, marked on the schedule with *Drive, drive, drive.* As it happened, after Atlanta they ended up playing a show every single night.

At that point Grover had only played in small theaters in Manhattan, and the actuality of leaving for tour made him chatter even more nervously than usual. "I'm going to miss my tangle box. If we make money, can we buy a battery-powered one for the van?"

"We *will* make money," Lexene said, "and it will go straight into the accounts your managers set up."

Carlos came downstairs with a stack of disks. "All done," he said, disgusted, and he handed them to Grover, who tossed them into the laundry bag he was using for a suitcase. "I don't know what you get out of that noise . . ."

Grover had coaxed Carlos into recording Hanes's entire collection of lute music from 1998, when the fad had been in full swing, spurred on by the constant media presence of Gerhardt Hess, the famous seven-foot-tall lutist. He toured the world with a single graphite lute and a roadcase full of scans of mezzo-soprano clef music. Hanes had a stack of hardcopy press on the guy too, all carefully encapsulated, waiting for the right collector. The amazing thing was how similar all the articles sounded. They all had headlines like, "UndiLUTEd!" or "Hess Takes Lute to New Heights" but the body text was mostly the same. A year and a half later, after an appearance on *Lifestyles of the Media Presences,* the listening public suddenly became embarrassed at its own taste, and Hess's product vanished.

Grover, of course, remembered Hess. "He looked like a big insect, grappling with that lute."

Lexene would later report that every day in the van, Grover carefully played all ten disks, in chronological order. Her earplugs, which she normally carried when she ran her designs for bands, were unfortunately left sitting in their plastic case on her drafting table.

Lexene and Hanes went to the Indian place on Willow Street. It had been the last restaurant without tangle in the front window, until the family that owned the place gave in and installed a secondhand Sony. They still ate there for tradition's sake.

The news was on. General Foods execs testifying before Congress, denying that they purposely made their designer fats addictive. The Supreme Court declaring automated facial recognition unconstitutional. The usual wars.

Then, a "new development" in the ongoing babble about Grover, which turned out to be an interview with his high school art teacher. "I always thought Grover was one of my most talented students."

Then Grover's head filled half of the screen, covering the old woman in her affected velvet suit. "We have this to report: Puppeteer Grover McKay is still dead."

Another head appeared. "I'm not dead yet," it chirped.

"Awww," said Lexene. "Can we get our stuff to go?"

"There's no escaping it," Hanes said. "You might as well get used to this. Anyway, it looks like it was triggered by the news. Maybe the Belgians are trying to send the press a message."

In the window, the two heads argued about whether or not they were dead. The tall Punjabi waiter came out and cycled through a few channels, but the heads were tagged onto every one.

"Maybe not," Lexene said.

By the time that first tour hit San Francisco, Grover's managers had run through three A&R people. They'd also rebooked the dates, each venue getting bigger and bigger until he sold out the Warfield three nights in a row, two shows a night. In New Orleans, the van became a tour bus, which just as quickly turned into a private jet. Grover christened the jet the *Gravy Dog*.

Every night, Lexene would call and relate the latest details on Grover's rapid ascent. Every night was "amazing." The first real press on the tangle was a bit from the Baltimore show. It snowballed from there, to a familiar scene that Lexene would relate:

All the kids in their seats, chattering away in a dull roar around Lexene at her light board. All the puppets hanging from their racks on the stage. Then Grover would shamble out onstage in his black coveralls, pick up the first two characters, and Lexene would announce his presence with a big flash of white light and a close shot of Grover's wide-eyed face on the monitors. Silence from the crowd, probably amazement at the big image of the tiny little man they'd come to see.

"Hi. How are you?" Grover would say into his headset mike, then he'd launch into the story of "Mr. Magic Teeth." For the rest of the show, Lexene's hands moved automatically across the board, helping it improvise on her basic program, as the puppets danced in front of Grover.

Before the tour, when Grover was explaining the show to the management team that Lexene dug up, they couldn't understand why he didn't want to be hidden—that much they could remember about how puppet shows were supposed to be done. He couldn't explain why. The management didn't want to know anything about breakfast cereals, or kung fu movies, or cartoons. Lexene had to convince them that it was really an elaborate deconstructionist riff, having Grover stand there with his puppets. They bought that.

At first, with no roadies to help out, he had to pause every time he wanted to switch puppets from the two he could manage. By San Francisco, there was a two-person crew just to hand him the right puppets. The People Channel gave him an Honorable Mention as their Best New Media Presence of the Year, since even they admitted that it was a necessity to see him live.

Lexene dumped all three sauces on her samosas, making the waiter cringe. She took a big bite and talked around it as she chewed.

"Well, I'm embarrassed to admit it, but this past week, holed up in the Great Northern, I spent a lot of time watching tangle. Not that crap where they tag Grover; that's creepy. But I clicked around, trying to get all the news I could. Trying to find out how much the management lied to us about what was going on . . ."

"It's their job to lie. That's why people go into that line of work—they're uniquely suited to constant dissimulation as a way of life."

"Well, yeah."

The waiter reappeared to refill the water glasses. "I am quite sorry about the malfunctioning window," he said. He'd given up on the channel selection and simply shut the sound off.

"'s OK," Hanes replied. Because it was there, they both took sips of water.

"So why did he do it?" Hanes asked the tablecloth.

"You saw that last tour. He was over the edge, and there was no one around him to say 'no.'

"The first few dates, everybody was up. Then Grover just started going sideways. First he wanted to cancel the tour, but he couldn't explain why. They smoothed that one over by tweaking the one last responsible nerve he had in his body: they reminded him how many people's livelihoods depended on him. By that time we had a roadie for every single puppet, five caterers, a masseuse, and that glorified babysitter who thought he was a road manager. Hell, I had my own crew; I didn't have to lift a finger until the show started. But it was stupid for them to remind Grover of just how responsible he was supposed to be.

"He got enthusiastic about the tour, but then he kept wanting to change things. He had all these ideas, and none of them sounding like the Grover I knew. Then in Mexico City, when he came out and sat on the front of the stage and just started talking to the people in the front row . . . god. They didn't tell us until we were already on the jet after the show that we were headed back to New York, not on to Guatemala. And Grover was headed back to a team of therapists and his new house in LA.

"Why did he do it? I don't know. Maybe he was just trying to walk away from everything . . ."

"Yeah."

"It just doesn't seem real that I knew who that was," she said, pointing at the heads in the window, "let alone actually rode around in a van with him."

When the waiter brought the main course, Grover's images vanished from the front window, uncovering the news.

"Try not to think about why, Hanes. Leave that up to the Enquirer channel; they'll figure it out and the world will still be the same crappy place." She elbowed him in the ribs, trying to take his attention away from the newly uncluttered window.

"Get out of town, take a trip. I'm going back out on this hip-hop reunion tour; that's what I set up while I was staying in Manhattan. Small places, mostly, but the gig's enough to keep my bank account from absolute zero."

"Where to?"

"Pac Rim, Japan, Oz. Starts there. You should think about doing the same. You got time. You've got money."

The last tour. Hanes rode down to DC; he'd been busy for all the New York shows. The opening act was Gerhardt Hess. Grover's managers didn't want to book the lutist, but at that point they didn't have much choice. If Grover had asked to tour the country on a fleet of chrome tricycles, they would have said yes.

He had dinner with Lexene, then once they got back to the arena she stalked off to check the work her crew had done. Hanes had his VIP laminate scanned by five different off-duty cops before he made it into the bowels of the arena, where Grover was sitting in a mint-green cinderblock dressing room. Upstairs, Hess was getting only derision from the audience, thousands who had shown up to see Grover and his puppets. The amplified lute music snaked down the stairwells, as did the dull roar of uninterested conversation, punctuated by an occasional scream, the age-old, "Get off the stage!"

Grover was drawing on the chalkboard. His road manager, whose name was either Carlin or Carlton, sat in a rocking chair next to the untouched catering table. The table had the usual cheese tray, meat tray, drinks on ice. It also had a row of boxes of Grover's favorite breakfast cereals, unopened. Grover put the chalk down, dusted his hands off on his coveralls, and then shook hands with Hanes.

"Hi. How are you?" he said blankly. Then, before Hanes could respond, he blurted, "Just a second." He backed away around the divider to the bathroom.

"Howdy," the road manager said, oblivious to Grover's hasty retreat. Hanes nodded and sat down on top of a cooler and waited. The road manager went back to flicking his fingers around on the computer screen in his lap.

Minutes passed, with no noise coming from behind the divider. Hanes helped himself to a wet bottle of Evian from the gray plastic trough filled with slush; it was something to occupy his hands and his mouth, so he didn't have to feel bad about not talking to the road manager.

Grover reappeared and shook Hanes's hand again. Then he gestured at the chalkboard.

"I want to do a new show, one with robots," he said. "Can I get the Omnibot 2000? Do you know where I can get a bunch of them?"

"It's pretty rare to find working ones—"

"OK, well, just ship the one you've got down to the next show. I want to get right on this. Carlton can give you the address."

Carlton started pushing things around on his little computer's desktop.

"Just a second," Grover said, holding up his hand. They were the last words he would ever say to Hanes. He scuttled off to the bathroom again.

Hanes set the water down and left without speaking to Carlton. He sat through the show, hugged Lexene goodbye, and got on a northbound train.

═══

After Lexene left with the hip-hop band, Hanes made arrangements for another trip to Australia via Edmonton, where he had a line on a roomful of Logical Davids, early eighties desktop computers that you could supposedly program in twenty-one different natural languages, if all you wanted to do was add and subtract numbers. He would meet up with Lexene in Sydney, where she had a day off.

The weekend before he left, he drove down to the Englishtown market. It was quiet. He glided through, nothing piquing his interest until he found the Greek at the far end of the cluttered field. The Greek had a video poster tacked up on a warped sheet of plywood leaning against the station wagon. The poster flickered out a little ten-second clip, hazy in the glare of the high sun. Then the clip started over again. Looping.

"Is busted. Play button is stuck. I give you deal," the Greek said.

On the poster, a thin silhouette, backlit from the waist up, manipulated two little puppets. The puppets were the bipedal horses, sneaking out of Dog City after they'd planted the bombs. Sneak sneak sneak. Then, at the end of the clip, one of Lexene's lights would go "pop" and that meant Dog City had blown up. The frame jerked for a second, then the clip started again.

"I'll take it," Hanes said. He paid the Greek, rolled up the poster, and walked back to the van.

The Master Key

"I am not my stuff. I am not my stuff." Jaki repeated this as she moved her dust-covered possessions out of the cardboard boxes she had shipped from Brooklyn and into the clear plastic tubs she'd bought in Austin. The purple ceramic candlesticks that someone had given her when her father died, the collection of hats that she never wore, the crumbling videotapes and Super-8 film she would never digitize. And then, after transferring all of the stuff that was not her from old box to sleek new tub, she came to an even older box. Her high school memorabilia, including a complete run of the school newspaper, the *Devil's Diary*. She had been the arts editor, and gained a tiny bit of notoriety by running reviews of R-rated movies like *Total Recall*. Also her high school diploma. And also, the master key to West Harding Central High.

She brought the key with her when she flew back to West Harding, the hometown where she no longer had a home. The houses were still there; her family had lived in three different ones in West Harding. She had no interest in the houses. The last one had been pleasant enough, with a terraced backyard and a hot tub. Oh, if that hot tub could talk. She even knew the current owners well enough to stop by if she wanted to. Bruce Toole's parents. Bruce was long gone, though, as were all of her other friends. All of them except for Arthur Wrenn.

Arthur, belying his regal name, had never been much for questing. He had gone to state college and received a speech communications degree. When his four years were up he headed straight back to West Harding and got a job as a staff photographer at the local paper. When the paper got bought by a conglomerate and shut down, he stayed put. He took a job photographing houses for real estate agencies. It was just enough work for a person completely lacking in ambition.

He and Jaki stayed in touch. At first, before email, the gaps between communication were months or even years. After her mother moved to Florida, she had no reason to visit West Harding for the holidays.

She had a soft spot for Arthur. They worked together on the school paper, and hung out together at night. Unlike every other guy friend she'd had in high school, Arthur never made a play for her. Never even flirted. When she didn't have a boyfriend, they went on trips together, camping in the mountains. Arthur had a couple of high school girlfriends, but neither relationship lasted longer than a month. The friendship with Jaki inspired a loyalty in him that did not leave a lot of room for romance.

So when the university budget went haywire, and she had to take a two-month sabbatical with no warning and didn't feel like spending it in Austin, she decided to go visit Arthur and West Harding.

"You missed the fifteenth reunion," Arthur said when he picked her up at the airport. He was driving a brand-new Mustang.

"There's a fifteenth? What anniversary is that, anyway?"

"Traditionally, it's crystal. On the modern list, you give someone a watch on the fifteenth anniversary."

"I should have brought you a watch," Jaki said.

"I should get you some crystal."

"I hate crystal. Except maybe for a crystal ball. I'd like one of those."

They cruised on the new downtown expressway, past a mountain of red dirt enclosed by a chain-link fence where Borofsky's bakery had been. Borofsky's was their after-school hangout, junior and senior year. Run by a couple of failed acrobats, it was where you could buy day-old croissants and deadly coffee for cheap.

"Oh," Jaki said.

"Yeah, they tore down Borofsky's. It's going to be luxury condos. A lot of those are going up. I don't know anyone who can afford a luxury condo. Maybe Bruce Toole. He's moving back to town; I saw his parents at the Saint Patrick's Day parade."

"What else is gone? Borofsky's, crap."

"Wait until we get to my place, then all will be answered," Arthur said.

She closed her eyes for the rest of the drive, afraid to see the spaces where things no longer were, or their style-less replacements. When the thrum of the Mustang died down and Arthur turned left into a drive, she opened her eyes. A sign read "Mirror Lake Homepartments."

"Oh, don't tell me—"

"Yeah."

Mirror Lake had been the outdoor pool and amusement park, open since the 1930s. The scene of West Harding's biggest racial conflict in the 1960s. The Peters family had owned and run the place. There was a little train that circled the property, and a carousel they'd imported from Germany. The pool itself had a fake waterfall. One side was built up against a big wall where a trompe l'oeil painting showed the water continuing on into a distant sunset in an enchanted land of waterfalls and giant mushrooms.

"Did they save any of it?"

"Not really. They dismantled the carousel and auctioned it off. Flattened everything else. The stupidest part is, instead of trying to save the old clubhouse and pool, they built new ones. The only thing I've found is parts of the old wall, back behind the dumpsters. I'll show you tomorrow."

Arthur lived in a ground floor unit. One bedroom, one bath. It was furnished in a hodgepodge: thrift store coffee table and dining table. An old beige computer teetered atop a child's desk. A sleek black leather couch sat opposite a giant wall-mounted television.

On the wall behind the computer was a blackboard. On it, the names of the establishments they'd frequented as kids, along with the names of other old businesses. Borofsky's was there, struck through. Most were crossed out. The Coliseum Grill, where they'd spent most nights eating cheeseburgers and drinking iced tea. Sunshine News, which sold exotic foreign magazines and those awful clove cigarettes that Arthur had affected senior year. The Terrace Twin, a suburban cinema that showed late night B movies. Snelson Elementary.

"Snelson's gone? Why the hell are they tearing down schools?"

"It was outdated, according to the school board. Cheaper to destroy and rebuild than to renovate. The new place there is Reagan Elementary."

"You're kidding . . ."

"Reagan's Raiders! Go, team."

"Why do you stay here, Arthur?"

"Got no place else I really want to go. Got no money to go anywhere. Why did you move to Austin?"

She had made up reasons to tell her friends in Brooklyn, to tell her co-workers in Austin. She could tell Arthur the real reason.

"They were trying to kill me in New York. They were trying to kill everybody.

"Put it this way: When I first got there, it was magical. Just walking around at night with my little gang of starving artists, before any of us had done much of anything. Right before I left? If a car backfired, there I'd be, flat on the pavement, shaking, heart pounding. I had to get out."

It sounded dramatic, and she thought she was past drama, but it was true. Arthur just nodded.

"You want to get something to eat? I don't keep a lot of food around," Arthur said.

"Where is there to go?"

She pointed at the blackboard.

"There's lots of new places. Taylor's is gone, but the new owners kept all the fixtures, so it's kind of the same."

He drove to Taylor's. Something was wrong with the Mustang; it took him four or five tries to get it started. It made a thin, wheezing sound when he turned the key before finally catching and coming to life.

Taylor's was an ice cream parlor that had been around since the 1950s. Back when ice cream parlor was a viable business model. For Jaki and Arthur it was the hangout spot after junior year football games. By senior year, they had switched to Angelo's Pizza, where you could usually get beer if the right waitress was working.

Taylor's was now the 345 Club, after its street address. The menu touted itself as "upscale homestyle" and featured dishes such as lobster grits and chipotle macaroni and cheese. The counter and spinning stools were still there, although the stools were now covered in black leather instead of gold naugahyde.

"What is it with black leather?"

"West Harding is chic now. Urban."

"Have you ever been to a real city, Arthur?"

He was silent.

"Sorry, sorry, I went too far."

They ate in silence, gazing out the big windows that faced onto Straightway, the old cruising strip. She started counting the SUVs as they went past, but gave up at one hundred.

The check arrived and she let him cover it.

"We've got a dim sum place now. We can get brunch there tomorrow. And there's a Vietnamese place. And lots of Mexican places now, run by actual Mexicans. Not like Pepe's Tacos."

"Sounds good," she said.

"Why did you come back?"

"I don't exactly know, Arthur. Call it unfinished business."

On the way back to Mirror Lake they stopped to stock up on alcohol. The liquor laws had not changed since she was a child. The liquor store closed at seven p.m., but you could buy beer and wine in the grocery stores until midnight. The selection was abysmal. She picked up a twelve-pack of Mexican beer.

He had an oversize bottle of Kahlua at his place. That was his drink, Kahlua and cream. Except now he drank Kahlua and skim milk, in a tall glass with ice. She had four beers as they plowed through the litany of Where Are They Now? Arthur knew all the answers. He stayed in touch with parents, and was on some alumni email list she'd never heard of. When he was bored he would search the Web on names from the yearbooks, which he kept on a shelf above his computer.

Bert Bradlee, the school mascot, had lost an arm in a car accident in the mountains. Charlene Stellter, debate team captain, had a couple of adult-oriented country hits. Phil Bagley, the prettiest boy in school, was now fat and bald. Debbie Wright, nondescript theater geek, was now a bombshell, with her own line of power yoga DVDs. Arthur fished one out of a pile below the television.

Now she was Deboura, not Debbie. And, if the photo hadn't been airbrushed to death, she was indeed a bombshell. More porn movie than yoga instruction.

"Do you actually do yoga?" she asked.

"Which is more embarrassing? That I tried it once and felt like an idiot when I couldn't even sit properly . . . or that I bought it just to drool over the apotheosis of Debbie Wright?"

"Yoga is hard, Arthur. You can't expect to do all of the poses right off. I took yoga classes the whole time I was in New York. I still can't do a split."

In Austin she hadn't bothered looking for a yoga class. She was taking self-defense. First she took a class called Maul-a-Mugger. Scream and try to kill the guy in the ridiculous padded suit. Eyes, throat, crotch. The guy in the suit was extremely short, and seemed only too happy to replicate rapist terror language. She graduated from that and had just moved on to aikido. It was supposed to be a "soft" martial art, all circular motion and redirected momentum. But her knees and shoulders ached after every class.

What did it matter what Debbie Wright was doing? What any of these people were doing? They were just other humans that she'd been near, years ago. Near to them physically, not necessarily near to them psychologically. Fifteen years later, she couldn't call up Debbie Wright to go hang out. Hey, Debbie, I need help with my side crane pose. She worried that Arthur did think he could call up Debbie Wright or Charlene Stellter or one-armed Bert Bradlee. That he was collecting all of this information for his own special reunion.

"I've got Charlene Stellter's CD, too, somewhere," he said. "It might amuse you to learn that the songs are terrible."

"But she always had such a pretty voice."

Charlene's show tunes were always the hit of the talent show.

"And absolutely nothing to sing about."

"Those are nice artifacts," Jaki said. "But I have something that tops them all."

"The skinny-dipping Polaroids?"

"No, not the skinny-dipping Polaroids."

Those fabled images were long gone. She realized that it was right here, on Mirror Lake, where they'd been taken. They'd broken in one night after graduation. Someone, she didn't remember who, had a camera, and had shoplifted packs of film. One by one the bravest souls crept up out of the pool to be documented. When the cops showed up, it was Jaki who grabbed the stack of photos as well as her tube dress. Everyone ran. Arthur got caught, stuck in the middle of the pool. He was made to stand there naked in the glare of the cop's flashlights while they called his mother. He steadfastly refused to name anyone else who had been there.

"I have this," Jaki said, pulling the key from her pocket. She glanced up at Arthur.

"That what I think it is?"

"Yep."

"It's been fifteen years. Won't work."

"Probably. But I want to try it."

It was a side effect of being one of the Good Students. Her senior year, the state finals in debate were held at dear old West Harding Central. She wasn't on the team, but Arthur was. She got yanked in as student coordinator. That was how, one bright Saturday morning, it came to pass that Mister Granera, the assistant principal who was supposed to chaperone the event but was desperate to go play golf with the three other Cubans who lived in West Harding, handed her the master key to the school.

She and Arthur went out to a hardware store over the lunch break and waited impatiently as the senior citizen behind the counter made copies of the key. They waited to get busted, but they weren't. The old man didn't even charge them.

After the debate finals (Arthur and his partner had been knocked out in the preliminary round), they planned all sorts of pranks based on their possession of the master key. But they never executed them. Real life intruded. Jaki kept the key, though, in that box with all her other high school debris.

It was unreasonable to think the key would still work. Surely high schools changed their locks. And surely there was an alarm system. But it was something that had been undone for so long, and she needed to resolve that.

That night she slept soundly on the leather couch.

The next day, Saturday, Arthur took her on a tour of town. They had coffee at a place downtown, organic free trade shade-grown by communists coffee. It was trying a little too hard.

"What about the mall? Anything left at the mall?" she asked.

But she already knew the answer. They went there anyway and walked the entire circuit, dodging the mall walkers in their white leather shoes. The Sears was still there, but even that was remodeled beyond recognition. The fountains had been filled in, and the shiny geometric sculptures were gone. Probably rusting away in a scrapyard. The only other extant store from her youth was the Cookie Machine, with the rotating oven in the front window and the pizza-sized cookies. But the oven didn't rotate there anymore. They got a cookie anyway, chocolate chip with pecans, and split that for lunch. They spent the afternoon in a forgettable movie.

Just after sunset, they drove to school. Arthur parked on the street near Stony Forest, which had managed to escape the rampant development. Probably the high concentrations of THC in the soil made it unsuitable for luxury condominiums. They locked the car and sauntered onto campus as if they owned the place.

"What if there's a silent alarm?" Arthur said. "What if we get arrested?"

"Who's going to arrest us? We're not thieves. We're not here to take anything. Besides, the key's not going to work anyway."

They circled around behind the main building. Three stories of bricks thrown up in 1920. In plan it was a figure eight, with two courtyards. The courtyards were always locked when Arthur and Jaki were students, but in some elegant past they'd been used. They had fountains and benches and planters, all of them empty when she had attended.

Down the slope from the old building was a modern addition, the cafeteria and science classrooms connected by a breezeway. They crept up to the main door near the offices. She tried the key but it wouldn't even fit in the lock, let alone turn. Arthur peered in through the windows past her and let out a long breath.

"Metal detectors," he said. "No way would I get in school these days." Arthur used to carry a Buck knife on his belt.

They went to the opposite end of the building, but it was the same type of lock. Her master key was useless.

"You know where we should try," Arthur said. "The band room."

The band room was on the opposite side of the school, set off by itself at the end of a long hallway that stuck out of the main building. The hallway was lined with lockers. They walked around the hillside to the band room, another modern addition. Flat roofed, with square panels of glass and steel windows. It did have its own outside entrance, though. You could get there from the school, or you could walk right in from the parking lot next to Stony Forest.

She slid the key in the lock and turned. The latch clicked open.

"Here we go," she said, and heaved the door open. No alarm bells sounded. Maybe a room full of music stands and cheap band instruments wasn't worth protecting.

"Did you bring a—" he said, as she pulled a flashlight out of her purse and flicked it on. They picked their way through the chairs and music stands to the other side of the band room, where the door to the long hallway was. The door was open.

"OK, we did it. Now what? Is this where you profess your undying love to me?"

"Shut up, Arthur. This is where we find something we've never seen before. The courtyards. The cupola. The steam tunnels."

"I know where the steam tunnels are. Tommy Burr showed me."

The entrance to the steam tunnels was in the hallway between the band room and the main building. Just past the lockers, a set of stairs went down to a narrow door. Jaki had walked by it hundreds of times.

The master key worked in that lock too.

"Still don't know what we're doing here," Arthur said, pulling the door to behind him.

"You're exploring, Arthur. Without even leaving town. Come on, let's see where this goes."

She tried to keep to the right to stay oriented. The steam tunnels, if that's what the passages really were, had been repurposed as a fallout shelter at some point. Old civil defense signs were still bolted to the cinder blocks. The ground faded between concrete and packed earth in places.

Rounding a turn, her flashlight caught something that was not a bare wall. Arthur gasped. From the rafters hung a stuffed panther by a noose. The Panthers had been their crosstown rivals. The panther's fur was covered in a luminous mold.

They got lost soon enough, even keeping to the right. She felt like she'd walked a circuit of the school several times, but the tunnels seemed to extend beyond the footprint of the main building. They were heading down a long straight passage, not sure if they were headed toward or away from the entrance. It sloped gently. She wondered if it was a connecting tunnel to the middle school nearby. The ground was now completely concrete, and damp.

So damp that Arthur slipped, and fell, and hit his head.

She said his name, screamed it, a few times. This had no effect. He was out cold. The back of his head was wet with blood. She felt his chest. It was still rising and falling. She set the flashlight down, propping it against the wall so that it would disperse a little light. She pulled out her cellphone, but had no signal. The pool of blood under Arthur's head was spreading. She was wearing a T-shirt and jeans, maryjanes with no socks. So, the T-shirt had to be sacrificed. She took it off and tore it in half, folded one piece into a compress she applied to the back of his head.

"It's like JFK back there, Arthur," she said. He made a groaning noise, but was still out.

The cloth soaked through when she applied pressure. She put the other half on the wound, trying not to move his head too much. What if he had a spinal injury? Don't move the injured, right. All she had to do was magically conjure a team of EMTs who would trek down here to the forgotten steam tunnels underneath her high school, bringing a stretcher and years of expertise.

She shined the light on the back of his head and saw that he'd caught himself on a shard of broken glass. Probably a beer bottle. If he was bleeding that badly, she needed to get it stopped soon.

"Arthur, you've got to wake up. And you've got to help me."

His breathing was labored. She didn't know if that meant he was coming to or getting worse. As her adrenaline rush subsided she realized that Arthur had clothes on too, and thus was a walking bandage cabinet for himself. T-shirt, jeans, socks, and maybe underwear. It might hurt to move him, but she decided to risk it, peeling his shirt off of him, moving his arms up over his head. Just as she leaned down to use his shirt as another compress, he came to. She could barely see the whites of his eyes in the light. He opened his mouth, then reached up with his arms and pulled her toward him.

She said his name again, sharply. He responded by relaxing, letting his arms fall on the back of her head and letting his mouth gape. Her nose ended up resting on his tongue. She tried to twist free from his semi-conscious embrace, but his fingers got tangled in her bra straps. She jerked herself up to her feet, which only made the bra strap pop, leaving it in Arthur's hands as her breasts swung free.

It was then, of course, that Arthur gained full consciousness. His eyes widened in the dim light. The flashlight was still pointing upward, illuminating her toplessness. She crouched down to shut it off, just when Arthur was pushing himself up into a sitting position. Their heads collided. This time she fell into a heap. Not knocked out, but shocked and in pain.

"Not like I haven't seen them before," Arthur said, reaching to feel the back of his head.

"That was fifteen years ago. There's a grandfather clause. Or in the case of these things, a grandmother clause. They are saggier."

"Bigger, too."

She swatted him on the ear.

"I'm bleeding," he said, looking at his hands.

"We need to get you to a doctor. For a minute there, I thought you were a lot worse off."

"I think I'm still in shock."

"It's just the breasts. Luckily I've just got them set to stun, not to kill. Can I have my bra back?"

He handed it back to her, now flecked and smeared with his blood. She put it on, then pulled his arm up over her shoulder to help him stand up. He sagged against the wall as she bent to pick up the flashlight. She put his arm over her shoulder again and started walking back up the tunnel's slope.

Lights came on, incandescent bulbs in little cages overhead. She was blind for a moment.

"Shit!" they both hissed in unison.

"What do we do?" Arthur asked, making the shapes of the words rather than speaking.

She gestured down the slope. Forge onward instead of going back to the school. So there had been a silent alarm, and a security guard or cop was checking out the tunnels. Maybe they would give up before discovering Arthur and Jaki, shirtless and bloody. Maybe there would be a hiding place at the end of the slope.

They crept along, Jaki still supporting Arthur. She kept stealing glances backward. She flicked the flashlight off but kept it in her grasp. The tunnel was long. The farther they went, the more luminous mold covered the walls. Moss grew on the tunnel floor. Finally she could no longer see any concrete, nor any light bulbs. She turned the flashlight on again. The tunnel stopped, or rather, it turned abruptly to the right. Up ahead she saw more light. Sunlight.

"Have I been in there all night?" Arthur asked.

His head was still bleeding. Rivulets of blood trickled down his back from underneath the makeshift bandage. They walked out into the sunlight. They had walked so far, they must be all the way at the little park near downtown. She had taken tennis lessons there. But they were not in a little park with tennis courts. They were in a forest, in a clearing next to a stream. There was a tent set up in the clearing, and a fire that had died down to coals inside a ring of stones.

The tent was orange nylon. She recognized it. It was her father's tent. When they were teenagers, she and Arthur had borrowed it to go camping.

"The first aid kit was in your pack, wasn't it?" she said.

Arthur didn't speak. He plopped down next to the fire. She opened the tent flaps. There was his pack, her pack, their sleeping bags, just as they'd been. His bag was serious camping gear; hers was Lisa Frank, with a rainbow leopard design. She was relieved that young Arthur and young Jaki were not in the tent. She fished out the first aid kit and went to work on Arthur. He just sat there, didn't even flinch when she cleaned out the wound with antiseptic. When she was done patching him up, she looked down and laughed. The back of Arthur's head was clean and tidy, but the rest of him, and all of her, was still bloody and half-dressed.

"We should wash up," she said. "Make sure to keep your head out of the water."

She led him down to the creek. They stripped off the rest of their clothes. She was carrying more weight these days, he less. She waded in to the deepest spot she could find, leading Arthur in by the hand. She splashed water on herself and scrubbed away at the blood. He mimicked her actions feebly.

When they were clean they went back to the tent and toweled off and then slept. The sun was high in the sky, but she had been awake for so long. As she drifted off she worried about Arthur having a concussion. But then sleep overtook her worries.

When she woke up he was gone. She panicked for a moment. She got dressed as best she could, putting on her jeans and bra, and squeezing into a coat from her pack. There was a trail nearby. She remembered: upstream led farther into the woods. Downstream led back to, what? Civilization? And of course there was the tunnel. Maybe he'd discovered the tunnel and gone shambling back. She didn't know which way to explore first. She emptied out both packs to assess her food supply. Some granola in a zip-top bag. Some astronaut ice cream.

"I hope you like fruit," he said, startling her. "There's an abandoned orchard in the meadow just over that hill."

He held out a bag of apples, pears, and plums. One of his old T-shirts still fit him. Hers was stretched to its limits. They ate the fruit.

"I can't just live on fruit," he said. "I have to go to work."

"I think I can stay. For a little while. I like it here."

She pulled the key from her pocket and handed it to him. "Come visit, if you want."

She spent a month there. He never did come back to visit. She explored the path in both directions. She found something better than an abandoned orchard. She found waterfalls, and giant mushrooms. The land from the destroyed painting at Mirror Lake. The mushrooms were delicious, it turned out. She meditated, repeating the word "the" over and over for hours on end. She lost some weight. She made lists of all the types of birds and butterflies she observed. She kept the fire going. She stopped caring about how bad she and her clothes smelled. She imagined herself as the star of her own reality television show. There were no predators in the forest.

And then, after forty days or so, marked out by a circle of stones next to the creek, she went to find the tunnel again. She walked back to West Harding.

She left the key with Arthur.

Circa

An email, from Virginia to Robert: "They're tearing the house down next Monday."

He closed the file he was working on and called her on the phone.

"Hey, Ginny."

"Hey, Bobby. What are you doing this weekend?"

"This is Whitemantle you're talking about?"

"What other place would it be? We should stay there again. Auld lang syne. One last chance for you to see your ghost."

"Our previous sleepover turned out so well," he said.

"That was a long time ago. I'm not eighteen anymore. I'm assuming that you're no longer eighteen."

"I thought your job now was like, grand high wizardess of historic preservation, or something. Whitemantle can't be preserved? It's historic."

"It is historic. We tried. There's another circa 1790 house downtown. City doesn't think they need two. We did what we could, but it's a goner. The land is too valuable. And our budget is already tapped this year from all the places we did manage to save all across the state. I'm heartbroken, even if it doesn't sound like it. With this job, you get used to being heartbroken."

"Is husband John going to be camping out with us? What does he think about this idea?"

"Eh, that ended last year. I thought I wrote you. What are you going to tell your girlfriend?"

Robert snorted. "You know relationship status—single, engaged, married, it's complicated? Well, it's complicated. I'll explain later."

And so Robert told Linda, the jeweler with all the piercings who had moved in the year before, that he was getting together with a group of old high school friends, and he packed some things and drove the seven hours back to Budleigh that Saturday. His parents were gone and it was not a place he visited often. Virginia was the only person from his school years whom he kept in touch with. He hadn't actually seen her in two decades. He didn't get an invitation to her wedding, and he had never asked her why. She didn't do social media beyond running an account for the preservation group. They exchanged email regularly and cards every December and then every few years they would have an epic phone call. She was always so busy, saving this old textile mill or that old school. He was much less busy.

But he remembered the house. He remembered the ghost. Ghosts were supposed to be scary, but he was not scared. It was just another memory, fading like all the others. Lots of people had seen ghosts.

Twenty-nine years earlier, when they were Ginny and Bobby and not Virginia and Robert, they graduated from high school and got summer jobs as counselors at a day camp for troubled kids, held on the grounds of Whitemantle. The house had been the center of a sprawling plantation started by Moses Eliezer, a Jewish attorney who married into an Episcopal family and changed his name to Leazar. In the 1960s the last of the Leazars had died, and what was left by then was just eight acres of land and the house. A local real estate agent with a flair for history bought the property, planning to restore it some day. He rented it out to nonprofits, but never occupied it himself. Ginny and Bobby were getting fifty bucks a week in the summer of 1984 to assist with ceramics and drawing classes, and to play croquet on the sloping lawn that led from the house down to the stand of trees that shielded it from the road.

The kids were the ones who said the house was haunted. "Old Miss Leazar comes out at night, everybody knows that," said one. "She wears a wispy gray dress," said another, "and she's all gray, and her long gray hair hangs down and she floats around and says, 'Where is my buried gold, hid from the Yankees?'" "And she plays the piano," said a third, but there was no piano in Whitemantle. "What piano?" said Virginia. "It's a ghost piano!" the third kid replied.

All of the Leazars' possessions, including any pianos, were gone, auctioned off in the 1960s. The necessities of the summer camp, the jugs of Flavorade and cookie cartons and the craft supplies, were piled into the front rooms. Ginny had been entrusted with a key, because she arrived earlier in the mornings than the woman who ran the camp did.

Ginny and Bobby had known each other since third grade. They had done a lot of things together: kickball, *Much Ado About Nothing*, hashish. There were a couple things they'd never done together: kiss, have sex. Also, they had never stayed in a haunted house.

As Robert drove, he visualized. That was his expertise. Robert was a freelance space planner; he designed mailrooms for corporate clients. He walked himself through the house: through the front door into a high-ceilinged living room. Four rooms on the first floor, each with a fireplace. Two rooms on the second floor. That was the original house. Out the back, step down into the first addition, step back up into the second addition, both of which were still old, pre-Civil-War. On the ground floor, a kitchen and bathroom and screened porch, then a big back room. On the upper floor, a long sleeping porch, and a master suite. Two sets of stairs connecting the floors. An attic, but he'd never been in the attic. He'd never thought about old Miss Leazar much, but he pictured her knocking around alone in there in the sixties, sleeping in an antique four-poster bed, watching *To Tell the Truth* on a black and white television.

He tried to picture Ginny now. Maybe she was one of those people who avoided social media because age had done its work on them? Age had done its own good work on him. His hair was almost gone, and what little was left was a mix of black and gray. For many years, he'd stayed in shape by playing handball, but then he blew out his knee and dropped his gym membership. He took the blood pressure medication that his doctor recommended, but only after a couple years of escalating threats and numbers. He did not do many of the other things that his doctor recommended, which all involved losing weight and getting in shape. He had some cheap reading glasses that he used while working at his computer, even though he needed a real eye exam and bifocals. He realized that he'd left the cheap reading glasses sitting on his desk at home. He took his memory of Ginny and applied some of the same transformations. Grayed her hair—her mother had had salt-and-pepper hair—made her bigger, slower, more hunched over.

Why had she invited him to recreate a bit of summer adventure? "Auld lang syne," she'd said. No more husband, she'd said. She had mentioned the ghost. She hadn't mentioned the other thing that happened. They would be just getting together as Ginny and Bobby, as they always had been, official lifelong friends. Never mind the intervening decades.

When he drove into town, he took the exact same route he always took. Exited the interstate, drove through downtown past the bakery that had been run by the twin Czech ballerinas. Past his elementary school, middle school, and then high school, three brick bunkers ascending a hill. Past the pizza joint that had been the prime hangout back then, now converted into a Starbucks. But then he drove right past the turnoff into the neighborhood where his parents' house sat, full of some family unknown to him. He kept going north, back into an area zoned for business. He stopped at an intersection where the four quadrants were occupied by an extended-stay hotel, a run-down shopping center, a members-only discount superstore, and finally a stand of trees with a lone mailbox and driveway vanishing up a hill into the forest. Hidden back there, on eight acres of absurdly valuable property, sat the remains of Whitemantle, the house of the Leazar family.

The previous adventure, in 1984, they met there on a Saturday. It was early August, still hot and muggy as the sun made its way down below the tops of the trees. The surroundings were different then. The nearby shopping center had just opened, but the extended-stay hotels and big-box stores were years in the future. All of the outside world was buffered away into silence after they made their way up the sinuous drive and into the meadow where the house stood at the top of the hill. Their provisions included: two sleeping bags, a deck of cards, a bag of cassette tapes, a boom box, three bottles of Blue Nun wine, and a Polaroid camera.

They set out their things in the living room, and turned on the fans that had been left there by the day camp. They opened the first bottle of Blue Nun and sat on the front porch and speculated what the first year of college would be like. She was staying close to home and majoring in history. He was going to DC, and was undeclared.

As the sun set they moved inside. Bobby pulled a table lamp from a stool and set it on the floor near the fireplace and plugged it in.

"Our campfire," he announced. "No way we could build a fire in those fireplaces."

"Agreed," she said. "What are you going to do when you see the ghost?"

"I don't believe in ghosts," he said. "I believe in *Ghostbusters.*"

"God, that was a great movie. Yeah, I don't believe in ghosts anymore. Now, eighth grade, that's a different story."

"Eighth grade you believed in everything: witchcraft, UFOs, ghosts, magic runes, pyramid power, Tarot. You had me convinced too."

"Of course I did. You were always copying my tastes," she said. He swiped the bottle from her and took a long drink, letting the wine gurgle out over his chin.

"Now we're the ghosts," she said. "I mean, if anyone was lurking outside, they'd think we're the ghosts."

"Put some music on, O Great Ghostly Tastemaker."

Ginny put a tape in the cassette player: Madness's greatest hits. They didn't dance. They passed the Blue Nun bottle back and forth, bobbing to the beat. She had a funny way of tilting her head when she listened to the music, as if she had only one good ear. They opened another bottle.

They decided to use up the Polaroid film doing dramatic poses together. She set the camera on the mantel, flipped the timer switch, and they stood in front of it and he blurted out, "Catty!" They instinctively twisted their heads in profile and raised an eyebrow just as the flash popped. They repeated the exercise: groovy, sullen, angry, wasted, robotic, patriotic, manic, distressed, happy.

After a considerable amount of wine later, and several more cassettes, they decided that they might perhaps still believe in ghosts to some limited extent. They decided to try and summon Old Miss Leazar. They sat facing each other, palm on top of palm.

"Old Miss Leazar, first off we'd like to apologize for calling you old," she said. "But we're curious, are you like Old Miss Leazar from 1790, or from 1840, or from 1903? Because these things matter."

"We're also curious as to whether you exist at all, so come on out!" he said.

They waited, his right hand on her left, her left hand on his right. She had her eyes closed.

"You can't see Old Miss Leazar with your eyes closed."

"I'm summoning. When she's here, I'll know it."

But Old Miss Leazar never showed up, so when the wine ran out they gave up on summoning a spirit. They were both yawning. They rolled out their sleeping bags and pads and lay on top of them fully dressed, because of the heat. They were right next to each other, next to the fireplace where the lamp stood in for a fire. Ginny clicked the light off and they lay there talking, spinning out a nonsense story about buying Whitemantle and living there with all their friends in a commune. Their eyes adjusted to the moonlight.

Finally they ran out of things to say and just stared at the ceiling. Ginny closed her eyes. Bobby couldn't close his eyes. He was counting to himself. One, two, three. Again. One, two, three. Then to ten. Then to three. Finally, after another one two three, he rolled toward Ginny, swinging his left arm over her and trying to slide his right arm under her head.

"I'm making my move," he announced.

Then he stopped. Neither one of them moved for a minute.

"Stop touching me, Bobby," she said.

He pulled his hands out of the awkward hug he was delivering.

"Roll back to where you were," she said.

"I'm sorry—"

"Roll back to where you were."

He did that.

"The me of third-through-eleventh grade was really hoping you would've made a move before now. And y'know, maybe I should've made a move then. But you didn't, and I didn't. And this isn't the right thing for me now."

"I'm sorry—"

"I don't want you to be sorry. I want you to understand. Do you understand?"

"I think so."

"That's good enough. Now, I have to go to the bathroom. And when I come back, we're going to go to sleep, and you are not going to apologize anymore, and we are going to wake up and be Ginny and Bobby, officially lifelong friends, and we are going to proceed on with our glorious lives. OK?"

"OK."

Ginny slid out of her sleeping bag and padded off to the back of the house. Bobby didn't watch her go. He clasped his hands behind his head and sighed.

The moon was slanting in through the front windows. He gradually became aware of another light source, something warmer than the moon, coming through the windows at the back of the room. Probably just the bathroom light shining across the yard. But it kept getting brighter, and when he turned to look, there she was, walking through the wall.

He instinctively slid away, pushing himself and his sleeping bag with his hands until he was backed up against the opposite wall. But the ghost was not a threatening ghost. There was no terror-inducing visage, no chains binding its tortured limbs, no threats to steal his soul. There was not even frenzied piano-playing.

She didn't wear tattered white sheets nor early American dress. She wore a green turtleneck and tan skirt. She was an older woman, as old as his mother. She stood in the center of the room, looking down at him with unblinking eyes.

Then she began to move, stepping quickly toward him. He gasped and shouted "Ah!" but made no move to escape. She stepped back just as quickly. Her skirt swirled around her legs. Her hips swayed from side to side. She kept her eyes on him as she moved, forward and backward, side to side. She continued this exercise, the flowing movements, several times. Then she vanished.

He realized that he'd been holding his breath. He took a deep breath, jumped up, and ran back to the bathroom. It was dark in the back hallway and he forgot to step down to go from the old part of the house to the first addition, so he went sprawling and then hit his head on the newel post of the stairs.

He cried out and heard a muffled response. He reached up to touch his head but felt no blood. It was a sharp pain dulled only by the Blue Nun. He felt like he might get sick. He got on his hands and knees and crawled the rest of the way to the bathroom, where the door was still shut.

"I saw it," he said to the door. "I saw the ghost and then I hit my head and it really hurts and could you please come talk to me?"

She cracked the door.

"There's no ghost," she said. "Are you bleeding? Did you get knocked out?"

"It just hurts a lot. There is a ghost. She was here but then she left."

"I'm not feeling very well," Ginny said. "I think I drank too much wine. Give me a minute. If the ghost comes back, yell real loud."

She shut the door. The pain and the nausea were subsiding, and at some point he dozed off in the hallway. He woke to Ginny standing over him. The light from the bathroom blinded him. She was checking his skull.

"You're right, no blood. I'll trust you when you say you didn't get knocked out. So, tell me about this ghost. Was it old Moses Eliezer himself, come to discuss Judaism and Episcopalianism with you?"

He described the apparition.

"What do you think it is?" he asked.

"I have no idea," she said. "I haven't seen any ghosts."

"I think we should leave."

"Neither one of us is in any shape to drive anywhere. I'll protect you from the ghost, as long as you don't try any more 'moves.' Come on."

He insisted that they go up and camp out on the sleeping porch instead of in the living room of the old part of the house, and so they did just that, and slept until the sunlight came pouring in through the windows.

Two weeks later he was gone off to Washington, DC, and college and life.

Robert parked on the side street where she'd told him, near the extended-stay hotel. He felt vaguely criminal as he pulled his pack and sleeping bag and his grocery bag out of the car. He started walking down the sidewalk back toward the intersection. There was an old mailbox at the bottom of the drive. He looked around, thinking he should try and sneak up to the house, but the world was oblivious. People in SUVs and compact cars zipped around from the grocery stores to the fast food restaurants and gas stations. They had no idea that hiding behind all those trees was Whitemantle, a house from another time.

The drive snaked up into the trees and disappeared. He walked up it as quickly as he could, but his knee was giving him trouble, especially with the added weight of his bags. Once safely in the forest, he stopped and caught his breath for a moment before continuing on up the slope. The drive switched back and forth twice before opening out onto the familiar view. Three giant trees staggered on a lawn of high grass, and at the top of the hill, Whitemantle itself. Something was different, though. He realized that all of the flora was grown up around the house. Where there had been neatly trimmed bushes and a manicured lawn, now the boxwoods and the ivy threatened to swallow up the house. The camellia bushes with their pink flowers were gone.

Virginia was standing near the front door, waving. He huffed his way up the hill, feet and knees and hips and lungs complaining all the way.

"You could've helped," he said, plunking his stuff down at her feet.

"I could've helped by telling you about the path," she said. "I just got here. Parked right behind you, in fact. There's a path through the woods now, a shortcut, but it's hard to see from the street."

She was different, of course. Although he didn't quite see why she wouldn't put her picture online. Her hair was completely gray, although her eyebrows were still black. There were some creases and wrinkles. When she smiled it was a smile of amusement tinged with sadness, not a smile of pure joy.

The house had changed a bit, too. The porch was all wrong.

"What's up with the porch?" he said.

"This is the one thing the caretaker managed to get done," she said, gesturing at the tiny stoop with one gable held up by two square columns. "He sent the porch back to 1790. The porch that you remember from when we worked here? It wasn't original. It was way too big, and had all that Queen Anne gingerbread on it. Totally wrong for 1790. Of course it doesn't matter anymore. It's all coming down next week."

"I liked that porch. It was a good hangout space. I still can't believe someone wants to tear down this house. And what about you? You been sleeping in a hyperbaric chamber or something?"

"I will take that as a compliment. I take my vitamins and do my yoga, sure. How about you? Where have you been sleeping?"

"I sleep on the couch a lot."

"C'mon, let's take a spin around the house. Remember the ceramics the kids made? There are still some here."

There had been paths through the boxwoods, but now the bushes were so overgrown that they had to skirt around them. Hiding underneath the bushes were some of the old pottery projects: lumps of white and brown and gray clay, sculptures and pots that never got taken home. They tromped through the high grass to make their way counterclockwise around the house. He called out identifications of some of the big trees that were going to be destroyed along with the house itself: Eastern cedar, black oak, American elm. The trees were in better shape than the house. The black shutters sagged from the windows, their vanes punched out like bad teeth. Green mold covered the back of the house where sunlight didn't reach. Near the foundation on the north wing, Virginia pointed out where some siding had been pulled away and not replaced.

"We were checking for termites and rot," she said. "And we found both."

They continued on, moving from the high grass into the English ivy that crept out from the woods behind the house. The ivy covered everything in its path, including a rusted-out Volkswagen squaretail.

"The caretaker's," Virginia said. "He left a car, and he left a lot of things inside. Technically he wasn't supposed to stay here, but I think he spent his weekends here for years."

"Hey, watch out!" he said, grabbing her arm. They stopped.

There was a tiny baby bird sitting on the ground in the ivy, underneath a dogwood. They both bent over to peer at it.

"Its eyes aren't open, are they?" he asked.

"Just barely. Can't you tell?"

"Sort of. Not exactly. I left my glasses at home. I have trouble with details up close. I probably won't be reading the newspaper."

He glanced up at the dogwood.

"But that's clearly the nest," he said, pointing. "This won't take a second."

He let go of her and stooped to pick up the bird.

"I thought you weren't supposed to touch baby birds. The parents will smell you and then kill them."

"That's a myth, pretty much. Most birds can't smell a thing. A bird this young, it's not a fledgling yet. We can put it back in the nest."

He cradled the baby bird for a few minutes, warming it up. She bent the branch down so that he could replace the bird. There was another hatchling in the nest.

"It probably got kicked out accidentally. I think it'll be fine. I should wash my hands."

They continued back around to the front and went inside. The air was stale in the house, but there were still a couple of fans, which they turned on.

He washed his hands in the kitchen, and then she gave him a tour of the current state of the house. They explored it from front to back, opening the few windows that had screens. Virginia had been there quite a bit recently, showing it to wealthy donors, trying to set up a plan to save the property or at least to move the house somewhere else.

"I guess my ghost keeps the vagrants out," he said.

"No, I'm pretty sure the caretaker kept any vagrants out. The caretaker never mentioned a ghost. And believe me, I asked."

There was a blue sofa, a green armchair, and a pink brocade armchair in the living room. There were more abandoned pottery projects in the adjoining parlor. The room beyond the parlor was where the caretaker had slept—there was a double mattress on the floor, a black folding chair with a desk lamp, and a little carrier for a cat or small dog.

There were more things left in the back room. There was a card table, an old office chair, and on the table sat a beige computer connected to a modem. At first, Robert thought the computer was on, because there was a droning sound in the room. Then he felt something whiz by his face. He looked up and saw a swarm of bees congregated in the corner of the ceiling. He dashed out of the room into the back hallway and on into the kitchen, looking back to see if he'd been followed by a bee.

"Hey! I can't stay here. I'm terribly allergic to stings," he shouted.

"So you've got an Epi-Pen?"

"Yes, I've got an Epi-Pen. It's sitting on my desk at home right next to my glasses."

She sighed.

"Stay right there, Bobby," she said. He kept an eye on the room as she backed out and then closed the door. There was a huge gap at the bottom. She went and got the comforter off of the caretaker's cot and jammed it into the empty space.

"Problem solved," she said. "I'll go close the upstairs door into the back room."

He went to the living room and started unpacking his bags and inflating the air mattresses that she'd brought. He shoved the furniture up against the walls to make room. When she came back into the room, he was sitting on the blue sofa, working a Rubik's Cube.

"Nice," she said. "Did you bring some parachute pants too?"

"I found it at my place when I was looking through a box of old things. I think I actually took it from this house."

He flipped the cube and spun the sides at random.

"I used to know how to solve this," he said. "Did it all the time in college, just to calm my nerves."

She came and sat at the other end of the sofa.

"Let me see that thing."

He tossed her the cube. She flipped and spun and had as much luck as he'd had with it.

His calf itched, and he pulled his pants leg up to scratch.

"Successfully avoided the bees, but, ugh, there must've been mosquitoes outside," he said.

"A mosquito flew up your pants leg? Let me see that."

He held up his leg: pale skin, purple veins, black hairs and all.

"That's not a mosquito bite. That's a seed tick," she said, tilting her head back and peering through the bottom of her glasses.

She rummaged in her bags and pulled out a multi-tool, flipped it open into a pair of needlenose pliers.

"Hold it up here in the light," she said. He stuck his leg out in front of the lamp. His knee twinged. She pulled the tick off and took it back into the kitchen. He looked at his leg where the tick had been, but all he could discern was a blurry reddishness.

"Holy shit!"

"What is it?" he said, even though he knew.

"Well, I've got five of them. So far. We must've got into them in the yard."

She walked back in, holding her shirt up and gesturing at her waistline. He couldn't see any ticks.

"We need to do tick checks," she said. "Hang on, let me get these off of me."

He stood up, imagining that the sofa was infested with ticks. He lifted his shirt to see if he could spot any ticks on himself. There seemed to be one at his waist, but after he picked at it he remembered that it was a mole, one he was going to ask his doctor about when he got around to another physical.

Ginny returned.

"Oh, right. You can't see. Take your clothes off," she said.

"What? Are you making your move?"

"No, I'm assisting you in not catching Lyme disease. My tattoo artist had it. Trust me, you do not want Lyme disease."

"You have tattoos?"

"Take your clothes off and stand over there by the lamp."

He slumped back down on the sofa.

"I'll take my clothes off if you take your clothes off."

She set the pliers down on the floor, and then pulled her top over her head while stepping out of her clogs. She reached behind her back to unclip her bra.

"OK, OK, I give up. Tick check," he said. "World's most embarrassing tick check." He stood up and started taking off his clothes.

"No, no, you're right, it's only fair." He glanced over and she was continuing to shuck her clothes. "I think I found all of the ones on me, and if there are any left on me, I doubt you can see them. But fair is fair."

He stumbled trying to get his pants off, tweaking his bad knee. When he looked over at her again, she was naked. He yanked his underwear and his pants off and then he was naked too, a deer in the headlights.

"Stand by the lamp," she said.

"Can we at least move away from the windows? Someone could see. Someone besides you."

"No one can see. No one's back here but us. No one knows this place exists. Lift up your gut."

He complied, looking away down into the yard. It was getting dark now. Even though they were surrounded by roads and shopping centers, he couldn't see any lights from beyond the forest. They might as well have been floating in a void.

"OK, turn this way. Grab your junk and move it to the left, and don't make any stupid jokes."

She found only one more tick, burrowed into the crease behind his bad knee. After removing the tick, she rinsed the pliers off and put them away, then pulled some ointment out of her bag.

"Here, put some of this on. It's called Miracle Mend. It fixes everything."

"How much do you have? Maybe I should just slather it all over myself."

"Couldn't hurt," she said.

He dabbed some ointment on the two spots where ticks had attached. It smelled of lavender and tea tree. She was putting her clothes back on and so he followed her lead, getting dressed without making any more jokes. Goodbye, naked Virginia. She put on a green turtleneck over her shirt.

"Well, I survived," he observed. "And you survived, too, and didn't go blind or turn to stone. Thank you. We should celebrate a successful tick check."

"I brought a bottle of Cabernet Franc."

"Are you kidding? I brought three bottles of Blue Nun."

He pulled a bottle out of his grocery bag and opened it. They started in on the wine and continued setting up their camp in the living room. He hooked up his phone and speaker, then pulled up New Wave Hits on his radio app. "The Metro" by Berlin came up, robotic synthesizers chugging along underneath an emotionless female vocal.

"Let me see if I can find something we actually listened to," he said.

"Here, use my phone. I've got Madness, the Waitresses, the Furs. I made us a playlist."

"You made us a playlist? Well, I'm afraid I can't skank anymore."

"You can't do much of anything, can you?"

"I can tell you where to put your bulk mail sorter, sister. And I can save the baby birds with my eyeballs tied behind my back. How about that?"

"How about adult dancing? Have you ever tried that? Swing, salsa, that kind of thing."

"Nah."

"The basic swing steps are pretty easy. A lot easier on the knees than skanking. And it's a great way to meet people, should you and your 'it's complicated' girlfriend, whom I should add you haven't mentioned at all yet, break up. Come on, stand up."

She swapped her phone in on the amplified speaker and dialed up some Benny Goodman.

"So, watch what I do and mirror it, OK? It's back, forward, side, side." She kept stepping, back, forward, side, side, in time to the music. He tried to match what she did, but something got fouled up in the connection between his brain and his feet. He kept stepping back, then back again. Finally she moved to his side, so he could replicate her movements exactly. After a few minutes, he got the basic step.

"Now we hold hands. That's all we're going to add, is holding hands. Just keep doing that step."

"I think I need more wine; maybe that'll make me a better dancer."

He took a big slug of Blue Nun, which was even sweeter and harsher than he remembered. But it didn't help. He had to concentrate so much, whereas she was effortless. And his knee hurt, even if it wasn't that strenuous. He stopped dancing.

"Do you ever wonder, Ginny?"

"There have been occasions when I wondered, sure."

"But you're not wondering now."

"Not at this moment, no."

"Hey, forget dancing. I brought you a present. It's what I was looking for when I found that Rubik's Cube. Something I've held onto for a while."

He went to his bag and unzipped a side pocket, pulled out a photograph. It was a Polaroid, one of the ten they'd shot long ago. It was "happy." He bowed ceremoniously before handing it to her.

She changed the music from Benny Goodman to the mix she'd made of their eighties favorites, but turned the volume down so they could just talk. After one bottle of Blue Nun, they both decided it would be preferable to drink the Cabernet Franc.

By midnight, they were both exhausted. They retired to their respective air mattresses. He was the first to get up to pee, only an hour later. Whereas Robert was a light sleeper, Virginia didn't move when he got up or returned.

He woke up immediately when she rolled off of her air mattress and left the room. He picked up his phone and checked the time. Three a.m. When he looked up from his phone, the ghost was there, standing in the middle of the room. There was no question who it was. It was Ginny, eighteen-year-old Ginny. She was not swaying. She was looking at Robert. He sat up to get a better look at her. Then they observed each other, neither one moving. She cocked her head, listening to a sound that he could not hear. Then, when she was satisfied, she started walking again, walking past where he sat on the floor, toward the front wall. She passed through it and out on to the porch, historically correct and also doomed. He moved to sit at the window and watch her glowing shape recede as she headed east down the front lawn.

He stayed there, watching her until she disappeared into the trees at the end of the slope. He thought about a ghostly young Ginny appearing on the other side, walking across the main road and continuing on, all the way to a rising sun.

The next Monday, the workmen arrived.

At the Fair

The fair was a blinding splatter of white light in the dark canvas of town, sending out spiral arms onto the dead grass, metastasizing onto the gentle slopes of the grounds. Held in check only by chain-link and barbed wire, counteracting the night with the modern miracle of halide lamps.

The fireworks go off at nine, and the fair closes at midnight, but in between, how long is that? Is there still a town out there in the darkness beyond?

There were three of us at the fair, me and Karl and Eva.

"Have we seen it all?" we asked each other.

"What's down there?" Karl asked, pointing at a space between two large tents. Hand painted signs on easels in front of the tents announced a folk-singing contest from earlier that evening. The tent to the left was for the "Religious" competition while the tent to the right was for "Secular."

Just beyond those tents was a spur of carts and wagons. The turkey leg vendor had already closed up shop. The Alpine Disaster ride no longer ran, but the grease-covered legs of a carny protruded from underneath. The clank of cotter pins and straining metal, as well as a variety of oaths, emanated from the ride.

One attraction was still open. At the far end a man still slumped against the podium in front of a canvas tent. He came to life when he saw us enter the clearing, pushing himself upright, tracking us with his gaze. The banner over him proclaimed "Beyond the Pale! Peculiar! Remarkable!" We advanced automatically, drawn to the only sign of life.

"Gentlemen and lady, step right up, see the one and only Nude Man, the wonder of seven continents, a rarity never before seen in these parts."

Karl snickered at this. The doorway to the tent, just another person-sized flap of canvas hanging down, stirred in the night breeze, beckoning in a subtle way that the talker could not.

"That's right, folks, only one dollar to see the Nude Man. He is eccentric. He is bizarre. He is so quaint and queer as to beggar all description, yes."

The talker might as well have been addressing an audience of a hundred, as loud and clear as he spoke. I turned back to see if, indeed, there were more townspeople in the clearing with us, but none were there. Beyond the two large tents, the electronic calliopes nattered on.

"Let's get back to the real fair," Karl said, not even attempting to hide his disdain from the man at the podium.

"Exceptional! Anomalous! Unprecedented!" the man cried defensively, pointing his finger straight at Karl.

"What's the matter, Karl, are you afraid of a Nude Man?" Eva asked.

She fished three dollars from her purse, walked up and handed them to the man at the podium. He smoothed the bills, folded them twice and stuck them into the slot of his moneybox. Then he pulled aside the canvas curtain, bowing and gesturing for us to enter with his other arm.

"Enjoy the show," he whispered.

We walked in, Eva then me and then Karl. A little foyer opened onto a square room. Not more than a dozen wooden folding chairs, with an aisle between, faced a low platform. There were no other entrances. There was a folding screen set up to one side of the stage, painted with a large coat of arms. On the coat of arms, two rampant gray horses flanked a leafless black tree, all on a brown background. We took seats in the front row. From behind the screen, whispers and giggles, followed by shushing noises and then silence.

In the middle of the stage was a wooden chair, heavy and institutional looking but painted gold and covered with sparkles.

There was a click and then the electrical hiss of a noisy speaker, followed by a blaring fanfare. This too emanated from behind the screen. Harsh tape-recorded trumpets announced the arrival of the Nude Man.

He was not behind the screen. Instead, he marched up the aisle from behind us. By the time we thought to turn around he was already upon us and then past, stepping up onto the platform.

From behind, the Nude Man was pasty even under the incandescent bulbs of the tent. He was short and stocky, with a roll of fat around his middle leaving a horizontal crease just above the vertical crease of his buttocks. He was also quite hairless. He spun in place in front of the gilded chair and stood there, eyes slitted, smiling out at the three of us.

The Nude Man wore a tiny crown on the top of his bald head; it had to have been glued in place. The Nude Man was not, in the strictest sense, nude. Covering his genitals was a wooden star, invisibly held in place, coated in the same sparkling gilt as the chair.

He waved his hand, as if the room was packed with spectators, as if the room was a large concert hall instead of a tiny canvas tent. From behind the screen, two women walked out, each with a bunch of roses in her arms. The women were not nude; they were both clad in gauzy gray dresses. They advanced and stood on either side of the Nude Man. He turned to each of them and as he did so he raised his hands as if to say, see the bounty of the Nude Man. The women began to bow and proffer the roses to him, but as they did so the blaring trumpets ground to a halt. The chewing sound of a cheap cassette dying in a tape recorder came from the speakers. Both women hastily handed their roses to the Nude Man, then they disappeared behind the screen again to switch off the tape.

The Nude Man, unruffled, settled into his chair with the roses in either arm.

"Greetings, my subjects," he said in a booming voice. "Let the lecture begin." He rolled his R's. Looking to either side for vases that weren't there, the man decided to simply drop the roses onto the floor of the stage.

"We paid for a nude man," Eva said, "not a semi-nude king."

"Ah, you noticed! Yes, I am also a king, and I sit on a golden throne."

"But you're not nude!"

"For a mere pittance I will remove both crown and star, young lady, if that is the satisfaction you seek."

He adjusted both of these accoutrements as he spoke.

"Yes, only ten dollars and I will present myself in all my radiant glory."

"Ten dollars?" Karl asked, but the Nude Man continued with his presentation instead of responding, rising quickly from his throne.

"First I would like to pose, to reproduce some of my favorite historical works of art," he said, rubbing the palms of his hands together and pacing back and forth at the front edge of the stage.

"Michelangelo's *Dying Slave!*" he blurted, then he twisted his body into the erotic rictus of that sculpture and froze there. It was quite a different effect, though, on a portly man wearing a tiny crown, genitals censored by a bright star. Still, he was quite good at remaining motionless. His breathing was undetectable. His arms did not shake there, raised over his head.

"Slaves," he snickered to himself, returning to normal posture.

"Leonardo's *Vitruvian Man!*"

This was not a pose but rather an exercise: the Nude Man did little abbreviated jumping jacks to indicate the multiple arms and legs. His star bobbed. It looked painful to me, but his expression for the duration was the blank stare of the original Da Vinci sketch.

"Rodin's *The Kiss!*"

He sat down on the chair, turning to clutch an imaginary woman in his arms. He closed his eyes and puckered his lips, holding the pose for longer than the previous ones. In the gap I noticed that I couldn't hear the calliope sounds from the rest of the fair, no shouts or cries, nothing but the breeze flapping the sidewalls of the tent.

One of the women emerged from behind the screen, strode over to him, and bent down to kiss him on his waiting lips. After a resounding smacking noise she turned and retreated. He sprang to life again, leaping up and bowing left, right, and center stage. We all clapped automatically, and from behind the screen came the sound of additional applause from the cheap tape recorder.

"I would now like to open the floor for questions from you good people," he said.

Eva raised her hand but began her question without waiting for an acknowledgment.

"Why aren't you nude?"

"Soon enough, soon enough, my hasty maiden. I am completely unclothed and therefore nude, insomuch as a crown and star are not clothing. But you will have your opportunity to see all. Any others?"

Again, he scanned the room as if it were packed with attendees.

"Are you a good king, or a bad king?" I asked.

"I am a king, there is no good or bad with kings. We are beyond all that."

"If you're a king, why are you here, a sideshow attraction?" Karl asked.

"I believe this is best answered by King Canute, who said, 'Let all men know how empty and worthless is the power of kings.' But let me add to this. Let me regale you with a story."

He sat back down in his chair, adjusting his star and crossing his legs so that his right ankle rested on his left knee.

Once there was a land where it was safe—safe to live, to work, to love, to dance. In this land, a valley nestled between a great forest and a majestic mountain range, everyone dressed in the colors of nature: greens and browns. There were flowers everywhere. No one was hungry, or thirsty, or tired, for everyone worked together for the common good to grow crops and make wine, but no one worked too much. No one drank too much, lest they be unable to get up the next morning to work in the fields. No one ate too much, lest someone else go hungry. Everyone understood the difference between "enough" and "too much."

No one questioned the way of things; it had always been thus. Children grew up seeing that if everyone worked moderately, everyone benefited equally. People were free to leave the valley as they pleased, but few ever did. The few that did leave never returned, though. The ones who left were ones who could not discern between "enough" and "too much."

One day a pair of assassins arrived from another place, from a kingdom beyond the great forest. They arrived on horseback, scarring the carefully plowed fields and trampling the beautiful flowers.

"Who rules this land?" they asked.

"We rule this land," the people replied, no matter whom the assassins asked. At first they laughed and reared their horses back and charged off to a different part of the valley, but soon enough, after hearing this same reply after each inquiry, they became angry.

In the evenings the people would gather at a hall in the center of their village, to drink some wine and sing and dance. The assassins discovered the people gathered in the hall, and they rode into the hall and smashed the wine bottles and the musical instruments.

"Where is the king?" they shouted. "We are here to see your king!"

But the people of the valley did not understand the word "king," and so they could only look puzzled, and wonder at how long it would take them to make more wine, and to repair their musical instruments.

"What is a king?" asked Johanna the guitarist.

"Yes, what?" reiterated Nicolas the grape farmer, stepping up to stand beside Johanna.

"Why do you continue to mock us?" asked the assassins. "Don't you realize we could kill you all?"

"We do not mock you," Johanna said. "We do not understand why you come here and destroy our wine and music."

"You have mocked us from the day you sent spies to our land, to confound our king and his people!"

For you see, the assassins came from a land where recently two scoundrels had duped the king and his court, tricking them with cunning deceits. The king had them imprisoned and tortured to find out their heritage. The two scoundrels were indeed from the valley, but before they could describe their peculiar homeland, before they could relate why they'd left it, the king's torturers beheaded both of them. But the king was unsatisfied with the deaths of the scoundrels. Then he sent assassins out to avenge the slight: he had been made a fool by these scoundrels, yes, but in turn he would have their king murdered. In truth, the king was ready to start a war.

But the king did not realize that there could be a land where everyone ruled and thus no one ruled. Once again the king, through his assassins, was confounded. The assassins, realizing that they had to kill everyone or no one, turned their steeds and rode off into the forest. The people set to repairing the musical instruments and making more wine, and they lived on in their peaceful land between forest and mountain.

When the assassins returned to their king with their story, it was so outlandish that it could only be true. The king was greatly amused by the thought of a valley full of people where everyone and no one ruled; he asked the assassins to repeat their story several times, and each time he laughed longer and harder at the story. His anger dissipated, and no longer did he think of starting a war with the people of the valley. Thus did the mercy of the great king shine down upon the people of the valley, because—even though none of them knew it—their lives had all been spared.

Sadly, the king's good cheer was short-lived, for his own people, seeing him duped by scoundrels and unable or unwilling to respond in a kingly manner, drove him from the throne and banished him from his own land, sending his two assassins with him.

"OK, look, it's ten dollars for the three of us," Eva said, proffering the bill. "No way are we paying ten dollars each."

"It is ten dollars for all three, yes," the man replied, "but you all have to remove all of your clothing, too."

We glanced among ourselves, looking to see who would contradict the man first, or conversely who would remove their clothes first.

"But I am only joking!" the man said, and he laughed. He bent to one side of the chair and picked up a single rose.

He leaned over and snatched the bill from Eva's grip, exchanging it for the rose. Then he extended his hand out to his side. Both women came out from behind the screen and one of them took the money. He reached up and, as if unscrewing it from his head, removed the tiny crown. He handed the crown to the other woman.

"Why did you come here?" he asked us. "What for?"

"We came here to see something remarkable and unprecedented," Karl said.

"And you are not satisfied seeing a king on a golden throne, seeing the great sculptures of history re-created, hearing a tale of olden times? Surely all of these are remarkable."

He shrugged, turned his back to us, and worked at the star attached to his crotch. Or perhaps he simply moved his arms for show, making this last removal seem harder than it really was. Finally he extended his hand, holding the golden star, to the woman to his right.

He spun back around, arms akimbo, but it only lasted a second. Just as quickly, he turned and dashed off behind the screen.

His penis, which all our gazes were drawn to when he turned, was utterly unremarkable.

"Did you see it? Did you see it?" he cried as he ran toward the screen. Then, silence.

"Thank you for coming tonight, the show is over," the women said in unison. We remained in our seats. They set down the crown and star and advanced slowly to the edge of the stage. They stepped down and stood before us, extending their hands to me and to Karl. We took them by reflex. My gray lady's grip was like iron, and as I glanced over at Karl I could see that he was in pain too, both of us with our fingers twisted backward. We stood up and tried to get out, to get away from the women, but they didn't allow a swift exit. Instead they paraded us slowly, paralyzed, down the aisle. I looked back to see that Eva followed, twirling her rose. Beyond her, though, the man had emerged from behind the screen. He stood there, still nude, watching us leave with a smile on his face. A smile of triumph—one of many triumphs experienced nightly, for a handful of dollars. Finally at the end of the aisle the gray ladies let us go and we passed beyond the canvas door of the tent.

We staggered out of the tent, past the empty podium, into the night and the town beyond.

Pete and Earl

Mrs. Stone has a new special friend. Her special friend's name is Earl. I've never met Earl before, but he knows my name. "Hello, Pauline, please come in," he says when he answers the big white door before I've even knocked.

Mrs. Stone lives in a big white house. The Stones lived in a series of houses of different sizes and colors, but the white one is the one they've had for decades. It was a nice place to end up, so after Mr. Stone died, Mrs. Stone kept the house. It has a pool, a tennis court, a pasture for riding horses, and woods for hiding in when you're nine years old. None of the Stones' three daughters are nine anymore, and, of course, neither am I. The three horses—Lucky, Happy, and Ronald—are all gone now too. They've been gone for a long, long time.

Earl is there, though. He takes my jacket and compliments me on my sweater, unaware of its thrift store origins. He knows that I'd like a cup of Darjeeling, information passed on from Mrs. Stone's previous special friend, Eugene. Earl dashes off to get the tea. I wander through the pastel rooms of the mansion to the sunporch where I know I'll find Mrs. Stone.

"I'm so glad you've come, Pauline. What a pleasant surprise."

I always come on the first and third Saturdays of the month. It shouldn't be a happy surprise to Mrs. Stone but then again most things are surprises, happy or unhappy, to her these days. She remembers me, but Earl probably prepped her for my visit. She offers her hand, which I grip for a moment before letting go and easing back into a wicker rocking chair.

Earl appears at my elbow, sets the tea down on the glass-topped coffee table between our chairs.

Then he leaps over the table, spinning in midair, and lands squatting down on his haunches next to Mrs. Stone. His hand on top of hers, his eyes wide and eager to help out. Ready to spring into action again.

Mrs. Stone starts the conversational litany in the present, requiring some help from Earl to relate the current crises. Julie, the oldest daughter, is having marital trouble with her fourth husband. Patricia is doing just fine in Washington, DC, but Mrs. Stone can't understand why she can't find a good man to settle down with. She doesn't mention Angela, the youngest daughter, and neither does Earl.

The place that's most comfortable for Mrs. Stone is the distant past, where her husband and all three of her daughters are still alive. Earl's been briefed on the distant past, I'm sure, but he doesn't need to help Mrs. Stone much once she starts rummaging around back there, telling the same stories she told two weeks ago and the same ones she'll tell two weeks from now.

Earl is someone's idea of perfect, but not mine. Millimeters make the difference between a handsome face and a disgusting face, and Earl's mouth bleeds over into disgust. His lower lip bulges, pouting, even though his upper lip is barely there. I don't need to concentrate too much on Mrs. Stone's stories—I've heard them all—but this leaves me with a little too much time to concentrate on Earl's face. His immobile smiling gaze, a clown's idea of readiness, is unnerving.

The beginning of her stories is the war. In the beginning was the war. It was when wars were fought by the poor, in large numbers, with bullets. On a bus ride from an indoctrination center to a training camp, Mr. Stone met my father. They were both poor then, but it's hard for anyone—Mrs. Stone, me, Mom—to imagine Mr. Stone as poor. My father, he carried his possessions in a shoebox tied with twine. No one can remember what Mr. Stone carried his possessions in. Mr. Stone doesn't really come into focus until much later, until after the war. Before that, he's just this vague blur who meets my father on a bus, who trains with my father at Fort Benning.

He's the vague blur my father grabs and pulls down behind an armored personnel carrier during an ambush, an ambush where the lieutenant in command of their platoon is killed. Mrs. Stone carefully relates this as my father saving Mr. Stone's life. I never once heard my father use that phrase, "saved his life," to describe the event, though.

It's only years after the war that Mr. Stone comes into focus, wearing his affected ascot ties, driving monstrous gasoline-powered cars that could hold both our families. Supervising construction on all of the houses—his houses, our house, all the houses in between.

Those were Mrs. Stone's good old days, and she winds through them, reminding me of riding horses with her daughters, of swimming and playing tennis with them. I was always a lousy tennis player, though. The Stones had given me a really nice titanium racquet for my birthday when I turned eleven. The only place I could play tennis was at their house, so I was doomed to be perpetually worse than Angela. It was Angela, not me, who finally tired of tennis. She was tired of trouncing me every time we played. It just wasn't a challenge anymore. So once we turned twelve we only rode horses and swam. No more tennis.

Earl doesn't have to help with any of these stories: the time that I was riding Ronald and he went haywire and charged off up to the highway, the time that Angela dyed the dog (and most of the carpet) pink, the time that Mr. Stone took my father golfing with an astronaut. Mrs. Stone knows these stories by heart.

There's still a grounds crew keeping the foliage tidy, the pool clean, the tennis courts free of debris. Does Mrs. Stone still hire a cleaning service, too, or does Earl handle that? What does he do all day?

I let myself in the basement door at Mom's house. When I was a teenager I took over the basement as my own domain, an incursion quickly erased once I moved out. I still like coming in that way and imagining, for just a second, that all my belongings and furniture will be there.

Today when I walk in, Pete's changing a lightbulb in the ceiling fixture. He's clambered to the top of a blue plastic stepladder, but since the stepladder's only three feet tall, and he's just over four feet tall, he can still barely reach the fixture on tiptoe with arms outstretched. He looks less well than the last time I visited, pale and skinny.

He teeters, grappling with the circular fixture, which I always thought looked like a weird nipple up there in the ceiling, trying to hold it up with one hand while unscrewing the lightbulb with the other. The blue ladder starts tilting sideways, but he doesn't notice. Finally it dumps him off onto the hard tile floor. The ladder falls on top of Pete, while the light fixture dangles in the air, suspended only by the thick black and red wires.

Pete looks up at me, his face completely blank. Then he pushes the ladder off, stands up, turns, and walks up the stairs.

I right the ladder, pick up the new lightbulb in its corrugated cocoon, and change the bulb easily. As I screw in the new one it comes to life in my hands, warm and blinding.

Upstairs, Mom is sitting at the kitchen table. There's a red mug next to her, steam coming up out of it. I ask her what she's drinking. "Hmmpf," she says. "Hey!"

Pete comes ambling into the kitchen. "Yes, ma'am, what can I dooo for yooooooooo?" Pete has started bursting into song a lot lately.

"What am I drinking?"

"Pete says green tea. It's full of health for yooooooo—"

"Thank you, Pete."

"Sure thing," he says, a little downcast that Mom cut him off mid-warble.

I look over into Mom's mug. It just looks like boiled water to me, no teabag or leaves or color at all. Pete's already trying to sidle back from the kitchen to the dining room. There's nothing much in the dining room—Mom sold all the nice furniture after Dad died—but Pete hangs out there.

It's not like we ever used the dining room, anyway. When the Stones built our house they built it with a dining room, a living room, a den, a playroom. They insisted on all of these rooms. We just used the den. It was the one room that had a television.

"Let me get you a fresh cup, Mom." I take the mug to the counter and start rummaging in the cabinets for more tea. There is no tea, and when I taste what's in Mom's mug it confirms that she was just drinking hot water. There are cans of mixed nuts, there are containers of yogurt, which should be in the refrigerator but aren't, and there are boxes of sugary breakfast cereal. There's Mom's ancient spice rack, still populated with labeled glass bottles containing flavorless dust from decades ago.

"Mom, you can't live on nuts and cereal. I gave Pete a shopping list the last time I was here."

"I'm just not hungry," she says. Then, "Hey, Pete!"

Pete peeps in from the doorway to the dining room.

"Yeah, she's not hungry," he says, knowing that she's probably already forgotten why she blurted his name in the first place. "Hun-gar-eeeeee!" he adds with an ascending operatic flourish.

Some special friend you are, I think. But instead of sneaking back into the dining room, Pete wanders into the kitchen. He pulls himself up onto the bar and sits there, spindly legs dangling in front of the cabinets.

"You have been taking your medicine, though, Mom?"

"Yes," they answer simultaneously, Mom and Pete. Then he adds, "She wouldn't be here if she didn't, now would she?"

Mom just smiles, showing her chipped teeth. Pete smiles right along with her. Their expressions remind me of Earl. I've been dropped into a universe full of smiling people.

"See, I'm just fine. It's you I'm worried about. How is Bert, Bernie, Ben—"

"Bill," Pete interjects.

"Bill and I broke up," I reply. Bill and I broke up a year ago, and if Mom doesn't remember, well, Pete should. What do they talk about, when I'm not here?

"I'm sorry to hear that, dear. Don't you worry, another man will come along."

"There's more fishes in the sea," Pete adds.

"Shut up, Pete," I say.

"Remember Lucille Canaday?" Pete prompts Mom.

"Oh, yes. Did you hear about this? Lucille Canaday, from church? Her first husband left her . . ."

"Last fall," says Pete.

"Last fall! Well, now she's found herself a trial lawyer. A *lady* trial lawyer. Which is fine by me, in case you were gonna ask. Trial lawyers make good money. Good money."

I try to keep the conversation steered away from myself. Mom's short-term memory seems to work best when she can focus on something to worry about. She's not good with names, but she remembers that I need a man (or a rich woman) in my life. That I haven't had a promotion or even a raise in years. That, until she dies and passes it along to me, I'll never be able to afford a house like hers, the one the Stones built.

We do manage to talk about Mom's favorite soap opera for a while. It's Pete's favorite soap opera too. He reminds her of all of the characters' names when she fumbles for them, but she can remember all of the events—the pregnancies, betrayals, affairs, lost loves—pretty well. As if they're all interchangeable. At least, Pete never corrects her when it comes to the events. I wouldn't know the first thing about what happens on soap operas, even though I should be an expert after listening to hours of enthusiastic commentary from Mom and Pete.

"How's that Bill fellow doing these days?" Mom asks, just before I leave.

For her sixteenth birthday, Angela got a little Japanese convertible with a V-6 under the hood.

When I turned sixteen, a few weeks later, I got a speech from my father about the economy, and about "staying out of trouble." Which meant boys. The Stones and their three daughters, the tennis court and the swimming pool and the horses, they weren't considered trouble.

So everyone was surprised when Angela slid off the road in her powerful Japanese car and plowed into a big pine tree. Me most of all, because I was in the passenger seat. I got minor bruises and lacerations. Angela got dead.

I never told anyone that it was me egging her on to see how fast the little car could go on those twisty backroads, pushing the speedometer needle up and up. As always, living vicariously through Angela. I never told anyone.

Then it's not the first or third Saturday of the month anymore. Then it's just my life. It's payday, so when I get off work at the archives I decide to treat myself to a whiskey in one of the neighborhood bars here in the deserted heart of downtown. Just one, before the sun sets, then I'll catch the bus to my apartment. At the Green Star I get a Jameson's on the rocks and an empty booth. It's dark in my booth, so I can people-watch in peace. There's soccer on the television and a sprinkling of regulars on stools at the bar.

They don't talk; they just grunt and point at the television or their drinks and exchange glances. This makes it easier to make up the stories of their lives. The tall one with short spiky hair, in his forties but still wiry and athletic, he's a tennis pro, I think. Or was, before a tragic accident. Like, he was on the Davis Cup team by the time he was twenty, but then there was some horrible automobile accident. He survived: outwardly he ended up fine but there was brain damage. He couldn't interact with people any more, could barely speak. But his memories were intact. He knew that he'd been a rising sports star, but there was nothing he could do about it except drink heavily and live out his life on the settlement money.

I'm halfway through my drink when the doors swing open and Earl walks in. Pete trails behind. They walk up to the bar and Earl carefully lifts Pete into place on a stool before pulling one up for himself.

One of the regulars, the one who's been nursing an Irish coffee, notices them enter. He nudges the tennis pro on the shoulder, cocks his head, and whispers one word. I don't have to be a lip-reader to tell what he said: "Specials."

The tennis pro turns, squinting his eyes in disgust at Earl and little Pete. He can't do anything, though. Special friends have rights too; the Supreme Court said so.

Pete gets a shot and a beer. Earl, the designated driver, gets a white wine spritzer. He has to explain to the bartender how to make the spritzer. I lean over and cup a hand to my ear so I can listen in better. Earl and Pete don't notice me.

"The previous guy," Pete says, "if I may continue, was a snooty bastard."

"Let's not speak ill of the retired," Earl replies, then he takes a dainty sip of his drink.

"Snooty ooty ooty!" sings Pete, a little too loud. The drinkers swivel their heads toward him for a moment, then back to the television.

"Besides," Earl adds, "the 'previous guy' almost got handed down to your current employer."

"Says who?" Pete downs his shot and looks sideways at Earl.

"Said Eugene himself, when he briefed me for the job. Yet another favor from the beneficent Mrs. Stone. Eugene was petrified she'd send him there instead of just letting him retire."

"Christ, retirement! Don't even bring that up. I sit in this empty white room half the day pretending that I'm retired."

The bartender asks Pete if he wants another shot. Pete doesn't reply.

"Yes, he'll have another," Earl says to the bartender. "On me."

"You're a stand-up guy, Earl," Pete says, slapping him on the back. "Not snooty like frigging Eugene."

"Frigging? What a colorful turn of phrase, Peter. Frankly, I'm surprised Eugene even associated with you. He didn't seem like the slumming type."

"What's that supposed to mean?"

"We're from different worlds, you and I. I'm from the top floor and you're from the 'as is' bin in the bargain basement. Surely you've noticed."

"OK, never mind, you're exactly as snooty as Eugene was."

Pete turns back to his drinks and downs the second shot. That's when I pick up my drink and walk to the bar and plop down on the other side of Earl.

"Tell me all about it, Earl."

"Pauline," Earl says, "what a pleasant surprise," mimicking Mrs. Stone's greeting even as his facial expression betrays the sentiment.

"No, really, what's going on, Earl? Why are you here with Pete?"

"Because Mrs. Stone asked me to be here, of course. I was going out shopping and she asked me to take Peter—not that she actually remembers him by name—along too. It's so much easier for him that way than the bus."

"You're too kind, Earl."

"No, Pauline, it is you who is kind. You visit Mrs. Stone twice a month, after all."

We all drink in silence for a moment. Then Earl starts giggling to himself.

"Nuts and cereal," he whispers, loud enough for us to hear. "Now that's good eating."

I start to respond but then Pete taps him on the shoulder.

Earl turns and Pete is standing there, teetering on top of his stool the same way he teetered atop the ladder. This time, though, he does not fall. Instead he whips his arm around, hand clutching his pint glass, until it contacts Earl square in the cheek. There's an explosion of glass and blood. Special-friend blood: it's clear, not red. It pumps out viscously, pooling on the counter.

The others sitting at the bar don't move from their stools, but the bartender reaches down behind the beer cooler and pulls out a pistol, leveling it at Pete.

"Get out, now," he says. Pete raises his hands reflexively, swaying on the stool.

"You little shit," Earl says, ignoring the gun, "you ruined my face!" He dives at Pete's legs, knocking both of them onto the concrete floor. Pete tries to curl up into a ball, while Earl starts punching and grappling.

"Just shoot them," I say. "Aim for the tall one."

The bartender looks puzzled. By this time Earl has Pete's hands pinned down and he's head-butting Pete with his gooey face.

"No, really, it's OK," I say. "They're paid for."

But he doesn't shoot, and the tragically brain-damaged tennis pro doesn't move, and after a few seconds of pathetic squirming on the floor, Earl lets up and Pete slides away. They get to their feet, both of them slick with Earl's special blood.

"Come on, Earl," I say, "why don't you drive us all home now?"

He just stands there, and no longer am I in the universe where everyone smiles. Earl sneers and gnaws at his misshapen lips before removing a white handkerchief from his pocket and squeegeeing most of the fluid off of his skull. He leaves while the rest of us are still frozen in place.

I put Pete on the bus with as much money as I can afford to give him to make up for groceries that Earl drove away with, then I take a bus home myself.

The next day I take the bus over to Mrs. Stone's house, to apologize. Or rather, to rectify Earl's account. To set things straight, or at least as straight as they can get.

Back in the time when Mr. Stone was a vague blur, it's probably true that my father saved his life. And back in the time when Mrs. Stone's daughter Angela and I used to be friends, it's probably true that I helped end Angela's life. How straight can things get? How even?

It's only the second Saturday of the month, but I go to Mrs. Stone's big white house anyway.

A pale man with short auburn hair answers the door.

"Can I help you, miss?" he says, cracking the door no wider than his slim face.

"I'm here to see—" I start. He waits carefully, blinking. Neither a smile nor a sneer crosses his face.

"Never mind," I say.

The next bus comes by the stop seventeen minutes later. It's hard to maintain a real sense of urgency when the bus is your primary mode of transportation, but the minutes blur by as I make the transfer to Mom's neighborhood and then march up from the stop to her house.

I run through the basement and up the stairs and find them sitting at the kitchen table. Mom and Earl. Earl, the latest hand-me-down, with his ruined face. Black stitches track across his face like a spider's web. Once again Mrs. Stone and her money have worked quickly, behind the scenes, to rectify a problem. If I didn't know how to even things up, Mrs. Stone surely did.

I don't know how Earl will treat my mother, if his sneering contempt will be any better or worse for her than Pete's loopy bitterness. But I pity Earl more than I hate him.

If anyone has won, it's Pete. He finally got what he wanted: retirement. No more sitting in the white room for him. And Mrs. Stone, she got what she always gets: a new special friend, a new toy, a new perfect thing to take the place of all the things she can't have. The things you can't buy with money.

The Ornithopter

"Do you think I could take the tank back to my desk?" Wilson asks. "Or maybe the cannon?"

Wilson is standing in the darkness with Roy from Accounting. He doesn't really want the tank or the cannon. He's just humoring Roy.

Roy continues working on the lock on the door of the enormous display case in the middle of the darkened lobby. "You want the ornithopter," Roy says. Roy hasn't shaved in a few days, and a line of dried blood is running down next to one ear. Roy's been eating candy bars, and he has chocolate smeared around his mouth. Wilson sees all this in the beam of the flashlight that's strapped to his head. Wilson has already had his daily candy bar, back when the sun was out. Just the one. Tonight Roy ate three in quick succession. Although Roy is supposed to be from the Accounting department, Wilson doesn't remember the company ever having any department called Accounting. They're not supposed to be breaking into a big museum case in the lobby. They're supposed to be monitoring the server during the emergency power outage.

"What can you do with an ornithopter?" Wilson looks up and illuminates the ceiling, three stories overhead.

"You can fly, you can escape," Roy from Accounting says. "I'll show you how. But if you don't hold that light still, we'll never get inside this thing."

"This was a bad idea," Wilson says, even though the idea of escape appeals to him.

"Oh, this whole place is a bad idea," Roy from Accounting replies.

****"Service Request? Dial 5-5 5 5 5 for Essential Maintenance."****

Wilson works at the company in the 100 Complex. Buildings 100 through 104, all of them giant white three-story boxes, strung together with three-story hallways. Wilson has worked there for almost eleven years.

Wilson works for Geeta, the team leader. Geeta has a metaphor that she uses to get through the day. For all Wilson knows, it's the metaphor she uses to make it through the night, too. Geeta's metaphor is the original *Star Trek*. She is the happy captain, as she has been since Wilson started his job there. She has a big plastic model of the USS *Enterprise* on a pedestal on her desk. Also a Tribble. Her office is a slightly bigger cubicle than the other cubicles in the 100 Complex.

Wilson doesn't have a metaphor that he uses to get through the day. Or rather, he keeps trying on metaphors and then discarding them. Lately he's been thinking about the stories of Edgar Allan Poe. But Wilson doesn't talk about his metaphors at work. Anyway, Geeta always finds a way to direct the conversation back to *Star Trek*. His first day at work (it was April 2) in her cubicle, she pointed to the model of the *Enterprise*. "I am not your Captain Kirk," she said, "nor even your Captain Janeway. I have always felt like Spock. Think of me as your Captain Spock."

First she held up her index fingers next to her ears, pointing toward the ceiling, little Vulcan ears. Then she threw the Vulcan salute. That was back when there really was a team, when there were many teams, and all of the 100 Complex bustled with life. Now there is one person on Geeta's team: Wilson.

Wilson walks the halls of the 100 Complex, smiling and nodding at anyone he passes, but he doesn't say anything and neither do they. They're on other dwindling teams, working on other fading products, all sailing into the same void together. Geeta and Wilson are not the only workers to think of the place as a starship. You walk in the airlock at eight a.m., you leave ten hours later, you might as well have been sliding through the corridors of interstellar space in that big thing, with its wonky air conditioning and its white noise generators humming in the background. Especially if you're in the core of one of the cubicle mazes, away from the windows.

The company is contracting—fewer and fewer people every month—but the buildings remain, nestled in the piney forest. Geeta and Wilson sit up at the far end of the third floor of building 104; the tops of the pine trees sway outside the windows. If the 100 Complex really is the USS *Enterprise*, it's the episode where most of the crew has left the ship to go live on Omicron Ceti III. Outside, though, life is all around: a family of foxes lives in the courtyard formed by the ring of buildings. Deer and wild turkeys wander through the woods between the parking lots and the complex. A particularly nasty corps of Canada geese has taken up residence as well, not migrating anywhere, just staying there and pecking for food in the drainage ditches, shitting on the crumbling sidewalks.

Wilson takes long walks every day, but he doesn't go outside as much anymore, because the paths are so overgrown now. The graves are outside. Inside the building, there's nothing as picturesque as the graves, but there are still surprises. One day he walked past one of the large conference rooms where a presentation flickered on the white screen in the dark, but no one was actually sitting in the room. Another time he went to use an elevator, and the doors opened and he barely noticed that the elevator car had not arrived. He almost stepped into the empty shaft, then he spun backward to safety at the last moment.

There was a company exercise program, one that Geeta cheerily insists still exists, where if you walked 10,000 steps a day you would get a bonus at the end of the year. It was on the honor system, but Wilson bought a fitness tracker anyway. He wears it clipped to his belt, next to his key card, but he doesn't really care much about the 10,000 steps or the mythical bonus. He just likes wandering around and exploring, watching the decay work. In the spring and fall he walked outside, on a little paved path that ran through the piney forest.

Geeta showed him the graves. You walked toward the main gate and then took a shortcut on a power-line right-of-way, down to an old footbridge over a little creek, then back up a hill. At the top was the Hopson family cemetery, dating from the mid-19th century. Geeta pointed and said, "Christians." She said it slowly, with a hard T. Chris-tea-uns, like they were some weird cult. There were the usual motifs: hands pointing upward, reclining lambs, tree trunks broken off. The biggest grave belonged to Janadius Hopson, and it had three eyes on it, laid out in a triangle.

"That grave is empty," Geeta said, and Wilson asked her how she knew. "Oh, the library computer told me," Geeta said. She said that fairly often.

Wilson researched the names on the graves, too, starting with Janadius Hopson. Evidently, long before the land got parceled out to giant technology companies, the Hopsons had run a mill and distillery and a carriage factory there. Hopson's Mellow Rye and the Hopson Wagonette were their main products. Collectors sold empty bottles of the rye online now, and the state transportation museum had a well-preserved Wagonette in their collection.

> *"Old Janadius was a deacon at Willow Fork Baptist, a pillar of the community, but he was known to tipple a dram of his own product now and again. One day he'd been drinking and a dark stranger challenged him to a harness race later that afternoon. Janadius said that his horse hitched up to a Hopson Wagonette was faster than anything in earth, heaven, or hell. So the race began and Janadius was beating the stranger pretty good. But the agreed-upon course had a sharp left turn, and Janadius was going so fast in that buggy that when the horse turned, he was thrown against a pine tree and killed. The horse trotted back home with the wagon, and the dark stranger left town as mysteriously as he had arrived. But Janadius Hopson's body was never found, not one bit of him, except some red hairs that are still stuck in the side of that pine tree to this day!"*
> —*Haints and History in Willow Fork*, 1927.

The cafeteria is shut down now. There's a sign taped up, purple Comic Sans and bad grammar, about how the food service company contract was terminated and staff should now "access" the coffee shop for drinks and light snacks. The coffee shop is open, in that the doors are unlocked, but the lights are off and no one is working the register anymore. There's no more fresh coffee and fresh popcorn, but there are still candy bars and bags of potato chips stuffed in the wire racks. When Wilson first notices this, he leaves the unguarded snacks alone. But then, as the weeks go by and there's no sign of the shop truly reopening for business, he goes in and snags a candy bar every day during his afternoon walk. He does not tell Geeta, who would surely disapprove.

Geeta stays in her office all day now, and she brings her lunch in an insulated bag. There is always plenty of work, because there are fewer people around to do the work. On the rare occasions that she takes a break, it's to watch videos to learn Klingon. She passes along the directives from upper management (aka Starfleet Command) about the company deconstructing itself, when Wilson has to get involved. Some servers, and the people who run them, were sold to another company, either in Canada or India, on two weeks' notice. He had to go meet with the one person, Naomi, who was left from the server department, to come up with a new data storage plan.

"Essential Maintenance will handle it now, all on the single machine that didn't get sold," Naomi said.

"I thought Essential Maintenance just did building services," Wilson said.

"No, they handle everything now," Naomi said. "Mrs. Ekwosi from Essential Maintenance, she's on top of it."

The servers were in a big room in Building 100. Key-card entry, but a window on the door. Now when he makes his rounds of the building, Wilson peeks in to check on the lone computer in the middle of the raised floor. There's also an office chair with a broken arm, and a bucket, and nothing else. The lights are on full blast, so it's a brightly illuminated nothing else. The door is still locked and his badge doesn't open it.

Out in the halls are enormous cardboard bins full of keyboards, monitors, assorted cables, ancient floppy drives. When Wilson first started, the bins were for recycling, and would fill and then be emptied regularly. Then the H-CAPs, the layoffs, started. They're never called layoffs. They're called head count allocation procedures. H-CAPs for short. All kinds of things started piling up in the bins: old framed awards, Lucite paperweights and logoed mugs heralding this or that achievement, all the detritus that builds up on a desk during a career or half a career. Then the people who cleaned out the bins must've been laid off too, because now the bins overflow. Wilson picks through them, looking for new treasures. Once he found an unabridged dictionary, and hauled that back to his cubicle. Every day he opens it to a random page and tries to learn some new words.

> *LABEFACTION n. A weakening or loosening; a failing; decay; downfall; ruin.*

A few weeks ago, Wilson stopped to piss in Building 100. Just as he was washing his hands, a gaunt red-haired man in a Hawaiian shirt entered the bathroom. He had on a baseball cap with some kind of rainbow logo, and he carried a disposable razor and a can of shaving gel, and he looked vaguely familiar. Wilson and the man didn't speak or even grunt, they just exchanged nods. As Wilson was leaving the bathroom the man was carefully setting out his shaving supplies on the counter. Later Wilson realized that the man looked like Harry Dean Stanton's character in *Alien*.

At their desks, Wilson and Geeta keep stringing together the letters and numbers that do the work of the world. Every week, money shows up in their bank accounts. Every week, it seems, the building gets emptier, or there's another reorganization. Sometimes it's the most trivial thing: a design team somewhere has decided to change the branding from yellow triangles to red hexagons. Sometimes work is being outsourced to a temp agency, or to some other team in another country. Sometimes it's news that a whole division got sold off, or laid off, or just plain disappeared. None of this dampens Geeta's enthusiasm. Whatever the latest changes are, she remains convinced that they have the company headed in the right direction.

Geeta doesn't seem to notice that the metaphor they're working inside of might be the *Nostromo*, the spaceship from *Alien*, not the USS *Enterprise*.

She still runs a morning meeting, every day, nine a.m. sharp. Used to be the morning meetings were a dozen people, all gathered in one of the big conference rooms. Katja, the high-priority customer support person, was always late, always threw the Vulcan salute when she walked in, her way of apologizing to Geeta. Now it's just the two of them, and Geeta makes a big deal over how much shorter the meetings are. They're still booked on the schedule for a full hour, but after fifteen minutes or so there's nothing left to discuss, no more slide presentations to view. "I give you forty-five minutes back!" Geeta says, every single day. Every day Wilson thinks, I wish you really could give me all that time back.

Wilson has started parking in the visitor lot, even though it's verboten, to save a little time—it's a shorter walk to the main door, and the sidewalk from that lot is not as overgrown with poison ivy and Virginia creeper, and the evil geese don't congregate there. There are never actual visitors anymore, anyway. Only the employee of the month is supposed to park in the visitor lot. There's a metal sign on a pole marking the space, but the pole is now askew and some of the letters are gone from the sign. PLOY OF THE MONT, it says now. Geeta still parks in the main lot, of course. It stretches for acres but is mostly empty except for the pokeweed and small trees sprouting up through the cracks. A cardinal nests in a sweetgum tree near where she parks, and it spends all day fighting with its reflection in the side mirror of her diesel pickup truck. The truck is white, like the USS *Enterprise.*

Geeta jokes with Wilson about writing him up for parking in the visitors' lot, reporting the violation to Human Resources. Wilson responds in deadpan, "I thought I *was* employee of the month." It's another ritual. Every three months she has to do staff assessments, has to rank Wilson on a scale of one to seven, one being the best. She always gives him a two. There's always room for improvement in Geeta's world.

It gets darker in the building. Part of it is the weather, which has been gray of late. Part of it is the vines that have crept up to cover some of the windows. One day Wilson is making his rounds and he notices something he has not seen before—the large windows in the connector halls between buildings are hazy, covered in some kind of translucent slime. More lights are burning out, too, even though they should all be ecological long-life bulbs. The women's restroom nearest them is completely dark. Geeta leaves messages with Essential Maintenance, but in the meantime she brings a headlamp to work and straps it on before she goes to the restroom.

At the far end of the complex, in the main lobby in Building 100, there is a big museum-style display case, bigger than Wilson's cubicle. It contains replicas of the inventions of Leonardo da Vinci. Or rather, it contains models of things that look sort of like some da Vinci sketches. There's a protean version of a tank, round with a conical top, wooden. There's a marionette dangling from a pyramidal parachute. Some of the models—the tank and parachute, for instance—aren't life-size but others are. You could really ride the bicycle. You could really strap yourself into the ornithopter. The Plexiglas walls of the case have yellowed. Wilson remembers seeing a similar exhibit when he was a child. For all he knows, this could be the exact same set of models. He remembers himself as a kid, idolizing da Vinci the technologist. He remembers watching *Star Trek* as a kid. His plan at the time was to grow up and invent things. His favorite character on *Star Trek* was Scotty, the engineer. He has never told Geeta this. He doesn't have her encyclopedic knowledge of the show. It was just something he watched after school, when he was supposed to be doing his homework. He just remembers bits and pieces. She can quote the episodes by heart.

Wilson walked all the circuits and grids of the building, and while there were changes every day, eventually he knew all the landmarks. The rare unlocked supply cabinet on the second floor of building 102. Yellowed pages from the free weekly newspaper tacked up on the outside of the cubicle of someone who was clearly a hero of the local poetry scene. The broken stair in building 100 that sounded like an old man groaning when you stepped on it.

The one place he had not been was on the roof. Each of the buildings had one (and only one) stairwell that went up a half-flight past the third floor to a roof access door. There were official "AUTHORIZED ACCESS ONLY" signs on the doors, red and black and white. There were unofficial barriers, where someone had used duct tape and string to block off the stairs to the roof, as if that would stop anyone. Maybe the doors are open, Wilson thought. Maybe they're alarmed. Maybe there are hidden cameras, and watchful eyes somewhere halfway around the world would see.

One day when Geeta was off at a dentist appointment, he carefully stepped over one of the string barriers and walked up the stairs to the roof door. He tried the knob and it didn't turn at all, but when he pushed the door opened anyway. The frame and the lock didn't line up anymore; maybe it was because the building was settling.

He peeked around the door, saw only sky, so he walked out onto the roof. There was nothing as interesting as an old Leonardo da Vinci exhibit, or *Star Trek* memorabilia, or even a cabinet full of office supplies. There was gravel and tar and puddles of dirty rainwater growing algae, and lots of bird shit. There were some antennas and satellite dishes bolted to masts. One of them looked like an old TV antenna, like the one his parents had on their roof back when he used to watch *Star Trek* after school. There was nothing much else on the roof. He was up there, though, so he started walking his circuit. He walked to the big skylight dome over the main lobby, which was covered in a moldy residue. He found a clear space and peered down at the barren lobby from three and a half floors up. There was the da Vinci exhibit, rotting away in its Plexiglas cube. He imagined himself down there in the lobby, staring at the da Vinci case and then slowly looking up to see himself in the skylight.

"You're not supposed to be up here."

He stood and turned. It was Essential Maintenance, Mrs. Ekwosi. She was standing very close to the edge of the roof.

"I'm sorry," Wilson said. "The door was open."

"The door might've been open, but the sign clearly states that access to this area is for authorized personnel only, and you are not an authorized person, are you?"

"No, I am not authorized."

"Time to go back inside, then."

Wilson bowed his head and started walking back toward the access door. Mrs. Ekwosi from Essential Maintenance fell in behind.

"There are cameras, and they still work?"

174

"Don't worry about my knowledge," Mrs. Ekwosi said. Then she added: "I understand the appeal of the roof . . . you can see the graves from here."

She pointed, and sure enough, there was a clear view of the grassy hilltop and the Hopson cemetery.

"You know about the graves?" Wilson asked.

"I work in Essential Maintenance. I know about everything."

Mrs. Ekwosi stayed on the roof. Wilson re-entered the building and checked his fitness tracker: 9,251 steps. Back in building 104, Geeta had returned from her dentist appointment and had a new list of tasks for him.

Before getting back to work he went to use a stall in the bathroom, the one nearest their cubicles. Someone still came in and cleaned at night, restocked the toilet paper and soap and paper towels, but he never saw the cleaning staff, no matter how late he stayed. It was quiet as he sat there, just the hum of the air conditioning system, but then there was a sudden noise, like a big truck skidding on gravel combined with the roar of the ocean. It was coming from a drain in the floor between the two stalls. All his obsessive cataloguing, and he'd never really noticed that the bathrooms had floor drains.

He sat there trying to puzzle out what the noise was, if it was something to do with the water supply to the whole complex. He imagined an underground river surging through a giant tunnel beneath the building. Then there was another, more familiar sound. The fire alarm.

Wilson hustled to get out of the stall, and in the process bashed his left knee against the metal partition. "Shit!" At first it went numb, but once he was out on the stairs, it was like someone jammed an ice pick in there.

Geeta was very serious (with a smile) about fire drills. He took the stairs one at a time, the pain increasing every time his left foot hit. By the time he made it out of the building, it was all he could do to walk instead of crawl to get to Geeta, who was already standing on the cracked pavement behind the white line. She frowned with concern as he limped along, but she didn't budge from behind the line. It wasn't her way. However much she revered Spock, she was not actually much like him, nor overly logical. Spock would've gone to help Wilson the instant he saw him limping along. Geeta confused logic with her optimistic obsession for following rules, directives, policies. As if that would ensure success, or ensure anything at all.

They were the only ones in that part of the parking lot. Off in the distance to either side, he could see a few other workers shuffling around, waiting for the drill to end. He counted fourteen total, including himself and Geeta. Maybe there were more people around the other side of the complex. Maybe some people just stayed inside and ignored the drills now. Maybe not. The pain in his knee had peaked, and he was taking long, deep breaths to try to stay upright.

When the all-clear sounded, Geeta offered him her shoulder, and he did not refuse.

* All staff must exit building within two minutes of alarm signal.
* All staff must stand in parking lot or wooded area behind white line demarcating 200 feet from nearest building.
* Do not return to building until all-clear signal is sounded or until directed by Essential Maintenance personnel.
* Do not use elevators. Use stairs only.

Wilson worked the rest of the day with his left leg propped up on an overturned trash can. His knee swelled some. He put some ice in a plastic bag and kept it on his knee, which seemed to help. By the end of the day, it didn't hurt to walk, but he couldn't go up and down stairs. He realized that he would have to start using the elevators, at least until the knee healed up. He went to the one nearest their cubicles. It still worked, but had only one flickering light bulb. The walls of the elevator were chipped black enamel, and the carpeted floor smelled of mildew from years of coffee spills, from who knows what. When it moved there would occasionally be a shudder and a loud noise, like someone pounding on an I-beam with a sledgehammer.

Some day the elevator will stop working, he thought, probably with me in it. There was a little panel and behind it the phone that was supposed to call Essential Maintenance or security or elevator repair or whoever. He wondered if anyone was on the other end of that line, so he opened the little door and picked up the handset. Silence. He waited a few minutes, punching the buttons that opened and closed the elevator doors to pass the time. The doors worked just fine, but no one ever came on the line. He imagined the monster from *Alien* on the other end of the line, its jaws silently extruding another set of jaws instead of language.

The next morning Wilson came in, now equipped with a cane, and found a small box on his desk, with a note stuck to the top reading "Happy Anniversary!" The box was wrapped in old printouts, taped together haphazardly. He realized that it was April second.

Inside the box was a tiny replica of the USS *Enterprise*, on a chain.

"It's from the 'Catspaw' episode," Geeta said, lurching into his cube.

"Shit!" Wilson said. Geeta was forever jolting him out of his concentration, scaring the crap out of him. Shaving time off his life, probably, time that she couldn't give back to him.

"Thanks," Wilson said, "but which episode again?"

"'Catspaw,' with the witches and spells and curses, as if William Shakespeare and Edgar Allan Poe wrote an episode together."

He remembered it vaguely, something about the main characters being trapped in a dungeon. "There's a cat in it?"

"Yes, a black cat that grows to enormous size, thanks to a matter transmuter wielded by the alien adversaries." She growled and pawed at the air to demonstrate.

"Thanks, Geeta."

He hung the model from his desk lamp so that it dangled over his pencil cup and box of tissues. He imagined ivy curling up the sides of the ship as it hung there. He imagined the Hopson family living inside, making their mellow rye and sharing it with Scotty, ever the whiskey enthusiast. There was old Janadius in the captain's chair, cruising along at warp factor eight, racing the dark stranger. Wilson wondered if you could buy a little model of the commercial towing vessel *Nostromo*.

Later that day Geeta got word of an emergency power outage test, an EPOT, happening overnight, where the company shuts off the power remotely. She asked Wilson to spend the night to make sure the server came back online with no problems. "Essential Maintenance will be here, of course," Geeta said. "But I want to make sure everything goes smoothly." It's a global business. A power outage in the middle of the night there was a power outage in the middle of the day somewhere else. It might mean a 1 instead of a 2 on his next performance review. So he said yes instead of pushing Geeta to stay herself.

He had a toothbrush in his desk, and there were microwave burritos in the break room fridge. Geeta finally left at six, poking her head in his cubicle one last time, startling him again.

She left him a key to the server room door, and her headlamp. He was already clocked out, reading a copy of *Haints and History in Willow Fork* that he'd bought the week before.

"Essential Maintenance called," she said. "Mrs. Ekwosi has gone home but she will return later, after dark. Live long and prosper."

"Live long and prosper, Geeta," Wilson said.

Wilson read for a while, then he went to the break room to microwave a burrito. He flipped on the television to the local news. A storm was coming.

"Muggy rainy week ahead," the certified meteorologist said. "But first, let's check the Mega Doppler radar."

Wilson read some more, but it was putting him to sleep, so he got his spare winter coat from his cabinet, and the polyester blanket he kept there for when the air conditioning was overactive. He curled up under his desk and tried to sleep there, thinking he'd feel less exposed. The rain had started up outside, strong enough that he could hear it tapping on the windows. But even though he'd been fading out while reading, he couldn't drift off to sleep. He was just lying there, staring up at the bottom of his desk. He realized that if he wrote something on the bottom of the desk, left his mark in some way, no one would ever notice. At first he couldn't think of anything to write. Then he got up and plucked a permanent marker from the cup on his desk. He lay back down and scrawled NOSTROMO on the underside, going over the big block capitals again and again. The power was supposed to go out a little after midnight. To escape the reek of the permanent marker ink, he got up and went to the couch in the break room, where he managed to drift off to sleep.

And then was awakened some time after midnight. He'd forgotten to set an alarm, and the power was already out. There had been a crashing noise, although he wasn't quite sure if that was in his dream or if it had really happened. He listened for the rain, and he could hear it louder than ever. Too loud, really. He heard a siren in the distance. He realized that something was wrong with the building itself. He slipped his shoes on and tried to figure out where the rain sound was coming from. It was on the third floor, where he was. Near the windows that overlooked the courtyard.

It was too dark to see, but he knew the paths and made his way over there. As he got closer he saw a dark shape up ahead between the cubicles and the windows. For a moment he imagined that the dark shape was the monster from *Alien*, but it didn't move. He could feel the wind and the rain blowing in. He crept closer and realized that a tree had fallen and smashed through the window.

The shatterproof glass had given way. Now there was no difference between outside and in. The distant siren stopped and there was just the sound of rain and wind, mimicking the white noise that they pumped in the building during the day.

He would never be able to get back to sleep. For all he knew, Mrs. Ekwosi, Essential Maintenance, was somewhere in the building, looking for him, doing her work. He wondered what Geeta would do in this situation. His priority was monitoring the server when it powered back on, but he thought about repairing the window. At the very least, trying to find some tape and some garbage bags to patch the breach. He stood there, trying to figure out what to do. That was when he heard the knocking.

It was steady, three thumps and then a pause, over and over. Muffled and barely perceptible, he could tell it was coming from the entrance to Building 104. Not just the wind lashing at a tree.

Wilson remembered Geeta's headlamp, so he went back to his desk and got it, and continued on downstairs to the airlock doors of 104. Slowly, one at a time, because his knee still hurt. Outside the doors stood the man in the Hawaiian shirt, soaking wet. He was pounding on the glass. He was pounding with the side of his head, not with his fist. When he noticed Wilson, he stopped and slapped his ID badge up against the glass. "Hey, friend!" he shouted. "My badge isn't working. Reader's not powered up. You Wilson?" He mashed his face up against the glass too. Blood trickled down from his scalp. "Let me in, friend. It's Roy, from Accounting. There's been another reorganization!"

"I'm expecting someone from Essential Maintenance," Wilson shouted.

"Essential Maintenance? There's been another round of H-CAPs. That whole group got decommissioned. Replaced by Accounting. Sorry I'm late. Push that door open, buddy."

"There's an emergency power outage, and a tree fell into the building," Wilson said. "I was going to go home. I don't know when the power's coming back on. I don't really know what to do."

And because he didn't know what to do, Wilson let Roy from Accounting into the building, because Roy's badge didn't work, and that's what you do when people have badges that don't work. You let them in.

Roy walked in and stamped his feet a few times. "So, yeah, another reorganization," he said. "Turns out you report to me now!"

"Wait, what? What about Geeta?" Wilson said. "She and I are a team. We've been together for years. She was just here a few hours ago."

"She's moved on to other opportunities. Things happen fast in this business, y'know? Speaking of business, are you ready to get to work? I wouldn't want to have to write you up on my first day as your manager." Wilson nodded, the beam of the flashlight waving up and down on the sopping wet clothes that contained Roy from Accounting.

First Roy tried to dry off with paper towels from the bathroom, and then he said he was hungry, so they went to the snack shop and he got some candy bars.

"Shouldn't we get to the server room so we'll be ready?" Wilson asked.

"I was born ready. Besides, the power's still out, so I'm re-prioritizing our task list."

Roy from Accounting stuck his finger in his mouth, scrubbed out the last bit of gooey chocolate from some crevice, then licked the tip.

"You been all over this building, am I right?" Wilson nodded, the light bobbing again. "But you ain't never been in that case with the ornithopter and all of Leonardo's other fine contraptions, have you?"

And it was true. Wilson had never been inside the case that held the ornithopter.

"First time for everything," Roy said. "Come on."

"This man will never accomplish anything! He thinks of the end before the beginning."
— *Pope Leo X, describing Leonardo da Vinci*

Roy finally gets the lock open on the da Vinci box. One whole side of the clear rectangular cube opens up like a door. He starts pushing out the inventions onto the lobby floor, flickering in and out of the beam of Wilson's flashlight. The tank. The wooden bicycle. The crossbow. The parachute. The cannon. At the far end the ornithopter hangs from fishing line attached to the roof of the cube. Roy from Accounting yanks it down. It doesn't look light enough to fly, but it's light enough for him to carry. He drags it out and hands it to Wilson. It's unwieldy, but indeed, it is not very heavy.

The ornithopter is sort of like a backpack frame with giant bat wings attached. The bat wings were folded up some to fit in the display case, but out in the lobby they unfurl. There are leather straps to attach yourself to the ornithopter, and cords and pulleys for your flapping arms and pumping feet.

"You know an ornithopter cannot actually fly," Wilson says. "Especially not one built for a museum display. Also, we need to get up to the server room, to be ready when the power comes back on."

"Don't worry over your power outage. The ornithopter was Leonardo's finest invention. We are going to ride this ornithopter to freedom. I'll show you."

Lightning strikes close to the building, making Wilson jump and illuminating the lobby in a flash.

Wilson and Roy from Accounting climb the main staircase up to the top of the atrium.

"Slow down," Wilson says. "I've got a bum knee. "

The rain pounds on the glass skylight dome over the big main stairs.

Wilson and Roy from Accounting trudge to the roof access. The door still opens, same as it did before. Rain drenches them almost immediately, but Roy from Accounting is undaunted. Suddenly Wilson is very tired again. "Now, are you sure this thing can fly?"

"I ain't never flown before, to tell you the truth," Roy says. "But I'm feeling good about this. Leonardo, you know?" As if that is any kind of explanation.

Wilson helps Roy get into the mechanism. Roy is hyperventilating, breathing quickly and deeply as Wilson tightens the straps. Finally Roy is fully installed in the mechanism, and he tugs the cords tentatively to test the monstrous wings. He backs up from the edge of the roof to create a runway. He gives Wilson a thumbs-up, his little hand flashing in the beam of the light. Then he starts running. He dashes across the wet gravel, falling forward the whole way, and at the edge of the roof he takes a leap.

And he flies off into the air, the black bat wings flapping crazily. Wilson can feel his own heart pounding in his chest, in time with the rhythm of the wings. He tracks the ornithopter for a time as it skitters through the air, bright against the night even though Wilson's flashlight beam is useless at that range. Then Roy's gone, winked out, vaguely in the vicinity of the cemetery on the hill, but who knows really?

Wilson waits but Roy from Accounting does not return. He thinks about the tiny USS *Enterprise*, hanging from his desk lamp. If he held it in his hand or wore it around his neck and then ran off of the roof, would he fly up out of there, escape to somewhere else? If he slogged outside and up to the cemetery on the hill, would Roy be waiting there for him? Or was Roy never coming back?

Finally he goes back in the building. The lights are back on, but very dim. Evidently the power has returned, at least a bit. Mrs. Ekwosi is probably waiting on him. His knee aches from all the activity, so he decides to take the elevator down instead of the stairs. Maybe he can just leave and deal with all of this in the daylight. The elevator car arrives. He gets in and presses 1, and the elevator whisks him down the two floors, but when it stops the doors do not open. He tries the button to open the doors, but it does nothing. He waits, wondering if he should pick up the handset. He waits for a very long time. Then the lights go off completely, and the elevator lurches, and begins descending again.

Stronghold

He had worked late again. The roads were empty as
he steered the little Corvette to the townhouse. He had the top
down, with the heat on to cut the autumn chill. It was after dark
but his part of the city was well lit by streetlamps and by the
glow of track lighting shining out through expansive windows.
Above him, beyond the roofs of the buildings, the sky was clear.
A crescent moon and all those stars.

He idled the car in the street for a moment before he
pulled into his basement garage. On the previous Monday, a
building across the street had been demolished. He tried to picture what had been there. The block was an eclectic mix of styles
and of old and new buildings, his being the newest and the most
stylish. There was a chain-link fence up now that had not been
there before. The lot was not empty: about halfway back sat a
curved metal hut, like something he'd seen in a war movie. It
did not fit at all on the block, and was surely just a temporary
office for the construction company who would be putting a
new building there.

He left his briefcase in the car, to avoid the temptation
of looking over the Bradley account again. He left both car and
briefcase under the watchful eyes of the ram carved into the big

teak door of the townhouse. The ram wore a top hat, its horns coiling up through holes in the brim.

In the ground floor hallway he slid the dimmer switch and lights buzzed up, shining on the terrazzo floor and on the paintings studded on the walls. All of the paintings were abstracts. He liked abstract art; it soothed him even when it was frenetic. It reminded him of stars. Random, but if you looked long enough you could see patterns.

One panel wasn't a painting at all. It was the window into the swimming pool. Like many features of the house, it was more for the benefit of guests than for himself. With no lights beyond, it was simply a black mirror. He walked up to it, putting his hands on the glass and peering in. He briefly entertained the fantasy of something horrific looming up out of the darkness. A shark, or a submarine.

It was quiet. The only sounds in the house were made by the heels of his calfskin shoes clacking against the floor. He walked to the elevator at the far end of the hall and took it up one floor. The stairs did not get much use, except by Houseman.

It was Friday night, the beginning of the weekend, and the thought gave him a pang. He had dated every woman he knew.

He hit the bank of switches to light up the pool atrium that separated the front of the house from the rear. Three floors of empty space hung above the still water, all the way up to the skylight roof. He thought back to the last pool party. It was just after he'd broken it off with Margot. Someone had lost her top. That same someone had beaten him at chess, too, but he didn't remember her name. As parties go, it was a wash. Someone else had knocked over a bonsai planter. Arthur? Arvo? One of those two. He was always getting them confused. Short men.

He flipped another switch and the curtains whirred back to reveal the dining room and kitchen in the rear part of the house. Houseman had not set the table. He expected to see the good silver, the red linen napkins, the candelabra poised with new unlit tapers. He liked the red linens the best against the bright white Formica of the pedestal table. He continued on to the padded bar, dialing up the overhead lighting so that it gleamed off of the stainless steel countertop. This was his favorite part of the day, the first cocktail after work. Decision time. He wavered between a Busted Knuckle and a Gilded Butterfly, finally choosing the latter. Something to get the appetite going. From the bar fridge he plucked a frosted glass and the ingredients. He measured everything carefully into an ice-filled beaker. Then he stirred one hundred and eleven times before straining the concoction into the glass. That was his secret flourish, stirring one hundred and eleven times. Won, won, won. Win, win, win, his own little cheer for that first drink. Go, team. Cocktail glasses were only meant to be filled halfway, but he made himself a double this evening. He took the first beautiful sip and held the fluid in his mouth, circulating it across his tongue, back to front, side to side, the cocktail as lover. When he had extracted all possible flavor, he swallowed.

"This party needs some music," he said as he walked to the central control panel.

He punched in the code for his favorite Brubeck record, *Time Out*, and turned the volume up. The piano crept in, quavering lazily in all of the rooms of the house.

Drink in hand, he took the elevator up to his study. It was here that the first sign of violence invaded his after-work reverie. On the couch, just under the painting that was the first piece of art he ever bought, were a pair of panties. He set his drink on the coffee table, took a pen from his jacket pocket and probed the stray undergarment. Finally he lifted them aloft, noting that they were torn and that there was dried blood on them. They did not look like any panties he had seen recently. They did not look like any panties he had seen ever, and he had seen lots of panties. These were lime green. What kind of lunatic wore lime green underwear? And while they were clearly cut for a woman, they were styled like men's briefs, right down to the pointless fly. Even stranger, they were printed with the design of a monkey's face on the front and rear. They were also clearly not new. The fabric was detaching from the elastic waistband.

He wondered if this was Houseman's attempt at a joke. Houseman had dyed the pool water green for Saint Patrick's Day. He dumped the panties on the coffee table, to keep them from staining the upholstery.

In the office bathroom, he washed his hands. Then he dialed the music down and took the elevator up one more floor. Nothing looked amiss in the guest bedroom. The books were still neatly arranged alphabetically in the headboard shelf of the bed. He hadn't had a guest since Margot, and that was months ago. Summer. And Margot, when she wore panties, wore ones made of white silk.

The recognition hit him that if this were not a Houseman joke, someone had been in his stronghold. Someone might still be in his stronghold. He stalked over to the catwalk and peered down. Nothing but the water of the pool, the scent of chlorine rising on thermals, the sloshing of his cocktail a tiny echo. He checked all the balconies. He continued across to his bedroom, pushing the sliding glass door back slowly. Houseman had not restocked the fireplace logs. He thought about docking Houseman a day's pay, but decided against it. He walked around behind the teak wardrobe to check the master bathroom. He stopped on his way out to shed his blazer and tie and replace them with a maroon smoking jacket.

Someone hiding, it occurred to him, might not necessarily be an intruder. He had given away copies of the key to his apartment so many times. Perhaps Britt was back, wanting to have a bit of fun. She'd left the absurd panties out as a calling card, and was even now playing hide-and-seek. Perhaps she was wearing nothing but one of his shirts. Britt loved his shirts.

There was only one other place to check. He descended the spiral staircase into the living room, crouching low in an attempt to spot the intruder first. But there was no intruder. He walked over to the stereo control center and shut off the Brubeck. The heating system shut off too, the house having once again reached an optimal temperature. He was left with the sound of his own breathing. He walked to the chessboard to check on his current game with Houseman. Lately Houseman had been playing a Modern Defense, with black bishops lurking on either side of the board, ready to slide in on the frontal attack he was mounting as white. But Houseman hadn't made a move all week. Now, he found the pieces scattered in a pile on the board. He assumed this was Houseman's way of conceding the game, although Houseman had never done this before, and he didn't think the position had been that dire. He carefully set the pieces back up to start a new game.

He finished off the drink in two gulps and left the glass sitting on the bar. He flipped up the center panel to see if Houseman had restocked the liquor there. He had stayed up late the night before, mixing himself one Broken Javelin after another. On the work shelf next to the line of crystal glasses was a pile of what appeared to be elliptical chips of onyx. He picked one up to examine it; it was a false fingernail. Blood was dried on the back of it. He pushed the pile around and counted them, ten in all. He thought back, trying to remember a woman with long black fingernails. He knew this had nothing to do with Margot. She had natural fingernails that barely protruded beyond her fingertips. She painted them red; "Rarely Red" was the name of the polish color. With all of the women, the ones who spent a single night, or the ones who stayed for weeks, he examined their cosmetics kits with diagnostic fascination. He tried to think of a name for the color of these nails, which had clearly been torn off of the person who once wore them. "Inky Madness," he decided.

He had planned to spend an evening by the fire, unwinding with a good spy novel before getting to bed early. Work had taken its toll on him. During the day he had struggled to stay awake while he worked on the Bradley and Sherwood accounts. The storyboards had been worked and reworked, but the clients were not satisfied. He had been forced to break off his Friday lunch trysts with Secretary, and still he was toiling into the evening. He took joy in his work, but it was not the be-all and end-all of life.

He decided that a survey of the evening sky would be even more calming than a spy novel. He took the elevator up to his private deck on the roof of the townhouse. Everything was as he had left it: the director's chairs, the striped chaise lounge, the jerkberry plants in their elliptical planters, the powerful telescope sealed away in its cabinet. There was one additional thing on the deck, and that thing was the body of a woman.

She was nude except for a pair of boots, prone, with her feet closest to him. His first thought was, *from this angle she doesn't look familiar*. Neither the body nor the boots. He stooped to examine them. They most closely resembled combat boots, although they had large buckles as well as laces. "Your mother wears army boots," was a well-known insult, but a young woman actually wearing army boots was simply absurd. Even through the lens of his need, he found nothing arousing about her. Her skin was alarmingly white, no tan at all. He knew his history—pale skin had once been considered quite attractive. But the unhealthy pallor held no appeal. She was small, smaller than Houseman. If there was an adjective that fit all of the women he had dated, that adjective was "statuesque." Blonde, brunette, or redhead; green, blue, or brown eyes, they were all statuesque. The strangest thing about the corpse was her hair, which was almost as green as the panties he'd found earlier. Her face was turned to the side, as if she were looking over her shoulder about to ask him a question. Her arms were at her sides. He checked the fingers of her right hand, bending down and planting his hands on the warm tar so he could see without disturbing the body. Her fingertips were bloody in places where nails had been torn away.

He couldn't decide whether to turn her over. He had read enough detective novels to know that it was bad to touch a corpse. Tampering with evidence. He shifted up to look at her face, but her hair covered it. He crawled around the body, looking for clues. She had a triangular red birthmark on her left calf. The nails had been torn from her left hand, too. He peered carefully up into her crotch, but could see nothing there to indicate a source for the blood on the panties he'd found earlier.

What a shame, he thought. He took the elevator down to his office and called the police.

"I've discovered a dead body," he said, then gave his address.

"We'll be right over," the high-pitched voice on the other end said.

He went down and unlocked the front door, then went to the pool terrace and changed into his swim trunks, the turquoise ones with white piping. He swam lazy laps, first the backstroke and then the crawl, while he waited for the police to show up. When he saw shadows through the porthole window, he got out of the pool. He swaddled himself in his smoking jacket and went down to meet the police.

He could see their shadows as he descended the stairs. They had been peering into the porthole, but turned and genuflected when they heard him approach. He had only seen policemen work once before in real life, when he'd been in a car accident, but he had read about them hundreds of times. They knelt with their badges upraised in their left hands. He knew the procedure, and carefully read and memorized their badge numbers.

"Hello, 453 and 062," he said. He said "zero" and not "oh." Policemen appreciated a man with a sense of precision. "Proceed with your investigation."

"Thank you," they said, and rose and showed their faces. 453 was stuffed into his uniform like a sausage. Coarse black hairs curled up from the tight collar of his shirt, but his head was clean shaven. His skin was greyish-brown, the color of a boiled tongue. 062 had size 12 features on a size 6 head, his eyes, nose, and mouth crowding each other. He was shiny with sweat, even in the cool weather.

They stood there, neither moving, so he pointed down the hallway and said, "Let's take the elevator, shall we, gentlemen?"

They went straight to the roof.

Once there, 062 reached to a shiny black pouch on his belt and unbuttoned the flap. A police parrot flew out and lit on the ground next to the dead woman's face. It shook out its wings and hopped up and down. Then it flew up and sat on the woman's face. It wrapped its wings around her head. It held her head so tightly that it shook. This made her head shake, indeed her whole body quivered. He looked up at the policemen but they did not seem to notice this as out of the ordinary. 453 had walked over and was admiring the glossy green leaves of the jerkberry bush.

After a minute, the parrot hopped up off of the woman's head, preening itself as it marched down her spine. Then it flew over to 453, who bent and allowed it to land on his shoulder. He leaned in as the parrot whispered something. Then 453 straightened himself to his full height, the parrot teetering to stay balanced. He was looking forward to showing the policemen his chess set and his collection of nude paintings.

"He says someone in a red velvet jacket did it," 453 said, pointing his thumb at the parrot. "A jacket such as the one you are wearing."

"Well, that's absurd. I'm the only person who ever wears this jacket. And I certainly did not commit this murder."

"Parrots never lie," 062 said. The other men pursed their lips and nodded.

"Hey, boss?" 453 asked.

"Speak freely," he said.

Once again, 453 genuflected, as did the parrot on his shoulder.

"You are arrested," 453 said.

"Oh my," he said. "I've never been arrested before." At least he didn't have any plans for this evening.

"We know," 062 said, and he was not genuflecting. Perhaps 062 was the bad cop, 453 the good cop. Neither one of them was much to look at, certainly.

"You are under house arrest," 453 said. "So, please do not leave your house. Agreed?"

"Agreed," he said.

"There will be drastic repercussions if you do," 062 said.

"Oh, I understand completely," he said.

062 pulled apart the flaps on his belt pouch and whistled and the parrot flew back into it.

"Would you gentlemen like to see the rest of the house?" he asked.

They shook their heads.

"There's no time. We have police work to do."

"Do you mind if I watch?"

"Suit yourself," they said. But he grew bored quickly as they prowled around the body, taking notes and drawing diagrams. 453 found a cedar log wedged behind the jerkberry planter. It was the kind of log Houseman should have stocked the fireplace with. "Probably the murder weapon," 453 said.

Finally 062 pulled out a body bag from another one of his belt pouches and they rolled the body over onto it before zipping it up.

"You probably don't want to look at this, boss," 453 said.

He did look, but not at the other side of the woman's face, the ruined side. He looked at her body. Between her breasts there was a tattoo. It was a question mark.

He had the weekend off to think about things. After he called and left a message with his attorney's answering service, he took a long hot bath. He tried to continue reading the spy novel and once again fell asleep on the couch. When he woke up the next morning, the first thing he thought about was solving the mystery. He thought of the dictum that his favorite burly detective used when cracking cases: "Which of these things is not like the other?"

It was clear which thing was not like the other. The metal hut on his street was out of place, and merited investigation. But he could not legally leave his house. It pleased him to solve this part of the mystery rather easily. He went up to the roof deck and brought out his powerful telescope. He set up the tripod near the ledge closest to the skylight and angled the telescope down to point at the hut. He had mixed up a thermos of Ram's Horn Toddies to fortify him during his surveillance. The drink was his own invention, one he was quite proud of.

He was into the third drink when he noticed movement at the hut. Someone walked up to the door. He scrambled to get focused but it all happened too fast. What he thought he saw was a person walking into the front door of the hut with a garbage bag over their shoulder.

So, someone was home. He thought of his white chessmen lined up, ready to mount another frontal assault, and decided to break the terms of his arrest to go investigate. It was just across the street and two doors down, after all. He polished off the third toddy before descending to dress. He chose a gray suit, white shirt, black tie. Something that spoke of authority without being ostentatious.

Leaving his house, he imagined a flock of police parrots descending on him the instant he was visible in the street. They did not materialize. At the lot where the metal hut sat, there was a rusted chain holding the fence gate closed, but loosely. He got a rust stain on his sleeve when he crouched down and squeezed through under the chain. He walked up to the front door and knocked.

No answer, so after one hundred and eleven heartbeats, he knocked again. This time, the door opened just a crack. A dark, blank face looked him up and down, not speaking. Was it a man or a woman?

"I'm your neighbor," he said, half extending his hand and smiling.

"You a cop?" the face asked, lips barely moving. He decided that she was a woman.

"Look at me," he said, straightening to his full height. "Do I look like a policeman?"

"How should I know?"

"As you can see from my physique, my demeanor and wardrobe, I am not a policeman. I am a citizen of the world."

"What do you want, Mr. Citizen?"

"As I mentioned, I am your neighbor," he said, more slowly this time, gesturing back at the sleek prow of his townhouse. "I want to welcome you to our neighborhood. We don't get many new people on this street."

"Houseman works for you?"

He nodded. "How do you know—"

"The name's Max," she said. "Get in here."

The curiously named person opened the door and yanked on his sleeve to pull him in. He was shocked by this, and made a mental note to have Houseman send this suit to the cleaners as soon as possible.

Inside was an open space, about the size of a basketball court. He wrinkled his nose. It was cold. Mismatched furniture had been scattered sparsely around. The walls were covered in crude, spray-painted designs, clouds and stars. There was a blue kiddie pool full of water. Cans of beer floated in it. There were destroyed armchairs. Even if they'd been pristine, they were not his style at all: overstuffed, antique. Some paperbound books with their covers torn off were splayed on the floor. There were some things in the hut that did suit his tastes, and that was because these things were his. In a nest of bedclothes on the floor, he spotted his sheets with the blue and yellow diamond pattern. He'd had them specially constructed for his round bed. On an end table with a missing leg were some canned goods that could have come from his pantry: orange slices in syrup, cured ham, grapefruit juice, sardines.

"Yeah, some of this stuff might look familiar," Max said. She was rummaging through a green garbage bag, pulling out half a loaf of bread and a tinfoil-wrapped piece of meat. "But what's in this bag isn't yours. I just liberated it from the garbage cans behind that French palace looking place up the street. Haven't you people heard of recycling?"

"No, that doesn't ring a bell," he said. "I'd like to ask you some questions."

Max was small, like the corpse. He found her unsettling. She wasn't attractive, but she wasn't obviously lower class, like Houseman or the police or any other servitors. She wore black nail polish, and she had small breasts (but breasts nonetheless). She wore dungarees, sneakers, and a white T-shirt. Her head was covered with a scarf. Underneath the scarf, she had black hair in tight braids. He'd never seen hair like that before.

When he approached the table to examine the filched goods, something shambled out from behind one of the chairs.

It was a dog. He had seen pictures of them before, but never one in real life, walking on all fours with white teeth and shiny eyes. Like a tiny horse with fangs. He quickly grabbed Max and held her in front of himself for protection.

"Can you control that thing?" he asked, pointing with his chin. Max worked to prise his fingers from her shoulders. She was surprisingly strong.

"You haven't seen a dog before?" Max asked. "This place is even more fucked up than I thought."

"I've seen dogs. So, it's a tame dog?"

"Don't worry, Skippy here won't hurt you. He is hungry, though."

It looked like something that could do quite a lot of hurting if it wanted to. It also looked extremely untidy, dripping spit and scratching the floor with its talons. Not at all a civilized animal. She tore a hunk of meat off and set it on the floor for Skippy, who swallowed it without chewing, regurgitated the lump, and then went at it again. He tried to stay focused on his investigation, but it was difficult. After the dog finished the meat, it walked up to him and sniffed at his crotch. He stood as still as possible as the dog snuffled carefully before finally spinning and sitting down on one of his calfskin loafers. "Don't make any sudden movements," he remembered, another dictum from a detective novel he'd read once.

"Have you seen Kendra?" Max said. "She left yesterday morning with your ugly friend Houseman and hasn't come back since."

"What's a 'Kendra'?"

"White girl, green hair? Hard to miss."

"Kendra is what I came here to talk to you about."

"Well?"

He told her about finding the body. She slumped down into one of the chairs as he did this. The dog went over and she stroked its back while staring off into the distance. He continued the story, starting in about the police parrot's investigation.

"Shut the fuck up, OK?" she said.

He had no idea how to respond to this.

After a minute, he said: "They think I killed her."

"She was already dead back there," Max said, pointing to the back door of the hut. "Just a matter of time. She'd made some bad choices."

The back door was a small metal door barred with a length of iron. He imagined that it opened onto a service alley.

She looked back at him. "I know what it's like to be falsely accused."

"Is that why you're here?" he asked.

"Yeah, you could say that. If you're asking me how did I get here, then the answer is fuck if I know. But as it stands, I'm making the best of a bad situation," she said. "Slumming."

"Where did you come from?" he asked.

"See for yourself, golden boy," Max said, pointing at the back door.

"Can I ask you something?" he said.

"Shoot," she said.

"What's the name of the nail polish color you're wearing?"

"I think it's called 'Inquisitive.' Any other questions?"

"Yes," he said. "Kendra had a tattoo on her chest. A question mark. I've only read of sailors being tattooed—"

"Listen, I need to think. Alone. If you want to go home, go home. If you want to keep going on your private investigation to crack the case, find your ugly friend, and visit the land of the tattooed ladies, feel free," she said, gesturing toward the back door.

He walked over, picked the iron rod up out of the brackets, and leaned it against the wall.

He opened the door and a blast of warm air enveloped him. He stepped through. The door closed behind him.

He was standing on a city street. The air smelled bad, like gasoline mixed with rotten eggs. There were many people about, all of them smaller than he. Giant motor vehicles whirred down the street, packed with people inside. Everything was grimy, and litter swirled about as the vehicles passed. He spun around— the door was still there. But as he spun, he noticed something. A sign across the street said "BAR." He was thirsty, and there might be interesting women in this bar. After all, he needed a date. So he waited for the flood of the giant vehicles to subside, then he walked across the street, straightening his tie as he went.

On a telephone pole outside the bar, a scrap of paper flapped in the dirty breeze. "MISSING?" the flyer said. There was a photograph and a number. In the photograph, Max and the other woman, Kendra, sat together on a couch.

The inside of the bar did not smell much better than the street. It was dark and deserted, though. He chose a stool near the back. The bartender was another one of the small pale people. He did not have a white shirt or sleeve garters or a sleek black vest as any proper bartender would. He had a shaven head, and had been in some sort of accident that gave him huge earlobes. You could stick a cigar through the holes. The bartender was doing a crossword puzzle.

"A Lemony Chimney, please," he said. "On the rocks."

"Yeah, I don't know how to make that," the bartender replied, not even acknowledging his personhood.

"It does require exotic ingredients, doesn't it. Something more mundane . . . a Supine Tingler?"

"Nope. No can do."

"Golden Frosted Inseminator?"

The bartender sighed.

"No, I do not know how to make that either."

"Of course you don't; there's no such thing. I was merely testing you. What kind of bar is this?"

"This is the kind of bar that serves beers and shots of whiskey, highballs and the occasional martini. Do any of those pique your interest?"

"What's a 'martini'?"

"You don't know what a martini is, chief?"

"No. Enlighten me!" He was always interested in learning how to make a new drink, and was gladdened that the bartender had used something resembling a proper epithet when addressing him. The bartender showed him the process. It seemed a bit too simple, not enough ingredients to manufacture a truly interesting drink. But the bartender used a little measuring glass, and that precision made him happy. The garnish was a spiral of lemon peel. The bartender slid the cocktail glass across the bar toward him. He picked it up by the stem—always by the stem—and took the first sip.

It was the drink he'd been waiting for all of his life.

"You can use an olive instead of the peel," the bartender said, but he barely heard this as he swallowed and then leaned into the drink to savor the aroma. It was like a brilliant razor of joy slicing through his skull, bringing comfort and clarity at the same time.

Behind the glistering array of bottles there was a dusty mirror. He examined himself as best he could between sips. His hair was mussed, and the knot in his tie had loosened. As he neared the bottom of the drink, it struck him that he was doing nothing to solve the mystery he'd set out to. He had a new mission. He needed to rescue this miraculous beverage from this filthy, noisy world.

"I'd like to buy those ingredients," he said to the bartender.

"What?"

"I would like to purchase the liquors you used in this concoction," he said, raising his glass and then downing the dregs. "Will you take a check?"

"No. Besides, there's a liquor store just a couple blocks from here."

This was not a response he was used to hearing.

"All right, then," he said. "How about another?"

The bartender carefully made another drink. This time, when the man pushed it across the bar, he picked it up and threw it in the bartender's face. A waste of a magnificent beverage, but there was nothing else to do. He reached behind the bar, grabbed the two bottles, and ran.

Into the street, across the sidewalk, to the door. The dog, Skippy, was sniffing around outside the door. He opened it and ran inside, Skippy close behind him. Max was in there. Also, Houseman was there, and he was holding the iron bar.

It had been so long since he'd actually seen Houseman. Weeks. And it had been months since he had seen Houseman without his veil. Houseman still had on his khaki uniform but the veil had been torn away. He could barely stand to look at that monstrous chin, at the little slit mouth and beady eyes.

"Put that down!" he said.

"No," Houseman said, backing up and turning to face off against him and the dog.

First Max, then the bartender, and now Houseman, all of them so contrary that it was wearying. It had been a long day, and he had martinis to make.

"You're fired," he said, and that was puzzling enough to Houseman to make him drop his guard. Max ran up from behind and locked her forearm around his throat. Skippy dove in and caught Houseman's ankle in his mouth. Houseman lashed out with the iron bar, but he only swiped air around Max's head.

"Little help here!" Max said, but he still held the precious liquor bottles. He set them down carefully on the floor and then scampered over. Houseman, still in Max's grip, switched to slashing away at him with the iron bar.

"Why did you do it?" he asked, dancing out of range. Specifically he was thinking of the cha-cha, a very quick cha-cha.

"Beautiful . . . and terrible," was all that Houseman managed to get out, before saliva foamed up through his clenched teeth. He dropped the iron bar and a few seconds later went limp. Skippy worried at Houseman's ankle until Max shooed the dog off.

"Hurry," Max said, as she let his unconscious body fall to the floor.

Together they worked to tear the sheets into strips which they used to tie up Houseman.

"That was quite an impressive display," he said.

"Tell that to Kendra," she said.

Back at the townhouse, he called the police to announce that he had solved the crime. He did not mention Max or the doorway. 062 and 453 came by and picked up Houseman, whose guilt made perfect sense to them. He was insane, after all, raving about oppression and a door into another world. After they left he thought about phoning in a request for another Houseman, but that decision could wait for another day.

Max stayed in the guest room. Skippy stayed down by the pool. Every day after he got home from work they drank martinis on the roof, and she told him stories. After a few days, the martini ingredients ran dry, but the stories did not. He tried to reconstruct the drink, combining ingredients from his capacious bar, but he could never duplicate its complex simplicity, its simple complexity. They also played chess. She beat him, most times, and taught him about the importance of pawn structure. Even though he grew to see her as attractive, their relationship did not progress into romance. After a month, she and the dog left. She took the black queen from the chess set with her.

He continued drinking on the roof, where he could lean back and look at the stars. He thought of trying to follow Max, into a world that was bigger than he'd imagined, a world that had gin and vermouth but no police parrots. But he never did. After another month, construction crews demolished the metal hut and began working on another townhouse. It was stylish, but not as stylish as his.

Delta Function

Gray had been so many places. They'd sent him to Oak Park, Deer Park, Menlo Park, Echo Park. Bangor, Miami, Seattle, San Diego. The technology had evolved over the years, digital recording replacing magnetic tape. Email and text messages replacing phone calls and faxes and beepers. He had clipped lavalier microphones on Oliver North, Judy Chicago, Karl Lagerfeld, Janet Reno. He had held boom mikes over the heads of winners and losers, anonymous victims and celebrity predators, the fortunate and the doomed. He had set levels on the voices of actors in convenience store commercials, corporate training videos, low-budget horror flicks, and independent feature films. He worked long days, straight time fading into time-and-a-half into double time. Golden time.

On a few rare occasions they'd sent him out of the country. He turned down most of the wars or catastrophes. Still, he had been to Iceland, Ireland, and Italy, all travel paid for by this or that broadcasting corporation. All expenses deducted from his extremely complicated taxes. He had been so many places, so finally after all that time working in video and film they sent him to the town of Poston. Where, thirty years before, he'd graduated from Poston State College.

Gray was staying in a Quality Inn near a new plaza of big box stores. It had probably been a farm outside of town when he'd been a student there. Driving in on the interstate, nothing had seemed familiar. Glass box office buildings, hotels and condos, a new sports arena. He found an organic grocery store and stocked up on almonds, sardines, beef jerky, and coconut water. Many of the people he worked with, both above and below him in the pecking order, had eaten craft services food for too long, and it showed. He had gone bald years earlier, but he was in much better shape in his early fifties than he'd been as an undergrad. Days at home were usually days off and days off were spent in the gym or at the pool. Work hard, play hard, that was one of Gray's mottos.

The job in Poston was an outsider artist who had toiled in relative obscurity all his life, on a farm just outside the city limits. The farmer/artist, Mack Walters, welded gigantic sculptures out of scrap metal and old farm equipment, looming stick figure people that he planted in a fallow pasture on his farm. Gray recalled hearing about the crazed welding farmer when he had been in college in Poston, but he'd never been out to the farm. It was a wonderland, and now it was news because the Hirshhorn was buying Mack's biggest piece to add to their sculpture garden on the Mall in DC. Mack, who had been getting by as a well-kept secret among art brut cognoscenti, was suddenly a superstar in overalls. For Gray, the job was a piece of cake. No tricky setups, no diva talent to cope with. Short hours, so no overtime, but the day rate that the networks paid was already high, even in these lean times. He built in extra days on the road on all of his jobs—in the years since the divorce, poking around roadside kitsch in America had become one of his hobbies. In Poston he was going to have plenty of time to see how well the town had aged.

It was a bigger town, sprawling further out into the county now. The Poston of his college years seemed to be gone. There were no old school friends to look up, because the friends that mattered had all left too. The ones that mattered were Kitty, Robert, Hilda, and Jerf. The other members of the band Delta Function. Kitty and Robert, bass and lead guitar, they had got married and drifted away and he hadn't heard from them in decades. Last time he googled them, on a whim, they were running a goat farm in the mountains of West Virginia. He exchanged email with Jerf, the drummer, every six months or so. Jerf was in Chicago, and exhorted Gray to visit anytime he was in town. Most of Jerf's messages involved a lot of talk about being sober, and faking it until making it, and doing things one day at a time, and being thankful and mindful. Hilda had found Gray on Facebook and friended him, but they didn't communicate there very often. As best he knew, Hilda had made a fortune in the computer business in the eighties and nineties and lived in semi-retirement in Hawaii, just doing the occasional tech consulting gig. Her Facebook presence consisted of news about her two teenage daughters, and photos of them. No photos of Hilda at all. In a sense he'd swapped places with Hilda—in Delta Function she had operated a computer synthesizer of her own design, a giant rig of patch cords and knobs, playing it from her post at the sound board. She wanted to be in the band but she did not want to be on stage. Working behind the scenes, as he now worked.

After a day of Mack talking in a high-pitched drawl about "my big people I make," and the curator from the Hirshhorn talking about "reveling in an innately enigmatic personal vision," Gray went back to the hotel, worked out in their fitness center, and showered. Then he drove over to the campus strip and parked. He assumed there'd be at least one restaurant or bar there that had stayed in business over the years, a place to get dinner and a glass of wine. But there wasn't. He parked at one end of the strip in a bank parking lot. Even the bank had changed—once the local bank where he kept his perpetually empty checking account, now it was Bank of America. A row of boardinghouses still stood, but they'd been taken over and refurbished into faculty offices by the college, which was now a university. Poston State University, the Fighting Angels. He made the Fighting Angels sign, upraised index finger tracing a halo in the air. It was the same sign folks made on the job to mean "faster!" or "let's wrap this up." Past the houses should've been the bowling alley, then the movie theater, and then a cluster of bars, restaurants, head shops, record shops, and bookstores. They were all gone or transformed. He walked along and catalogued their fates. The bowling alley was now an Apple Store. The restaurants were now national chains instead of a dairy bar, a diner, and a vegetarian hippie place. The bars had moved elsewhere, and besides the drinking age was 21 now, had been for years, not 18 as when he'd been in college.

The place he was most interested in finding, The Outpost, had been obliterated. It took him a minute to realize that the two-story brick building he was looking for was now a parking lot. The Outpost was where he and the band had played most of their shows. They played plenty of other places . . . frat houses, outdoor benefits, a couple of out-of-town gigs, the student union on campus. But The Outpost was their home. He walked around the parking lot, looking for a trace of it—the foundation, anything. The newsstand next door was now an upscale dining place, global fusion street food, whatever that was. He didn't want to give them any money. Still hungry, he walked up to the light and crossed the street over into campus.

At least on campus, some of the buildings were the same. The door of the English building was locked. He kept walking. There seemed to be a new cafeteria where the math building once stood; it was closed. He was starting to feel a little dizzy; he was prone to low blood sugar. But he kept going. He went to his old dorm, one of the oldest buildings on campus. The door was locked there, too. He looked up at the window to what had been his room. A woman appeared there, a girl, who stared back at him for a moment before pulling down the shade.

He kept walking, still pretty much in a straight line, and that took him to the old student union. It was still there, still a hulking white brick building. The doors were open, so he went inside.

The first familiar thing he spotted was the Warhol. The union was home to most of the college's art collection, including a Warhol Campbell's soup can silkscreened on a shopping bag. It was in a Lucite box on a pillar on the first floor. The old information desk, a curving piece of mahogany, was still staffed by undergrad volunteers, although now they stared at phones and laptops with looks of boredom instead of thumbing through magazines and newspapers with looks of boredom. The study lounge tucked away underneath the grand staircase to the second floor was now something called the Student Operations Resource Center, but the lights were off and a metal grate was pulled down over the door, so these operations would remain a mystery to Gray. The floors were still blue-and-white terrazzo, the school colors. The globe-shaped light fixtures had not been updated, although he could tell they were now populated with CFLs instead of incandescents. There was a brand-new drink machine selling energy drinks and bottled water, and next to it three recycling bins. All of this space had been free-form for hanging out or studying or napping; now it was much more well defined. There were three iMacs set up as information terminals, a Fighting Angels branded Google page beaming out from each. Where the "need a ride" board used to be bolted to the wall was a flatscreen TV, tuned to CNN. Beyond the information desk he could see that the snack bar was still open. For Gray, the most jarring feature that survived in this landscape was the bank of pay phones next to the restrooms.

He walked up the steps to the second floor—on the landing stood the eternal sentinels, the American flag and the state flag. At the top of the grand staircase the space expanded into the atrium of the theater, three stories high. Overhead, the knockoff Calder mobile, a collaboration between the art and engineering departments, still spun lazily. The box office was closed. The minimalist sculpture was still there, three panels of black steel. He wondered what Mack Walters would think of the sculpture. Back in 1979, Jerf had written "ART?" on it in white paint marker. The actual title, on a little bronze plaque set into the marble base, was "HELL/LUST/ACID." The sculpture, and its enigmatic title, had outlived Jerf's commentary. The vandalism had always pissed Gray off, anyway. He was no aficionado of modern sculpture, but he knew a Philistine when he saw one in action. Jerf could keep time behind the drum kit, and he liked all the right bands, but beyond that his conversational skills had always been limited to how cheap the beer was, how easy (or not) any given woman was, and the extent to which this or that thing sucked.

Gray looked up past the mobile and spotted security cameras mounted in the corners of the ceiling. Any would-be Jerfs of the present would be caught on video if they tried to tag their graffiti onto HELL/LUST/ACID.

There was one lone student camped out on one of the couches, lying there with a laptop on his stomach, typing in furious blasts. The student glanced over at Gray, looking through him for a moment, before turning his attention back to the little computer. Gray walked to the far set of doors that led into the theater. Like so many doors on this campus, it was locked.

By this point he was extremely hungry, and feeling a bit dizzy. He thought he'd go down and grab whatever marginally healthy something he could find at the snack bar. A bag of cashews, maybe. It was then that he remembered the steak place.

That was its name, The Steak Place. Run by the college dining service, with students as waiters, serving beers in frosty mugs and steaks on sizzling iron skillets. Except of course you couldn't serve beer at college anymore. And he figured the tastes of most students ran to sushi or samosas now instead of steaks. But surely The Steak Place had evolved with everything else—maybe it was a sushi bar or a global cafe now.

He walked down the main stairs to the first floor, then over to the little side stairwell that led to the basement. The terrazzo was slick here—he did not see any housekeepers, but a mop and rolling yellow bucket sat on the landing. The terrazzo was so slick, in fact, that just before he made it down the last set of stairs, he slipped sideways and pitched forward, falling and banging his knee and then the side of his head at the very bottom.

He lay on the floor for a few minutes, breathing in the piney smell of the cleaner. Slowly he rolled up so that he was sitting on the steps. Nothing felt broken or sprained, so he experimented with standing up. He walked slowly through the stairwell door and around to the doors of the old restaurant.

He pulled open one of the big swinging doors. Whatever The Steak Place was now, it was dark and smelly on the inside. It took a second for his eyes to adjust. His legs felt weak and he decided that he needed to sit down as quickly as possible. He went to the nearest empty booth and slumped down onto the blue vinyl, resting his elbows on his knees.

He looked over at the menu sitting on the sturdy oak table. On the front, embossed in gold, it read "The Steak Place."

"Some things never change," he mumbled to himself, dabbing at his temple tentatively to see if he was bleeding. He was not bleeding, and so he sat up and looked around the room.

It was still The Steak Place, just as he'd remembered it. Probably some kind of retro night, as the students were all dressed up in ski vests and jean jackets, sporting mustaches and long hair.

"May I get you a beer, sir?" the waiter asked, setting a glass of ice water on the table. He was sporting the ridiculous hair as well, although his garb was the timeless garb of the waiter. White shirt, black bow tie, black pants, black apron.

"Sure, how about a Sierra Nevada?"

"I'm afraid we don't have that brand, sir. We have Schlitz, Old Milwaukee, and Michelob. Michelob is a dime extra."

"I'll have the Michelob," Gray said. He touched his temple again—the pain was starting to kick in, but he still couldn't feel any swelling. As the waiter walked off toward the kitchen, Gray plucked an ice cube from the water glass and held it against the side of his head.

Something was wrong with the room, and that something was this: the students who were dressed up in their retro gear were also drinking beer. And smoking cigarettes. And on the tiny television he could see at the end of the bar on the other side of the room, a staticky picture of Jimmy Carter jumped and crackled in glorious analog black-and-white. It was middle-aged Jimmy Carter the President, not old Jimmy Carter the charity homebuilder. Gray had walked into 1979.

Instinctively he reached for his cell phone. Time to text one of the couple hundred friends he had on Facebook. He pulled it out, but there was no signal. No bars. The camera still worked so he casually held it out and snapped a few photos, panning it around the room. Fending off the realities of 1979, mediating them with his pocket computer. Then he turned in his seat and took a photo of himself, with the room as backdrop, before stashing the phone as the waiter returned.

I am lying at the bottom of the steps in the stairwell, Gray thought. In a moment, I'll come to. Until then, I'd better play it cool. Gray was good at playing it cool. All those famous people he had clipped microphones on, around them he was laid-back, friendly, professional. Never in awe, never bedazzled.

It was a moment later, as the waiter was setting the frosty mug and the curvy brown bottle of Michelob down on the table, that Gray realized he had no way to pay for it. He didn't carry paper money, and besides, most of the paper money had been redesigned. He was strictly a debit and credit card guy. It drove his coworkers crazy, how he'd buy a buck-fifty cup of coffee with a credit card. Everything on the menu, which had a handprinted insert with the specials, dated "April 20th, 1979," was cheap. He was pretty sure that The Steak Place didn't take charge cards. And he was pretty unsure as to how quickly his banged-up knee would carry him out of The Steak Place if he dined and dashed. Besides, if he dashed out the door, what would be there? 2009 or 1979? How far did he have to run to get back to where he'd come from?

He decided to split the difference. He was still starving. He ordered some tomato soup and a salad. It arrived quickly, the soup probably from some giant industrial can, the big brother of the can printed on Warhol's shopping bag. The salad was a wedge of iceberg lettuce glopped with Thousand Island dressing. He tucked in and resumed watching the crowd, looking for familiar faces.

He didn't expect to spot anyone he knew, though. The Steak Place was not much of a hangout for his friends and acquaintances. Maybe if he'd blundered into some past version of the record store, or The Outpost. Here it was big guys in sweatpants and rugby shirts and guys with mustaches in fraternity shirts and caps. Women in fuzzy sweaters with carefully feathered hair. Delta Function had played The Steak Place, but it was like playing a sorority party. You did it because it was a job. And in 1979 in Poston, getting paid to play mostly original songs was not particularly easy. The New Soul Seekers, five middle-aged white guys, they got a lot of work, because they played covers.

As he finished up the salad and soup he thought he spotted Aqualung. He never knew Aqualung's real name. The guy was in his Economics 201 class, and had interesting tastes in music. King Crimson, weird prog bands from Sweden, German art rock. Named Aqualung, Lung for short, because he looked just like the cover of that Jethro Tull record: big hairy bearded dude in a trenchcoat. Before Gray could think about it he was up and headed across the room, further into the stench of cigarette smoke. His knee still ached from the tumble down the stairs. What was he going to say? "Hey, Lung, I fell down the stairs from the future! What's up?" It didn't matter, because before he made it all the way there, the guy in the trenchcoat turned. He was clean-shaven, and way too skinny to be Lung. Just some weirdo, probably another time traveler. Gray took a quick left toward the restrooms. On the blue cinderblock wall between the doors labeled "Angels" and "Devils" there was a bulletin board awash in flyers and posters. Summer jobs, roommates wanted, hi-fi equipment for sale. Smoker parties, keg parties, Purple Jesus parties, Green God Damn parties, toga parties. Flyers for bands. In fact, a flyer for the Delta Function. They were going to play The Steak Place. The show was April 21. The next night.

He went back to the table and finished his salad and soup. He was beginning to feel less jittery; his blood sugar was leveling off. The waiter stopped by to take his steak order. The waiter seemed exceptionally attentive. Gray realized that the waiter's natural indifference toward the older people— mostly faculty—who dropped in to The Steak Place had been defeated by some uncanny twenty-first century something about Gray.

"What's your name?" Gray asked.

"Boyd, sir."

"Boyd, here's the thing. I don't want a steak, because I can't pay you. Can't pay you for a steak, can't pay for the beer and soup and salad. I have, uh, left my cash in another place. But I promise you, Boyd, on my honor as a Fighting Angel," and here he made the halo sign, "if I come back tomorrow night with money, will you let it slide?"

Boyd did not hesitate.

"Certainly, sir. We'll put it on your tab. Would you like another beer?"

"No thank you, Boyd. You're a stand-up guy."

"Thank you, sir. See you tomorrow night."

Gray stood up, shook Boyd's hand, and walked out of The Steak Place. He kept walking. Campus was dark and quiet. At first he thought he'd walked into yet another world, this one empty. But as he approached the library, two students crossed the path in front of him, both staring at their cellphones. He had made it back.

The next day when he woke up in the Quality Inn, his head felt fine. Not a bump, not a scratch there or on his leg. If he had been hurt, he'd left that back in 1979.

He emailed the photo he'd taken of himself in The Steak Place to Jerf with the subject line "No Comment." Jerf responded in two minutes: "Nice Photoshop work. Why did you go to the trouble, though? The past is a burden, and by dwelling on the past we only increase the weight of that burden, Gray. Learn to let go! BE HERE NOW. Love (but not in THAT way), Jerf." Gray didn't bother to respond. He had let go so many years before, without even realizing it.

He went to the ATM and got out some twenties, then went to the front desk and asked for change in one dollar bills. Some of the bills were still crisp, so he asked for older ones. The man behind the counter obliged. They were still relatively new, but they were one dollar bills. The one dollar bill hadn't been redesigned.

There was one more day of work, mopping up the B-roll shots around town. Interviewing local collectors who had been hip to Mack Walters before his overnight success in the art world. Gray rode in the cab of a big white Dodge pickup driven by a 22-year-old production intern who kept calling him "bud" and "chief." Gray usually worked with three different types of people. Quiet professionals, which is what he tried to be. Colorful characters, like Dastardly Dobey Diggs, the crazy redneck cameraman. The colorful characters all had nicknames. Square Deal. Double Stuff. Bastard Amber. Dastardly Dobey would celebrate the end of a particularly hard job with stuntman shots, where you snort the salt, drink the tequila, and then squeeze the lime in your eye. Gray did it once, just to prove he would. Dobey was always cutting up, but he never complained on the job, and he never missed a shot. Work hard, play hard, he was with the program. The third type was the garden-variety asshole, which is what this kid was. Some local trying to get started in the business. Probably got the gig just because he had a truck.

Gray tried to let it slide, tried to avoid saying at any point "I'm more than twice your age, if you call me 'bud' or 'chief' again I'll strangle you with a mike cable." He tried to avoid thinking about age too much, although he was not always successful. Back home he ran with a crowd of folks of all ages, but with only a couple of exceptions, they were all younger than him. They went to art openings, they hung out at the pool, they ate low-carb food, they even went to see bands together on occasion. But they didn't talk about Gray being in a band all those years ago, because Gray never talked about it. Every now and then Jerf would put an old photo up on Facebook, and they'd ask when he was going to digitize that box of cassettes he had (the only preserved output of Delta Function) and then the idea would fade, scrolling back with all the other photos and status updates and likes and dislikes. As for the cassettes, they'd gotten soaked when his storage space flooded. He was pretty sure they were unplayable now. He hadn't mentioned this to anyone.

The kid driving the truck had yet to grow out of his punk rock uniform. Misfits T-shirt, ripped jeans, black Chucks. His hair had probably been bright green at one point, but now it was just the color of weak tea, with brown growing in at the roots. Gray was reminded of Errol, one of about six punks who came to Delta Function shows. Probably the entirety of the punk scene in Poston at the time. Delta Function were not smooth nor were they slow, but they were smoother and slower than the Dead Boys or the Germs. The local punks didn't have much choice. Errol would valiantly pogo when they did "Rat Patrol," one of their faster numbers. The other punks would nod vague approval when they played songs like "Badge of Hell," where the lyrics were nihilistic even if the music itself sounded like the Knack, if the Knack had incorporated the burps and farts of Hilda's homemade synthesizer.

I am living the dream, Gray thought. "Living the dream," that was another mantra. He used it any time he hit a rough patch of work. A long day, a particularly assholish producer or co-worker. He repeated his mantra silently and thought of all of his friends who were working in beige cubicles in overly air-conditioned buildings, doing the same thing every day. Or his friends like Jerf, who seemed not to be working much at all. He had money, a nice condo downtown, dependable friends who were always there when he got back into town, ready for the swimming pool or the sushi bar. He had the occasional date, which was just fine with him given that crazy time after the divorce. If there was something he wanted, he couldn't define it. Couldn't conjure up an image of it. He was as happy as he was going to get.

Riding in the white pickup, it had air conditioning that worked and seats that were comfortable, and the kid had said: "Dock your iPhone and play some tunes if you want, chief." It was not like riding around in Jerf's 1977 Chevy Suburban, aka the Deltamobile. That vehicle was a hand-me-down from Jerf's parents. The Deltamobile was puke green, at least the parts that had not yet rusted. But it could hold five people and all their musical equipment with ease. The few shows they played out of town, they were lucky to make enough gas money for the thing.

Gray pulled his iPhone out, but just as he was plugging it up to the kid's car radio, it buzzed. It was Sandy, the producer, so he answered the call.

"Mack Walters just died," she said. "Just keeled over while he was eating lunch. We need you out at his farm."

"Why? What's the rush?"

"Have you heard of a little thing called the news? Acclaim arrives too late for local artist, et cetera. Get out here and start documenting the teary aftermath."

"Got it," Gray said, and then he hung up.

He told the kid to drive out to the Walters place. He also told the kid to drop him off at the university first. Sandy would be pissed, but he'd be back on the job the next day, and she'd get over it.

The sun was setting as he walked across campus. At first he was sauntering along, but then he started walking faster, and finally broke into a jog. He couldn't wait to find out if 1979 was still just around the corner. But as he ran up to the student union, he noticed a group of campus cops, three of them, standing around a man seated on a bench just outside the doors to the building. He slowed to a brisk walk, keeping his eyes on the police officers. The man on the bench was big, wearing a tattered gray sweatsuit, his skin burned to a shiny red by the sun, his beard and hair long. An overstuffed black garbage bag sat next to him. He was looking up at the policemen, pleadingly, but what he was saying was "Fallen angel! One more red nightmare!" over and over. Clearly the cops were puzzled by what to do about this.

Gray was sure it was Lung. He hesitated for a moment, thought about walking over and trying to defuse the situation. He wondered what path Lung had taken to get from Economics 201 to this bench. It didn't look like Lung was in any shape to relate his life story. Gray kept walking. One of the cops, a tall woman with a weak chin, glanced over at him. Gray smiled, indicating that he was nowhere near as much of a threat as the philosophical gentleman seated on the bench. The cop turned away and Gray entered the student union.

As he walked down the stairs, he paused. Listened, but heard nothing other than the faint whir of the HVAC. He wondered if he would have to take another tumble, conk himself on the head. He continued on and around to the big double doors, which yielded when he pulled on the enormous brass handle. The Steak Place was open for business.

He slid into the same booth to take in the room. It was mostly the same—frat boys, white boys, spending their parents' money on meat and alcohol. The sight that made his breath catch in his throat was, on the little triangular platform in the far corner of the room, the Delta Function prepping for the gig. Closer to him, there was Hilda, setting up her computer on a folding table that also held the mixing board for the PA. You had to bring your own PA to The Steak Place, so they were using the underpowered Shure that they'd bought used from a Baptist church. Hilda pulled a cassette tape recorder from a thrift store suitcase. Gray knew that she carried three or four recorders, as backup. Her computer software ran off of the tapes.

"Good evening, sir," Boyd said. Gray had been so focused that he hadn't noticed the waiter. "Another Michelob?"

Gray fished the wad of ones from his pocket. He brandished them at Boyd and said, "Yes, please. And I'd like a steak, too. A ribeye, rare."

"Certainly, sir."

Jerf was leaning against the bar, taking long pulls on a Budweiser tallboy, his head swiveling around any time a woman walked past. He was wearing a plaid flannel shirt underneath a suit jacket, with a red bandana around his neck. A bohemian cowboy dressed up for church, that was Jerf's idea of style. Everyone in the band wore black suit jackets, that was their look. Black blazers over whatever the fuck else you wanted to wear. Gray had favored a sleeveless T-shirt under his jacket, even though he was paler and doughier then. He had curly hair, and let it grow out long enough to form a halo around his head.

That was the Gray of 1979's look, but that person was not here. Gray waited to see his twenty-two-year-old self walk out of the bathroom, but it never happened. What would he say if he encountered his past self? What wisdom could he deliver? He couldn't think of anything beyond, "Work hard, play hard."

On stage, Jerf's drums were already set up. Robert and Kitty were grappling with their amps and with tuning their instruments. Kitty was in her turtleneck and sunglasses, all black. Kitty had a good heart, but she tried way too hard. Probably would've taken half as long to get set up if she'd have taken the sunglasses off. Robert was carefully setting all the dials on his Fender Twin, which teetered atop a wooden chair. Robert's uniform was pure new wave: skinny tie and dress shirt. The lapels of his jacket were covered in badges. And his hair was even more ridiculous than Gray's had been. Kitty cut it for him, razoring it into a Johnny Thunders mullet. Robert sprayed the whole thing down with Aqua Net before a gig, so even when he was an airborne guitar hero, his hair didn't move a millimeter.

The steak arrived, sizzling on an iron skillet but already doused in Heinz 57. The little red plastic sign stuck in it said "Rare" but it was medium at best. Gray sawed away at the leaner bits and washed them down with a second Michelob. He tried to remember this gig, but could not. It had been a long time. Jerf probably obsessively documented their shows, took notes and saved flyers. To Gray it was all a blur. He remembered images, sounds, songs, venues. But if asked, "How was that April 1979 gig at The Steak Place?" he would've been unable to answer.

After he finished the steak, he picked up his beer and wandered over to the stage. The tiny cadre of Delta Function fans milled around. There was Errol, his hair bright blue and his face a riot of acne. There was Bragg, the black woman who always wore combat boots and surplus fatigues.

Errol and Bragg were both smoking. The past smelled like cigarettes, and except for Bragg, this past that he'd walked into was populated only by white people. But Gray felt giddy. Happy. Glad to be there. It felt like that moment when, after searching for your car keys for half an hour, you realize they've been in your pocket the whole time.

Jerf was on stage, having a heated discussion with Kitty and Robert. Gray moved up closer to listen.

"Fuck this," Jerf said. "Let's fire his ass."

"No," Robert said.

"We'll play some instrumentals," Kitty said, "and Rob can fill in on vocals on the songs that are in his range. That way we get paid. You want to get paid, don't you, Jerf?"

Jerf nodded, but then turned and spat on the stage.

"Hey, uh, hey. Excuse me," Gray said. "Big fan. I know all your songs, and I think I'm a pretty good singer."

The three musicians on stage looked over at him.

"I don't remember seeing you at any shows, captain," Jerf said.

"Shut up, Jerf," Kitty said. She turned to Gray, and spoke very slowly. "You . . . are a singer? And you know our songs? I don't know whether we should call the mental hospital, or feel flattered."

"I'd go with flattery," Gray said.

"I don't know," Robert said. But then it didn't matter, because from the sound board, Hilda had started playing the Delta Function Anthem on her computer. Fed up, she'd started the gig on her own. The rest of the band scrambled to their positions and joined in on the second stanza, triumphant guitar chords and cymbal crashes. It was supposed to be a goof on the Presley thing, starting a show to "Also Sprach Zarathustra," but the band got behind it, pushing each line into a slow marching crescendo, daring the occupants of the room to do anything other than focus and listen.

The anthem brought Gray all the way back. He didn't know whether to be embarrassed or overjoyed at the sight of his old band catching up a roomful of college kids, making them stop chugging their Schlitz, making them pause over their steaks. Kitty was swinging that gigantic Jazz Bass around like some kind of medieval weapon. Robert was already jumping or high-kicking at the end of every crashing line.

And then the anthem ended, and Jerf clicked off a fast 1-2-3-4 and they slammed into the first real song, a fast one. A familiar one. Gray started jerking, dancing in place, without even realizing it.

The song was "Living the Dream." Kitty locked eyes with him, and then shrugged and nodded toward the lonely mike stand. Gray jumped on stage.

He stepped up to the microphone, and began to sing.

Give Up

Forty-three is not a milestone birthday. Forty-three, it's a prime number. Richard "The King" Petty's number when he won stock car championships. In 43 A.D. the Romans began their conquest of Britain. Jim knew all of these things about the number forty-three. When he turned forty, Charlotte had given him a bigger television and a genuine Eames Lounge Chair. A month before his forty-third, when she asked him what he wanted, he had lied. He said he had no idea, that gifts were not important to him anymore. She believed him, but bought him presents anyway.

As a child, he had obsessively read encyclopedias. As an adult, he entered trivia contests at local bars. They were a team, Jim and Charlotte, and they won most of the contests they entered. To the other trivia regulars, Jim was known simply as "Trivia Guy." As in, "Hey, Trivia Guy," delivered broadly with a big smile, the way you'd smile and point out the meteorologist from the local news if they wandered into the fake Irish pub.

On the morning of his forty-third birthday, Jim had an admission to make. He was opening the drapes in the den. "I got myself a birthday present," he said. "I was keeping it a surprise."

"It's tough to keep surprises from yourself, isn't it?"

"People do it all the time," he replied.

The drapes opened and out in the yard sat a giant blue structure, a geodesic dome covered with an opaque membrane. "I hope it wasn't expensive," Charlotte said.

"I've been saving up."

"What is it?"

"It's a Backyard Everest."

It had started with a trivia question, a few months prior. The question was, name the two British explorers killed on Everest in 1924. Charlotte knew that one of them was George Mallory, famous for his "because it's there" motivation. Neither of them knew the name of the second Brit. This planted a seed in Jim's mind. He read a book about Everest, and then he read another book, and then he read all the books they had at the library concerning Everest and mountaineering. Everest was, he read, not the hardest mountain to climb, and in fact did not require what alpinists would consider hard-core technical mountaineering skills. Still, people died every year attempting to reach the summit.

On his birthday, while he carefully read the instruction manual for the dome, she delivered the presents she'd bought for him: a subscription to the *OED*, a cashmere scarf, a wool hat, and a pair of fur-lined leather gloves. The clothes were luxurious and stylish but not particularly appropriate for climbing the world's highest mountain. All the gear he would need for the expedition was already inside the dome.

"Can I come see what it's like?" she asked.

"No, I only bought a single-user license," he said. "You have to sign a pile of waivers just to walk into the thing." He picked up the gloves and pulled them on, looped the scarf around his neck, then yanked the hat down over his head so that it covered his eyes. "Besides, as the manual says, eventually everyone is alone on the mountain."

"Let me guess, you've already scheduled the time off work?"

He nodded. "You know how much vacation I have saved. I never take vacations."

She plucked the hat from his head.

"Ten weeks?"

"Twelve weeks. And this won't take nearly that long."

"And if I complain, you'll mention China."

Charlotte had spent most of the previous summer visiting her younger sister, who was doing missionary work in China.

"Yes, if we argue about this, eventually I will mention China." The television was tuned to a twenty-four-hour news station. In the real Nepal, not the Nepal inside the dome in the backyard, monsoons had caused massive flooding. Hundreds dead, thousands displaced. The tragedy had nothing to do with Everest. It was August; it was monsoon season. No one was on the real Everest this time of year.

His tent at Base Camp was also a blue dome, much smaller than its counterpart in the backyard. When he got in, he sat on the cot for almost half an hour, just listening to the wind whipping against the nylon. Finally he stood up and left the tent. The world out there on top of the glacier was an expanse of snow and garbage, dotted with tents of all shapes and colors. Rising up on three sides were sheer faces of rock and ice. He could feel that the oxygen was thinner. He was disoriented for a moment, then he followed the sweep of the river of ice, the Khumbu Icefall, around and up and then there it was. Everest, the top of the world. He could barely see the summit pyramid and its plume of icy cloud.

He stared at its malevolent beauty for a while, and then finally fished around in his parka pocket and put in the earpiece.

"Righto, I was beginning to think you'd gone wacky," the voice in the earpiece said. "Shall we begin?"

Jim had ordered a neutral accent, but the guide spoke in clipped English tones. It was as if old dead George Mallory himself were guiding the expedition.

"Before we begin, tell me: which is the mess tent?"

"Mess tent, the large green tent to your left, old man."

He started toward the mess tent, past a pile of spent oxygen bottles. A light breeze blew, smelling faintly of rot. Colorful prayer flags flapped in sunshine. A large rock spun under his foot and he almost turned his ankle. He resolved to be more careful.

Inside the mess tent, a cup of tea was steaming on a table. He picked it up but decided not to sip it. Too hot. Be careful. He found the water cooler and mixed some in with the tea, then he drained the tepid cup and went back outside.

"Ready for some skills work? Proper planning and all that. Get your gear, old chap."

At the far end of the plain, the jagged edges of the Khumbu Icefall spilled down between two ridges. He went to his tent and retrieved the ice axes and crampons, the main gear for climbing the mountain. The axes were much lighter than he expected. The crampons were hard to fit onto his mountaineering boots. After he geared up, he walked back toward the icefall, to the giant pillars of ice.

The guide coached him through ice axe and crampon skills. He picked a spot that was not quite vertical, lifted his right foot, and kicked it into the ice. Then, as he lifted his left foot, stepping up into the air, he swung the right axe, embedding axe and the other foot simultaneously. It seemed pretty easy. The sharp fangs of the crampons supported his weight. The axes slid into the ice without much effort, but then felt secure. He continued up the pillar until he was twenty feet off the ground. Nothing compared to how high he'd be on the summit of Everest, but an accomplishment nonetheless. He looked up, but now the summit was obscured by the icefall. Far overhead, a crow sailed in the breeze. He hadn't realized there would be animals in the simulation.

He could feel his hamstrings tightening up, so he made his way down.

"Good show, good show!" the guide said as Jim jumped the last few feet back onto the plain of Base Camp.

The climbing he had ahead of him was treacherous, but none of it would actually be as tough as a sheer ice wall without ropes. There would be plenty of ice, but not as steep. There would be rock walls, but they would be fitted with ropes. He was up to the task, had that same feeling of confidence as when he was the only one in the room who knew the answer to some particularly obscure trivia question.

On his way back to the tent he passed a couple of rats fighting for scraps in a trash pile. Once inside the tent he stripped down to his underwear and called Charlotte on the satellite phone. He stretched his hamstrings while he talked, hopping around the tent like a crane: first on one leg, then the other.

"Honey, this is amazing," he said, just after she picked up the phone. "It's absolutely real. There are birds, even."

"How far up are you?"

"I'm still at Base Camp. But I've already done some practice climbing. I feel great."

"That's good. I want you to make it all the way. But when you stop feeling great, I want you to do the right thing."

"I love you too, my dear. How are things at home?"

"Well, I'm heading off to trivia night without you. That feels . . . weird."

"Good luck!" Jim said.

"Right back at you," Charlotte said.

He was climbing the Lhotse Face. His expedition had started days earlier. How many days, he didn't remember. He just did what the voice in his ear told him to do. Climb from Base Camp to Camp One, through the Khumbu Icefall. Climb to Camp Two and spend the night. Back down to Base Camp. The orders came in and he executed. Up and down, up and down to get acclimatized to the altitude. From his position on the Lhotse Face, he could not see the summit. The mountains were impossibly steep, impossibly high. He was cold, and hungry. He had already started using bottled oxygen.

The day had started at Base Camp. He had tea and oatmeal in the mess tent just before dawn. Then up into the Khumbu Icefall, the scariest thing he had encountered here so far. The Khumbu was a jagged spill of enormous splinters of glacier, as if a giant had cracked ice to make a cocktail the size of Lake Erie. A maze of giant blocks and deep crevasses. He started climbing before dawn so that the ice was less likely to melt and crack and move. That morning was his seventh run through the Khumbu. It was only slightly less horrifying than the first time. The guide coached him constantly to keep him moving through the maze, across the ladders that spanned the crevasses. Jim had started thinking of the disembodied voice as George. Sometimes George gave precise instructions and sometimes George delivered more general motivation.

"If you are going through hell," George said, "keep going. Winston Churchill." Jim was paused at the lip of a particularly wide crevasse. It was spanned by three aluminum ladders, fully extended, lashed together at the ends with bright red rope.

Churchill never climbed Everest, Jim thought. And Jim wasn't going through hell. He was climbing a simulated mountain. He wondered if they made a Backyard Hell that came delivered in a dome, and if so, what it would be like. And who would want to rent such a thing. With Everest, there was a clear test. You either made the summit or you didn't. Whereas hell had no victory condition.

Hell or no, he did keep going, out across the bouncing bridge of ladders. It was terrible, but it was better than the first time he had clipped in to a safety rope and ventured out onto a ladder. Then he'd gone across on his hands and knees. When he had reached the other side after that first crossing he collapsed, retching up breakfast. The vomit lay there on the snow, glistening in the first rays of the rising sun. He had thought about using the safe word. There was a kill switch that would pull him safely out of the simulation if need be. It also ended the expedition immediately, all that money and time down the drain no matter how far you were from the summit. The safe word he had picked out was kakorrhaphiophobia. Fear of failure. Not a word one can say easily.

That first day, lying there after the first crevasse, he had thought long and hard about the safe word. Pondered why the hell he was doing this, spending so much money to do something that was not real. Or rather, was as real as a movie or a book or a song. Those were real. People cried, people laughed, people changed their lives because of books and movies and songs. He was going to change his life by climbing virtual Everest.

The Lhotse Face was a steep ice slope. It was over half a mile from Camp Two at the bottom of the slope to Camp Three. Camp Three was just some tiny ledges cut into the ice halfway up the face. Where the icefall had been terror alternating with calm, the Lhotse Face was steady panic and slow, tiring work. Kick with one set of crampons, step up and kick with the other foot. Swing one ice axe, pull up and swing the other. Every two hundred feet, where the safety ropes are clipped in to ice screws sunk in the mountain, fidget with the hardware on the safety harness to move from one two-hundred-foot rope to the next two-hundred-foot rope. One mistake and all you can do is fall for thousands of feet. Jim had thought that the vertigo would pass, that he would get used to the dizzying height, but this was not the case.

Climbing Everest by himself, the one thing Jim did not have to worry about was coping with others ascending faster than he was, or descending. Traffic jams had killed many people on the mountain, both near the summit and farther down. The lack of company made it less deadly, but not necessarily that much easier. The brochure for Backyard Everest had promised that the virtual climb would be every bit as hard, and thus every bit as satisfying, as real Everest.

Thinking about the lack of others, imagining the mountain with other people on it, this had distracted him enough from the climb that he kicked in but not forcefully enough. The ice was worn into a series of shallow steps here, but the steps were still hard and slick. When he lifted his other foot to kick he lost purchase completely, bashing his knee into the icy face and falling. He twisted as he fell, his back crashing into the mountain, but the safety ropes held. He hung there for a while, stunned, wondering if he had broken anything. At first he just felt numb, but when he began to twist back around and haul himself up again, his right knee hurt with a pain he had never felt before. He wondered if he had permanently injured himself. It was all he could do to pull himself back into the moment, away from visions of walking with a cane, of lying on an operating table while a band of surgeons and nurses in scrubs huddled around his poor shattered knee. At the very least, it felt like he'd be walking with a limp for months.

He slid back down and let the rope hold him, not completely confident in its ability to do that. Below him, the Lhotse Face stretched all the way to the tiny colorful dots that were the tents of Camp Two. Above him, Camp Three was only a few hundred vertical feet away. If his knee held, it made more sense to head for Camp Three than to descend.

Or he could give up completely, say the ridiculous safe word, and forfeit the money and the chance to climb Everest. He couldn't envision a second chance.

"What have you got for inspiration, George?" he said into his radio. George was silent. Panic set in. His heart was pounding. He became convinced that he was about to pass out, that he was too weak to haul himself back up the rope. He had visions of the safety harness failing, his body sliding down the ice uncontrollably. He realized he was having an anxiety attack. He steadied himself and took long, deep breaths. He reached around to the regulator on his oxygen tank and cranked up the flow to maximum. There would be more oxygen canisters at Camp Three.

That was when he spotted the corpse.

Just off the climbing route, resting on a slight ledge in the slope, was a pile of something shrouded with purple nylon and tangled in ropes. At first he thought it was some gear that had slid down the mountain from Camp Three.

He tried to think back, to recall if the brochures and manuals had mentioned that there would be corpses of the people who had died on the climb left in place on Backyard Everest just as they were on real Everest. Distracted from the pain in his knee, he was struck with the fantasy of making his way over to inspect the corpse more closely. To see what was left—flesh frozen in place, or bones picked clean by the crows? Or what if it wasn't a corpse? What if it was a person who was still alive?

He tried to spin and get back in place on the mountain. It felt as if someone had jammed a screwdriver into his kneecap. He tried not to care about this. He hauled himself up on the safety rope, but it was slow going. Breathing was even more difficult, as if the oxygen mask was robbing him of air instead of providing it. It was hard to focus on the task at hand. He was sifting through everything he'd read about Everest, trying to recall if he'd read anything about what or who this thing might be. A tent, a hot cup of tea, a sleeping bag, these were all waiting for him at Camp Three. Tomorrow would be another day: rest and tape up the knee, then back down to Camp Two, then another final push all the way to the summit.

He looked over at the body again. He thought he could see strands of brown hair caught by the breeze. Every landscape feature on Everest had a name: the Geneva Spur, the Yellow Band, the Chinese Ladder, the Mushroom Rock. Corpses were considered landscape features on the mountain.

"Sleeping Beauty?" he said. "You shouldn't be here."

Sleeping Beauty was the name given to the corpse of Francys Arsentiev. But Fran had died on the other side of the mountain, on the northern route. Her husband had been lost there as well, but while his body was never found, Fran remained clipped to the safety line for years. So high up, higher than even the crows could fly, the climbers who passed her had dubbed her Sleeping Beauty. A few years back Fran had finally been cut free from the ropes and pushed further off the route, to where her body was no longer visible. Whoever this was, it couldn't be Sleeping Beauty.

The simulation had to be breaking down. There was no other explanation. This only increased Jim's terror. What kind of horrible things could a broken mountain do to you? What if the demons from Virtual Hell showed up, raining fire and brimstone down on him from the summit of Everest?

There was another explanation. *I could be hallucinating,* Jim thought. He blinked thick tears from his eyes, which rolled down and froze on his cheeks. *If I were a real climber on real Everest,* he thought, *I would not be dangling here arguing with myself over whether this was a hallucination or a computer malfunction.* This only made him feel more hollow inside.

Did it matter which explanation was true? He tried to concentrate. It was as if he could feel each individual synapse firing in slow motion. Inspiration surprised him: he had turned his oxygen all the way off, not all the way on! He reached back and cranked the regulator in the opposite direction. He tried to breathe regularly, slowly. Four counts in, four counts out.

Just when he thought he had his breathing under control, he started coughing. He stayed as still as he could, trying to will the sensation to stop. Finally he coughed something up. He pulled his mask aside to spit it out. It was blood.

As he examined the red stain he'd left on the mountain, he thought he saw the woman, or whatever it was, moving. Another realization struck him: he could use the safe word at any time. If he began to fall, he could just blurt it out. He was pretty sure that was how it worked, but it didn't make the slope any less terrifying. And he was pretty sure he remembered the safe word. Cacophony? Cacophobia? Cacophobia. He tried to keep the word perched on the tip of his tongue, as precariously as he was perched on the mountain.

"To climb steep hills requires slow pace at first," George said. George sounded a little drunk. "That's Shakespeare. One of our boys. What do you think of Shakespeare, Trivia Guy? Have you ever read any Shakespeare? Or did you merely memorize the years of his birth and death?"

Jim pulled out the earbud. George had clearly gone insane. Or malfunctioned. He slapped at it with his other gloved hand, the way you'd rap a phone or a television to get it working again. Then he screwed it back into his ear.

"No stopping to examine strange women," George said. "We have a mountain to climb, Trivia Guy. We must stamp to the top with the wind in our teeth."

Jim yanked out the earbud again. He could hear George babbling away, indecipherable British static. He considered stuffing it in his pocket. Instead he chucked it down the slope. It skittered and bounced for a few seconds before he lost sight of it.

"Goodbye, George," Jim said.

He didn't need George any more. He kicked in hard with his left leg. The pain in his knee made him yelp, but it did not feel as bad as it had a few minutes earlier. Jim reached down and unclipped his safety harness. Untethered, he traversed toward Sleeping Beauty. He worked slowly, three points of contact at all times, swinging hard and kicking hard.

Once on the ledge, he jammed his crampons down into the mountain as forcefully as he could before he knelt and pulled back the purple nylon. He could still feel the pain in his knee but it was a faraway kind of pain.

Her skin was glassy and gray. Her eyes were closed and both arms were raised over her head. Lying next to her in the snow was an empty syringe. Dex, he knew that. Short for . . . short for a much longer word. A steroid used in emergencies to fight the effects of altitude sickness. He had a syringe of dex in one of his pockets, somewhere. She did not look alive, though. He leaned over her, close enough to kiss her, to see if she was breathing.

"What are you doing to that woman?" Charlotte said. Charlotte seemed to be an amazing climber, too, because she was standing on the slope just above him. She was barefoot, wearing a T-shirt and jeans. The T-shirt was her lucky trivia night shirt, black with a four-leaf clover. Charlotte was holding the birthday presents: the hat, scarf, and gloves. "I thought you might need these. It's cold up here."

"And steep, too," he said, gesturing down the slope.

"It's okay, I don't have acrophobia," Charlotte said.

Acrophobia, that was the safe word. He thought about saying it.

He turned but his wife was gone. In her place was a bird, one of the crows, watching him. Its talons were sunk into the rime.

The traverse had made him very tired. He thought about lying down there next to Sleeping Beauty, just to rest a bit. Then later he could rescue her, and rescue himself. He planned it out. He would tie her to his harness, then drag her back over to the safety lines. But wasn't there an easier way to rescue Sleeping Beauty? A kiss, and the curse was lifted, he remembered that much. Surely rescuing her, even if she was a corpse, was as much of a feat as climbing a mountain. More important.

He bent down to kiss her, but before he could make contact he lost his balance and tumbled over her. He scrabbled for purchase on anything but he was already sliding out of control down the ice, shocks of pain coming as he bumped along. The fear of the moment pushed one last bit of adrenalin into his system to clear his thoughts. He was thinking about how much he hated himself. He was thinking about failure. And in that moment Trivia Guy, the part of him that tended to all those dates and facts and figures, remembered the safe word.

"Kakorrhaphiophobia," he screamed, and then he blacked out as the world disintegrated around him.

And then the company paramedics came and pried him out of the mechanism, and his hospital stay began, but Jim was not conscious for much of this, not at first.

Life became fragmented.

"I expect a full recovery," Dr. Singh said after the knee surgery. "You really messed yourself up good, but you do your physical therapy and stay rested and you should be walking unassisted again in, let's say, eight weeks." Charlotte spent her nights at the hospital, sleeping in the reclining chair. The first time he saw her, they both burst into tears. After three days of helping Jim and avoiding the issue, she finally asked, "What happened in there?" He told her everything, as best he could remember it.

At the hospital, he received fifty-five minutes of counseling from a short woman who looked like she'd shaved her head the previous week. She talked about how the mountains he needed to climb were inside himself. He scribbled notes as she talked. The "never say die" spirit is admirable, she said, until you wind up dead because of it. This just made him think about Sleeping Beauty, about all the real people up on the real mountain left there frozen in the snow, while he was there safe in a warm bed.

The physical therapy was more lengthy and more frequent than the mental therapy. It was something like torture, if torture involved elastic bands and ankle weights. He performed it dutifully, even after he'd moved back home, trying not to make too much noise when he cursed. He had felt worse pain. And he was a champion at resting up. He had been reading the *OED* on his tablet, jamming it in the pocket of his robe as he shuffled from the bed to the couch and back, making his daily rounds. He had taken to wearing the wool hat around the house. Everything was happening on schedule.

Outside the guest bedroom window, the blue dome still sat in the backyard. A monument to his failure. He couldn't even climb fake Everest, let alone real Everest. He felt queasy every time he saw the dome. He'd been released from the hospital a couple weeks earlier and was now able to shuffle around the house by using a walker or a cane. Charlotte had been working from home.

She brought him lunch: a grilled cheese sandwich with extra pickles. She set the plate on the bed and went to the window.

"When are they going to come and take that thing away?" she asked.

"As it turns out, there's a significant discount for the second attempt," he said. This was true. It wasn't something the company advertised, but in the aftermath, the sales rep had told him that they would leave the dome there until he made up his mind. The second attempt would be half off.

"So I was thinking—"

"You were thinking of taking another shot at getting killed? At getting killed by something that isn't real?"

"I don't know," he said. "You want me to give up?"

"I'm scared. I'm worried that I don't know who you are anymore." She left his phone on the nightstand, so that he could call and have the dome taken away any time he wanted.

He woke up and turned to read the clock on the nightstand. His ribs still ached when he moved. It was 3:15 A.M. He had to pee.

Charlotte was asleep in their bedroom. He was staying in the guest room on the first floor while he recuperated, unable to climb the stairs. There was a little bell on the nightstand that he could ring if he needed her. He didn't feel like asking her for assistance, though.

He tried to wait it out, to see if he could drift back to sleep, but by 3:30 he was still awake and he still had to pee. He looked out into the yard, the dome lit by a full moon. He could save up and try again. That was just moving some money around, saving instead of spending. He knew how to do that. Not trying again, that was more of a mystery. What is it that you save up so that you can try not to do something?

He flipped the covers aside, and put his feet on the floor. He'd done it before he knew he was going to do it. The walker was there next to the bed and the cane was propped against the nightstand. He had tried walking with the cane the past few days, with some success. He grabbed the cane, took a deep breath, and heaved himself to his feet.

Step number one, fine. Step number two, feeling no pain. Step number three, his knee felt like it had turned inside out, and he collapsed on the carpet.

He winced, squeezing his eyes shut. He reached down to rub his knee, as if that was going to make it stop hurting. He couldn't get to his feet by himself. He thought about yelling for Charlotte, but squelched that when he realized he could use the cane to retrieve the bell from the nightstand.

When he opened his eyes, Sleeping Beauty was there, standing over him. She was wearing her purple snowsuit, with the hood down. She looked quite alive. Her long brown hair fell into her face, half-lit by the moonlight from the window.

"Let me help you," she said. He reached up to her. She ignored his hand and knelt by his side.

He started laughing to himself. It didn't seem to bother Sleeping Beauty.

"I need to tell you something," she said. "Are you ready?"

He stopped laughing, and nodded. They were holding hands now. "Never give up, Jim," the dead woman said. "Never, never, never." Then she leaned in closer. They exchanged kisses on the cheek. He didn't feel like a curse had been lifted. He felt like he was kissing her goodbye.

He let go of her hand and turned away from her and started crawling, pulling himself with his arms, letting his legs slide while trying to protect his knee. He didn't look back to see if she'd gone. Maybe she was still there behind him, along with the bed and the telephone and the little bell and the blue dome.

He kept crawling. It was going to take a very, very long time.

Chemistry Set

There are things I know and things I don't know and one
of the things I don't know is why my father had the corpse of a
possum in a bucket of formaldehyde in the garage. But this isn't
about my father. This is about Brett Bradley and me.

Brett Bradley came over to play when we were both ten
years old; he was wearing combat boots and jeans. They were
Toughskins, but they were still jeans. I don't think I got to wear
jeans until I was thirteen or so. It was the beginning of summer
just after fifth grade. In fifth grade, Brett sat at the desk to my
left, and Helen Aigner sat to my right. Brett brought a magazine
to school one day that had photographs of Cheryl Tiegs in it. He
was really excited to show it to me, but I didn't get it. I was not
particularly moved by Cheryl Tiegs. I was still infatuated with my
fourth grade teacher, Miss Quarry, a real actual person and not a
photograph. She didn't teach at the school anymore, though. She
had moved to the beach with her fiancé to sell kites for a living.
She kissed me on the forehead on the last day of fourth grade.

"What's so great about Cheryl Tiegs?" I had asked Brett.

"Ummm," he said, stabbing his finger at the magazine, at
Cheryl Tiegs's chest. All it did was make me wonder what kind
of bathing suit Miss Quarry wore when she wasn't selling kites.

Brett didn't bring a magazine when he came to my house that day. He brought a football. It wasn't brown, like most footballs. It was red, white, and blue. I guess from the Bicentennial? His mother probably dropped him off, but I don't really remember. I couldn't tell you what she looked like or what kind of car she drove. I'm not even sure whose idea it was for him to come over—mine, his, my parents, his parents? What I do remember is what Brett looked like. He was exactly five feet tall that year, a fact that he announced constantly. Towering to me, then, and the combat boots just made him even taller. He had brilliant blond hair in a buzzcut. His eyes were two tiny sapphires set deep in the ridges of his tanned, or more often than not sunburned, face. He had perfect teeth, on the small side. Somehow this mattered in the fifth grade. At one point there was a solid two or three weeks where Brett was getting teased by the other kids in the class about the size of his teeth. "Tiny teeth, tiny teeth, tiny tiny tiny teeth!" Of course I got teased for a lot of things.

I tried to suggest that we watch television. It was about time for the *Fat Albert* re-run to come on. "I'm tired of *Fat Albert*," he pronounced, tossing the football from one hand to the other. I tried to show him my collection of rocks and minerals (most of which I'd bought from the hobby shop instead of collecting myself) but he didn't care. Nor did he care about the wide variety of leaves that I had pressed between the pages of an unabridged dictionary. Tulip poplar, *Liriodendron tulipifera*. Sugar maple, *Acer saccharum*. He did not want to hear about the compound leaves of the devil's walking stick, *Aralia spinosa*, which I didn't actually have a sample of because it was rare and didn't grow in our yard, which is where I got all the leaves. He just wanted to throw the football, punt the football, maybe place-kick the football between the two trees at the far end of the back yard. Southern crabapple, *Malus augustifolia*, but I didn't say that at the time.

I tried to think of other distractions that were not football related. I was pretty experienced in distraction and diversion, at getting out of things that I wasn't good at or didn't really want to do. The year before, my parents wanted me to start helping them rake up the leaves in the yard. I did a terrible job of it, on purpose, thinking that it'd get me out of raking. When that didn't work, I spent a long time secretly rubbing the rake handle against my index finger until it raised a blister, which then popped dramatically while I was out raking with my mother. That got me out of the task for a solid couple of years.

There was one potential distraction that I couldn't mention because I wasn't supposed to know about it myself. Down in the very back of the garage there was a shelf that was off limits for me. It was my father's shelf. The chainsaw sat there, among some other tools. On the bottom shelf there was a gas can and rat poison and there was a five-gallon bucket that had "Do Not Open" written on it in Magic Marker and of course I had snuck down there and opened it once and inside there was the corpse of a possum (*Didelphis virginiana*) floating in what I guessed was formaldehyde. I never knew why my father had this. Brett would've probably been really into it but rules were rules, so I didn't mention the possum in the bucket.

This makes Brett sound like a caricature, a ten-year-old version of a crass jock, and me the stereotypical nerd. But there was a lot more to it than that. Brett was trying to help me. To get me up to speed on the important things.

"What about the cliff? Can we climb down the cliff?"

We lived at the top of a hill, and the backyard ended in what then seemed like a fairly steep drop down to the parking lot of a dentist's office below. My parents dumped leaves and grass clippings over the edge to try and control the erosion. It wasn't really a cliff, of course, but I was still forbidden to go near the edge. Mostly I just stared at it when I was riding up the hill coming home from school. I wondered if there were any interesting rocks in the hillside, something to add to my collection, but it might as well have been Mars, as far as me getting access to it. It couldn't have been more than twenty-five feet from top to bottom, but it was as much a cliff to me then as it was to Brett. Except I didn't particularly want to climb up or down it.

"The cliff is off limits, according to Mom and Dad. *Way* off limits."

As a last-ditch effort, I mentioned my chemistry set.

"What can you do with that?" he asked.

"Well, you can test different foods to see how much starch they contain . . ."

"That's boring."

"Yeah, it is. You can make a really strong blue dye, except we probably shouldn't do that. You'd be surprised at how much a little dye can do. Um, make a volcano?"

"Like the one you brought to class that time? Nah."

"Got anything you want to plate with copper?"

"Nope. What about a bomb? Can we make a bomb?"

"Let's try," I said. I didn't think we could make a real bomb. But whether we could or not, it was better than throwing the football.

We went downstairs and I dragged the ChemCraft set down off the shelf in the playroom. It was a metal box the size of a small suitcase with shelves built in for all the chemicals and the other gear: test tubes, an alcohol burner, even a little set of scales. There was a big photograph on the outside, of a red-haired kid in a buttondown shirt and cardigan smiling as he gazed at a beaker full of some blue stuff. Probably that dye that stains everything. I opened up the set and pulled out the test tube rack.

Brett flipped through the experiment booklet, but quickly gave up on finding any bomb-making plans in there. I was just winging it. I mixed up some ammonium chloride and sodium silicate solution in a test tube, but nothing happened.

"You don't make a bomb in a test tube," Brett said.

So we used one of the blue plastic bottles that the chemicals came in to make our bomb. We dumped in a little from each of the other chemical bottles until it was full. Maybe mixing everything together would make a bomb. Maybe both Brett and I were still tacitly playing let's-pretend even though we were graduates of the fifth grade. A feeble gray foam started to pillow up over the lip of the bottle, so I screwed the cap back on.

"Is it going to blow up?"

"I don't know," I said. It didn't seem to be doing much of anything.

"Maybe we need a fuse. Bombs have fuses."

I rummaged around in the garage, trying to find something that might work as a fuse. Brett just stared at the little bottle that had once contained only tannic acid, $C_{76}H_{52}O_{46}$, but now contained our experimental bomb. If the thing had exploded, Brett would've caught it right in the face.

I found a ball of string to use for a fuse. I went to pick up the bottle and it was warm enough to make me pull my hand back, but not hot enough to burn me.

"It's getting hot! I think it's going to blow!"

"Quick, outside!" Brett said, grabbing up the bottle and rushing out the basement door. When he got to the backyard he paused and heaved it up into the air, grenade style, so that it arced and fell to the ground on the other side of the old bird feeder.

Nothing happened. No explosion, no flames, no sound. By the time we went and retrieved it, it wasn't even hot anymore.

"What a dud," Brett said. He unscrewed the cap and started to dump out the contents on the ground.

"Stop! You might kill the grass or something. My parents will get angry."

"This couldn't kill anything," Brett said, and to prove it he poured some out into his palm. It was just a glittery white paste now. He reached up and slid his hand down one cheek, then the other. "Now you. Here, I'll do it."

I couldn't say no. So he poured some more out and painted my cheeks too. I thought about cracking a joke about girls and makeup, but I stayed quiet. Whatever compound it was now, it didn't burn or sting. It wasn't even warm.

"And now it's time to throw the football," Brett said. "Come on, you know you want to."

I was convinced that instead of making an explosive, we'd made some kind of deadly poison, trace elements of which were still seeping through my cheeks into my bloodstream, into my skull, deep into my brain. The whole football thing helped take my mind off of that, at least from thinking about the worst possible scenario.

Brett was actually a pretty patient teacher with the football. He started passing it really softly, just tossing it back and forth underhand, and then he'd take a step back, and so on. Before we got too far apart, he showed me how to throw a spiral. He wasn't just zipping the ball at my head full speed, which plenty of other kids did on the playground or at summer camp.

He taught me to punt the ball, too. We tried one place-kick, me holding the ball for Brett, but he sent it way past the crabapple trees, over the fence and into the Spruills' yard next door. He scrambled after it, climbing the tall wooden fence that until that point had seemed like an impenetrable barrier to me.

It would never have occurred to me that you could just jump up and pull yourself over it successfully. We went back to passing the ball. Now we were far apart and I was discovering that while I could throw the ball pretty far, I had no aim. Brett could always throw the ball so that I could catch it. He even had me start running, going out for a pass, and while the ball often slid right through my arms he was always on target. I had no idea where the ball was going to end up when I released it; I was thinking too much about spinning the ball with my fingers.

And so, of course, before too long I sent the football spiraling up into the air and over the not-actually-a-cliff. Sometimes you remember thoughts and more often you remember feelings and most of the time you don't remember anything at all, but I remember both the feelings and thoughts I had when that ball went flying over the edge. The feelings were shame, humiliation, and inadequacy. There were two thoughts. Thought one was, whatever you do, don't let those feelings show. Thought two was, who is to blame? I was to blame, I threw the ball. But wasn't Brett to blame too? He brought the ball. It was his idea, and he'd been insistent. Surely the blame was mostly his.

Brett immediately ran to the edge and got down on his hands and knees, while I stayed back behind the bushes that marked my parentally imposed border. Sacred bamboo, *Nandina domestica*.

"I think I see it," Brett said.

"You're not supposed to be that close to the edge," I said. "Mom and Dad—"

"Oh, we're going *over* the edge to get the ball," he said, looking back over his shoulder at me. "It's not that bad. It's not . . . what's the word?"

"Vertical? Perpendicular?"

"Perpendicular. Didn't I see some rope in the garage?"

He went silent and after a few moments, moments when I was thinking about the sheer impossibility of climbing up or down the cliff, his expression changed.

"You did that on purpose," he said, as he got up and walked over to me.

"Did what?"

"Threw the ball over the edge!"

I started to tell him that I hadn't, but before I could make a noise he clamped his hand over my mouth.

"Shut up. I looked at your stupid chemicals and your stupid rocks and stupid leaves, and then you throw my football away? No. Hell no. We're going to go get it."

He took his hand away.

"Brett, we cannot go get the football," I said.

He lashed out and smacked me on the side of the head. It stung and I yelped and crouched instinctively. While my brain was pinging between two conclusions—had I been merely inept, or was I craftily inept? —my body lurched forward, and I tried to grab Brett around the knees to tackle him, so that he wouldn't hit me again.

The year before I had carefully memorized the diagrams in the encyclopedia article on judo. I remembered none of those techniques in that moment. But it didn't matter, because I managed to run into him low enough and fast enough to knock him off balance. So far off balance that, in fact, he fell over backward, bounced, and went over the edge of the bank, but not before clocking me in the head with one of his combat boots. I'm pretty sure that was as much an accident as all the rest of it except for him hitting me in the first place.

I don't think I lost consciousness, but I do think I was lying there a minute or two before I realized that Brett was yelling up to me.

"Hey, hey," over and over. I crawled over to the edge and looked down. My vision was blurry and spinny and it seemed like there were two Brett Bradleys splayed out about halfway down the little slope.

"Go get the rope," they both said, once they saw me. "Go get the rope and we won't get in trouble."

I rolled back away from the edge and slowly got to my feet. Unsteady, but mobile. My vision still felt a little like looking through a kaleidoscope, but I managed to go get the coil of rope. I tied it off to a pine tree that was near the edge. The rope was old and grayish and had black electrical tape wrapped around both fraying ends. I tossed it down to Brett. I was waiting on my parents to come out and end all this, but I guess they were busy with other things. I didn't want to get in trouble. To be clear: getting in trouble didn't mean anything like corporal punishment. It meant no television, which was a horror that I couldn't chance.

He slowly made his way up the slope. He was only pulling with one hand on the rope, kicking his combat boots into the hillside. I wanted to go stand back behind the bushes. It felt wrong to be where I was, but I stayed.

As he got close to the edge I realized that he didn't have the retrieved football in his other hand. He was injured. It was his throwing hand, too. I reached down and tried to help pull him up the last little bit, and then we both rolled onto our backs at the edge.

"Are you OK?" I asked.

"Of course I'm not OK. My hand is messed up. My wrist."

He didn't say it like he was mad. He said it like he was a robot, talking to the sky.

"I'm messed up too. My vision got all blurry. I thought I saw two of you down there."

That was his cue to say something like "that's stupid" or "you're a dumbass," but he didn't.

"You owe me a football," he said. Same robot voice. "How long before you can buy me another football?"

"A month?" I had no idea.

"One month, one football. It's got to be the same colors."

"Sure thing, Brett."

We used the garden hose to clean up before going inside. He was cradling his right arm in his left and I could see that his wrist was swelling up but when I asked about it and suggested that we put ice on it, he just told me to mind my own beeswax. We watched television in silence until Brett's mother came to pick him up. *Fat Albert* was still on. They learned a lesson about not eating too much junk food and then sang a song about it. After Brett left I tried to go back to what I'd been reading that morning, which was a big article in *Newsweek* about the neutron bomb, but I was still having trouble focusing on the tiny print, so I gave up and watched more television.

I waited a week before telling my mother about losing Brett's football. I only said it went over the edge. I skipped everything else. I thought she might take it out of my allowance (three dollars a week then) but she just asked my father to take me to the sporting goods store out past the college. They had some red, white, and blue footballs in what they called "dead stock." Dad bought one and then drove me to Brett's house where I dropped it off, handing it to him through a barely open screen door. He had a bandage that covered most of his right hand.

"I'm going to miss football tryouts because of this," he said. "Because of you."

It wasn't because of me. It was his fault, but I didn't feel like arguing with him about it.

"You can work on your ambidexterity. Do you know what ambidexterity means?"

"Shut up, dumbass. Go home."

When I got back in the car, Dad said, "Be more careful the next time you're playing with your friend, OK?" But I never played with Brett Bradley again.

Days and then years piled on top of that day with Brett, and soon enough it was a memory that would only very rarely wash ashore unbidden. Whatever happened to Brett Bradley, I would wonder for all of five minutes, and then I'd move on to more urgent matters. Sometimes, I wondered if Brett Bradley ever thought of me. We had still bounced around through the same middle and high schools before I went off to college. Tenth grade English, eleventh grade history, I think we were in the same classes. We acknowledged each other on occasion but we were never as close again as we'd been up until that one day in the summer after fifth grade. He just became another in a cast of thousands, someone who might show up in an odd dream, someone I wouldn't think about for years at a time.

I skipped my tenth high school reunion. Turns out that Maurice Payton, the most famous guy from our class, had attended. Maurice directed music videos, and he'd brought one of the original MTV VJs as his date to the reunion. I heard all about that from Helen Aigner. She kept up with everyone and everything. According to Helen the VJ was really nice, personable, seemed really interested in meeting Maurice's old classmates. Helen had a Polaroid of the two of them. So when the next reunion came around five years later, I thought about flying back to the ol' hometown to attend. Another bit of incentive was that my first marriage had ended the year before. "Amicably" is the word you're supposed to use.

Maurice Payton didn't show up to that reunion, though, and thus no MTV VJ nor any other C-list celebrity of any kind. It was me and Helen Aigner and a sea of folks who were mostly paired off and having babies, kicking out the jams for one night, wearing name tags that featured their old yearbook photos. Helen and I were too cool to wear the name tags. I said hello to the few people I recognized, but ended up off in the corner with her, drinking my beer as slowly as possible because it was a cash bar.

The head of the reunion committee gave a speech and quoted Wordsworth. "As William Wordsworth wrote: 'There was a time when meadow, grove, and stream, The earth, and every common sight, To me did seem apparelled in celestial light.'"

"I sure do miss celestial light," Helen said. She offered me a flask from her purse. The committee head was plowing on, now moving somehow from Wordsworth to the *Challenger* disaster. It had happened in January of our senior year. There was a whole section dedicated to the *Challenger* crew in the yearbook. They misspelled Ellison Onizuka's name.

"I have no such recollection myself about celestial light," I said, then I unscrewed the cap and took a discreet swallow. "But poetry was never my thing."

"Oh, you say that. But I bet you could recite Chaucer, and Shakespeare. It's all in there still." She reached up and tapped my forehead with her middle finger.

"Maybe. Remember that assignment, we all had to write poems based on something from nature? I wrote about the birds that came to our bird feeder. Got to use both 'vermilion' and 'viridian.' I always liked using big words. I think I got an A minus."

"I wrote about my gerbils," she said, "who lived in plastic boxes and ate cardboard when they weren't eating each other and were about as far from nature as you could get. Remember Brett Bradley? Remember what he did?"

"I remember Brett Bradley. What did he do?"

"He copied a poem and handed it in as his own work. 'The Chambered Nautilus' by Oliver Wendell Holmes! It got him suspended."

"Now that you mention it, I do remember that," I said. Helen was always better at remembering.

"I mean, how dumb do you have to be, to hand in some flowery Victorian crap like that as your own original sixteen-year-old creation?"

"Guess you have to be pretty dumb. Have you heard anything about Brett lately?"

"I *have* heard about Brett," she said. "I ran into Leesa Stewart one day at the Caboose." The Caboose was an actual caboose converted into a hot dog stand, and Leesa Stewart was even better at keeping up with hometown goings-on than Helen. "He'd been working pumping gas into passenger jets, but he went back to school. He's finishing up a criminal justice degree. He wants to be a state trooper, Leesa said. But she and I agreed that he'd be lucky to make city cop."

"What I hear you saying is that if I'm out driving around after having too much of whatever that vile stuff is that's in your flask, I might get busted by Brett Bradley?"

"*Oui.*"

"Well, it's good that I don't drink and drive," I said.

That was kind of a lie. It was not the first lie I'd told that night. I also lied about voting for Al Gore when Helen wanted to commiserate about George W. Bush now being our nation's president. I didn't vote for Gore or Bush. I voted for Nader. Not because I agreed with his platform, or even knew what his platform was. I didn't vote for Gore because I hadn't forgiven Tipper Gore for the Parents Music Resource Center.

"Hey, there he is," Helen said, pointing to the bar. "There's the author of 'The Chambered Nautilus' himself."

He was hard to miss. He was taller and sturdier, but had that same blonde buzzcut. Helen and I walked over just as he was paying for a light beer. I watched him make a big show of stuffing a dollar into the tip jar, which was a dollar more than I had tipped.

"How's football going, Brett?" I said. He looked at me blankly, then smiled.

"Haven't really played since high school." He paused, looked over at Helen, scanned our chests for the missing name tags. "Do I know y'all? Which one of you went to—"

"We both did," I said, at the same time that Helen said, "We're not married."

We introduced ourselves, but Brett still seemed sheepish. He took long pulls at his beer.

"Did we have classes together?" he asked, moving his index finger around the triangle that we formed.

I laughed. "Yeah. Remember fifth grade? Cheryl Tiegs? Hell, you came to my house once when we were kids, don't you remember?"

"It was all so long ago, y'know?" He shook his head. "I'm back in school now. I've barely got enough room in my brain for all of that. School is a lot harder when you're in your thirties."

I understood forgetting, but this felt like an insult. How dare you forget me, Brett Bradley. Me and my chemistry set and my cliff that wasn't a cliff and my crappy football-throwing and bomb-making skills? Instead I said, "Helen's got a flask if you want a little something to go with that beer."

"No thanks," he said, smiling faintly, showing off those tiny white teeth in the warm glow of the fake chandeliers. He crushed the beer can. "I'm one and done. Gotta go study. Hey, it was nice talking to y'all."

"Nice talking to you," Helen and I said in unison. He walked off toward the restrooms.

Helen and I stuck around long enough to dance to "Party All the Time" and "Nasty" but when the DJ put on "Rock Me Amadeus" we took that as our cue to leave. The flask was empty.

The next year after the reunion I got a letter from Helen Aigner. No letter, actually, just a newspaper article that she'd clipped out, with a Post-it attached where she'd written three big exclamation points.

"Police officer Brett Bradley confronted Manuel Munoz as Munoz was driving away from the scene of an alleged domestic dispute with his niece. Bradley was given erroneous information by a police dispatcher who claimed that Munoz was a repeat offender on a variety of domestic violence and petty theft charges. Bradley ordered Munoz, in English, to get out of the car and to put his hands up. Munoz responded in Spanish, and began to pull something from his waistband. Bradley shot Munoz twice, believing that he was in danger. The item that Munoz was attempting to retrieve was his wallet. Bradley is on administrative leave pending further investigation."

I took four years of German in high school. Did Brett take Spanish? I don't know.

I didn't go to any more high school reunions. The years slid by. Another marriage came and went. Helen Aigner and I moved from the occasional letter to much more frequent exchanges in email and then on social media. She talked about her kid a lot. She never mentioned her spouse. We dissected the goofy plots of the latest Hollywood blockbusters, which I watched in corporate cinemas in bland shopping centers, while she got to see them in the old Art Deco theater that was still limping along in downtown.

My father died, and then eight months later my mother died. When I had been helping her with his estate, she said more than once, "I'm going to follow him soon," and she was right. And so it was time to tie off all the loose ends, and the biggest loose end was that house on top of the hill.

I had already missed a lot of work after my father's death, and so with my mother gone I was trying to do as much of the work long-distance as I could. But then the appraisal report came back from the house inspector, via the real estate agent, who in turn was a friend of Helen's. "Cracked foundation." Did I want to try to sell it as-is, or did I want to spend the money to get the foundation fixed, and to do a few more things around the house, to increase the value? This was a good question, so over Memorial Day weekend I drove there to try to come up with an answer.

First I met with a service that ran estate sales and disposed of anything that didn't sell, basically a one-stop shop for getting rid of a family's worldly possessions. Then to a meeting with the house inspector, to hear him explain in person what his form already said. "Cracked foundation." Did he have any idea when it started? No. Did he have any idea what might've caused it? Well, all houses settle. But being on that hill, and not far away from that bank—he called it a bank, not a cliff—that's eroding, well, that might have something to do with it. It's not uncommon. He, of course, had no direct ties to any construction companies but he did happen to have a business card for a service, Hare Brothers, the Masonry Professionals!, that he handed me with a smile when I handed him a check for five hundred dollars.

I was driving back to the house, up the hill, like ten-thousand times before. This time I was cursing that hillside, the red clay and the pokeweed and the years of decaying grass clippings and shredded leaves. And as my mind and my vision wandered away from the road to the hillside, I thought I noticed a dark spot right in the middle. A shadow. An opening.

Back home I fixed a makeshift gin and tonic with supplies I'd gathered, and started feebly sorting through the things in the basement. The chemistry set was still there, but when I opened the case it was empty, just some rust-colored stains on the inside. I started using it as a case to put small trinkets in, things I thought I might want to save. I couldn't stop thinking about that shadow, that opening. I started going through things in the garage, but there was nothing much left there that I wanted to save. I imagined taking all this dead weight out into the back yard and pushing it over the bank. Off the cliff. Throw all the hand tools and flower vases and aluminum extension ladders and the moldy bag of golf clubs over, and then climb on to the riding lawn mower and set it on fire and drive it over the edge too, zoom. I looked for a coil of rope, and there it was.

Even older, just about rotten, but it was the rope all right. It still had that black electrical tape on the ends. I went to make another gin and tonic.

I fell asleep on the couch while I was reading a Hardy Boys book that I'd found tucked back behind the worthless set of encyclopedias. *The Haunted Fort.* There were stolen paintings and hidden treasures and Joe and Frank were on the case, and the book itself reeked of mildew. I nodded off in chapter five.

I woke up in the dark, unsure at first as to why, and then I heard something in the basement. The garage door had raised itself. It happened from time to time; my parents always blamed ham radio operators but they never bothered to get the garage door opener fixed or replaced. That was all it was, and I just had to go close it. But my anxiety kicked in. Maybe it was some kind of garage-door-hacking thief. If it was thieves, well, they were welcome to take what they could carry. Eventually I got up the nerve to go investigate. I pulled out the little keychain flashlight that I always carried, and took the largest volume in the encyclopedia set ("M") along as a weapon. Suddenly I remembered the amazing color plate in that volume, the one that went with the Mineralogy article, a rainbow of rare minerals and semiprecious stones. I crept down the stairs, through the playroom. I threw open the door from the playroom to the garage and shone the light around, holding the encyclopedia aloft.

Nothing. But before I hit the button, I thought about that dark spot in the hillside again. It was almost five a.m., pre-dawn, and it's not like I was going back to sleep. I set the encyclopedia down and walked out into the driveway.

I made my way through the backyard and toward the edge of the bank. The sacred bamboo bushes were gone, part of a landscaping push in the nineties where my parents took out all the things that, they had discovered, were invasive species. The pine tree was still there. I wondered if I should've brought the rope. Once I got to the edge I realized that I didn't need the rope or the tree. There really wasn't much of an edge. Between my flashlight and the light of pre-dawn, I could see where the grass of the lawn faded into the red clay soil of the bank, riven with cracks where rainwater drained down. I stuck the flashlight in my mouth and got down on my hands and knees and peered over, and about halfway down, yes, there was an opening. I turned around, with my ass toward thin air, and kind of spread my arms and legs out and backed my way down the side of the hill. There were enough roots sticking out, skeletal fingers that I could grab to keep from sliding too much.

I backed down past the opening so that I could look in first. All I could see was more red soil and beyond that darkness where the flashlight's beam couldn't reach. I pulled myself up and inside. Surely the solution to the mystery of the cracked foundation was in here. Of course the foundation of the house was cracked—there was a freaking cave that ran up underneath it. Hollowed out by . . . animals? Native Americans? nineteenth century farmers? Whatever natural forces make caves? I tried to remember the encyclopedia article about caves as I crawled along.

After a while it opened up into a bigger chamber, although I still couldn't stand up straight. I pulled the flashlight from my mouth and scanned the floor and walls. The boy was in the far corner.

He was sitting on a large rock. He leaned back against the clay, as if he were scared of me, not me of him. He wasn't threatening. So small to me now, even though he was exactly five feet tall. Skinnier than I remembered. Sickly, even. His skin shimmered, coated with the sparkling paste from the thing that was not a bomb, would never be a bomb. He bent down and reached into the darkness, and when he sat back up he had a football in his hands. Red, white, and blue.

"This is for you," he said. "Do you want to play?"

He lobbed me the football and I caught it with my free hand. Whatever he was, the football was real enough. The football looked as anemic as he did. Underinflated.

"With you?" I replied. "Maybe. You were a good kid, but wow, did you grow up to be a shit."

And the kid said back to me: "So did you."

I thought about slinging the ball at his head, maybe knock some of that glittering paste off. Instead I tucked the ball under my arm and turned to crouch down and leave, beckoning him to follow.

"Come on, let's go do some passing, some punting, some kicking. You're still probably better at it than I am," I said.

"Wait," he said, "I have another thing to give you. You have to come over here."

He stood up on top of the rock and held out his hand. I walked over to him. What was the alternative? When I got there he reached up and slid both hands down my cheeks, sliming me with the glistening paste. His hands were as cold as iron. When he touched me, a perfect memory came to me, like a bone-white buoy popping up on the surface of a murky sea. I remembered that one day from so long ago absolutely, holographically.

Not just the sensations but the thoughts and emotions, too. The fear and the anxiety, which had always been memorable. Now I also remembered a great sense of accomplishment, of success, at beating Brett Bradley at a physical contest, knocking him over the edge. I remembered that when he hit me, for that one moment, I really hated him, and I wanted to hurt him. Hurt him badly. Kill him.

"Take that and go," he said.

"I'm sorry," I said. I started backing away. He didn't respond. When I turned and looked back he was gone. There was only the rock where he'd sat.

I crawled out and scrambled up the hill. It was light outside now. I grabbed my phone and called Helen, to see if she wanted to come over, maybe toss a football around, maybe listen to me apologize some more.

Under Green

The town had become a city, but a gentle one, and there were places to hide if you knew where to find them. Leah had lived in San Francisco, and in New Orleans. Those were not gentle places and she had not done gentle things. Going home was not the right way to disappear, but she bought a bus ticket anyway. She had changed, and she wanted to see how the town had changed. Her childhood was like a story about someone else, but maybe the town was a place where she could be reborn one more time.

The house where she grew up was still there. Her parents were long gone. Some people who she did not know lived in the house. She watched them from a bench on the greenway. When Leah was a child there had been only woods behind the house, no greenway. There was a creek she had played in. She had talked to the trees. There was one tree that talked back.

When she returned as an adult, her first order of business was to find a place to stay on an extremely limited budget. A nonexistent budget, really. She ended up in the Rose Garden. There was an abandoned amphitheater at one end and a thick stand of trees at the other and in between there were rose bushes growing on arbors and trellises. The roses and the trees there provided shelter, but they did not talk to her. The police did not seem to notice that she was camping out there. Other people who lived outdoors stuck closer to downtown, where there were shelters and opportunities to make money on the sidewalks. It was a gentle city, and she found a place to hide.

She started passing the time on the greenway. She got a map at the public library and started walking the entire circuit. There was an access point near the Rose Garden, where a swath of asphalt led off from the road, down past a culvert and then on. The greenway spiderwebbed across the whole county, following the creeks mostly. And, it turned out, it snaked up beside the creek that ran behind the house where she grew up. The creek even had a name, which she never had never known as a child: Cemetery Branch. It made sense, because it ran out from near the original town cemetery, out into the suburbs and finally into the reservoir lake north of town. Leah was more interested in hydrology as an adult. In the flow of things.

She got a decent pair of running shoes at the Goodwill; they fit her perfectly and were a ridiculous shade of red with gold trim. When she got tired, there were benches, and there were water fountains in the parks. People stared, but people had always stared at her. The city of the greenway was a mirror of the city of roads and buildings. Walk south and there were other people who camped out in the thickets and the high ground in wetlands. Most of them were harmless but word was that someone had been murdered in a parking lot of a convenience store, and the cops came and destroyed a site where a bunch of folks had tents. Maybe one of them was the murderer. Probably not. Walk far enough south and there were needles, crack pipes, and human feces on the greenway. The gentleness of the city was worn down in these places. The greenway ran through tunnels under the highway, and when Leah walked through them she thought about being back in New Orleans or San Francisco again. About her former life, where part of the job description was handling situations that could break out into irreparable violence. She used more of her precious stash to buy a knife at a head shop, a cheap thing for teenage boys, with a locking blade and a dragon embossed into the handle. She had never stabbed anyone, and didn't like the idea of stabbing or being stabbed, but it made her feel safer to have the knife in her pocket. It was safety but it was also a foolish risk, because she still had an outstanding warrant in San Francisco. Nothing violent, but enough, if a cop stopped her and ran her in all the cop databases.

Walk north and there were people on new bicycles, many of them wearing colorful jerseys. Lots of people, most of them white, walking dogs or running or even birdwatching. One of her first days back in town, Leah passed a Boy Scout troop out cleaning up a stretch of greenway, and she thought she recognized one of the adult leaders. They had been in some of the same classes in high school, PE and health and Latin. He was staring at her as she trudged up to them. She tried to think of a name, tried to take the age off of the guy the same way he was trying to subtract the years from her. Rusty, that was his name. Maybe he was different now too; maybe he was Russell instead of Rusty. But it was all over in an instant. She passed the Scouts, said a quick "hello" to the staring man, who returned the greeting with a blank expression and a "hi." She kept going. They had nothing to talk about. They had too much to talk about.

There were other things to stare at on the greenway. There was the backwards woman. The first time Leah saw her, it looked like the backwards woman was falling, twisting and trying to catch herself. Leah felt the urge to go help. But the woman wasn't falling. She was running backwards. She wore glasses with little mirrors on them to see where she was going, and a cycling helmet. Leah hated questions, and she hated it even more when she was the one who had a question. "Why are you running backwards?" sat there on her tongue, waiting to leap out, but she kept her mouth shut. Questions and answers were bad news most of the time. From then on she saw the backwards woman every day. Here she'd come and then there she'd go, except she'd be facing Leah as she went, smiling but staring into her little mirrors. Leah never saw the backwards woman fall, even though the greenway was bumpy in places where tree roots were re-emerging, and slick in the moist shady places where moss grew.

Leah's favorite place on the greenway was the spot behind the house where she grew up. There was a bend in the creek there, and on the other side a little hill, and on that hill was the brown house where she had lived from age zero to age seventeen. She sat on the bench and looked up at her past. That was part of the routine she fell into. She did not do drugs anymore, but she had done her share. She had been intimately connected with the consumption and sale of drugs. But now her drug was to take care of daily business—find food, wash up—and then to walk the greenway, and to end up sitting and staring up at that house. She half imagined that she'd see her younger self in a window there. A man and a woman lived there now.

She'd been doing this for a week before the tree finally spoke. The woman was working out back on the deck. Leah realized that she was the backwards woman from the greenway. She was potting flowers and smoking a cigarette. It made Leah want to smoke, but she'd quit that too when she quit the drugs, and so they were linked in her mind. It was a "negatively involved association," that's what a social worker in San Francisco had said. Besides, cigarettes were expensive.

"You do not need to smoke, and fire has no place here anymore," is the first thing the pin oak said to her. Not the first thing in her whole life. The first thing since she returned.

"Well hello, friend," she said. "I was beginning to think that you were gone. Or that you'd never been there. A figment, or a fragment."

When she was a child, she could hear noises that the plants near the creek made. Talking noises, breathing noises. The ones who talked, most of them didn't make words, or if they made words they didn't make sense. The honeysuckle vine, she could just hear it breathing. Sometimes it would sigh heavily. There was a redbud tree that babbled nonsense constantly, but quietly. You had to get right up next to it, and even then it was just a ghost like wheeze. "Bifurcated revolving plasm angle in Z block," it would say. "The thing that was left in the place there at the bottom was no longer in that place but moved instead into the protoregium," it would say. Sentences but then sudden words she didn't know, as she strained to hear and make sense of it. You could try talking back to the redbud, but it wasn't listening. It just kept up its quiet patter. "Plainly Paris pinhook pie pencil pirouette buffalo turquoise flange protocol."

But there was one plant who talked quite plainly, and who listened to her, and that was the pin oak. "Hello. I am a pin oak," was the first thing that it had said. "Or you might call me *Quercus palustris*. But my name is Cleverwell. What is your name?" At the time, Leah's name was Lee, and Lee was in need of a friend, and thus not particularly startled by a talking tree. In fact, quite happy to have a special friend. They were friends all through Lee's childhood. Cleverwell gave advice. It was usually better advice than Lee's parents gave, when you could figure it out. Cleverwell said, "I must stay here, but you can go anywhere." And so Lee did go somewhere. Cleverwell said, "I will

always be Cleverwell, and a *Quercus palustris*, but you can change."
And so Lee changed. At first into Leaf. When she was Leaf a lot
of things changed. She grew her hair out and dyed it pink and
then she let it mat up into dreadlocks, which she quickly regret-
ted. She started wearing dresses that she got at thrift shops.
She started hanging out with a different crowd at school. She
thought that she had found herself, and by doing that, she left
Cleverwell and the other plants behind. She didn't spend much
time in the woods anymore. She didn't spend much time at
home. She was out, staying on couches and in basements.

"Can you read my mind?" Leah said, sitting there on the
bench. "I mean, in my memory I can hear your voice. What was
I hearing, all those years ago?"

"We don't need to make noises to communicate, if that is
what you mean," the tree said.

"And why have you waited so long to communicate? I've
been back for days now."

"Time moves differently for you and me. You know that.
We used to discuss that at great length when you were here
before. You were smaller then, and looked different."

An older couple went by, power-walking as best they could.
Leah had seen them often since she'd returned, and they were
friendly enough. She waved. They both smiled. The man tipped his
baseball cap. The Giants. She wondered why he liked the Giants,
San Francisco's baseball team. She had gone to a Giants game
once with Manny. Manny was the dealer she had worked for in
San Francisco, and in New Orleans. "You're going to go straight,
that's funny," Manny had said. "No way you can go straight, girl."

"Can you hear what they are thinking?" she asked Cleverwell, speaking of the older couple.

"No," Cleverwell said. "Do you not remember? You asked
me that when you were a child."

"That's so long ago, tree."

"It is not a long time, not for me. And my name is Cleverwell."

"My name is Leah."

"I know. Lee, Leaf, Leah. What will your next name be?"

"I think I'm sticking with Leah for good." And she said that, and it was sort of true, but it did make her wonder if she was in a terminal state. Was there another change ahead of her? She felt the same on the inside. Maybe less confused.

"What else have you forgotten?" Cleverwell said. "Did you forget about the sun?"

A memory slotted itself into place. Leah saw herself, under Cleverwell's guidance, stretching her arms out and facing the sun.

"Tell me about the world, Leah," Cleverwell said.

"You know as much about it as I do."

"Yes. But tell me of your travels. I want to hear your story."

And so she told the tree her story.

Drop out. Try to get back in. Fall in with a fun crowd. The wrong crowd. Burn bridges. Take drugs. Sell drugs. Move away. Party on. Brushes with the law. Brushes with death. Brushes with ignorance. Move back.

When she was done, Cleverwell asked, "What are the trees like there?" She did her best to describe them. She didn't really remember them that well, though.

Cleverwell said, "What is the line from the poem that you read to me? 'The transformation of waste'? Perhaps you could get a job transforming waste. There is a lot of waste in the world.

There is more of it every day. Everything falls apart." And so she did get just such a job.

She got work doing the cleaning and recycling for a bar near the university. The owner had a line on a cheap garage apartment, too. She liked the Rose Garden. She knew it wasn't really safe but it felt safe. Even though someone was clearly tending the roses, nobody much came there. Every Sunday afternoon people would show up to take engagement photos. But all in all it was a peaceful place. The plants there did not talk to her.

One day she asked Cleverwell, "Do other plants talk to people?"

"Some do," it said. "But it is not common. You and I are rare. Mostly I just talk to the other plants here. We sing."

"Sing me a song," Leah asked. "Why have you never sung me a song?"

"You cannot hear my songs," it said. "I am singing one right now, but you cannot hear it. I am almost always singing a song."

Then when she worked at the bar, which she did every day until it opened in late afternoon, she started singing too. First she tried singing songs she remembered from her youth. Then she just started making up noises and stringing them together. Humming tunes that twisted and changed and reformed into different songs. Making space alien noises when she felt like it. No one could hear her in the back parking lot next to the dumpsters as she pulled the sticky, smelly empties from garbage bags and sorted them. Glass, metal, plastic, paper, trash. No one could hear as she sponged and swept and mopped up the previous night's stains and debris. The bar owner's name was Dwight.

And then the rain came, the first real soaking rain since she'd returned, and she realized that the garage apartment made sense, even if she'd be away from the beautiful mute roses. She moved her worldly possessions, which fit into a backpack and a large garbage bag, from their hiding place in the Rose Garden to the apartment. She didn't have many possessions but there wasn't that much space in the apartment.

Dwight gave her an old bicycle too, a rusted Schwinn Sting-Ray. It was older than she was, but it was the right size for her. She started riding it on the greenway, making herself that much more conspicuous. There was no way that she could blend in with the people in Spandex on their sleek new bikes. She didn't have a helmet, and felt bad about that. But she could cover much more ground on the bike, roaming over the whole county. In the afternoons she still ended up back behind her childhood house, talking to Cleverwell, and meditating. The bench had a little plaque screwed into it. "In memory of Pemba Reendar," who was someone she did not know. She felt like she should look up the Reendars, give them a call and ask if it was OK for her to spend so much time on the bench dedicated to Pemba. She'd read an article at the library about meditation, how it was good for you. Cleverwell quite respectfully did not talk to her when she meditated. It could read her mind, though, so for all she knew it was listening in as she breathed and tried to think of nothing but breathing. What does a tree think of nothingness? She never asked.

She rode the bicycle and when the hills were steep she got off and walked it. She catalogued the greenway: the rocks in the streams that looked like faces or like whales, the wetlands and the meadows, the backs of all the houses. As curious as she was about her childhood house, she had no desire to move back there. She did see a lot of places that inspired fantasies of owning a home, though. Houses that looked like mountain chalets, with big open windows. Older houses that were very close to the greenway, with sheds full of junk right there and "NO TRESPASSING PRIVATE PROPERTY" signs nailed up. The greenway was never boring. You could fantasize yourself into hundreds of lives on it, whether in the people that you passed or the houses that you could see. And Leah did just that, thought about a path to a new life. How would that even work?

She would get one of the more modest houses around the lake. The real estate around the lake was fairly exclusive but the lake itself was a great equalizer. The greenway encircled the lake, which had been built by the Corps of Engineers, and it was a park attended by people of all races and ages. The house she liked was up on a ridge, a little 1970s cabin, with big glass windows that faced the lake. The backyard was fenced in but there was a gate down at the bottom and a little path that led to the greenway. In the mornings she could make coffee and look out and see Canada geese, mallards, and the one heron that seemed to hunt in the lake. There were deer that prowled the underbrush. She would pay a neighborhood kid to mow the grass for her, and let the backyard go completely natural. There was a stone fireplace and chimney. She could get a big flatscreen television to hang over the fireplace. She imagined a big open kitchen, a laundry room, and a garage with a treadmill and her car, one of those electric ones. Just enough room left for a master suite and a guest room.

That was as far as she got, because while she could imagine the insides of the houses, she couldn't imagine anything else about her existence. Even if this was all powered by a winning lottery ticket, there was nothing else inside.

One day she realized that these beautiful houses were still full of unhappy people. And in fact if she were to occupy one of them, she'd still be herself. With her same problems. Even if she had some money. She would still be alone. She would still be not the biggest fan of herself.

This made her happier, though. The realization that all these fantasies dangled in front of her, as daily she traversed this strip of nature or pseudo-nature, that they wouldn't solve many of her problems, it helped. She'd have more space, but she wouldn't be that much safer, living in one of those places.

One day she'd fallen asleep on her bench, exhausted because the night before she hadn't got much sleep. While she was meditating the next day she dozed off, the Sting-Ray leaning against the bench. She had asked Cleverwell if it minded if she leaned the bike against it, and while it didn't care, she still thought it was more respectful to lean the bike against the dead wood of the bench. When she woke up it was dark. She didn't know where she was for an instant. She'd been dreaming about a punk rock toothbrushing contest, between Billy and Stewart, who were both actually dead now. Billy had OD'd and Stewart had jumped off the top of the college library, eleven stories up. In her dream they'd been stomping around in their engineer boots, frantically sawing away at their foaming mouths, trying to best each other at daily oral hygiene.

Cleverwell was silent, and when she reached out to it with her mind she didn't get a response.

"Cleverwell," she said aloud. Still no answer.

Around her the trail was dark but there were lights from the houses that bordered the greenway and the creek. Including in the house where she'd grown up. She could see the people in the kitchen. She sat and watched them. Her eyes were already adjusted to the dark, and her distance vision was good. The couple was having a fight. The woman paced back and forth behind the man, who was standing at the sink, facing out into the dark. Leah was still sure that this was the backwards woman, although now she walked in the normal direction. Neither the man nor the woman were wearing shirts. Maybe they were both completely naked. The fluorescent light was a sickly hue, not one of those new ones that were the same color as the sun. Maybe it was the same bulb from when Leah had lived there. She started thinking about all the other things in the house that might be the same. The place where she'd first written her new name, L-E-A-F, in cursive on the inside of her closet with a Sharpie. She had sat in there crosslegged on the floor, in a piled jumble of Converse and Vans shoes. Was the lock still broken on the downstairs back door? Had they replaced the 1970s wallpaper in the upstairs bathroom, all oranges and greens on a silvery background? Was it still the same house, or was it a different house now, and when exactly did it change from one to the other?

The man had a knife in his hand, a big chef's knife. She couldn't see the woman. The man held the knife up to his wrist and brought the blade across. Leah's first thought was "that's not how you commit suicide." Everyone knew you cut lengthwise. That was something you learned . . . where? How did this terrible nugget of wisdom get distributed to the world? Then the surprise hit her, and she realized that she was actually seeing this. It was actually happening, not just a movie projected on a tiny screen up in the night. The man was screaming in pain, doubling over, but then there he was standing up again, turned toward the woman and still yelling. Maybe crying. The woman came over to him, but instead of dropping the knife and letting her tend to his wound, they began physically fighting. Grappling. His knife hand slipped free and that's when she saw it. He thrust the knife into the woman. It wasn't like in a movie. The woman kept moving. They kept struggling. But it was clear now, the man was trying to kill the woman. He stabbed her again, and then they moved out of the frame of the kitchen window.

Leah remembered the first time she saw a dead body. People died all over, not just in ungentle cities but in gentle ones too. Maybe there was no such thing as gentle.

Leah had no idea what to do. She had no phone. Run to a nearby house and demand they call the cops? That was a recipe for disaster, for her getting in way over her head when she was already just treading water. Run up the hill and break in to the house, brandishing her little dragon-handled knife? She asked Cleverwell what to do, but again got no answer. She waited for a long time, maybe an hour, but nothing happened in the house that she could detect. No change in the lights. No one visible in the kitchen window. Maybe they were both bleeding out on the kitchen floor. Maybe she'd been confused by what she saw, still asleep and dreaming there on the bench, and they were fine. Leah decided to try and find a pay phone. They were thin on the ground these days, but she remembered one near the bar. She pedaled the bike back to the bar (which was closed, a Sunday) and went to find the phone. The little kiosk was still mounted to the side of a brick building next to a gas station. The phone was there but the handset had been torn off, and a piece of bright blue gum had hardened in place on the coin slot. Leah had no idea what to do. So she went home and went to sleep. She was used to sleeping under stressful conditions.

The next morning she got the paper from the mailbox in front of the bar—Dwight still "took the paper," as he called it. Nothing in it about a murder. She biked over to the public library and checked the local news sites, but there was nothing there either. A fatality in a DWI accident. A train derailed. A possible hurricane on the way. No mention of blood in a suburban kitchen.

She did the morning recycling, just trying to focus on the colors of the glass. A working meditation. But after she was done, she cycled the greenway over to her childhood house. She passed some of the mid-morning regulars, although she didn't see the backwards woman. Instead of parking at her bench, she took one of the access paths out to the neighborhood itself. Something she'd not done since coming back, worried that the confused pain of nostalgia would knock her over. But there she was, walking up the slope of Edgewood Drive. There were no sidewalks, because it was a suburb built when people rode in cars everywhere. Some of the houses were unfamiliar—newer McMansions built where smaller houses had been. Then up the last curve, and there was the driveway to her old house. The mailbox was different, which didn't surprise her because it was always getting knocked over when she was a kid. It was a strain to pedal the bike uphill with only one gear, but still she rode slowly past instead of stopping. Swiveled her head around to see if anyone was out in their yards. Were there any neighbors there who remembered her? When she was a kid, the Wainwrights had split up, and Mrs. Wainwright had kept their house. Maybe she was still there, although now her house was covered in English ivy and had trees planted close to all the windows. Mrs. Wainwright had gone crazier than anyone else in that neighborhood. Until now, at least. As far as Leah knew, knife murder was a new thing for the neighborhood where she grew up.

Leah turned and rode back down the hill. She tried to be casual as she stopped and flipped open the mailbox lid. Printed in there, in marker on a white card under some packing tape, were two names. She committed them to memory. She wasn't sure what she was going to do with the information. She needed advice. And so she went to see Cleverwell.

She explained to it what she'd seen the night before. "Do you go to sleep at night, or something? I tried to talk to you, but you didn't answer."

"We do not sleep, not the way you do. But we never talk after the sun goes down. Only singing."

"So you saw what happened?"

"Yes, I did."

"What should I do?"

"Something brave, I think. You should do something quite brave."

"What's that?"

"You will think of it, I am sure."

Cleverwell logic. Tree logic. No point in trying to push past it. They talked about how nice the weather was now. Leah tried to explain Daylight Saving Time, but Cleverwell didn't comprehend her. The light was going to last longer in the day. It was going to get warmer.

She rode to the library again, checked the local news sites again. Nothing. There was more news, but none of it was about a bloody knife murder. Or murder/suicide. Or whatever had happened in there. She was getting more comfortable with deciding that it hadn't happened at all. Or maybe it had been staged. A play fight. Some kind of fantasy kink. She'd seen plenty of that kind of thing in San Francisco. Maybe it was even for her benefit—Leah was a denizen of the greenway, and there were plenty of regulars who saw her on it every day. Maybe the people in the house wanted to freak out that strange woman who sat on that bench down by the creek.

The crisis of what she'd seen made her think about the greater crisis of existence. She was getting stronger, riding that bike all over the county. But she still had no idea what to do with her life. When she left, Manny had said that she was welcome to come back and work for him any time. She'd be the one taking all the risks, though. Manny couldn't afford a third strike. His operation now was so big, he didn't need to touch the business directly. He flew around, checking on production, checking on supply channels, making sure product moved from point A to point B without actually getting that close to the product.

She realized that she had to go back into the house, all these years later. That was the only way to find out what had happened. And she knew exactly how to do it, maybe, if the old back door still worked the way it once did. It locked, but it wasn't a deadbolt, and the lock was broken to where if you lifted the door up just so you could coax the latch to open. She discovered this when she was twelve, and in her teens Leah had snuck back in the house late at night many times by this method.

She rode back out to her bench, her headquarters, and waited. The sun went down and Cleverwell fell silent. They'd been talking about mountains. She was describing mountains to him, how it got colder the higher you went, even in summer. She had a sneaking suspicion that Cleverwell knew all about mountains and weather and axial tilt, but was just playing dumb.

It was like watching herself in a dream, when she got up and started walking to the nearest access path, the one that would take her to Edgewood Drive. She didn't know why she was doing it or what she would find, but she was slowly making her way to the house. A ghost looking for a place to haunt. She moved up the street. All the other houses were full of people, probably all staring at their televisions. When she got to her old address she turned and walked quickly down the drive to the back.

So close, so close to her personal history, running on adrenaline now and feeling kind of faint. But she had passed the point of turning back. She had a bandana and she used that to keep her prints off the doorknob of the back door underneath the deck. It worked exactly as she remembered. Lift it slightly, work it back and forth, and it clicked open with ease. She thought about the murderous man in there; she thought about alarms. She decided that a murderous man was more probable than an alarm system, and she decided she preferred that scenario. No alarm went off. She walked into what had been, and what still clearly was, the laundry room. Moonlight streamed in through the windows, and her eyes had adjusted. The familiar old wood paneling was gone. Now the walls were white. The floor was carpeted. She left her shoes in the laundry room and continued into the house in her socks.

She went upstairs to the kitchen, thinking that she was either about to solve a crime or become the victim of a crime. But there was nothing out of the ordinary there. She looked out of the kitchen window down toward the creek, toward Cleverwell. She thought of the woman. There was no one in the house, she was sure.

She walked down the hall to her childhood bedroom. The door was open. It was darker in this room, more shaded from the moonlight. She could make out the shape of a desk and computer, and a lot of boxes. Probably used for storage or an office now. She walked over to the closet and opened the door. She walked in, right into the clothes hanging there. She turned and lifted her arms and felt for the pipe that ran just below the ceiling of the closet. She slid her hand across it until she felt something that was not a dusty pipe. It was a ribbon tied around the pipe, down at one end. It was the ribbon she'd tied there years before, when she was Leaf, before she left home. She stood there and worked at the knot until it came free.

When she finally got it loose, she panicked. Her eyes had adjusted to the deeper dark and she could see everything now, and she realized that she was standing in a house that she'd broken into, one where quite likely a serious crime had been committed. She took the ribbon, went and padded down the stairs and got back into her running shoes. She pulled the back door shut behind her and the wonky latch clicked into place. She thought about trying to stumble down the hillside through the trees and brush, but that would attract more attention and could break an ankle. After ten deep breaths she walked up the drive and back down Edgewood. Back onto the greenway, to her bicycle, and then to the apartment. A light rain had started. She had the old ribbon in her pocket. She wondered if it was still bright green, or if it had faded.

Days passed. Leah checked the news constantly but saw nothing. She became convinced that she'd seen a play, a bit of misdirection for her benefit, and that the couple had gone on vacation. Backwards woman was no longer on the greenway and so that was definite, it had been backwards woman living in her old house. The house stayed empty and dark and she would sit down by the creek watching the sun go down, talking and then waiting for Cleverwell to fall silent.

One morning when she arrived at her spot she saw something yellow flapping in the breeze, surrounding the house. Police tape. So something was amiss. She couldn't risk talking to cops, though. She pedaled back to the bar as fast as she could. She was getting faster, and stronger, even on the ridiculous bike.

The television was already on when she got to the bar.

"They caught the guy who killed that woman," Dwight said, pointing. The shot was of a reporter standing in the front yard of her house, just outside the police tape. The reporter was saying something but Dwight talked over the noise of the television.

"I mean, they've got him in Canada, trying to extradite him. A jogger spotted his wife's body dumped at a construction site. All carved up and soaked in bleach. I don't know why people do this stuff. You know they're gonna get caught. Don't they watch TV?"

"Can we listen to the news story?" Leah asked.

"That's about all there was to it. They've already done the autopsy. Didn't have much family, just a cousin from Montana. Gonna bury her in the old town cemetery."

Dwight was kind enough to give her a job and find her a place to stay, but he wasn't much on conversational skills. She wanted to talk to Cleverwell. Leah thought about the woman lying there out in the elements. About her getting stabbed. Could Leah have saved her?

Before she could leave, the emergency broadcast system kicked in on the television. A tornado warning. Funnel cloud spotted. Take cover immediately. So she and Dwight went into the back office. The rain came, and the power went out, and the wind blew hard enough to rattle the building, but they were not in the direct path of the tornado. Dwight was prepared. He had a little battery-powered radio, so they didn't have to try to converse.

Eventually they both fell asleep in their chairs. In the morning, the power was back on. She got up and went into the bar and flipped on the television. The tornado had touched down in the city, skipping through in a path just north of downtown. An image of a map was displayed, with the line of the tornado superimposed. She already feared the worst. Then they cut to the live feed. Oh, the irony, that a neighborhood shocked by a bloody murder would be hit again, this time by a force of nature. Shreds of police tape, trees and power lines down everywhere. The camera panned around and her house was crumpled under the weight of two big trees, the roof mostly torn off and sitting in the front yard. The camera zoomed to show the path of the tornado. How it had come up the hill from the creek.

And there, at the end of the shot in the distance, was Cleverwell, now fallen, lying across the greenway, completely uprooted.

Leah raced back up the greenway, to sit with the corpse of her friend, but she could hear noises before she got to the bend in the creek where the tree had been. Pemba Reendar's bench had been crushed when Cleverwell fell. Leah heard voices, and the roar of a chain saw. She ditched the ridiculous bicycle and started running. There was the Boy Scout troop, and Rusty was wielding a chain saw, cutting up the corpse of Cleverwell into sections. The Scouts were heaving these into a wheelbarrow and carrying them over to dump in the creek. Others were picking up limbs and piling them in the woods. It was more than Leah could bear, even if it made no sense. What was the city, the gentle city, going to do, leave a tree lying across the path? Leah ran over to the far end, near the top of Cleverwell's corpse, away from where most of the Scouts were working, trying to hide herself in the branches that still bore green leaves. She bent down and put her hand on Cleverwell but she heard no voice.

Rusty stopped his chainsaw and told the Scouts to take a water break. He walked up to Leah, who still knelt turned away from him.

"This tree meant a lot to you?"

"Yes, it did."

"Well, it's going to mean a lot to the beavers now."

"I want to keep part of . . . the tree," Leah said.

"What, you want to roll a log out of here? That sounds a little impractical, uh. Remind me your name?"

"My name's Leah."

"Sorry. Leah. How about a branch? Maybe you could make you a crooked walking stick or something. A memento."

"Yes, a branch."

Rusty went and got a bow saw and started cutting on a branch about six feet long, a straight branch that bore green leaves and acorns.

"I can do that myself," Leah said, and she got up and took the bow saw out of Rusty's hand and finished the job.

"Thank you," she said, and she carried the branch away in her arms.

She carried it up the greenway. She passed the whispering redbud, unscathed by the tornado, but didn't even try to listen to its random babbling. She passed the modern house, and the swim club, and she made the precarious road crossing near the Catholic school. She started talking to Cleverwell along the way as she carried part of his remains. She carried him back to her apartment.

The next week, at the cemetery, she found the grave of the murdered woman. She gently laid the branch on top of the sod. There were no flowers, nothing beyond a simple marker set in the ground with a name and dates. She introduced herself and Cleverwell to the dead woman, and then she pulled a ribbon from her pocket and tied it around the top of the branch. Faded green against the bright green leaves. She sat on the ground with her feet tucked under her, picturing all of Cleverwell as if it were still here, a giant tree standing in the middle of the graveyard. Picturing the woman walking backwards, smiling, unknowable. She started humming a made-up tune, wordless, something to commemorate the two of them. She wanted to sit there all night, but she spotted a little golf cart in the distance, puttering up the paths of the cemetery. Some kind of graveyard cop. So she left, going back the way she came.

When she returned the next day Cleverwell was gone, and there were some flowers on the marker. Three red roses. There was also a woman at the grave, standing and staring down at her feet as Leah walked up.

"Oh, hello," the woman said, as she looked up at Leah. She waited a moment, and then asked, "Did you know her?"

"I saw her . . . around town. On the greenway, mostly. We never really talked."

"Greenway, yes," the woman replied, nodding. "I was her friend."

A breeze blew, rattling the roses on the bronze plaque. The woman stepped sideways toward Leah and held out her hand. Leah took it.

After a moment, Leah opened her mouth and began to sing. Not even a melody, just a long, low drone. The woman joined in, harmonizing. Leah changed pitch and the woman followed, slowly moving up an unknown scale. It was like meditation. Finally they stopped.

"Thanks for that," the woman said. "I was feeling really lonely today, and now I don't feel so lonely anymore. Maybe we'll see each other again tomorrow."

And they did see each other again the next day, and every day after that, and so they became friends, Leah and this new woman. In the days they worked and talked and held hands, and they walked the greenways and they hiked on trails, sometimes forward and sometimes backward, although Leah wasn't as good at that. In the nights they did not talk so much. But there was always singing.

Sunnyside

The rental that she booked was in the Meatpacking District. They both knew it was going to be small, and yet they still weren't prepared for how cramped it was. How to fit themselves into the puzzle of the studio apartment, which was half the size of the guest bedroom in the house back in Georgia. The house where she still lived, the house he had not lived in for sixteen years. They both thought of making a meatpacking joke, but then decided against it. Viv was unloading her cosmetics bag into the tiny bathroom when she finally decided to bring up the one aspect of the gathering that she had not yet mentioned to Stephen.

"It's going to be mostly virtual," she said.

"A virtual wake?"

"Yeah. I don't think the word 'wake' was technically used. We have to get in these things, abnormative clamps they're called."

"What?" He was grappling with the fold-out futon, which she had offered to sleep on so that he could have the bed.

"Abnormative clamp. Full body virtual rig."

"You know I can barely stand to look at my phone," he said.

"This is a lot better than your phone. The letter from his assistant explained it. You can take a drug before if you want." She left the bathroom to fish around in her purse for the letter. It had been addressed to them both.

"I don't take drugs anymore. I thought you stopped too."

"Not those kind of drugs," she said. "Stuff so you don't get sick."

"We came to New York to get into some kind of virtual thing with a bunch of people we don't really know? Couldn't we have stayed in Georgia and done that?"

"They don't have abnormative clamps in Georgia." She threw a tube of lip balm at his head.

"As violent as ever," he said. "What else are you not telling me about this wake? Do you know who else is going to be there?"

"The letter didn't say. Just said that it was going to be a small gathering of his closest friends. Maybe you can add to your autograph collection. You know everything else. We go to his place, meet the bright lights, clamber into the virtual world, pop some virtual champagne, I guess."

"Champagne for my real friends," he said. "What's the executor's name again?"

"Keerthi. His executive assistant right up to the end. I guess her address database is kind of old, having us both at the same address."

"Maybe Jimmy left you a little something you can hang over the couch. Something tasteful, without too many buttholes."

"Maybe that's where the wake is going to take place," she said. "Inside a virtual butthole."

"Do abnormative clamps have smell-o-vision?"

"That would be so very Jimmy." She plunked down on the futon, which made Stephen stand up. "I sure miss that guy. I mean, I've missed him for years now."

"You mean James Saint Jack."

"Jimmy Jack. I think he liked that I called him that. I hope he did. Hey, at least you got to see him the last time he came home. I had to work."

"Story of our lives. 'I had to work.'"

"You want to walk instead of taking the subway? We've got plenty of time before the party."

"Yeah. Search for churches on your precious phone. We should go pray for Jimmy's soul. He'd hate that."

"My dear, my ex-dear, he would love it," she said. "Half of his works—"

"His *phaintings*."

"Yes, his phaintings, half of them might as well be hanging up in some old European cathedrals we'll never see."

"Except for the buttholes."

They had dinner at an overpriced Italian restaurant in Chelsea. It seemed to be the only place that didn't have a line out the door or a two-hour wait for a table. He didn't finish his fettuccine Alfredo. They both got double espressos after the meal, clinked them together. "To Jimmy, who taught us about espresso, and so many other things," she said.

"The gateway drug to bohemia," he replied, trying and failing to replicate Jimmy's voice, equal parts gravel and squeak. "I drove by the ol' Rainbow Cafe the other day when I was getting my oil changed. It's a law office now. I didn't see any commemorative plaque, though. 'From 1978 to 1981, renowned artist James Saint Jack drank espresso and stole magazines here, while wearing a sequined frock coat and rings on all ten fingers.'"

They walked north on the High Line. It was hot for October, and the path was crowded. After getting jostled for the fifth time, he suggested that they sit on a bench. "We're still running early. Let's gather our energies." They plunked down facing east, into the city. The neon sign of the New Yorker hotel beamed down at them. She took a photo.

"That's where Tesla died, it says," she related, after fiddling more on her phone. "You think his buddies got together and hooked themselves up to some alternating current to celebrate?"

"Tesla died in poverty. Probably friendless. Let's think about Jimmy, not Tesla."

"That time we came to visit, when was it? Eighty-seven? A whole different city."

"No, must've been 1986. It was right before Warhol discovered him, and Warhol died in '87. I just remember how hot it was in that shoebox he was living in on Eldridge Street. And it reeked of vinegar, from that darkroom he had set up in the toilet."

"We tried to get really fucked up so we wouldn't mind sleeping on the floor with the rest of the vermin," she said.

"We succeeded. I remember even then, his little hospitalities. He was broke, and all around him his friends were dying. But he got us into drag night at the Pyramid for free, because he knew the bouncer."

"And then after one last lost weekend we got on a bus and went back home, and a few months later he got touched by the hand of Andy."

"Thanks to *Smurfette Anadyomene*."

"Yeah, Smurfette. My last modeling job."

"You ever look at that one? Phainting number one?"

"Can't stand it. I just think about how hard it was to get that blue stuff off."

The crowds thinned out and they got up and walked the rest of the way to Jimmy's apartment, a long hike up to Central

Park. The doorman looked at their invitation and made them show ID as well, then he let them through to the elevators. And then they were there, in Jimmy's place, high up in the corner of a big new glass building. The floor-to-ceiling windows looked out onto the green lawns, the trees, and the massive outcroppings of bedrock in the park.

The walls were surprisingly devoid of art. Almost everything was either black, gray, or clear. When they walked in, a woman clad all in black asked their names. She directed them to a bar counter where a phalanx of glasses of sparkling wine stood.

"That's Keerthi," Viv said.

"The executive assistant."

"Yeah. She's got her own band, too. The Half-Tones."

"You really keep up."

"You never read the articles about Jimmy?"

"I don't read the articles. I just look at the butthole phaintings."

"Of course."

Then Keerthi was back, helping herself to a glass of wine. "I'm glad you're here," she confided. "James always spoke of you fondly." She was wearing a tiny enameled pin on her lapel, of the Bad Big Wolf. The Bad Big Wolf was one of Jimmy's creations, sort of a trickster nemesis character. The Bad Big Wolf appeared somewhere in all of his works.

"That's great to hear," Viv said.

"His will was very clear as to who was to be invited. Of course, there's no way to force people to conform to his wishes."

"That'd be a real jackwagon move, to be invited to this and not come," Stephen said.

"Indeed," Keerthi said.

With that they all took another sip of wine. There were a few others there already, all of them at the peripheries of the big main room, next to the windows or back in the dark recesses. Stephen thought he recognized an old friend, then realized it was just an actress he'd seen on TV. Vera something-or-other. He tried to remember if he'd seen her naked. Viv noticed Stephen staring. The door opened again and Keerthi went off to attend to it. He drained the rest of his wine.

Viv made the old signal, her hand cutting the air over her glass, that he should slow it down. She'd barely touched hers. He set his glass near one of several giant sinks cut into the black granite countertop. "Why can't we just tell stories here in the real world?" he said. "Why can't one of these people give me their annual shoe budget, which I could probably live off of?"

He shoved his empty hands into his pockets, fiddling with the change.

"We'll tell stories," she said. "It'll just be inside this virtual world that Jimmy left for us. I'm going to find the bathroom. Wish me luck."

Keerthi checked back in with him, offered him another glass of champagne, but he waved it off.

There was an enormous spread of food, too, but he was still feeling bloated from the Italian place, so he just stood there trying to look fascinated by the tiers of sushi and macarons. He thought about drinking champagne with Jimmy. The only time he'd done that was at their high school reunion, of all things. The tenth, maybe the fifteenth? One of those. Jimmy was famous by then and he made a rare visit to town and hired a limo. They spent ten minutes at the reunion itself before leaving to just ride around drinking the most expensive champagne that was available, playing a mix tape that Viv had made. They sang along with all the songs at the top of their lungs, sometimes while standing up out of the moon roof. Squeeze's "Another Nail in My Heart," Talking Heads' "Once in a Lifetime," and their song, "Ça Plane Pour Moi" by Plastic Bertrand, three minutes of French new wave nonsense. Jimmy had found some local heavy metal boy to hang out with, a skinny blond guy with long hair and a top hat.

Recently, the last two times Stephen had a pizza delivered to his apartment, he could've sworn it was the same guy, just older and bigger and now bald. Stephen tipped him extra both times and the guy said "thanks, bro," both times, but they didn't mention Jimmy.

Viv came back from the bathroom just as another guest rolled in the door. "Hello darling," he said at top volume to Keerthi. He did the triple air-kiss and then immediately turned and started shaking hands and air-kissing with the other folks who were standing near the giant windows. He was wearing a black leather jacket and a white silk scarf, more black, and then some crazy running shoes that were green and yellow and blue and red. Parrot shoes.

It was that British actor guy who also sang and danced, a real triple threat. Joe Ardmore. One of those guys who would do character roles in movies, then be on tour singing songs to benefit East Timor or wherever, and then on Broadway in a revival of *Camelot*. A video had been making the rounds on social media recently, Joe doing a song at a grand piano on an otherwise empty stage in an old theater. Red velvet curtains, gilded woodwork. The song was about all the little complaints everyone has about life but how all our lives are special and individual and should be appreciated in the moment at all times. In the close-ups, you could see tears in Joe's eyes. Standing ovation at the end.

Joe made his way to the drinks counter. "Hey, it's great to see you," he said to Stephen, even though they'd never met. Joe kept going, greeting Viv and then moving on, and the party reconfigured itself around him. Folks drifted toward him in the center of the room instead of occupying the periphery. Maybe they thought he was about to burst into song.

"He's tinier than I thought he'd be," Viv said.

"They usually are."

"Jimmy wasn't."

Stephen nodded and then did his one party trick, moon-walking the length of the floor behind the kitchen counter. Everyone else was focused on Joe Ardmore, and didn't notice. Viv clapped without making a sound.

"We need to meet these folks," he said. "We could make some connections. Maybe Joe Ardmore needs an office manager."

"And you could be his personal bartender."

"Wacky adventures ensue."

"I get the feeling he's got an office manager and a bartender, and probably lots of other staff. A personal trainer and a smoothie chef. I bet none of them have wacky adventures, at least not while on the clock."

He pulled in a long breath, and then sighed it back out.

"What is it?" she said.

"It's hitting me again. Never. I hate how never feels."

He pulled a handkerchief from his back pocket and dabbed at his eyes. She reached for it when he was done. Keerthi had pulled a stool over to one end of the room and stood on top of it. Viv handed him back the hanky and he carefully folded it before putting it away. The others were still clumped up and talking and drinking.

Keerthi opened her palms to the crowd. "Good evening, everyone. I'm so glad that you all could be here. We're just waiting on one more guest and then we'll get started. If anyone needs to use one of the bathrooms, please do so now. Once you're inside the abnormative clamps, you'll be in for the evening." A woman with a salt and pepper ponytail and snakeskin cowboy boots groaned. A hunky older guy in a tight white T-shirt strode off purposefully down the hall. Keerthi stepped down from the stool and pulled out her phone.

Snakeskin boots lady came over to them. She seemed to be about their age, about Jimmy's age. "You guys must be the home-town gang," she said, "Jimmy's school chums." She extended a hand that bore a ring with a giant purple stone. Neither Stephen nor Viv could tell if she was earnest or making fun.

"That's us," Stephen offered, and shook her hand.

"Well, let me tell you, I am charmed to finally meet you two darlings," the woman said. "I'm Dimanda Langlois, James's gallerist. He always liked keeping his friends segregated."

"We're kind of self-segregated," Viv said. "It's nice to meet you."

"We're waiting on the ballerina, Marina Vrsovic. James talked about her constantly, and of course she was in so many of his later phaintings. But could I ever meet her? No. And he knew I loved the ballet!" Dimanda emptied her champagne glass and then reached for another.

Before either of them could respond, Dimanda continued.

"Now Andy, if he liked you, he would introduce you to anyone. But James had to keep us all in separate boxes. I guess it's something to do with his generation. So many of them died so young. I don't really know. He had such a knack for changing the subject. If I asked about his other friends, suddenly we'd be talk-ing about shoe shopping. If I asked him why he hadn't produced much work these last few years, suddenly we'd be talking about the comic books we read as kids. We were both big fans of Aquaman."

Keerthi started up again from atop the stool. "She's on her way, so let me just go over the ground rules again, which you should've received with your invitation." Dimanda looked at them and rolled her eyes and shook her head, as if actually reading an invitation was something far beneath her. "I don't know how many of you consume virtual reality on a regular basis. Jimmy has been working inside the abnormative clamp for a few years now." Dimanda knitted her brow; evidently this was as much a surprise for her as it was for them. Jimmy was known for his altered photographs, which he called phaintings, psychedelic rococo tableaux that usually featured one or more extremes of existence—celebrity and pornography, blood and guts, ballerinas and bodybuilders. Jimmy working in a feathered suit while a team of assistants handed him cameras, that was easy to picture. Jimmy hacking on some kind of virtual reality tech, that was harder to imagine.

Tight T-shirt guy was back from the bathroom, and he was fondling a version of the Bad Big Wolf that sat as a centerpiece on the food table. It seemed to have a mouth made of precious stones—rubies for a tongue, pearls and shards of quartz for teeth. Maybe T-shirt guy was appreciating it, or maybe he was wondering if he got it in the will. The door flew open and in came the late arrival. It was Marina Vrsovic, principal ballerina, recently retired. "I'm so sorry," she announced cheerfully.

Marina heaved her huge purse onto one of the couches as if she lived there and continued on in a beeline for the champagne. Keerthi nodded and continued. "Once you're in the clamp, if you come out, you cannot go back in this evening. If anything is uncomfortable when you first get in the rig, have the technician assist you. That's why she's here. Mr. Saint Jack left no further instructions for this event, and in fact explicitly stated that there were to be no more instructions. I am to say this, however: Ne Obliviscaris. Do Not Forget." Keerthi opened a side door and gestured for them to descend the stairs revealed there. Everyone trundled down, Stephen and Viv last in line.

"There are engraved invitations to indicate which unit is yours," Keerthi said.

They stood in what looked like an exercise room or a dance studio, with mirrored walls and a rubberized floor. Some dumbbell racks and other gear were pushed to one side of the room. There were a dozen abnormative clamps in a circle, all tethered to a console in the middle where the technician sat, making adjustments. "I didn't expect an engraved invitation," Stephen said, and Viv elbowed him in the ribs. They found their pods, which were next to each other. To either side of them was tight T-shirt guy and the ballerina. The markings on the units were simple and clear. You stepped in and leaned back and double-tapped a switch with the back of your head, and the unit sealed up around you. "Oh, I can't do this, I can't do this!" the ballerina said. "I had a panic attack during my last MRI and I can't do confined spaces anymore. Why can't we have a nice wake on the roof or something?"

"I'm with her," Stephen whispered.

"Yeah, I bet you are," Viv said. "Good luck with that."

Keerthi and the technician came over and had a hushed conversation with the ballerina. The only thing he could make out was something about "the transition is instantaneous and you won't feel confined for more than a second." The tech stuck a patch on each side of the ballerina's neck. The ballerina looked over at Stephen and glared, and he blushed as he realized that he had been staring. He leaned back into the pneumatic supports of the pod, and then jerked his head back twice. The suit closed up around him. For an instant everything was black and quiet and he felt as if he were floating. Then gravity zoomed back and he was standing in the apartment exercise room again, outside of the clamp.

"This is it?" he said, turning to look at Viv, who was as puzzled as he was. She looked the same, but she was dressed differently. Red mariner's sweater over a plaid shirt. He looked down and noticed that his clothes had changed as well. He sported a down vest, navy corduroy shirt, jeans.

"You are in the antechamber of the experience, just for calibration purposes," the voice of Keerthi said, but he didn't see her in the room.

"So what's next, charades?" said Joe Ardmore. "Name that tune?" He had lost his black garb and parrot shoes. Now he had on a white Lacoste shirt and short shorts, and a white tennis visor.

"Walk down the new hallway next to the front door."

And indeed there was a new hallway, a narrow passage leading off into what should've been another apartment in the building. Viv and Stephen went in, neither first nor last. It was almost completely dark except for some luminescent dust on the baseboards. It was a maze that switched back on itself, and he became completely disoriented, although part of his brain was telling him that he must've walked outside the bounds of the building, into empty space over Manhattan. She couldn't see the person in front of her and kept one hand out front, and still bumped into the person ahead of her at one point, because the whole line had stopped in the dark.

The passageway opened up and they were outside, although not fourteen stories above Manhattan. They were in a park full of trees and rolling hills. They had emerged from a dark doorway set in a brick wall, all of them in their 1981 finery. Stephen and Viv both knew exactly where they were. They were at the picnic shelter in Sunnyside Park, back home. It was the golden hour; under the shelter itself it was dim, and a weak streetlight had just come on. "Well, this is quaint as fuck," Joe Ardmore said. "Hide-and-seek in the middle of nowhere. Reckon they've got booze in here?"

"It's Sunnyside," Stephen said to Viv.

"Yeah, and it looks pretty good."

"The picnic shelter at Sunnyside has been gone for decades, hasn't it?"

"I don't know," she said. "I haven't gone there since high school."

She turned and went to explore under the shelter. There were wooden picnic tables there, laden with extravagant amounts of what had been their usual supplies. Instead of just one bottle of cheap liebfraumilch there were a couple dozen on ice in a big metal tub. There was an entire carton of Kents and a pile of plastic lighters. Joe Ardmore plucked up a corkscrew and a bottle of wine and had it open in seconds. "I was expecting more a stroboscopic orgy of visionary excess, not a hoedown. Let's see if we can get this party going, shall we?" He upended the wine bottle and chugged the entire thing. Stephen walked over and slit the cellophane on a pack of cigarettes, then tapped one out and lit it. He sucked deeply, but it didn't taste of anything much and didn't burn his lungs. But after a few seconds he felt an old familiar head rush. He'd stopped smoking years ago.

"Fucking close to water," Ardmore said, setting down the empty bottle. Viv went to get a bottle, but when she tried to pull one out of the tub, the neck snapped in her fingers. Stephen rushed over, but she wasn't bleeding. She grabbed the lip of the metal tub itself and easily bent it between thumb and forefinger. "My calibration must be off," she said, but no one beside Stephen paid her any attention. She sat down slowly and carefully at one of the picnic tables. The rest were all exploring, looking for something of interest in the barren wasteland of 1981.

There was a big silver Panasonic boom box, so Stephen pressed the Play button. The cassette spun silently for a few seconds, and then "Ça Plane Pour Moi," the one-hit punk wonder by Plastic Bertrand, erupted from the speakers. Salt-and-pepper hair lady, the gallerist, who had been trying to talk to the ballerina, came over and punched Stop. "Sorry," she said. "Too loud."

Viv scanned the table with her fingertips. There were hearts and initials and profanities there. She found the one that she remembered, the one that said "Gape Hour." Jimmy had carved that one night, with Stephen's pocketknife. She bore down on the table with her thumbnail, easily digging a ridge into the wood. She carved a big heart around Jimmy's old graffito.

"The level of detail is amazing," she said.

"I was talking to a customer at the bar last week, he'd done some of these . . . Everest and the *Titanic*. He said it was pretty realistic stuff except without all the freezing and drowning."

"I'd rather be here at Sunnyside than in the wreckage of the *Titanic*."

"I bet there's some wreckage here," he said. "Let's go try and find it. Just be careful, Superwoman." He started off toward the swimming pool, and she followed.

"You think the pool's here?"

"For all I know, the entire Earth in 1981 is in here," he said.

"That'd be something."

"Only one way to find out."

"Slow down—walking feels funny to me."

"Walking always felt funny to me," he said. "As did every single other thing."

"This isn't about you or me, it's about Jimmy."

"One last enigmatic joke."

"One more chance for understanding."

He stopped and turned and went back to the picnic shelter. She waited out there in the twilight. There were crickets chirping, or maybe they were frogs. If Jimmy were here, he would know. That was one of his secret talents. He knew all sorts of nature lore, and could identify trees by their leaves and birds by their calls. He always said he learned it in Boy Scouts, before they kicked him out. Stephen came loping back, with a bottle of wine in each hand and a magazine clutched in his teeth. The magazine was the February 1981 issue of *Playboy*, which they'd shoplifted one night and then pored over, cackling, before stashing it in a crack in the wall. Miss February's bottom half came flapping out of the center as Stephen jogged along. They walked in silence toward the pool.

The pool was always locked at night, fenced off with formidable chain-link topped by angled barbed wire. The pool and the changing house were down in a hollow and there was a concrete viewing platform with benches above, and so when lurking under the picnic shelter got boring, lazing around on the benches beneath the stars was the thing to do.

He sat on the cool concrete and swigged from the bottle, then tipped it over her open mouth as she lay next to him. He poured as carefully as if he were feeding an orphaned bird, so that she wouldn't need to grip the bottle and maybe smash it.

"Quick, think of a poetic platitude," she said after a gulp of wine. "A life lesson to share, just as we did in the days of yore. I always liked ol' Carl Sagan: 'We are made of starstuff.' Except so is garbage, and shit."

"That sounds like something Jimmy would say. Stardust and buttholes. Is that all this is, just an opportunity for his celebrity friends to see the old hometown as it was? Compare and contrast young broke fun with, in their cases at least, old rich fun?" She just shrugged and asked him for a cigarette. He popped two out of the pack, lit them, and put one in her mouth. She gingerly closed her lips around it and inhaled. He took a big swallow of wine and offered it to her again, but she waved him off.

"Or it's a scavenger hunt. Maybe there'll be a mystery to solve. Or like, puzzles we have to figure out before we can leave."

"I don't think it's a mystery. It just is."

"Let's see that *Playboy*," she said. "Find me a Nagel illustration, suitable for framing."

He held the magazine up in front of her face, flipping pages as she instructed while they read in the light from the pool. There were Nagel illustrations—Jimmy had always been a big fan and a proponent of the hidden depths of meaning behind the sleek minimalist white women that Nagel drew in endless but narrow variations.

In the distance, someone screamed. Then another person screamed. She pointed in the direction of the sound, back to the picnic shelter, just a little illuminated roof in the distance. He returned her shrug and set the magazine down.

"Well, that's alarming," she said calmly. "Maybe this thing is like a haunted house. Remember that time we went to the Christian haunted house with Jimmy, and he was in his cowboy outfit? I think they were more scared than we were." He corked the bottle and set it on the concrete. "Maybe Jimmy the Sparkling Ghost is going to pop out here in a second and give us a jump scare."

"Attention, slackjawed yokels: Look out, here I come," said the darkness. It was Joe Ardmore. "We're up here," Stephen shouted back. She reached over and tugged at his cuff to get him to shut up, but ended up ripping the whole sleeve off his shirt. Soon enough, Ardmore came bounding up the steps to the viewing platform. His white clothes were covered in blood, and he had the jagged broken neck of a wine bottle in each hand. "Who wants to join James Saint Jack in the great beyond, huh? Which one of you is going to be first? Johnny Appleseed or Ellie Mae Clampett?" He circled toward Stephen.

Stephen flicked his lit cigarette to the concrete and stubbed it out. He reached into his pockets automatically, feeling for a knife, but there was no knife. Not in the down vest, not in the Wranglers.

Joe noticed the *Playboy*. "Wanking at a funeral, were you?" Joe lurched forward, a drunken fencer, and speared Stephen in the neck. Stephen dropped instantly.

"James hated this podunk town," he continued, "and all the people in it. He told me so. He hated your idiotic school, home of the Battling Farmers, or the Leering Cossacks, or whatever. He hated the teachers, the ones who sneered at him and the ones who took advantage of him and the ones who didn't care when he got beat up. He hated people like you, supposed friends, who didn't care about the real James. So allow me to be a battling farmer. Or rather, an avenging angel." Satisfied that Stephen was down for the count, he turned to Viv.

"He loved us and we loved him," Viv said. She was sitting now. "Glrrmmph," said Stephen, who was lying there bleeding out from the neck.

"Oh, how could you know what he loved?" Joe said. He wiped the fresh blood from Stephen off on his shirt.

"You're going to regret this," she said.

He lurched toward Viv with his makeshift weapons. She was much faster, and stood and slipped to one side and seized his arm. He dropped the bottles, but she wasn't done. She grabbed his waistband with her free hand and spun him off the platform, sending him sailing over the fence and into the swimming pool. He surfaced, gasping and splashing, unable to conjure up words beyond a scream. She picked up the jagged bottle necks carefully and chucked them into the pool as well. Then she turned back to the body lying on the deck. Stephen looked up at her and said, "I don't actually seem to be dying." There was a pool of blood under his head, but it stopped at about the diameter of a large pizza.

"Yeah, it hurt when he cut me, and I can't seem to get up," he continued. "But given all that I feel fine right now, no pain at all." She picked him up and put him on the bench. She was getting better at controlling her strength. She took the torn sleeve and daubed away the blood that remained on his neck, and picked out shards of glass too. From the pool, Joe Ardmore was yelling occasionally, as he splashed around in the deep end. "Jimmy always said you were the strongest one of us," Stephen said.

Joe hoisted himself up out of the pool. He was dripping water and his clothes were dyed pink now and he'd lost the ridiculous visor in the pool. He had a constant profane patter going about how much James Saint Jack did not care for his old friends one bit. "You work in a bar, you get used to hearing stuff like this," Stephen said.

"No you don't," she said, looking down at Joe Ardmore. Joe tried the gate but it was locked. Then he started climbing the fence, the chain-link making a sizzling sound as he scrabbled against it. She turned back to Stephen. "We need to lose this clown. He can't do anything to me, but he's a nuisance." She picked up Stephen again and walked quickly and quietly off into the night.

"The elephant," Stephen said.

"Yeah, the elephant."

The elephant was a huge rock outcropping erupting from a hill at the western edge of the park. The hill sloped up to a side street and then continued on. At the top was an Art Moderne mansion that everyone in town had called "The Boat." It had been torn down around the same time as the picnic shelter. Here in the constructed 1981, it still stood on the hill, lit up. Viv jogged along in the dark toward that edge of the park. At one point she stepped in a hole and fell, dropping Stephen in the process. It was the same as before for him—a sharp jolt of pain but then nothing. He still couldn't move his limbs. She scooped him up and kept going. "I think we lost Mr. Joe Ardmore," she whispered. "I'll never be able to listen to his songs again." And then they were at the elephant. Except unlike everything else in this version of Sunnyside, the elephant was different.

The boulder had never really looked much like an actual elephant. It had been more of a landmark than a convenient hangout spot—if you climbed to the top of it, you were visible to any passing car, and those might be police cars. If you sat at the bottom, you were just sitting in the grass next to a big rock. But if you got bored or pissed off while sitting at the picnic shelter and wanted to take a little walk by yourself, maybe you went over to the elephant. At least it was like that until March of senior year, when Jimmy had come back from a solo walk to the elephant missing his fake fur coat, and with the hair burned off one side of his head. He refused to talk about it. He also refused to go anywhere near the elephant again. A few days later, he shaved his head.

Here, in this artificial Sunnyside, the boulder had been transformed. It had been carved into a giant sculpture set into the hillside, with the Boat looking down from above. Jimmy's Rushmore, his Petra, was like a depopulated version of one of his phaintings, a complex altarpiece that featured three large neoclassical thrones. At the top, also carved into the rock, was a banner with the motto: Ne Obliviscaris. Do Not Forget.

On each side, a heraldic version of the Bad Big Wolf crouched, but these Bad Big Wolves were neither bad nor big.

They were docile, friendly; protectors and not predators. Each throne was winged and topped with a seven-pointed star. Except for the wolves, there were no other creatures in the tableau. Not Jimmy himself, not a celebrity nor a supermodel. And instead of the psychedelic kitsch frenzy of his paintings, there were just the striated browns of the rock itself, illuminated only by the light pouring down from the Boat. Stephen looked up at the house and saw the flicker of someone moving in the window. It looked like a man holding a champagne glass, or perhaps a cocktail glass.

It started to drizzle. Still carrying Stephen, Viv mounted the steps to the central throne, turned, and sat. "You're speechless," she observed.

"Yeah, struck dumb."

"This is amazing. I wonder how he did this? Was he standing inside here with an imaginary chisel, hammering away at this imaginary rock?"

"I wonder if there's a way to get a picture of it."

"Doubt it."

"Yeah, knowing Jimmy, it's impossible."

"You just have to be here."

They sat there for a while, a middle-aged Pietà staring off into the night, then she took him back out to admire the view again. The drizzle let up. They were more damp than soaked. The rock now had a sheen under the lights from the Boat. The figure had not reappeared at the window, though. "Motherfuckers!" Joe Ardmore shouted in the distance. "Where are you?"

"Just stay quiet," she whispered.

"It's a memorial, and we're the only ones remembering."

But Joe Ardmore never intruded on them. They could hear the occasional shouts and yelps but the noises were receding, back toward the picnic shelter or maybe toward the bandshell, another old landmark. Behind Stephen, Viv sat with her legs to either side of him, keeping him propped up. Connected this way, they both convulsed as she started crying.

"I sure miss all this," she said.

He tried to turn his head to look back at her, but it just lolled to one side. "I miss some things. Stuff like this."

"I guess I never thought that Jimmy would miss it too."

The lights in the Boat dimmed. "Did you see that?" she said. "What do you think would happen if we left the park? If we walked up to the Boat and rang the doorbell. Or if we just broke in."

"I bet we can't leave the park."

"Only one way to find out."

"Well, I'm still paralyzed, so you'd be carrying me the whole way."

"Lucky for you I'm an amazon in here." She stood up, and hoisted him into her arms.

Minutes later she was walking through the entrance gate to the Boat, which was just a gap in the low flagstone walls. The soles of her Chuck Taylors slapped against the wet paving blocks on the driveway ellipse. She stepped up onto the covered terrace and tried the front door, but it didn't budge, not even with her super-strength. She rang the doorbell, which they could hear clang from inside the house, but no one answered the door.

"Yeah, I figured there would be limits," he said.

"Back door."

"It'll be just as locked, even against you, Wonder Woman."

"Windows"

"Unsmashable."

"Chimney!"

"Good luck, Mrs. Claus."

"You always were a glass-half-full type," she said. "Or really, a glass smashed to bits type."

"It's a fair cop. Hang on a second. I think I can move my arms and legs again."

"It was all in your mind to begin with."

"All of this is. It's in our minds. From Jimmy's mind to our minds."

"From the abnormative clamp to your cortex. The next best thing to being there."

"Yeah."

"Sort of," she said.

"I feel pretty good. Let me down."

She lowered his feet to the stones of the terrace, and stood him up. He wobbled a bit but remained standing. She took his hand and they walked around past the garage, and down a row of Japanese cherry trees to the back of the house, the side that faced the park. There was another terrace, but then floor-to-ceiling windows into the huge living and dining rooms. Gauzy curtains blocked the windows. "Look through here," she said, peering into the space between the window frame and curtain. "I think there's someone sitting in that armchair, the one next to the big vase of calla lilies."

He leaned over and looked in. "My eyes are as bad in here as they are in the real world," he said.

"Let's get closer," she said, and continued on down the terrace.

She made her way to a sliding glass door. He followed her. She tried it but once again it didn't budge. A gentle breeze rippled the air.

"Frankly," he said, "I was expecting more buttholes."

"Surely this will all be ending soon."

"Yeah."

"And I bet ol' Keerthi won't be inviting us back for another round in here, even if we could afford the trip."

Viv made a fist, and at first he thought she was going to try to smash the glass, but she just rapped on it. It seemed to startle the person in the chair. "Wake up," she said. The wind was picking up now. The person in the chair stood, with his back to them. He was dressed like a cowboy, from boots up to a tiny hat that was now visible outside the confines of the chair. Jimmy Jackson, unmistakably. Stephen and Viv pressed their noses against the glass, straining to see. He felt her take his hand. She felt his fingers interlace with hers. They stood there in silence. "Is it really him?"

She nodded.

"Jimmy!" he yelled, but the figure did not turn around.

Instead Jimmy walked over to a console stereo and dropped the needle on a record. He cranked the volume up. It was easy to hear on the terrace.

It was their song. It was "Ça Plane Pour Moi," by Plastic Bertrand. The enciphered energies of three distorted guitar chords crunching behind French gibberish, instantly familiar.

"Well, we've got about three minutes," she said.

Inside the Boat, something that looked like Jimmy Jackson danced, flailing around with his back to the window, his elbows and knees as mobile as a marionette. It started raining again, heavier this time. Outside, on the back terrace, Stephen and Viv began dancing too.

Acknowledgments

My writing is not a solitary craft; these stories exist because of the help I've received from editors, writers, and other friends. The original editors are: Andy Cox, Kelly Link, John Kessel, Mark Van Name, Christopher Barzak, Meghan McCarron, Gavin J. Grant, and Gordon Van Gelder. Gavin and Kelly also edited this collection, which includes several previously unpublished stories, and for that I give them thanks, and thanks, and ever thanks.

Almost all of these stories have been run through the Sycamore Hill Writers' Workshop, and I thank everyone who read and critiqued my work there. I must also thank my friends Lewis Shiner and Wilton Barnhardt, both of whom are exceptional writers and insightful critics. Barb Gilly is the first person to read everything I write and her encouragement is invaluable.

In particular and in closing I thank my best unbeaten brother Christopher Rowe for his advice, friendship, and support.

Publication History

"Holderhaven," *Crimewave 11: Ghosts,* 2010.
"Ash City Stomp," *Trampoline,* 2003.
"Horses Blow Up Dog City," *Intersections: The Sycamore Hill Anthology,* 1996.
"Circa," *Interfictions,* 2014.
"Pete and Earl," *Lady Churchill's Rosebud Wristlet,* 2004.
"Give Up," *The Magazine of Fantasy & Science Fiction,* 2012.
"Adventure," "Scenes from the Renaissance," "The Master Key," "At the Fair," "The Ornithopter," "Stronghold," "Delta Function," "Chemistry Set," "Under Green," and "Sunnyside" appear here for the first time.

About the Author

Richard Butner's short fiction has appeared in *Year's Best Fantasy & Horror*, been shortlisted for the Speculative Literature Foundation's Fountain Award, and nominated for the Shirley Jackson Award. He has written for and performed with the Little Green Pig Theatrical Concern, Aggregate Theatre, Bare Theatre, the Nickel Shakespeare Girls, and Urban Garden Performing Arts. His nonfiction, on topics ranging from computers to cocktails to architecture, has appeared in *IBM Think Research*, *Wired*, *PC Magazine*, *The News & Observer*, *Teacher*, *The Independent Weekly*, *The North Carolina Review of Books*, *Triangle Alternative*, and *Southern Lifestyle*. He lives in North Carolina, where he runs the annual Sycamore Hill Writers' Conference. He and Harry Houdini have used the same trapdoor.

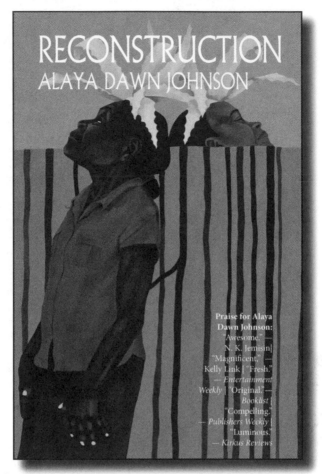

"In the title story 'Reconstruction'—one of two stories original to the collection—Sally uses her grandmother's spells to help protect a Black Civil War regiment while meditating on anger. These ten immersive stories embrace multiple speculative genres and take place in worlds both real and unreal. Much like *Lovecraft Country,* the stories combine horror and fantastical elements with anti-racist themes." — Margaret Kingsbury, *Buzzfeed*

"Johnson is one of the few writers in the genre who handles high emotion without preciousness, and she brings an almost unbearable pathos to many of these stories." — Simon Ings, *The Times of London*

"Vivid, imaginative, and often brutal prose." — *Chicago Review of Books*

paper · $17 · 9781618731777 | ebook · 9781618731784

"Each and every story in *Big Dark Hole* stands distinct in my memory. . . . Ford employs the tools of fantastic fiction to explore the strangeness of twenty-first-century American life." — Matthew Keeley, Tor.com

"One can encounter a myriad of strange and otherworldly things in a big dark hole; sometimes, we discover these holes in the most unexpected places. This new short story collection explores the extraordinary that lurks just behind everyday life. . . . Seamlessly blending the surreal with the mundane, Ford gives readers an innocuous ride to places they never knew they wanted to go." — *Library Journal*

paper · $17 · 9781618731845 | ebook · 9781618731852

"A synthesizer of the domestic & the fantastic, of soaring myth & the grittiest realities, of lewd dialect & high lyricism."
— KAREN RUSSELL

DANCE ON SATURDAY

ELWIN COTMAN

"Inventive, incandescent stories, rich in strangeness. Elwin Cotman's writing is a tonic to ward off drabness and despair."
— KELLY LINK